The nights without her were torture in a dozen ways. Julie had aroused me to such a pitch of desire that I couldn't be satisfied with the one day a week she spared for love. The more she fulfilled me, the greater the hunger she created.

Those Thursday nights, when she came to me, we spared little time for the ceremonies of courting. We didn't need to. We were too hungry for each other. We went directly to my bedroom. When we made love, I knew I was being loved—even adored. Every woman I knew afterward was to be pale in comparison . . .

THE

HUNTRESS

Mitchell Wilson

A FAWCETT CREST BOOK

Fawcett Publications, Inc., Greenwich, Conn.
Member of American Book Publishers Council, Inc.

PRINTING HISTORY
Doubleday & Company edition published September 9, 1966
First printing, June 1966

First Fawcett Crest Printing, June 1968

Published by Fawcett World Library
67 West 44th Street, New York, N.Y. 10036
Printed in the United States of America

To Stella

CONTENTS

THE

HUNTRESS

PART ONE—
HAL PRESCOTT: I

1

RECENTLY I HAVE BEGUN TO THINK OF JULIE AGAIN.
The few people still alive who knew her in the same strange
way that I did keep the same sort of silence that I do; and
so the public picture that remains is that of the frail, wraith-
like woman with luminous eyes of age and tragedy as she
gradually receded from view and became a living monument
to science like those others of her time: Einstein, Freud,
Curie, and Pavlov.

The Julie I loved, though, was in the midst of her life. She
was only beginning to wear the public halo of immortality.
She still had the startling beauty, the vitality, and the passion. I
was almost twenty years younger than she was and as sure of
myself as a man can be, but I had no advantage over her. In
the end, she was the one who rose with that fantastic dignity
of hers and walked out of my room, her soul untouched,
while I was the one who lost whatever there was to lose—and
I lost it forever.

Fame strikes in a very special way people who are in their
twenties: exhilarating, but, my God, how cruel! Because at
twenty you really believe that the applause and noise is going
to last forever, that all the new friends will go on being
friends no matter what happens. I was twenty-eight when
luck exploded like a bomb in my laboratory. Twenty years
earlier, the same thing on a far larger scale had happened to
Julie, and she had been only twenty-six.

Twenty-six and world-famous! Arc lights beat down on
her, limelights flared in her eyes and blinded her, thousands
of faces stared up, admiring, wistful, but without a shred of
comprehension of what she'd done or what she felt.

Julie could have seen her picture—if she had bothered to
glance at the newspapers—alongside the latest news of *l'affaire Dreyfus,* the flights of *les frères Wright,* and the most recent exploits of the daring *automobilistes* racing down the

Champs Elysées. The very words that were associated with her work—*colloid* and *enzyme*—had a magical sound in those days. Blood was the field of her research, and her name carried the aura of life and death. Even when I was a student, she was already being presented as a Joan of Arc of the laboratories.

She and I came from different times, and we came to science along different paths. She came to Paris as a young woman wearing a street-length skirt, a peekaboo blouse, and leg o' mutton sleeves, from a McKinley America of small towns, Sunday brass bands in the park, boardinghouses and horsecars; an America that sang "Take Me Out to the Ball Game," and felt exalted at words like "progress" and "square deal." Most of all, it was an America that believed in itself and everything it possessed with absolute passion, unaware of its dirty factories, its brutal mines and mills, or that its best colleges and universities weren't worth mentioning in contrast to the Sorbonne, for example, where Julie went to make her way even though it turned out to mean student years of starvation, and loneliness.

In Montparnasse in those days there was a bohemia of science, smaller than the Montmartre bohemia of the arts. It was poor but far more exclusive. She came to it all alone, provincial, shy about her awkward French, and ashamed of her inadequate training in biochemistry. The world of the laboratory then had room only for men, not women. Yet she had no intention of going back to America to settle for some teaching post in a New England girl's school like her former classmates at Radcliffe. It was pure research she wanted: without any idea of why, where, and how it would happen; or that such a profession really didn't exist then. She didn't even know she was beautiful.

For me it was all very different.

I came to Paris in 1922, just about twenty years after she did; not from a small town, but from a New York still remembering and celebrating its war victory and trying to drink whatever stocks of whiskey remained on hand, even though Prohibition had already become law. She had been poor, and of course, I wasn't; even though my father was still holding three things against me: one—I had been the first of the family not to go into banking; two—I had stubbornly insisted that since I was going to go my own way, I'd better pay my own fare; and three—I turned out to be two inches taller than he was. My father was a big man by anyone's count, and he had the kind of presence that made both men and women turn to look at him when he walked into a room. He didn't like it when he began to feel that people were looking not only at him, but at me too. Those were actually the least of our difficulties. The fact is that I was too much of a rebel to fit into any pattern laid out by my family. I studied things they didn't study; the people I liked they couldn't stand; their values bored me and the consuming fascination which science had for me seemed like madness to them. I couldn't even share their politics.

Another difference between Julie and me was that she arrived as an unknown student without anyone's recommendation, while I, in comparison, was received at the Pasteur Institute almost as if I had come with trumpets heralding my arrival because I'd already published my work on fibrinogen, and I brought Vaillant the letter from Collins at Johns Hopkins, which I still have and which I still read. Vaillant put me to work at once, although not until after six hard concentrated months did he come jingling impatiently into my lab to talk at random for a few minutes without meeting my eye, then growl out just as he was leaving that I satisfied him. That was the accolade you dream about, so of course I stayed on.

It was a tough, demanding life. There was hardly any money, but the work was fascinating, and, when you came up for air, so were the people. I thought I was covered with luck just to be able to be there with them.

So I worked in Paris that way for a year and a half before I even ran into Julie, and then it was in London—at the Royal Institution. I had been invited to come over to read a paper at a sectional meeting of the Royal Society. The September day and my mood had the same crisp brightness: my work had taken a sudden turn, and so I was in the happy position of being able to report good results on a research that had been infuriating me up until then. The world, I felt, was on my side and shared my pleasure.

Just within the entrance, though, like a dark challenge to the Georgian atmosphere, stood the small delegation from the Sorbonne, too visibly French in dress and feature to be mistaken. They were grouped around a woman whose face I couldn't see very well, but whose quality I instantly recognized from her pictures: Madame Julie Claudet. They surrounded her, proud and shabbily elegant like court attendants to some majesty who made careless simplicity her royal style. What did she look like to me? Let's turn it around and put it this way: if I, as I am now, were to see Julie as she was then, I would see standing there in the hall a blond woman of medium height and rather delicate build with no sense of clothes or style, perhaps, but a woman like nobody else in the world. This you saw at once. Her careless appearance even seemed a sort of distinction because what saved her was her marvelous figure, which you sensed as soon as she moved, her absorbed gray gaze as she looked up at you, the fragile intelligence in her face, which you continued to see even after she had turned away. Lines of sorrow and feeling had already deepened the quality of her eyes, and to me now a face isn't human until time and character have begun to mark it.

To me then? An entire field of science owed its existence to her. Her classic five-year experiment had been famous for so long that I almost expected to see a halo of light around her head, as though her intellectual brilliance had a luminous emanation of its own—like radium. I saw a woman about forty-four or forty-five, but even I was too awed at being in the same room with Julie Claudet to notice more at the moment. I was blinded by her presence.

I finally commanded enough courage to go over and present myself. I couldn't tell if she herself recognized my name, even though everyone else with her bowed and made it graciously clear that they did. I had come just as she was saying something about entropy as a guide to reaction rates. She looked up at me with surprise, and I noticed the startling clarity of her light gray eyes, and that her lips were surprisingly unlined. Her smile though, was brief, perfunctory, and full of polite dismissal. I bowed and left, and the meeting began.

I had been diverted from my own anti-coagulant work to follow up something from Julie's second big work—the pyrrole research with which she had discovered the similarity between chlorophyll and the haemin of hemoglobin. It had been sobering—even slightly terrifying—to have her show that one of the essential differences between all forms of animal life —screaming, growling, talking, swimming, flying, crawling across the face of the earth and the silent rooted world of forests, meadows, and sea bottoms—was perhaps largely due to the replacement of one single metal atom for another in a molecule of about seventy-five atoms. How remarkable that the evolutionary split might really be traced back to one single chromoprotein molecule! How lucky she was to have discovered it! How much courage it had taken to start out on the work and how much day-to-day laboratory drudgery to complete it!

What I was trying to do was simply to substitute other bivalent metals—copper, cobalt, nickel,—for the iron and magnesium in the pyrrole structure, just to see what would happen. That she of all people would be sitting in the audience meant infinitely more to me than all the praise I had ever received put together.

When I finished, I stood there waiting for questions. There was sharp but fair discussion from the floor, rigidly confined to the physiology of the matter, until Madame Claudet casually raised a finger just as one might in an auction room. My heart began to pound a little with anticipation. I wanted her approval of what I had done. She didn't get up on being recognized, but continued to sit comfortably in her chair, speaking in a friendly voice. She said nothing at all about the essence of my work. She ignored it completely to concentrate on some passing reference I had made to bivalency in terms of electronic theory. To me, it had been a side issue. This was 1924, after all, and biochemists were still unfamiliar with quantum ideas. In retrospect I had a right to be unclear. I think the truth is that I was simply wrong.

I stood at the lectern—completely exposed to everyone's view—and from where she sat, she spoke directly to me— American English with a pronounced New England inflection. Not Boston Brahmin American at all, but small-town New England. I tried to evade her, but she persisted. She was polite, but without mercy. It became very clear that as far as Bohr theory was concerned, she knew I didn't know the essentials. She was also making it clear to everyone else. She understood exactly what I should have said and was saying it for me.

For once, a top-ranking scientist was putting me in my place—with a gentle smile, it's true, with sympathetic light eyes, but with a ruthless insistence that I unmuddy my report by withdrawing what I didn't know from what I could be experimentally positive of. I wanted to re-establish myself in her eyes. I accepted her corrections, and went to my seat in the rear of the amphitheater, burning with anger at her and at myself. I felt like a fool.

I had accepted an invitation for the weekend, and I hadn't left too much time. As it was, the car that had been sent for me was waiting outside. It would have to wait a little longer, though, because I suddenly had an important debt to the research I had carried out so laboriously: I had made it appear less than it was. The thing to do was to wait until Mme. Claudet left the amphitheater during the intermission. I had to talk to her.

She sat quietly through the reports that followed mine. She didn't get involved in discussion over any of the other papers. Only mine—or my error—had awakened her interest. She listened attentively to everything else that was being said, leaning her chin on her hand in that characteristic gesture of hers. At the time it meant no more to me than the absentminded way she would brush back her dark blond hair with her hand while the talk went on about her. Someone once said that the motion was the gentle caress of the mother she never had.

During the intermission, I made my chance and caught up with her as she strolled slowly along the dark wood circular hall that surrounded the century-old amphitheater. She turned with some surprise. I towered over her and she made me feel my size. I said I'd like to continue the discussion, but she smiled in the shadows and said that this wasn't the time for quantum theory. At a respectful distance, a number of other scientists stood waiting to talk to her too.

"Some other time?" I asked. This close and alone she was no longer an Olympian being to me; she was almost someone from home. She looked up at me with appraisal, still smiling slightly. Then she put me off and replied by removing the question from my words.

"Some other time," she agreed.

"While we're still in London?" I went on. "Perhaps dinner together?"

Her eyes widened slightly. After a moment though they became softened by slight mockery, and with embarrassment I remembered the difference between us.

"Oh!" she said. "Impossible. But come to see me in Paris any time." She took back a little of what she had just given. "Just telephone first."

"Will you be back in Paris Monday?"

"Yes."

"Then Monday at ten o'clock?"

She laughed: and without self-consciousness, she put a hand on my wrist as if in a friendly warning to constrain me.

"All right," she said. "But at eleven."

"And I don't have to telephone?"

"No, Dr. Prescott," she said gently. Her smile was amused but guarded. "At eleven, at my laboratory."

We spoke a few minutes more about one of the other papers, a matter of physical chemistry—the one chemistry that most deeply interested her because it is so close to physics and mathematics. She seemed completely unhurried by the sight of the constantly growing crowd of people waiting to speak to her. It wasn't arrogance but independence. She refused to acknowledge any pressure from the outside world as to how to spend her own time or live her own life. It made her easy to talk to. No criticism, no hostility—only a deep and concentrated interest in what I thought. It was the first time I had ever had so direct a communion with a woman's mind, and it was intoxicating to find my curiosity coursing along with someone else's, running thigh to thigh, shoulder to shoulder, with swinging arms touching, and with a sure sense of shared identity and feeling.

Later, when I finally did arrive, I told my host, a man I hardly knew, but a friend of my brother's, that I was late because I had spent the morning with Julie Claudet. I had talked to her all alone for about fifteen minutes while she had allowed a dozen truly brilliant men to stand by and wait for her attention. I thought it had been the greatest compliment a man could have had, but my host and his friends lived lives very far removed from science, and they didn't understand.

"Good God, is she still alive?" someone laughed.

"What do you mean, alive! She's the most marvelous woman I've ever met!" I said.

Again there was laughter. "As a woman or a relic?"

"I mean as a human being, a person!" I said stubbornly, and for the rest of the day I was a little angry with everyone.

2

PROMPTLY AT ELEVEN O'CLOCK MONDAY MORNING, I was at her Institute, a gray stone building, stained by a gentle summery rain. It stood just off the Panthéon—at the corner of two narrow streets—the Rue d'Ulm and the Rue de l'Estrapade. Above a cracked gray cement wall, chestnut trees made an unexpected green bouquet on the dingy old street of schools, institutes, and mottled four-story stone houses two hundred years old. I came by a way I was to get to know very well: up the twisting, narrow cobbled hill of Rue des Fossés St. Jacques, past the old printing shops, past the florist, past the horse-meat butcher up to the triangle of the Place de l'Estrapade. Later I discovered that two hundred years before, Diderot walked up this same hill; a hundred years before, Pasteur trudged this way to his laboratory down the street; and only twenty years ago, the Curies had worked on radium not far away.

In a boxlike little gatehouse, the concierge was shelling peas and ignored my passing. Roses grew untended in the scraggly garden; windows were uncurtained, rusty pipes lay in a heap on the bare ground. To the people who worked in the Institute, there must have been beauty enough in what went on in the flasks, test tubes, and centrifuges. Roses in the garden were drab by comparison.

I pulled the antique bell-wire a second time. Deep within the dun-colored building, I heard the jangle. Nothing happened; outside, the rain stopped as softly as it had begun. Within seconds, sunshine lit up the day, making the heavy black clouds white and soft in a washed blue sky. While my head was turned to look back at the changed world, the door was opened by an elderly lady who was the librarian.

She led me along corridors lit by bare electric bulbs set in heavy porcelain sockets that could have been made at the turn of the century. Wiring ran overhead in heavily insulated cables thickened to twice their size by accumulation of dust. Yet through open laboratory doors, glass apparatus, nickel, and brass glistened more brightly than they probably did in the homes of the researchers. Where it mattered here, there was fastidiousness.

I counted a staff of about twenty men, all of them older and far more experienced scientists than I. Their names, on little cards posted on their doors made me walk with respect for where I was and what I knew these men had done and lived through. Actually, after the war, there were very few French scientists my age. My immediate contemporaries, the classes of 1912, '13 and '14, had gone directly from the *écoles* and *universités* into uniform. Nineteen out of twenty had been shot or bayoneted within weeks of reaching the mud of the front-line trenches. Men too young to fight during the war were still too young immediately after the Armistice to do advanced research, and so in 1919 and 1920, research posts and research problems that would normally have been competed for by an entire generation had been offered as gifts to the few of us who were still alive. I felt it sharply here. As I went, I counted another dozen men at work on the construction of the apparatus for the researchers. The distinction was plain and very French. The scientists wore white coats—the technicians wore blue smocks—just as in my own place.

Julie ruled over this group with a peremptory majesty. I could see it in the way she came walking toward me in the dim light, her hands deep in the pockets of the white unbuttoned laboratory coat. Her manner was severe, almost surgical. You scarcely noticed the face that went with all this happened to be beautiful.

I looked for a sign that over the weekend she too might have thought of our talk, but she only smiled up at me a little absently; then, without a word, she turned abruptly and went back the way she had come. I was to follow her. She was interrupted half a dozen times by researchers wanting her advice or her signature or to report to her. Her replies were quick and her authority went unchallenged. She knew what everyone was doing, and she had that fine researcher's sense of what happens within an apparatus. She herself had suggested and designed more than half the experiments going on.

I asked if any of the apparatus we had just passed was one that had been used for the famous experiment, but she shrugged off the question: it had been dismantled years ago to make way for more advanced work. I remarked that it would have had historic value.

"This isn't a museum," she said, and I was reminded that

along with her warmth which I had felt during our talk, there
was always the critical side that had attacked me in the first
place. I was wary of her.

She led me through her own lab, which was quite small,
into an adjoining room—a combination storeroom-anteroom-
sitting room. It was high-walled, narrow, whitewashed, and
cluttered: an old-fashioned black leather couch, a few pieces
of battered furniture, piles of research journals, bundles of
glass tubing of various diameters, and a blackboard.

Two photographs were thumbtacked to a wall. The one of
Georges Claudet taken just before his death was the original
that afterward had been duplicated in newspapers and in
textbooks all over the world. He had been almost fifteen years
older than she when they had married; but in the picture he
was younger than she was now.

His high starched collar, his longish hair, and his mustache
had the old-fashioned look of the pre-war years a decade earlier, but his eyes were young and alive. He had been a great
man and a man of great sensitivity, and it showed in his face.
The other picture was a fairly recent snapshot of a twelve-
year-old girl—a thin, shy-faced child, squinting sulkily against
the cold stare of the lens. I disliked the child at the same time
that I realized that the expression on her small face was one
of anger and heartbreak.

"Your daughter?"

Julie had been watching me, her expression wary. But my
question touched her where she was vulnerable, and she
smiled quickly. She told me the girl's name.

"American Susie or French Suzy?" I asked, and it was now
my turn to look at Julie squarely for the first time. I wanted to
see whether, after the weekend of thinking about her, she
would seem young or old. There were lines about her light
eyes, and darkness beneath. I looked away from what I was
sorry to see. It was my way to protect her, I guess.

"French Suzy, I suppose it will be," she was saying. "That
doesn't seem strange to me at all. Suzy has never been to
America, and I haven't been home in"—she laughed again
and waved her hand in a typical New England gesture of
Land sakes! that was unexpectedly old-fashioned and en-
dearing—"over twenty years!"

She looked at the snapshot again, and her face softened, not
so much with love as with loving pity. "Poor Suzy!" she said;
and before I could ask or even guess what she meant, she

turned to me with a slight questioning smile: "Well, Dr. Prescott? What was it you wanted to say to me?" She spoke courteously enough, but the implied request to state my business and be done with it had the same distant sound as her reply to my question about the classic apparatus. With anyone else, I would have begun to be angry. I asked myself where was that warmth I had so strongly felt in her in London?

"You don't see what I'm trying to achieve," I said. "Other people in the field seem to be getting it. Yet I want your interest more than anyone else's."

She shrugged. "Then explain it to me," she said simply, and folded her arms. I couldn't help myself: I watched the movement. Her breasts fitted snugly into the framing rectangle. The unbidden thought flashed at me: this is a woman who should always sleep curled up with a man's arms around her, with a man's body pressed to her back.

I glanced up to find that she had been watching me all the time. I was embarrassed. I turned away at once to the blackboard to begin to diagram and explain my work. I did badly. I gave an over-detailed description of the procedure I was using to break the metal linkage at moderate temperatures, and I completely lost my way. I kept asking myself why I wasn't furious with her for making me feel so ill at ease, but there it was: she had stripped me of my temper, my anger, all my quick protections. All the time her eyes held me with a cryptic expression that made me feel that she had known what I was thinking.

I kept talking. I drew diagrams. I wrote equations. Was she paying me back for my impertinence? A few times, I paused, tempted to break off the scientific discussion and ask her directly what she was thinking, but each time her glittering gray eyes arched a little as if to say: "Well, keep on!" Then just when I was absolutely positive she hadn't been listening at all, she took the chalk from my fingers and went to my diagram and, as easily as if she were writing her name, her chalk sped over the blackboard, improvising a brilliantly improved version of my apparatus. I was so impressed that I was left with nothing to say. Then, thank God, her improvement suggested a still further refinement to me, which I added to her diagram, so I could at least look as if I were holding my own. She watched what I did, the chalk still in her hands. Then she nodded slightly, put the chalk down, dusted her hands on her smock, and put a kettle of water on the stove. I asked what it was for.

"Tea," she said, "I'll make us something to eat."

"Here?" I asked.

"Of course," she said simply. "I have some cheese, bread, and wine."

"But if you're willing to have lunch with me," I said, overwhelmed at the extent of her intention, "for God's sake let's go someplace where we can really eat!"

"A restaurant?" she asked, as if the idea were too absurd to take seriously. She threw her head back and laughed with a rich full sound. It made her beautiful, with a vitality I hadn't seen in her before.

"I, in a restaurant? Who has the time?" Then she smiled. "You're right, but it's impossible. Of course, if what I have doesn't seem enough . . ."

I told her that it was more than enough.

"Then go on with what you were saying," she said and went about slicing a long bread into manageable pieces and removing a Camembert from its round box. Thank God, I thought, I finally have caught her interest. I had hoped that she'd invite me to participate in the Institute's famous weekly seminars. My chances looked good.

I sat down and spoke with a new enthusiasm because at last I was completely sure of myself again. On the table she added a can of sardines with its top rolled back, and a bottle of red wine. I drank and ate steadily as I spoke. After a while I looked at her frankly again. Either she was younger than I had thought originally—younger and more delicate—or else it was the wine she had had. Or else it was the wine *I* had had. I said ardently—sounding even to my own ears like a high school kid—that I thought her hemoglobin-chlorophyll research the most brilliant thing she had ever done.

She took a deep breath, as if something was finally finished. Had I overstayed my time and got on her nerves? Could that cryptic expression have meant no more than boredom? That couldn't be. Only a moment ago . . . yet, something in her had vanished before my eyes—leaving her lightless and remote.

I gave up and rose from the table. She was a woman I understood less than ever, I thought hopelessly. Perhaps it was I who had vanished for her.

"I'm sorry I went on so long," I said, "but I wanted you to have some idea of the work and why it's important to do."

She smiled up at me absently and said nothing. Or could she be still punishing me?

"I'd better go now," I said; but I stood waiting, silently hoping that in spite of my fiasco, she'd still invite me to contribute to the seminar. How could she pay me the enormous personal compliment of having lunch with me, and yet refuse the professional favor of the impersonal invitation to attend the meetings? With a burst of impatience, I wondered again where, for God's sake, was that side of her that had appeared so warm in London? I willed it to reappear, but she only looked at me as if surprised that I hadn't already gone.

"Good-by," she said. I took my dignity through the corridors to the front door. Then I stopped and went right back to her. She was already at work in her laboratory, standing in front of a table, watching the tall twin glass cylinders of a titration apparatus. Some green liquid had been running out of one cylinder into the common beaker; then a colorless liquid began running in drops out of the other. She stood there turned away from me with her hands alert on the stopcocks of the two cylinders, her eyes moving continuously from the beaker, where the fluids mixed, to the graduated marks etched on the glass, waiting for the indicator in the beaker to change to some characteristic color when the end-point was reached.

I remained at her door, waiting for her, aware too that I was seeing her as she had, and would, spend most of her hours of the days of her life. At just such a worktable. Wearing just such a white coat.

Most other chemists of her importance would have given the titration to a lab assistant; but she did all her own work herself: it was all chemistry and that apparently was what she lived for. The phenolphthalein in the beaker suddenly became red, and she caught the instant of transition with exquisite precision. The stopcocks turned, and only now that the measurement was over could she see who had been behind her all this time. She looked at me with surprise.

"I'd like very much to be able to attend the Tuesday seminars here," I said, straight out. "Could that be arranged?"

"Of course," she said, as if there had never been any need for me to ask. "Any time you think it will be interesting, please come." But then again she took part of it back, because she added: "Make it two weeks from tomorrow. Tomorrow and next week I don't think are for you."

I walked briskly down the corridor again. Until that moment, I had never once thought or cared about "my position" as a scientist. Yet she piqued me. She was continually ruffling a pride I hadn't even known I possessed!

By the time I had walked no further than the Place de l'Estrapade, I decided that I'd be damned if I'd go to any of the seminars! Then, with the sun still shining, the soft Paris rain began again. I took momentary shelter in the center of the triangular Place under the trees, which were jeweled with rain and sparkling with sunlight. As I stood there, all my anger with her collapsed. Of course, I'd go! And be damned glad of the chance!

3

REGULARLY, ONE NIGHT A MONTH, UNTIL THEN, I HAD been going only to meetings of the Société de Physique in the old Société d'Encouragement on the Place de St. Germain des Prés just opposite the church. Perhaps a fourth of us at those monthly sessions were foreigners—American, English, Japanese, Rumanian, Polish, Swedish, but we all spoke scientific French. The entire audience—French and foreign scientists alike—would descend like a regiment after each meeting, all talking and laughing at once, into the darkness of the street. Some of us, concerned with a topic that had come up during the evening, went only as far as the lights at the corner and settled down at the Brasserie Lipp across the boulevard where the argument went into high gear. The rest of us, still talking, continued through the night along the boulevard. Another group, impassioned about another problem, fell away, headed toward the Café Cluny. The main body of us used to turn off to the Rue de l'Ecole de Médecine up the slanting hill, across the Boulevard St. Michel to the Café Balzar where the main post-meeting sessions could boil with feeling. The Balzar was our territory—when I say *our,* I mean of course the French scientists—because by my second year there I had begun in the back of my mind to think of myself as a Parisian.

The meetings themselves were rather cold and unexciting, entirely unlike Julie's seminars, which could generate fire even before you got there. Simply to pass through the door into the crowded room on the top floor of her Institute was an electric experience.

The first time I entered, the room was hot with men's bodies and already close. Some thirty or forty men were standing around and talking to each other in small groups, giving the impression of two hundred conversations. The meeting began at once. The large room—bare except for blackboards, cheap folding chairs, and blue cigarette smoke—became quiet. The men took chairs and set them haphazardly facing the blackboard, the thin men with arms and legs folded in angular patterns; the fat men with heavy buttocks sagging over the sides of chairs like blue serge saddle bags. Their eyes, however, sharply intelligent, penetrating, impatient, defined the men and told you who they were and what standards they set for original creative thought. More than anything, though, you knew that these men actually worked—some for years—on experiments of historic value. Also, they were without money and never thought about it.

Julie was the only woman present. She wore a dark dress without her lab coat and sat among everyone else. An impromptu air gave an easiness to the meeting. Everybody seemed to have just walked in from his laboratory full of his immediate problems. Julie controlled the selection of her weekly guests by a standard more brutally exclusive than that used by any Parisian society hostess, but she looked as if it had all just happened to her too. No one was invited—man or woman—unless he or she had already given concrete proof of an unusual mind at work. To this day, men still boast of the time they were in Paris and attended a Claudet seminar. And if presence at only one meeting carried such an aura of honor, imagine what it meant to be a "regular"! Each Tuesday meeting was brilliant in a different way. You were always hearing a progress report on work, months, or even a year before it would make its appearance in the *Comptes Rendus,* the *Proceedings of the Royal Society,* or *Der Annelen der Chemie.* In the brief time I went to the Institute's Tuesdays, I can think of at least two papers describing early stages of what turned out to be Nobel Prize researches.

Discussion after each paper was just as creative and penetrating as the papers themselves. You were continually gasping at the brilliance of what was being said around you. Then you discovered that all along your own mind had been racing on with the stream. Suddenly you too were on your feet adding still another possibility to the ideas already raised, and in the crush after the meeting, you too were sought out by the bearded man who had spoken before you because he wanted to continue the discussion along the lines on which the two of you agreed passionately or disagreed violently. I used to come away from each Tuesday meeting in a kind of intellectual fever.

The first time I sat in silent appreciation. After it was over, I pushed my way through to Julie to thank her. She merely smiled up at me, accepted my gratitude, and turned away. Once more I had to put down my pride and ask if I could come again.

"In three weeks there might be something," she said after a moment. "Come on the twenty-seventh."

Once more, I felt challenged by her indifference, and during those three weeks, I swore I wouldn't go. Yet when that particular Tuesday came, I pulled my trench coat collar up about my ears, pulled my hat down so far that the rain dripped off my hat brim as if it were a country eave, and trudged off to the Institute until a tram came clanging along. I couldn't stay away.

Again this second time the fever of excitement caught me. Again I sensed my life being heightened to some maximum capacity I had never suspected in myself.

I had to ask for my invitation to all the other meetings that followed. I put it to Vaillant finally, when he was in the lab. "What is it with her? Or with me? I never met anyone before who affected me that way."

He stood there thoughtfully, the stocky, powerful little man with the foppish-looking eyepiece (he wore a monocle, I discovered, only because he came out of the war with one eye), the clipped white hair, and my question.

"I myself never go to her seminars," he said.

"She was rude to you too? To *you?*"

"She is never rude," he said gently. "It's that everything now is locked up inside her. She is too preoccupied. She simply doesn't see one any more."

"But she does when she wants to; and it's like having ten thousand searchlights on you."

"Ah, her warmth!" He smiled a little as if this were all an

old story. "Yes, there are probably moments when one sees it again, but—" He shook his head. "Listen, if the sunrise were to begin to come once every five years or so and then only for a few minutes at a time, people would soon give up counting on daylight! I choose not to go to the Claudet seminars—brilliant as they are—because I prefer to remember another era entirely—another Madame Claudet, for that matter."

"The sunlight's there, all right," I insisted. "I saw it once."

"Then by all means continue to go."

"No," I said. "That's finished. I will never ask again. She's the one who has to ask now."

4

I STOOD BY THE RESOLUTION FOR SEVERAL WEEKS.

Then I heard through a friend of mine—the American wife of a well-connected French businessman—that Julie had accepted an invitation to dine at the home of some people in Passy on the Avenue Kléber—one of the very rare evenings she consented to go out.

"I want to be invited too," I telephoned to my friend. "Arrange an invitation for me."

"Oh, I can't," she said, laughing. "You know I can't."

"Try," I said. "I want to see what she's like outside of a professional contact."

Misunderstanding accomplished what I couldn't do directly. The host heard my name and mistakenly assumed that I was in Paris representing the family firm. The invitation was easy, and I had no qualms about ethics.

I arrived before Julie, but the moment I entered the long hall with its bronze-flowered lamps, its length of Persian carpeting, its massively carved dark wooden staircase curving up into the mysteries of a large household, I knew that I had only worked my way back into a French version of the very atmosphere I had left at home on Eighty-seventh Street.

Recognition became still stronger when I was led to join the company in the oak-paneled library. It was lined from floor to ceiling with books hardly anyone read any more.

Even the furniture was what I had fled from: curved antique woods, draped pale silks, tapestries, tassels, and fringes. The men and women radiated the same calm sense of their own worth I had always felt in my own family. However, one obvious difference was that the women were more sparklingly alive to a flattering look from a man. Another was that the men obliged, when they remembered, with a heavy gallantry. Just as at home at dinner they never mentioned money, but everything they spoke about—horses, painting, châteaux, shooting—implied money. These people were my relatives intensified in every way: richer, more refined, more brutally complacent behind their refinement. What Julie had to do with them and this atmosphere, I couldn't imagine.

Her arrival splattered the party with contrast. Her plain dress was of some kind of black material; it had no style, but it made all the other women seem crisper, more smartly groomed, yet uniform. Julie at that moment looked like nothing so much as a woman who had jumped furiously out of bed, pinned up her hair, thrown the nearest garment on, and, with her mouth still full of hairpins, her hands behind her still hooking her brassiere, her feet still finding themselves in her pumps, had come running all the way up the Avenue Kléber only to pause for a moment at the door to catch her breath and shake herself together. She was probably a shock to each woman's sense of style, but to every man there she was violently animal; one could almost smell her overheated body, almost feel her warmth, almost see her full-bodied white nudity. The partial disarray of her hair didn't seem slatternly, but simply a sign of excitement. It was hard for me to think of her without desire.

I greeted her like an old friend. I was right: the atmosphere was not congenial to her. I thought wryly: even I look good to her here, because after greeting her hostess she came directly to me. We were fellow countrymen in a foreign land, not only as Americans in France, but as scientists among the latter-day medievalists. We arranged at once that I was to drive her home. Then we went in to dine.

The dinner itself was extremely formal. It went swiftly, but not swiftly enough for me. My partners gave me up as hopeless: my attention was only for Julie. I couldn't take my eyes off her. Her manner with these people was reserved, even a little shy, but actually she was so used to being the most distinguished woman present wherever she was that she was completely poised. She had a queenly simplicity.

The men around the table addressed her with a certain deference that was very different from the gallantry with which they spoke to the other women. The greatest compliment these men could pay Julie by their own standards was to treat her an equal, yet even as she spoke their eyes took on the warm awareness that she was female.

She was frank about her opinions. Sometime in the past, she had gone out a great deal into intellectual Paris, but it all had stopped about ten years ago. She spoke easily. Either she was serious about something, or else she dismissed it entirely.

As an American, I was not used to scientists who were also cultivated outside their science, and I sat there as impressed as they were by the breadth of the interests for which she had real feeling. The only hint of difficulty came with politics—hers were uncompromisingly left in the tradition of French science—but this was a dinner party in the stronghold of the French right. She had known Jaurès, and the faces of the men around the table turned colder and colder. The man sitting opposite her bore as much as he could, twitching like a goaded bull. Then political passion overbore gallantry, and over a certain point he broke out: "But not in France, Madame. We French—"

His mother-in-law cut in to remind him that Madame Claudet was also French now.

"One does not *become* French," the man said coldly. "One is *born* French of French parents!"

Protests were instantly made by some of the ladies pointing to other naturalized Frenchmen of whom France was proud, but without too much conviction, and I saw the loneliness on Julie's face. Outside of her laboratory in the Rue d'Ulm and her French colleagues, France had not really given her a home. And when, in addition, someone airily dismissed the poor translations of Shakespeare into French by saying: "France has so many great poets of her own she has no need of translations from other languages!" Julie and I glanced at each other in helpless fellowship: the company didn't even know they had excluded us. French chauvinism made us close friends.

We left together. As we drove away in my car, I asked why she had come here of all places. She told me that she owed a moral debt of sorts to the host's father: twenty years earlier when she and Claudet were in the midst of their great work, there had been no money to continue the research, and the elder Trussac had helped Georges with some kind of grant.

"That's why I came," she said. "Why did *you* come?"

"Because I knew you were going to be there," I said. "That was reason enough for me."

She was silent for a moment, and the wind blew past the car's canvas window flaps. The autumn air was almost crystalline in its dark brilliance. We were driving along the Seine toward Auteuil.

"Can't we go someplace?" I asked, glancing sideways at her.

"Go where?" she asked at last, very cautiously.

"Oh, I don't know. Name a restaurant or a café."

"I'm afraid that I can't."

"That's the third time you've refused me. Is the reason that it would embarrass you to be seen?"

"No," she said quietly. "The reason is that I have a young daughter waiting for me who's afraid to go to sleep if I'm not home."

The house was a modest one on a dimly lit street in St. Cloud. We stopped. I didn't know whether I was expected to go in with her, or to say good night and drive away. I could have happily done either. I got out of the car and opened her door for her. She shook my hand as she got out, automatically saying: *"Bon soir, monsieur."*

"You're so damn French sometimes!" I said. "How do you manage to remember to speak English to me? Are you sure you're aware that I'm an American?"

"Don't worry," she said, and she could have been laughing in a soft, low insinuation. Only then did she withdraw her hand. "I'm aware of you."

I was as dizzy as if she had suddenly touched me intimately. She hadn't said good night. She walked right past me up to her door, reaching into her bag for her key. I followed her. In the drawing room—small, squarish, densely furnished with green-tapestried furniture, fringed lamps, and tables that stood on gilt-balled feet, a single soft light glowed from a table lamp with a gold-tasseled green silk shade. From the hallway where I stood, I saw a whirl of whiteness speed down the stairs and run into the room with Julie. I heard a gasp, and then Julie's laugh, saying in French: "Darling, please,

I've brought home a friend, an American gentleman, a colleague . . ."

"But, *Maman!*" I could hear a passionate objection. "I have no robe on!" Then a fierce whisper which was not supposed to be for my ears: *"Is he old?"*

"Old enough, but also young," Julie replied with a stage whisper.

At this point I came into the room, and saw a dark thin girl with enormous dark eyes standing barefoot in a voluminous nightgown. Her straight hair was brown, and a little red ribbon made a bow over her forehead. Her features were very regular and delicate. Without being pretty she had great sensitivity. She stared at me, holding a green book open at her side. We were introduced. She said, "How do you do?" in very precise English. I tried to make her smile but she continued to look at me with great watchfulness. She left, after kissing her mother. Julie said: "Call me when you're in bed, and I'll come up."

With a small, sad smile, Julie picked up the green book left behind. It was Shaw's "Man and Superman." Julie handed it to me. "For my benefit," she said. "She thinks she has to show me what serious books she reads. She feels she has to live up to me. Poor Suzy! How I wish I were a better mother!" Then the girl called down to her from above, and Julie went out of the room to her. For at least ten minutes, I heard their low voices above me in a passionate discussion. At one moment I thought there were tears, but then the girl was laughing, and the talk rushed on. I sensed the girl's intensity and her passion for her mother. If I hadn't been there, they both would have been far happier. I thought of calling up the stairs that I was leaving, but then I remembered her remark as she was getting out of the car. She had promised me something and I wasn't going to leave until I knew what it was.

I wandered about the room. One of the tables was covered with snapshots standing in little metal frames—pictures of Julie and Georges Claudet on bicycles when she was in her twenties; pictures of them both seated in a field of daisies; pictures of them standing against the fender of a 1912 Renault; Julie holding a baby and waving her hand at the camera. What a handsome man Claudet had been! Her face was serene, intelligent, and somewhat aloof. There was a picture of him smiling. He had intensity, but there was no humor in his eyes. He was probably idealistic, perhaps fanatically so. Yet he was not what I would call a masculine man. Whatever he had been, here was the evidence of a close-knit family.

I felt very much out of place. I had probably misinterpreted the meaning of what she had said getting out of the car. The more I thought of it, the more ridiculous I looked to myself. The whole thing was insane. Paris was full of girls—wonderful girls—and here I was out in the suburbs waiting for a woman who had accomplished far more than I could ever hope to in my wildest dreams, who was not only infinitely superior to me as a scientist and almost old enough to be my mother, but was devoted to the memory of a dead husband who also towered over me in stature. She was tied to a child who hungered for every moment she had to spare. There was something horribly wrong, even ugly, about my waiting for her.

I took my coat, started for the door, then instead went up the stairs. One room full of soft light was open to the narrow hallway. Suzy was in bed, her thin body making only the slightest outline beneath the white blankets. Her pipestem arms were folded behind her head. The girl who had sat up for hours holding a copy of Shaw to impress her mother was now very happy to let her mother read to her a chapter of a fairy tale before going to sleep. They both looked up, slightly guilty, when they saw me standing in the doorway.

"I am afraid I've got to go," I said. "Please don't bother to come down and let me out. I'll find my way."

Julie rose and looked at me intently. I think she was relieved.

"Good night," she said. Her voice was gentler than at any time she had ever spoken to me. "And thank you."

"Good night, Suzy," I said to the girl, and smiled, but Suzy did not smile back. She simply looked at me with wide dark eyes and waited.

I hurried down the steps. At the front door, I paused hopefully for a moment. Upstairs I heard the smooth low voices. She had no intention of calling after me. I left the house.

Nothing had been said about the seminars. I hadn't even thought of them. But when I did, I decided to continue to stay away.

5

DAYS BECAME GRAY. THE SKY ITSELF SETTLED DOWN on the city as a single massive cloud and streets and boulevards disappeared in vapory mist. The air turned colder and snow fell. My experiment on electrophoresis was time-consuming and I was making little headway. One Tuesday morning, I received a *pneumatique* which read: "Due to illness, Villefort-Augustin will not be able to give his paper. Instead M. Yang will talk on *Kinetics of Protein Precipitation and Fibrination*. At two o'clock at the Institut Claudet. Please come. J. Claudet."

At last she had invited me of her own accord, and I was free to go! Julie was the center of the room for me from the moment I entered. Even when Yang began to speak, I had my eyes on her, on the play of her face, on the way her fingers touched her chin, her cheek, her hair in an unceasing, unthinking caress. I hardly heard what was said. In the talk that followed the paper—even though I was more qualified than anyone to appraise it—I sat without a word. She interrupted the discussion at one moment to turn and ask me specifically if I had any comment. I shook my head and she tightened her lips. After the talk, Julie beckoned to me.

"You were a disappointment today!" she said, looking up at me as I stood over her.

"I?"

"When Villefort-Augustin had to cancel, I wondered which would make a better program—a paper by you with discussion afterwards led by Yang, or Yang's paper with a discussion afterwards by you. Was your silence diplomatic, or what?"

A touch of color came into her cheeks and she frowned. She couldn't bear being laughed at by a man. "What's so funny?"

"I'm not amused—this is helpless rage," I said. "If you had wanted me to perform, you should have warned me."

"There wasn't time."

"Of course there was! A paper as important as this shouldn't have to be a last-minute substitution."

Her brows rose. Her entire head lifted. Had I committed *lèse-majesté* by criticizing her arrangements? I should have been terrified. Instead, I was so damned tired of the whole business that I couldn't have cared less. I pulled over an empty chair and placed it before her. I straddled it as I sat down facing her.

"Please, let's forget it," I said. "Instead let's talk about dinner some time." The invitation—certainly impulsive, probably impertinent, was a surprise to both of us. Her eyes widened slightly and I tried to remember when the lines about her eyes had seemed anything but entirely natural. I loved her.

"When will you be free?" I asked again.

"Suzy is in the country visiting her grandparents."

"You mean this evening?" I asked.

"Why not?" And again she used the same quiet tone which she had used getting out of my car the last time I had seen her. Once more I felt the burst of brilliance in my blood but her composure was perfect as she rose and turned away to speak to someone who came up to her.

Soon the room began to thin out. I asked her if she wanted time to go home to change her clothes. She shook her head. "Let's not go to a select restaurant!" she said. I had to smile— an American using the word *select* in so French a fashion. I teased her about it. "Oh, I'm no longer an American, I'll never be French. I'm simply a woman—a woman tired to death," she said. "If you can arrange an evening for me so that I don't have to *do, be,* or *think* anything, that'll be fine. Otherwise, I'll make an egg and some tea by myself downstairs and go on working."

"No, it'll be as you say. But if you're so tired, what's all this talk about taking an evening off to go on working?"

"Ah, you don't understand," she replied. "It isn't work that tires me, it's living that does it. I hurt people! People hurt me! Work is easy! Work is simple!"

6

IT WAS SNOWING WHEN WE LEFT TO GO OUT. FEATHERY flakes whirled and flickered through the yellow spheres of light that surrounded each street lamp on the Rue St. Jacques. Our footfalls were as hushed when we walked past the Sorbonne as if we were walking down a long slope of white velvet. An occasional automobile floated down the hill by us without a sound.

"There's something I've been wanting to ask you," I said.

"What is it?"

"Do you remember that London meeting when we first spoke to each other?"

"Yes."

I hesitated a moment but then took the plunge. "Why did you sail into me like that?"

I heard her laugh softly. "Did I?" she asked.

"You know you did."

"Probably because you weren't honest," she said. "Your paper had been so good and then you spoiled it for me. You made me angry—aesthetically angry."

"But you were so damn personal about it!"

"I was not," she said at once. "I took great pains to be pleasant to you—I liked the research you had done."

"You didn't say anything about that side of it."

"The very fact that I took the trouble to talk about it proved I did. And then you had a certain quality that I liked —behind that façade. Actually there's something I've been wanting to ask you too."

"Go ahead."

"Why did *you* do it? Rather, how could you let yourself bluff like that? Because what I saw was someone who is honest and sensitive."

"If I was bluffing, and I'm not ready to admit it, I could have done it only to impress you."

"Me?"

"Of course you! You know damn well that I worship you! I can't think straight when you're around."

She said nothing, but I felt the light weight of her hand on my arm as her willingness to acknowledge me. I tightened my arm to press her hand against my body, aware of how disingenuous a gesture it was, terrified when I stopped to think who she was, that she would glance up and laugh at me, or what was worse, look bewildered because she didn't understand the impulse. Yet in another instant, within the shelter of my heavy overcoat, her gloved fingers seemed to tighten surreptitiously on me, and her face, in the murky snowlight was also as drawn and somber as I felt my own to be.

"I don't want you ever to bluff again," she said. "There are too many trivial things in life you can be dishonest about, but never about the work—not with what you have."

I nodded my promise. I saw only her face and her intention, not the plain coat or her unbecoming hat. A surge of feeling for her swept through me. Her pride was at my mercy and I protected her. She was the most brilliant, the most gifted, the finest woman in the world! She looked the way she did, I made myself feel, because that was the way I *wanted* her to look, by God; and this was the way we would be walking together next week, next month, next year, ten years from now—

Then came the shock of pain: in ten years I would be thirty-eight, and she would be in her middle fifties, edging towards sixty! My God, how deathly it sounded. Whatever she would be in ten years, that night she was what I wanted desperately. And just because there was obviously no long future ahead for us, my tenderness increased! I saw myself as the beginning of her death.

I tightened my arm again on her hand and once more her hand seemed to press back ever so faintly. We walked down along Rue St. Jacques to Rue des Ecoles and turned into the Balzar in silence. I was full of love, full of grief for our eventual sadness, yet underneath everything else, I was taut with a thrusting pride that I, with no premonition at any point in my life, had grown up enough of a man and a scientist to rate Julie Claudet as my woman. It never occurred to me that there could be any other reason for her interest in me than a feeling on her part as deep as mine.

We sat at a corner table, ate oysters, drank muscadet, and said nothing. We were sitting together: for me that was happiness enough and there was nothing I felt like talking about. When she had finished her oysters, she continued to sit, quietly, looking down at her folded hands on the table. Her interlaced fingers slowly turned a wine glass around and around.

"Would you like to go someplace and eat now?" I asked.

She shrugged.

"Or would you like to walk a while more and then go to your place?" The glass stopped its turning, her fingers poised in waiting. I went on: "Or to mine?"

The glass resumed its slow turn again, but now in the other direction.

"How sure you are of yourself!" she said thoughtfully.

"You make it sound ugly. I was thinking how good it was that we could know what the other was feeling."

Again the glass stopped and now she glanced up at me. "How can you think that you know what I feel? Or what I am?"

I said nothing.

"But based on what?" she insisted. "I don't know anything about your life. And you know nothing of mine. The differences between us are so fantastic—"

"What differences?" I asked. "What important difference?"

She shook her head after a moment. Fifteen years of things too poignant for words were in that weary gesture. "What's the point of talking?" she said. "I'm out of my mind. And as for you—" she paused and then said abruptly and without expression. "It's too bad! Really too bad!"

We left the café and walked again for a while. At the Carrefour de l'Odéon, a snoutlike Renault taxi loomed out of the snow-fog of the Boulevard St. Germain. Without asking Julie whether she wanted to go or not, I stopped it and gave the driver my address. She said nothing. Seated side by side, I slipped my arm through hers, and still no change of expression acknowledged the touch. I was frightened. In my heart I knew I was in the presence of majesty—she could crush me with a flick, but then she let herself lean against me, and finally I relaxed too.

She came into my room, and before I pressed the wall switch, I kissed her. She held me to her lightly, then released herself and moved away in the darkness.

"Put on the lamp," she said quietly. I did. Her face was thoughtful. She was only mildly curious about where and with what I lived. Then she glanced at me. "You know, beyond a certain point, things make no sense. I am forty-six, you're twenty-eight."

"Well?"

She smiled slightly. "Now, exactly what does that *well* mean? That it makes no difference to *you?*"

"Exactly."

"Then I must tell you that it makes a difference to *me*," she said.

"But who cares—?"

"It's not a matter of *who*," she said. "It's a matter of *what* —of what happened to me in all the years between us. I felt more than I ever wanted to feel; and I don't want to feel any of it ever again. And it's all beyond your experience, beyond your present capacity to understand. You're attractive, you're even brilliant, and probably you're more of a man at your age than many men who are older. But there's still my whole lifetime between us."

I called her name and reached for her, but she simply shook her head, and I couldn't touch her. She didn't remove her hat or coat, and within twenty minutes she asked me to take her home. I did. We rode all the way in silence to her house, and I took the same taxi back to my place.

We had dinner several times after that, and we talked only about work. Far in the back of my heart I was deeply insulted in a way I could never explain to her. I resolved never to try. Then one night she suddenly put her coffee cup down, looked at it for a long time thoughtfully and with a frown: "I'm ready," she said in a low voice.

I didn't know what she was talking about. "To go home?"

She shook her head, still frowning, still not looking up.

"To go with you," she said, and I felt as if I had been stabbed in my lungs by sweetness, that a miracle had happened.

The true miracle came when she dropped the disguise of the shapeless dress, the old-fashioned underwear, for beneath it all, her skin was soft, rounded, unbelievably smooth and fair. Across her shoulders were childish golden freckles. Her waist was small and moved convulsively with the intensity of her breathing. Even the way she moved was young, her arms held close to her body, her barefooted steps short and quick as if she were shy and ashamed—yet there was neither shame nor self-consciousness in the way she took me to her. She was languorous and compliant, her eyes closed, her forehead slightly frowning, her lips parted by the tip of her tongue as if she were absorbed in the most intense concentration, or the coming of a sound almost too delicate to hear.

Then when she had me in her control exactly to her satisfaction, she took command with a seeming wildness that was really the most exquisitely explored self-knowledge. She overwhelmed me with her vitality, and the opulent generosity with which she used and gave herself.

She rested then quietly, satisfied for a while, but not spent, her eyes still closed as she lay on the pillow next to me; and with her palms and fingertips—like little questions—she lightly pressed my lips, my cheeks, my ears, asking their shape and texture. She felt that my eyes were open, then closed them like hers, and she caressed my lashes with the lightest exploring touch, even smoothed my eyebrows. Then later, she put her fingers on my lips to be kissed, then her palms, then her wrists, and gradually worked her arms about me again, and herself to me. Once again her breath was quick, and for another time I was caught up in her rhythm.

She rested, and now her eyes were open and looking at me levelly as we lay with our heads separated by only half the width of the pillow. Her gaze was candid, searching, serene; but I found it hard to believe the whole thing had happened.

I leaned over and kissed her gently. She closed her eyes.

"That's what I wanted to do in London the first time I saw you," I said.

"You hated me in London."

"Yet that's what I wanted."

She nodded slowly, her eyes remaining closed.

"I wanted you," I said. "But what I wanted was nothing like this turned out to be. I had given up hoping it could ever be like this. When I was a kid, I used to torment myself with delirious dreams of what it might be like to make love to a woman. By God, I used to imagine transports of ecstasy that could have melted steel!"

Her closed lids and lips smiled slowly.

"But it was never like that with anyone—except with you now," I said, and her eyes came open at once, seriously, sharply, with a frown, to test my truth. Then she was reassured and her gaze softened. "And I have a terrible premonition that it'll never happen again for me with anyone else."

She said nothing, not surprised by what I said, still searching my face.

"What are you looking at?" I asked.

"Your eyes."

"And what do you see?"

"What you feel."

"And that is?"

"What I feel too."

I leaned down and kissed her. "And if I'm in love with you?" I asked.

She rose abruptly resting on her elbow, her face changed and became serious. Her hair streamed down to the pillow, and she held the weight of her breasts in her hands.

"But you're not in love with me," she said at once. "Don't talk like that! Please!"

"But if it's the truth?"

"It's not. There will be no love between us, or even talk of it. What you and I feel is something else—something simpler, thank God!" She was getting out of bed now, but she glanced back at me, her instinctive alarm replaced by an imploring little frown. "But not love. Oh God!" she sighed. "Not love, please!"

I watched her from the bed as she put her hair up again. She stood before my mirror, her arms raised, her head slightly bent as she put in the hairpins with quick deft motion. I deliberately avoided looking at her neck and throat. It was as if having seen her as young as a girl, I was afraid that I would now see her once again as she really was, but I loved her so much, it made no difference what she looked like.

"My God, what a marvelous surprise you were!" I said again, because the burden of tenderness for her in me was actually a tangible weight. "I meant it when I said I can't imagine that there'll ever be anyone like you again for me."

She worked away at her dark blond hair, separate strands in back falling from her control a moment after she had pinned them in place. Still she managed, and at last she said: "I thought you said you knew exactly what I was like."

"Ah, who could have guessed!" I said. *"Madame la savante! Madame la directeur!* And that disguise you go around in! Where do you find those dresses?"

She laughed, flushing slightly, as she worked on her hair.

"I can't help the dresses," she said. "Clothes don't interest me."

"That's what I mean. Only a genius could have guessed what you're really like!" She was smiling at my ardor; then like a fool I went on to say: "But then of course that's what he was."

"He?" she said absently.

"Georges Claudet, of course."

Her hands stopped, still paused in her hair, and she stared at herself in the mirror, then at me. Her face had looked expressionless, but now I could see in her eyes the sudden weight of her pain. She just stood there, mute. For the first time in my life, I think I was terrified of another person because for the first time in my life here was someone against whom I had no true defense.

"We won't talk about Georges," she said at last. "Not ever!"

We left and I took her home. We said very little. The snow had stopped, and the night had a still, dark transparency. The low houses and the high walls along the narrow suburban street made two black ribbons converging above the fallen snow to a distant darkness. I took her key and unlocked her door for her. She seemed absorbed, only half present. She had gone away from me. I was sad with the premonition of loss. I loved her more than I had ever thought I could love a woman.

"When will I see you again?" I asked, giving her the key.

"I don't know. I'll call you."

"I'll call *you*," I said quietly reclaiming my masculine prerogative. "In any event, I'll see you next Tuesday."

"Oh, the seminar?" she said mechanically. "No, next Tuesday won't be of interest to you."

I stared down at her, speechless with hurt, but she was already thinking of something else. Then as if we had been intimate for a long time she continued a conversation we had dropped hours before.

"Georges didn't ever see me as I really am," she said thoughtfully. And then she added a remark that went off like a time bomb: "I think he must have been the only one who never did!"

7

SHE HAD THE MOST EXPRESSIVE EYES I'VE EVER KNOWN. From forty years ago, they still look at me: light and gray. They could be cool with amusement, icy with contempt, or—when glittering black pupils were enlarged—smoky with desire. It seemed to me that I was always being appraised by a serene intelligence so penetrating that I was absolutely transparent to her. Then too they could turn a listless dreary gray with a boredom that was maddening to watch. She, in her turn, could be so irritated with me that she could scarcely speak. Once when we were sitting in a café I accused her of not being interested in anything that happened to me before I knew her. She cloaked herself with the appearance of teasing.

"Because *nothing* ever happened to you," she replied. "All you've ever had was a good time in different ways. What Tolstoy said about happy families applies to you too: all good times are alike."

"You're wrong about good times, and Tolstoy was wrong about happy families," I retorted.

She smiled a little.

"That's better," she said. "Sometimes I even think you have promise!"

"Thanks for that *sometimes!*"

She sat back, and those gray eyes held a light, sardonic glitter. She was hurting me and she knew it. Later she would be sorry and try to take it back or make up for it with kindness, but now she was running with the wind in her hair.

"That's not enough?" she asked. "Am I supposed to admire you all the time?"

"No," I said. When she was like that, I became cold and short. How could I expect her to feel anything for me when she had known Georges Claudet? She never mentioned him directly or indirectly as "my husband," but I always knew that I was being compared to someone who stood behind me.

In the middle of a conversation, she would lose touch with me and her eyes would go deep with inexpressible longing for a time before pain began. The silence of remembering made her unreachable. Then she would look at me with a frown, wondering what this stranger was doing by her side at a moment like this. One of the reasons she attacked me so mercilessly from time to time was that I wasn't the absent being for whom she longed. It was pathetic, in a way, but it was cruel, and once I told her angrily that the very location of her lab was symbolic. One street, the Rue d'Ulm, was the scene of some of the greatest work in French science—Pasteur's old lab at one end and the Curies' near the other. Yet at Julie's corner, this street intersected with the Rue de l'Estrapade—and the Place de l'Estrapade's triangle of six trees marked where— centuries ago—military deserters and thieves used to be weighted with stones and dropped down on rocks from a high wooden platform, again and again, until all their limbs were dislocated.

"At the corner of the Best and the Worst, that ought to be your address!" I said. "Print it on your cards! It's you!"

When I said it, instead of giving me the angry retort I expected, her eyes filled with tears: "And you were the man who said he knew what I felt. I was foolish to expect you to understand me!"

I looked at her helplessly. I couldn't imagine what there was that needed understanding. More than twelve years had passed since Georges Claudet's death. He was an experienced Alpinist and had never done anything foolish or rash except for that one time. In the two weeks before his death, Claudet had become taut and self-absorbed. Someone said he looked as if he were trying to make himself comprehend something beyond comprehension. Someone else said the same thing differently—he seemed to be trying to accept some horrible fact that was unacceptable.

According to his pictures, he had been a slight, fair man; erect and at the same time almost ethereal, in a way a fencing foil vibrating in the sunlight can glitter like gossamer. In a group picture of a meeting of Nobel laureates a week before his death, he looked like a man who was mortally sick.

As to his actual death, I knew only what everyone else had read. On the day the accident happened, Julie had come home from the laboratory at her regular time, surprised to find Georges not there too. On that particular day, he was to give a morning lecture at the Sorbonne. He had not given his lecture. Instead, he had taken the nine o'clock train for Zurich, where he made an immediate connection. By five o'clock in the afternoon, he was at the base of the Winterfall and already climbing. He was well known to everyone in the town, and no one tried to stop him or even to ask him what he was doing. They all took it for granted that he was making some preparation for a climb the following morning, since he invariably began just before sunrise.

But that particular day he climbed into the winter evening darkness for three hours, according to the smashed crystal of his wrist watch. The hands were pressed flat against the face of the watch. At five minutes after eight, whatever had happened, happened. There was even evidence that he had gone over four thousand feet up the steep west face of the mountain.

I used to wonder what it was that Julie was staring at in the moments of absorption. Was she thinking of the night she had spent wondering where he had gone? Or of the telegram she had received in the morning from the burgomaster of the mountain village? Or the sight of his recovered body when she arrived there? Or of the moment of explanation to her small daughter that her father was never coming back? Whatever it was, she was staring at one of the faces of death, if not all of them.

She used to come to my place every Thursday at about six o'clock straight from her laboratory. Sometimes, she had even research notes with her. I always arranged to leave my own lab a little earlier to be there on time, and stayed later on Wednesdays and Fridays to make up for it. I had the apartment above the coach-house at Number 23 on my street, and when I looked down and saw her hurrying across the cobbled courtyard my heart began to pound. Through the porte-cochere, the wheels of the taxi that had brought her were already glittering with the movement of departure.

That winter she often used to wear a pepper-and-salt tweed suit that had a matching cape. It had been made for her as an act of devotion and homage by Paul Poiret, but Julie wore it as if she had thrown it on to run down for the mail. I remember too that she wore a dark gold velour broad-brimmed hat pierced by a cluster of gold and brown feathers. The brim curved at a piratical slant and put half her face in shadow. She wore the same hat almost every day that winter, not only for the laboratory, but to meet with the President of the Republic along with six other scientists for the formation of a French Advisory Committee on Research; she wore it to

Prague to read a paper there; she wore it for an interview she impatiently gave H. G. Wells; and she wore it while presiding over the World Science Congress held in Brussels in February.

She hated these demands on her time as futile interruptions to her work, but it was continually being explained to her that as a Famous Person, appearances were required of her. She rationed herself to accepting one out of about every four hundred requests that came pouring in on her. And one of the factors that influenced her was whether or not she would have to give more than an hour of her time.

Even then, to get her out promptly one assistant had to come with the tweed jacket and take off the smock, and while Julie was impatiently buttoning the jacket and arranging the cape, another assistant would bring that piratical hat which Julie put on without even glancing into a proper mirror, but into any glass surface that she passed on her way out, whether the front of an instrument cabinet or a balance case—no matter how distorted a reflection it gave back to her.

What I remember most about that hat though was the way she would toss it off her head and whirl it on the couch as she closed my door behind her. It was a jaunty gesture to the nine hours a day she put in, five and a half days a week at her laboratory, as if saying: to hell with everything! It made me feel that she was really happy to be with me. But then she would meet me hurrying to her and hold her face up to be kissed, her eyes half lidded, with the small, self-deprecating smile on her lips, and a sigh which either could have been happiness or her way of saying to herself: "God help me, look what I'm doing!" I could never help but give it the more bitter interpretation because it hurt me to love her so much more than she cared for me. It was because I felt helpless that I was always a little angry with her in self-defense, and I hated myself for it. I hoped the time would come when I'd feel easier, when I'd love her less, but it never came. I would watch her eyes close slowly, and then kiss her, always holding her face in the shadow of mine. The lines of her age would be softened, and blurred, but I loved them now even though I yearned to see her again with my first eyes—as a woman too old for me. I wanted my freedom from her. I longed to be released from a love that could bring me only disaster, but the terrible bondage held no matter how I distorted her features in my mind. More than anything else, I loved the feel of her mouth even though I swore I could sense that little smile through her kiss.

A hundred times I said to her: "If it means so little to you to be with me, why come?"

Sometimes my exasperation called up an equal feeling in her. More often it called up pity.

"How do you know how I feel about you?" she once said.

"I hear it in the way you sigh, I see it in the way you make fun of me; I feel it in the million things you do!"

She shook her head. "There's only one thing you know about the way I feel about you," she said, "and that is that I'm here with you like this. You torture yourself so—you can't let yourself enjoy whatever it is we *do* have that's good."

So many things she did hurt me, I told her; I admitted that I even kept wondering how many other men she had taken as lovers.

"Why should that make a difference?" she asked gently, almost pityingly; yet I knew that if I pressed too hard—I would be challenging someone far more experienced than I, someone with far greater depth of character than I. She could intimidate me with the threat of a fierce temper which I hadn't even yet seen.

"I want to know," I said stubbornly.

Her expression hardened a little. She was wondering how much truth I could stand; or how much truth I could be trusted with. I knew that whatever truth she told me would be veiled. I was heartsick.

Then she stood directly in front of me—put her hands on my arms and said deliberately: "Hal, you're the only man I've met since Georges died with whom I've had an affair."

I remember the moment she said it, and I remember the wonderful relief that came with accepting it as the absolute truth. It turned out to be the absolute truth, except that it was not the particular truth I thought at the time. Years passed before I realized that she had *not* said that she had not had an affair since Georges died. She had not practiced duplicity, only ambiguity; not out of deceit, but out of protectiveness. A long time later, I knew enough to realize that the tacit lie was the measure of how much she had wanted me to be happy, and the woman who could be angered by a lie about science had no qualms about telling a lie of kindness. She herself had said: "There are so many trivial things one can lie about—" Did it mean that love was one of them for her?

Thursdays, when she came to me, we spared little time for the ceremonies of courting. We didn't need to. We were too hungry for each other. We went directly to my bedroom. When we made love, I knew I was being loved—even adored. Every woman I ever knew afterward was to be pale in comparison.

Then we would sleep together in the Paris dusk, fitfully. She was the first to come back to the life we had left only half an hour earlier. I could never hold her because she was anxious to get on to dinner and then home because she knew that Suzy would not go to sleep without her. I could almost feel her anticipating the moment she'd leave me for Suzy. I was never told what fiction explained her absence from home until ten o'clock, except perhaps that *"Maman* is busy." I took her home in a cab, but I was never permitted to come into the house, or even leave the taxi. I rode back alone in the empty taxi, aching with the emptiness she had left, blind to the bright, crowded cafés that beckoned to me from all sides.

On other nights occasionally I was invited to dinner to catch a glimpse and a sullen, restrained curtsy from Suzy; but there was never any possibility that I could be identified with Julie's Thursday night absences. Iron walls kept me outside her life, no matter how often and desperately I flung myself against them.

In April, just before leaving my apartment one evening, I suggested that we arrange for a Sunday drive into the country for a picnic. She had been about to take her coat from me, but now she turned around.

"But you know that Sunday is the day I spend with Suzy!" she said.

"Of course. The picnic is to be for Suzy," I said.

She frowned at me. "Why?"

"But what a question! I want to do something nice for her. I want her to like me."

"But why?" she insisted. She came back to take her coat and put one arm into a sleeve.

"Well, damn it, she *has* to like me if you and I are ever going to be married!"

She turned to look at me and stood there with her coat half on. For the first time I saw someone really struck dumb. I was almost as shocked as she was, but I had spent nights wondering about it. On any level you looked at it, the idea was absurd, yet I felt that I owed it to her to give her what was—even at its most innocent—once pompously called "the protection of my name."

The coat slipped off to the floor as she burst into laughter. And now for the first time, I caught a glimpse of a wild capacity for enjoyment she must have had when she was young—a kind of endless appetite for pleasure, gaiety, fun, a willingness to dance until she dropped with exhaustion, laughing with her last breath at her own inability to dance any further. She pressed her hands to her stomach, and tears streamed down her reddened face. She gasped for breath.

"Oh, you poor man!" she cried. "You poor darling boy! Come here!" She reached for me, touched utterly; but in my humiliation, I pushed her away until she fell back against a table. I could have killed her I was in such a rage. Relief too because I *didn't* want to marry, but how dare she laugh at me!

She looked at me through her tears helplessly, but she shook her head. "Ah, you don't understand," she said. "Don't be angry with me. If I ever loved you, it was just then, so don't please—please—be angry!"

"Don't talk to me," I said. "Pick up your coat, put on your hat, and go home! I don't want you here. Get out!"

"No, please!" she said, sobering herself at once because she saw that I was absolutely serious. "I apologize for laughing, and I thank you from the bottom of my heart for the offer. You'll never know how sweet it was!"

"Sweet? Jesus God! I know how stupid it was!"

"You don't, because it wasn't," she said sincerely. She came to me, put her arms about me, refusing to acknowledge my anger. How familiar was the weight of her body against mine! There had been real sincerity in my demand that she leave: it was the one way to break off what had become an intolerable relationship, and I had half hoped she would go, but now that she was holding herself against me, I saw there would be no escape, neither through marriage to her, nor through parting. "Why do you want to marry me?" she asked.

"Because I love you."

"Thank you," she said. It was an infuriating answer.

"And because I want to help you. Every time I see that terrible sadness come over you, I sit there helpless. There you are, right before my eyes in agony, and I can't do anything for you! It's horrible to watch! I want you to be happy, damn it!"

Now she slowly released herself from me. "Ah, what a burden it must be to you!"

"I'm talking about what it must be to you."

She shook her head. "It's not as bad as it looks. I'm getting used to it. In seven years you ought to be able to get used to anything."

Seven years? Georges Claudet had been dead for twelve years! At first I thought Julie had made a mistake in arithmetic, then gradually I came to the shocking realization that her grief was not for Georges at all, but for another man, a man she had never mentioned.

8

WHO WAS THE MAN? I DIDN'T ASK. MY PRIDE WOULDN'T hear an answer. For the same reason, I suppose, I refused to ask why I couldn't be one of the "regulars" at the Tuesday seminars. Instead, in my secret heart, I was angry with her. Just the same, the angrier I was with Julie, the better were the ideas I had, and the more easily they came to me.

I used to walk away from Julie's Tuesday seminars so exhilarated that it would take hours for me to calm down and put my own ideas in order. Occasionally I left with her by my side. I did most of the talking as we would walk down to the quais and turn east along the river. Here the traffic was light, and Paris was old. If my mind went down a line of ideas that seemed faulty to her, she cut me off with a word and sent me on another line. At such times I was exuberant with invention, but she was detached and thoughtful.

To Julie the Tuesday seminars were no more than companionable gatherings. She was so at home in those rarefied altitudes that brilliance was run-of-the-mill to her and only true genius was worth remarking.

The first electrophoresis experiment suddenly seemed to solve itself and turn out well. I went on to develop the generalized technique for analysis. I published fairly often. Visiting American scientists began to look me up. When authentically creative people called it was exciting. When the man on the other end of the phone introduced himself as Professor of Embryology from the University of Upper Nowhere looking for a Good Time in Gay Paree it was irritating.

But if I was irritated by the unimaginative men among my

visitors, I was also irritated with Julie, who was the most ingenious person I knew.

From everyone else I got appreciation and even pleasure in my inventiveness, and I'm talking about men like Vaillant, Roq, Pemberton, and Weisenfeld. From Julie, no more than a shrug and a little smile: "Possibly," she'd say, or, "Not bad," and always, "Do you know whether it will work out?" And I'd have to say that I still hadn't tried it out in the lab. "Let me know what happens," would be her last word. Nothing I did seemed to impress her.

I was wrong about her though; for as lightly as she seemed to be treating my ideas, she was in fact listening carefully and critically. At one seminar discussion she tried to solve a certain dilemma by telling them of a possibility I had suggested to her at least two weeks earlier. Everyone turned to me for more details. I was forced to admit that it was still pure speculation.

"But I thought you said you were going to try it in the lab," she said. In her own eyes I had made her look foolish.

"I just didn't get around to it," I said; but now I was angry. If she had shown the slightest encouragement when I had first mentioned it, I would have raced to rig up some temporary test to see if it was worth further investigation.

"You're hard to figure out," I said to her after the meeting. "I never know exactly what you mean. I never know what you expect from me. I never know what you want me to do!"

"There's no mystery," she said shortly. "I'm waiting for *you* to show me what I have a right to expect from you."

"On Thursdays there's no big mystery about your expectations. What am I to you anyhow?"

She didn't answer me for a long time. I had finally reached her, I thought. I was beginning to be sorry. I'd been too blunt. Her eyes were reflective.

"You can do the whole thing with a Mayers flask, a reflux, and a concentration cell," she said. "In half an hour you can have an answer."

"And in less than that you can go to hell!" I replied, infuriated that my insult had gone right by her.

If there was any connection between my desire to prove myself to her and my inventiveness—as there inevitably had to be—I didn't feel it. She was a burden. I was too engrossed in an angry love. She was costing me time and energy, and for what? Satisfaction? There was none. I used to choke on the frustrated pride which she alone had called up in me. I was young, I was new, but certainly I had achieved enough already to be one of her Tuesday companions, yet I felt that I was treated that way only when I wasn't with her.

Those nights without her were torture in a dozen ways. Julie had aroused me to such a pitch of desire that I couldn't be satisfied with the one day a week she spared for love. The more she fulfilled me, the greater the hunger she created.

A thousand alternatives, some of them enormously attractive, could be found on the boulevards and in the cafés. Paris was full of women, but I simply couldn't make myself pick one of them up. It wouldn't have worked. I knew that about myself from when I had been a student. My curse is that I have to care. The few girls whom I might have cared about were so much less than Julie that I would have been bored with them in half an hour.

There seemed nothing to do but to bear my hunger. I might have been able to do that if only Julie had given me any of the things I needed from a woman, but really she gave me nothing —not even a full evening a week—only a few minutes here, a couple of hours there. If even as a fellow scientist she had given me what I wanted, I might have been able to go along on the starvation diet to which she had condemned me. I wished that I didn't give a damn about her or what she thought. I think I almost hated her in the intensity of my desire to be rid of the burden of her.

Finally I was driven, out of self-preservation, to find some sort of life of my own. I went out by myself: I prowled the cafés, cabarets, the theaters, but found no one to ease the angry frustration that was choking me until an evening of sudden rain, late in the spring when I came home with a portfolio full of work; and pushing my way through the tunnel-like arch that led to the courtyard, I recognized a girl among the people who stood waiting for the rain to stop. I had spoken to her several times before at her work in the stationery store down the street. This was the first time I was seeing her out of her shop smock. She had make-up on, and she wore high heels, a tightly belted coat, and silk stockings. She had beautiful slender legs, dark eyes, dark hair with absurdly premature strands of gray. What struck me about her in my ugly mood was the good-natured manner and smile of someone who had been a child in an affectionate and agreeable family We exchanged surprised greetings for a moment, and although she smiled, she shivered in the gusts of wind. Without the slightest sense of what was coming, I said she might as well come up to my place and wait for the rain to stop. For my own part, I added to reassure her, I had work to do. What she had that I wanted near me was her air of affability.

In my apartment, she hesitated before unbuckling her coat, but I had no patience with her standing on ceremony. She took it off and gave it to me, hugging herself because she had been so thoroughly chilled. The gesture made me notice that she was thin, but with a good figure. I was irritated that she was distracting me, so I made some tea for both of us, then went to work. I forgot about her. Two hours later, I looked up to see that she had prepared a supper.

I was deeply moved by the unexpected care. I felt an impulse to take her hand and kiss her palm the way I used to kiss my mother's hand when I was small and swept by bursts of uncontrollable tenderness. I was astonished that I could feel anything at all for any other woman when I was so deeply engrossed in Julie.

I had actually forgotten that a woman could take care of a man, be concerned about his comfort and needs, and even want him for more than the moment of desire. It made the girl a hundred times more vivid for me than she probably was —a treasure—someone I couldn't allow to pass out of my life after only one meeting. And so step by step we moved quickly toward intimacy. What made her exciting was her simple delight in what was happening. She made me conscious once again of the detail of life. She loved the awakening of desire. She loved making love and was always ready for it. She gave me back a sense of myself—an awareness that I existed. She took care of me, she would stop in on her way home and cook for me; she sewed buttons on my shirts; she told me when I needed a haircut; when my suits needed cleaning. But more than caring for me—she wanted *me*—me as a person.

Once she opened one of my books, and her face went blank with astonishment. She held out to me a page of chemical formulae and mathematical calculation—"*Tu comprends ça?*" she asked, as if it were incredible that anyone could understand such gibberish and her shrug showed wonder.

She preferred to talk about simpler things. As she became more used to me, she chattered on without waiting for, or even needing, an answer from me; and so I was free to think my own thoughts or work—as I pleased. I had affection for her, I was grateful to her, but I felt nothing deeper. It was as if she were a bird that came twittering into my room and then flew away still making its soft noises. All spring long she made me happy in a quiet way. When I knew she was coming, I used to go out in the rear and stand on the narrow stone balcony outside my bedroom and look for her coming from the street toward the river. I'd see the line of stone houses and mansard roofs, softened to a creamy gray by the bright haze of late afternoon sunlight.

The promise of a Paris summer was in the sky—cloudless and yet shimmering—as if a universe of pearls had exploded their bluish iridescence into the air, suffusing the entire atmosphere. Two orange awnings—so far down toward the Seine that they looked the size of postage stamps—were the only touch of vividness in the soft glowing world of blue and creamy pink. You could feel something like love just looking at it, and as soon as I'd see that quick trim figure below me I'd smile and step back into the room.

No matter how hard I tried to erase every mark she left on my apartment, Julie very quickly sensed the intangible atmosphere of her presence. Her eyes would narrow, and then she would point a glance at me—searching, reproachful, demanding, as if a wisp of scent, or the faintest of echoes had caught her attention. For a moment we would be held that way, then she would slowly look away. She was like a leopard with whom I had come face to face across a chasm too wide for her to leap. "There's a change in you," she said at last. She was sitting at my table, looking around my room. "What's happened?"

"Nothing. What kind of change?"

I was frightened. I had thought I would be making myself independent of her, but I hadn't. Instead, I learned even more sharply that for me there could never be a woman to replace Julie because for me there was no other woman who even came near her. In a very real sense I was being unfaithful to her; but what Julie was capable of giving was so far beyond anything within anyone else's power, that it was foolish to consider the act to be the same in both cases.

One day—early in June—Julie did something she had never done before. Still half dressed, she went directly to my wardrobe armoire and flung open the doors. I watched her from the bed, paralyzed and mute with panic. She pushed my suits back along the center rod; and there on the rear wall, she exposed a pink dressing gown. No garment ever looked more foolish or pathetic than that piece of silk. Then Julie did something which shocked me with its utter primitivism. For a long time after, I kept telling myself that it was simply the act of a trained chemist; but I always knew that it was more atavistic than that. She slowly took out the dressing gown and held it to her nose, smelling it carefully. Her face was white except for red blotches on her throat. The whites of her eyes were murky pink with feeling. For a moment she couldn't speak.

"Hal, when that woman was here yesterday," she asked at last in a low, controlled voice, "and it must have been yesterday, did you tell her that I was coming today?"

"She doesn't know about you. Julie, she's not important——"

"Neither are you!" she said as if I were distracting her from some important reflection. "It hurts!" she said, sounding distantly surprised. She was short of breath. "It really hurts!" Her lips were trembling as she looked up at me again. "Even when you don't care at all!" Her eyes filled with tears; then suddenly the tears began to stream down her face. I kept saying how little any other woman meant to me. I promised I would never see her again. I said it had happened only because Julie herself had made me feel small and unimportant; but Julie never heard a word I said. She dressed hurriedly. How beautiful her long legs were now that she was pulling on her stockings! Every movement she made while she was dressing reminded me that she was beautiful. She made no attempt to halt her tears or even to brush them away. From time to time, the intensity of her weeping was so great that she shook with sobs, but she went on with what she was doing.

I pulled together the courage to go to her because I was stricken with guilt. She was the most beautiful, the most vulnerable woman I had ever known, and I had humiliated her.

"Julie, listen, darling, don't cry, please," I said. "Nothing terrible has happened! I was with a girl a couple of times. I was lonely. She's nothing compared to you. There never will be anyone for me but you. I'll never see her again. Let's just get by this one thing, and you'll see; you'll have no reason to reproach me ever again. I'll promise it to you any way you want, or anything you want. Just don't cry."

Slowly her sobs subsided. Then she raised her tear-blotched

face; her bloodshot eyes were actually merry and surprised. Then she patted my face. My blood began to turn cold with a terrible premonition.

"Ah, Hal, what am I going to do about you?" she sighed. "You thought I was crying over you? I wasn't. I was the ghost of someone crying over me instead. And not little tears like mine, but heartbroken tears, and a long, long time ago. Don't reproach yourself." She went on wearily. "*You* did nothing wrong. I would be horrible to make you feel guilty; it would be trying to hide the fact that I've learned an awful lesson . . ."

"Julie, please, if it's nothing to you, fine; but don't let it change anything between you and me."

"It doesn't change anything, it simply ends it," she said.

She was all dressed and ready to go. The rhythm of her weeping was suddenly broken by limp bitter laughter. She stood there with that flamboyant pirate's hat in her hands, unable to put it on. I was paralyzed by sadness at the thought of losing her. Never again in my entire life would I know another woman so gifted, so large-souled, so lovely.

"Isn't it cruel how sooner or later you pay for everything! Wouldn't life be wonderful if we could learn all the lessons beforehand, and not as afterthoughts!"

"Julie, please don't go!"

"I meant what I said. It's ended. That'll be the first sensible thing you and I have done together. Why we even started, I don't know—"

"Because I wanted you, Julie, I still do—"

"—Unless I was pointing towards just such an end as this," she went on, without hearing me. "Just to prove something to myself. Only I proved the wrong thing! Or maybe all that's foolish too. How shriveled and unhappy you look, and you've done nothing to deserve it! I'll tell you what I'll do. Skip the seminar this coming Tuesday, because I still won't feel like seeing you, but after that, come as often as you please. You'd like that, wouldn't you? That's what you wanted in the first place, wasn't it?"

"Julie—!" I gasped.

"Good-by," she said, and left. I looked down through my window and watched her cross the courtyard beneath me. My heart ached, but there was no point in going after her.

I did what she told me. I didn't go to the next seminar, but to the one after, hoping that by that time she would have softened. She spoke to me as graciously as she did to the others about the work but when, afterward, I tried to speak to her privately, her eyes turned the unfocused gray of boredom. From behind that façade she hid from me. It seemed to me that it would never be different, and so even though I had at last what I had wanted more than anything in Paris—to be a "regular" at Julie Claudet's seminars, I never went back again.

9

THAT'S ALL THERE WAS.

I remained in Paris for another entire year and didn't see her. Who she was mourning, what had happened to Georges Claudet, what she even thought about him—I didn't find out.

Seven years passed before my life touched hers again. Then it was through someone who had known her long before I knew her, long before she was famous.

It happened when I went to Cambridge to give my six Winthrop Lectures at Harvard. Montgomery Crocker of the *Transcript* was then in his mid-fifties, about twenty years older than I at the time, a big, heavy-boned, sparely fleshed man. He had just recently won the Pulitzer Prize for science reporting. He looked awkward but strong. I had the sense that once he must have taken some kind of beating or defeat he had never forgotten. He didn't smile much. He dressed expensively, and he was used to his success. He moved slowly, but the slowness was a mild affectation: he enjoyed a picture of himself as the country boy come to town. "You've gone far ahead of everyone else in your field," he said to me during his interview. I accepted the praise. I was in my thirties and still sure that I would fulfill all the promises. "Ahead of everyone except one person." The slow-speaking country boy suddenly disappeared as he got to the point. "I'm wondering whether you ever came across her in Paris. I mean Julie Claudet."

"I met her," I said cautiously.

"What's she like these days?"

"Like everyone says she is."

"She was important to you?" he asked. He was looking at me sharply now that my answers were constrained.

"I met Madame Claudet after I'd already started my own work. I—"

"She was important to you?" he asked again.

"I told you—Julie is important to everyone who knows her—"

"Julie?" he said, still frowning. "Julie was also important to me."

We met several times while I was there. The one time he didn't speak of Julie was when he invited me to his home in Lexington. Then I met his wife—a pleasant enough woman —with the languid accent of a certain type of expensive boarding school. His two sons were also members of his wife's class.

After that, over the years we kept meeting. He had no illusions about life, about himself, his wife, his career, or even his sons; and so I knew he wasn't being romantic when he said that Julie had once changed the entire course of his life.

Eventually, in bits and pieces he told me how. By now, all the parts have long since fallen into their chronological order. He told it all to me rather differently, but this is the way my own memory has rearranged his way of telling it:

PART TWO—
MONTY CROCKER

1

THE FIRST TIME I SAW JULIE (CROCKER ONCE SAID)—I was riding along on the new Massachusetts Avenue electric trolley car in a blinding snowstorm. I was going out to Cambridge to visit a cousin of my aunt's, feeling sorry for myself because this was too tame a way to be spending the last day of the last week of the century. That very morning, the paper—I was with the Boston *Globe* then—had given me the second raise in the six months I had been with it. And so, for the record, at least, the young man riding the trolley was no kid reporter fresh from the New Hampshire hills; he was a young Boston journalist of promise, receiving a dignified twenty dollars—week in and week out. With my two-dollar raise, I had bought a cane to swagger into the glorious twentieth century. I sat there, the cane firmly planted on the trolley floor, my hands regally resting on the handle.

That cane was more than a disguise to hide a country boy. I had come down to Boston to conquer the world. Instead, the city had paralyzed me with shock. In those days, the *Globe* specialized in murder and murder trials. My daily assignment was horror. I saw murdered men and rape-stunned children. The very day that one trial ended, a new murder was on the front page, and New England's factory slums gave us plenty of choice. Other reporters took the assignments calmly enough. I tried to pretend that it was all in a day's work, but I longed for the time when I would be able to take everything in my stride. That cane on which I rested, and the very pose itself, represented the nonchalance I needed to keep from going mad.

My disguise also included an elegant starched white collar two inches high and a derby hat. I yearned for *style*, particularly because in those days newspapermen were not considered very high tone unless you owned the paper, or were a star like Richard Harding Davis. I lived in a boardinghouse on Brimmer Street, at the foot of Beacon Hill, just below Louisburg Square, and every morning on my way to work I promised myself that today would be the day when I would run into a young Cabot, Lodge, or Higginson of the female persuasion and end up keeping house with her on Beacon Street or Commonwealth Avenue, where no one ran shrieking from murderous madmen; where no one died of starvation.

Each day I repeated the litany: hang on, grow a tough skin, and everything will turn out fine. The salary raise that morning was proof that it was all possible. And so there I sat in the trolley leaning on my cane, reassuring myself that I was an odds-on favorite of God, and that all I had to do was to wiggle a pinkie just like that for the miracle to happen. And it happened, all right. The trolley car stopped at Guthrie Street, and the prettiest girl I ever saw in my life—she seemed about nineteen or twenty—stepped right out of the whirling white nowhere and got aboard. Pretty—but at a second look—too shy, too poor, too reserved, her clothes too wrong, for her to fit my idea of the rich young society girl I had promised myself. She was everything I *didn't* want to want.

She was thin. Her long frogged coat was worn; her high laced shoes and her street-length skirt were old; her gloves were darned. Yet if there was a natural aristocracy in this world, she was its essence. Her light eyes seemed serene and sensitive.

For minutes at a time, she sat as if those startling light eyes of hers beheld some shining rapture. Then she'd realize that she had been staring at someone who was staring back at her. She'd quickly glance down at her hands folded in her lap and blush. People terrified her. A couple of times she came out of her self-absorption to see me watching her. She'd turn her head away, irritated, and even angry. I didn't want to look at her; I didn't want to care about her. My mood was for something gayer and brighter—but I couldn't help myself. I was starved for decent things and decent people, yet I would rather have died than put it that way.

The trolley was cold in spite of the coal stove at one end and the straw on the floor. The girl kept sniffing to keep her reddened nostrils from forming pearly drops. It made her look that much more helpless and in need of protection.

She rode all the way to Harvard Square, where she got out, holding her skirt to keep it from trailing. I followed her down into the snow and wind hurrying to keep up with her. She remained on the university side of the Square. Sleighs, wagons, and carriages drifted by—drivers white with snow, horses steaming in the cold. Then she turned into the Harvard Yard. No respectable girl visited men's dorms without a chaperone, but nobody bothered her. Every student we passed turned to look at her after she went by. She kept going though, her head straight and front.

I followed her into the old Sever Hall and down to the basement. Gas light flickered in the early dark. In front of a small public lecture hall a placard said that the second Winthrop lecture of that year was going to be given. Nobody was collecting tickets, and I slipped in and sat on a wooden bench right behind her, my heart was pounding with the imposter's terror of being discovered: I had never been to college. The girl's silent entrance created a slow explosion in pantomime. About forty men in the room were turning to look at her— some with natural interest, others with annoyance. Only one man—white-haired and bearded—nodded as if to reassure her, and she nodded back. One other woman was present— heavy-set and in her seventies—whom the older men addressed very respectfully as "ma'am." The girl looked at the dumpy, dowdy woman with all the awe you'd expect her to feel for a queen or some great beauty.

I discovered later that the old lady was Jane Wetherill, the astronomer. I had to learn about scientists in general and lady scientists in particular in my own way.

The lecturer was a foreigner that year. I was so green that I didn't even know his accent was French because according to all music-hall comedians, Frenchmen were named either Gaston or Alphonse and said ze for the. I hadn't the wildest idea of what he was talking about except that it was the first time I heard the word "osmosis." Mostly, though, I paid attention to the girl. She had taken off her hat. Her hair was piled up in a pompadour, but a few small curls at the nape of her neck had worked free. They suggested nakedness—for my eyes alone.

When it was over, everyone fired questions at the young fellow. The older men appeared to be upset by what he had said. His answers were soft-spoken, but so sure of himself that nobody asked him a question a second time.

The girl got up and went out, her eyes shining. They were light, clear, and virginal. I could have been a speck on the wall for all she saw me. I nodded to her though, and she nodded back vaguely. If she remembered me from the trolley, there was no sign. She seemed aware of nothing, except some kind of inner Joan of Arc voices.

The following week, I went again. Sure enough, the girl from the trolley car showed up wearing the same clothes she had worn the week before. Again she was the only young girl in a world of men. Again she sat as rapt through the lecture as if she were in a cathedral. Again I merely nodded, and again she vaguely nodded back.

Not until we were filing out from the fourth lecture, did I make some remark that caught her attention. Her agreement had an almost passionate sadness.

"That's what chemistry really should be!" she sighed. "Imagine how it would feel to be at the Sorbonne or one of his students at the new French Collège des Sciences!"

I had never before heard anyone—let alone a girl—speak of chemistry with more fervor than most Americans speak of the United States. She sounded almost religious. I didn't know what to say as I walked along with her, but I had to talk to her if ever I expected to be a man of the world. I composed this sentence: "My paper ought to send you to Paris, then you could write us weekly articles: *On the Front Lines of Science.*" I forced myself to say it out loud.

She stopped short. "Then you're only a reporter?"

As long as I live, I'll never forget that *only*. She looked at me in surprise as I told her that at least a newspaperman stood a chance of making a living. Unless a scientist also happened to be an inventor like Edison, or Bell, or somebody like that, he didn't stand to make a dime. Whereas a newspaperman—

"You're not serious!" She was pale.

"I'm absolutely serious. If I'm here, it's only because I followed you in one day. You're the best-looking girl I ever saw. And in order to keep coming here, I had to tell a lie to my paper: I said that I'm covering a great revolution in science."

She thought I was a lunatic. "You shouldn't talk to me that way," she said quietly, and walked away.

I caught up with her. "I'm going to lose my job," I said. "I can't even write the first line of the piece without your help."

She kept on, but now I had to stay with her.

"I'd put in the words, and you'd put in the chemistry."

She walked upstairs and out into the Yard.

"This is a professional request," I said. "I get paid for the articles." There was no such assignment, but I didn't care. "I'd split with you. I'll get five dollars an article," I said. "And perhaps we could do six."

She walked on for another few minutes of silence. She was calm and pale. She told me later that her head was spinning —she didn't know whether to thank me for the offer or to call a policeman. Then abruptly she stopped, took off her patched glove and held out her hand to me. Her fingers were streaked with brown. Were they burned or did she smoke? It turned out to be only nitric acid stain. Her grip was firm: the way she thought men shook hands to bind a deal.

"You write the first draft of the article and then mail it to me: Julie Porter." She gave me an address on Appian Way.

I took a long breath for another burst of nerve. "Couldn't we go somewhere now and talk over the ideas?"

Immediately she was wary again. She didn't trust me an inch. "I'll have to get permission from the Dean first anyhow."

"The Dean?"

"I'm a student at the Annex." In those days, no one said Radcliffe. She was one of those mythical creatures—a Harvard Girl! But she wasn't rejecting me out of hand. "You just write it, as I said, and mail it to me," and she walked away without me.

Now I had to make good on my lie to her. I went to the Sunday editor and really tried to sell him the idea. I reminded him of the Roentgen-ray sensation of '95, only five years earlier. The Curie sensation was even more recent, '98. He was unimpressed, but he penciled the idea on a pad.

"What's the name of this young Frenchman you're going to make famous?" he asked.

Of all the names I ever wrote about, it's one of the ironies of my life that this was one I had to look up in my notes.

"Claudet," I said, "with a T. Georges Claudet."

I had no premonition that I was touching history. Nor, do I think, had Julie.

2

ONE AUTUMN IN THE WOODS BACK HOME WHEN I was about twelve, I suddenly found myself face to face with a huge-eyed young deer. Both of us stood terrified. My heart pounded in resonance with the deer's, and through that silent telegraph I sensed its panic and wonder: Will you kill me? it was asking.

Our pulses raced in unison moment after moment—then *ffshshtt!*—it whipped itself around and went leaping away. The way the deer looked at me before it ran was the way the girl looked at me when we finally had our first meeting in French's Bakery on Church Street.

She stood there, clasping the manuscript in her hands, afraid of me, yet forced to come. At every moment she was aware of who else was going in and out of the shop. While I read, I noticed she was wearing the same hat and coat—even the same old shoes, dress, and gloves she had worn each time before. This time, her fingers had a new violet-red stain—potassium permanganate.

She told me hurriedly that she was on her way to do some studying. The girls had access to the men's library—this was one of Radcliffe College's assets—but they had to sit in a room apart—railed off from the men. Even that was considered a great privilege. She was telling me what an important mission I was interrupting, and that I had better hurry up reading what she'd done. I assured her our meeting wouldn't take long.

"Your part of the article sounded as if you had actually met Claudet personally and had spoken to him," she said accusingly. She made lying sound as bad as murder, only uglier.

"Of course, I met him," I said. "I had to. I'm a reporter. I simply wrote him a note and told him I wanted to interview him."

Her expression changed a little.

"You really *saw* him?" she asked again, and I could see now that she was looking past me to this other man; it was who had brought her to me, not the article.

Claudet was about ten years older than I—say thirty-four or -five at the time—but he seemed less. He was fair, slight, dressed with a discreet elegance, and with a personal quality I was too self-conscious then to try to get down on paper. It was as if he had grown up in a dream, or in some sort of hypnotized forest full of cruel wild animals which were tame to his touch. It was impossible to think of him afraid of anything. He was the only man I ever knew who I could imagine dying of disgust. I wondered what he would have thought if he could have seen what I was seeing in the muddy alleys, the clapboard shanties and tenements not too far away from Harvard Square.

I told him that I had no technical questions to ask except in the most general sense, but that I *did* want to know about his personal background and life. He changed before my eyes. He became bored and answered my questions as if he were brushing dust off his clothes. He got up casually as he spoke, paced a little, and before I knew it, I had been ushered out of his room.

"That's exactly the way I thought he'd be!" she said. Her eyes were shining with admiration—not for me, but for him. Her voice was gentle, but I had a flash of feeling that she had a cruel streak in her somewhere even though she sat down submissively across from me. I asked Mrs. French to bring her a bun and coffee while I finished reading through the copy.

It was, of course, unprintable as it was. Whatever excitement and fervor she herself felt about her science, in the presence of paper and ink, she stiffened and became dry, shy, and forbidding. Just the same, she had given me almost all the information I needed.

"The only thing you didn't tell me was what it's good for," I said.

"What do you mean?"

"What's it for? How can it be used?" Her cool expression was making me stammer. "People want to know that kind of thing."

Her lips tightened slightly.

"When an important banker asked Michael Faraday: 'What good is electricity?' his answer was: 'What good is a newborn baby!' "

"You mean that someday all of Claudet's work can lead to an important new industry?"

"You don't see at all!" she said angrily. "Even if electricity had never become an industry, what Faraday discovered would still be of first importance!"

"I see," I said slowly. Actually I didn't, but I wasn't going to argue with her. "Well, I'll just have to rewrite it," I went on. "I'll put it into my own words."

"I never claimed to be a writer." She hesitated before asking: "Are you saying that my share will be less?"

I didn't have to look at her coat and hat to know how to answer that.

She was relieved. She finished her bun and coffee in only a few minutes. I asked if she wanted another. She shook her head, but I could see she would have been happy if I insisted. I insisted. She had said nothing about having sought the Dean's permission, and I had no intention of raising the matter. Obviously she hadn't asked because she didn't want to risk a refusal.

"Do you have any idea when the payment will be made?" she asked.

"First I'll have to do the rewriting. You'll have to explain some more things . . ."

"But you're sure it'll be accepted . . . ?"

"Oh, I'm sure, all right!"

Again she hesitated, but only for a moment and then she went on: "Could I have part of my share in advance? Five dollars? It would make a great difference to me."

I was about to remind her that she wasn't supposed to care about money, but I said nothing. I had only six dollars and change in my pocket until the end of the week, but I gave her the money even though I knew it was all going down the drain. I had known for several days ever since I had mentioned to my editor that I had seen Claudet.

"Stop right there," he said. "I've decided I won't be able to use it."

I felt sick. "Will you at least read it?"

"I'll read it," he said. "But I'll still turn it down."

I couldn't tell her that. So at that first meeting with Julie, I was very businesslike. I pretended that still another session was required to finish the job. "The day after tomorrow then?" I said.

She nodded after a moment of hesitation.

"Same place, same time?"

Again she nodded. She looked like a shy little girl when she made the gesture, except that her eyes were shining.

"Before we start the second article," she said, "do you think it's possible that I meet Claudet too?"

That was one meeting I was now determined not to arrange; but again, I put down any qualms about lying to her. The role of the hard-boiled big-city seducer was becoming easier and easier for me to play. "Sure," I said. "When the time comes, I'll fix it. It's a great idea!"

When we met once more at French's Bakery, it was snowing outside again, and she came in shaking the white flakes off her. This time I was less businesslike and asked her about herself. She said she came from Holmes Hole, which I knew as a small town somewhere down on the Cape. She stiffened with local pride, and her coffee mug came down hard on the table when I said so.

"The *Cape?* Holmes Hole is on Martha's Vineyard, mister, and the Vineyard is an island, all by itself!"

She was suddenly an indignant country girl talking about her home town. The set of her head was very erect and high on a young girl's neck. At once, I said that I had heard nice things about the Vineyard. She calmed down enough to allow that the Vineyard *was* one of the most beautiful places in the whole world.

"Is that your experience?" I asked with a straight face.

She shot me a look which taught me never to try to get around her. She was very pretty when her eyes glittered that way and color went to her cheeks; but I was wary of the temper of any girl who could work up such a passion for chemistry.

"My experience consisted of listening to people who *have* seen all the most beautiful places. That's how you learn. By listening. Should we go on with the article?"

I said that she had the manner of a schoolmarm. She laughed.

"I *did* teach school from the time I was fifteen." Then in an altered voice, she said: "And I grew up watching my own father teach school. He used to be Headmaster of Dukes Academy." She seemed to think she was speaking of a school like Exeter or Andover. I had never heard of the place, but I nodded.

When she explained to me what she had written, she put down her coffee mug and her bun to free herself for enthusiasm. Her excited eyes, her flashing hands, the way she lifted her shoulders made me long for the day when she would feel for me one tenth the passion she felt for the wonders of the hydrogen atom. She sounded as if she hadn't the vaguest idea of what could really exist between a man and a woman, yet obviously she had more love in her than she could handle. I didn't care how poor she was. I was crazy about her.

She was restless with her studies, she told me. She yearned for something else.

"Life is funny, you know. The Annex isn't all I thought it was. Papa had such dreams and I spent I don't know how many years longing for something far less exalted than this, never dreaming that it might be possible. Then when I finally *did* inherit—" She broke off impatiently. She tapped the manuscript on the marble-topped bakery table. "Let's get on with this."

"But I thought the Annex was one of the finest women's colleges in the country," I said. "Certainly it's the most serious. Maybe it isn't *college* that you're dissatisfied with."

"Oh, I know what it is, all right," she said, misunderstanding me completely. "We're supposed to have the same professors as Harvard teaching the same courses they give the men, but I can't believe it. Our courses are far too easy. We don't really have a physics laboratory. And the chem lab isn't much better. It's so unfair! And such a cheat, too!" Her voice altered. "All that was left of so much love was the money for this, because he knew how badly I wanted an education. The will said expressly that it was to be for college. The money is too little. What I'm getting for the money is too little. What a waste and disappointment! I hate death!" she said with quiet passion. She was the first person I ever heard say it aloud, and she didn't mean that she was afraid of her own death. She seemed to think she and death were equal adversaries. It made me admire her intensely. I couldn't face giving her up. I tried to stretch this second meeting into a third. Her mood of freedom suddenly disappeared. All her suspicion of me returned. She asked for—and got—a further advance.

"I thought we weren't going to start the second article until I met Claudet," she then said, and in my heart I said good-by to her. She and my money were dissolving before my eyes into thin air. I held her gloved hand for a moment. It was warm, firm, and small through the thin leather. This was to be the end.

Still I made one more attempt with the editor. He took my pages with a sigh of disgust. He read the first paragraph and tossed it all back to me.

"Why do you waste my time?" he complained, "I told you we couldn't use it, and we can't."

I waited a few days, but that was as much as I could hold out. I was so drawn to that thin, poor, discontented girl with the marvelous exuberance for what she loved that I couldn't help myself. I didn't even feel guilt as I sent her this telegram: "Entire series accepted. Meet me Friday five o'clock at French's Bakery. Can pay further advance."

3

IN NO TIME AT ALL, MY LIES HAD PUT ME IN A HOLE SO deep I couldn't turn around. I owed money. Also, I still hadn't delivered Claudet. I invented a number of appointments which were canceled at the last minute.

Still beyond that, my telegram had created trouble for her. She was living in a boardinghouse recommended by the college, and the lady who owned the house was responsible for her. By and large, she was a reasonable woman, asking only that the girls be home by ten o'clock in the evening and to do nothing to make themselves conspicuous. My wire, "Meet me at French's Bakery" had sounded like an assignation. Julie had to explain to her landlady what we were doing and the landlady insisted that I come to the house and do whatever needed doing there. We were given a back parlor to work in undisturbed—although the door had to be left open. Julie accepted it, but she was annoyed with me for having been so tactless. Those nights she didn't even bother to put her hair up. She wore it in a long blond braid down her back tied with a large bow at her neck. It made her look about fifteen and very pure.

Soon she began to press me for the date on which the series would begin to appear in the paper.

"But I already told you that your name won't be on it," I said, alarmed at this additional cause for her dissatisfaction.

"I know that," she said. "And I told my father so. But I still want to send him a copy of the articles."

"Your father?" Then, I said like a fool: "But I thought you told me he was dead."

She was indignant. "How could I have said that?"

"You were talking about him and how you had inherited the money to come here."

She looked at me helplessly in a way that reminded me of Claudet as if she too were thinking: how does one convey information to the primitive mind? Then she said: "I *did* inherit the money—but *not* from Papa!" Before I could ask who from she laughed gently. "Poor Papa, he couldn't leave me enough to pay for trolley-car fare. And I wouldn't want him to," she added, in case I got any idea she was disappointed in her father.

"Papa gave me a mind to think with, and then he taught me how to think. There isn't one girl in my class who brought as much from home as Papa gave my brothers, my sisters, and me."

"I didn't even know you had brothers and sisters! Are they all as smart as you?"

"Smarter!" Her retort was clipped. She was angry. She smoothed out the papers on the table as if she were anxious to resume work and end our talk.

"And where are they?"

Again I had asked the wrong thing. This time all I got was a cold look and a cold word. "Dead!" she said.

She was a mystery to me, all right; but the biggest mystery was why I persisted in considering myself a hard-boiled big-city man out to seduce an innocent college girl, when the truth was that I was a love-struck country boy without any experience, getting deeper and deeper in debt for a girl who didn't give a damn whether I came or went. My most helpless victim was myself.

When I look back at that time, I see mostly her profile—cool and regular—with that big bow at the back of her head. Yet she was never girlish. She scarcely looked at me directly when we were together in that little gas-lit back parlor, unless we talked about her work or the chance of meeting Claudet. Sometimes she would walk excitedly up and down the room. She used to wear a stiff high-collared white shirtwaist with a watch pinned over her heart, and a long gray skirt that touched the floor. Her fountain pen and pencil were sheathed in a case pinned to her belt or scattered on the table where she had put them down a moment earlier. A loop must have been missing from the skirtband in back, because the belt always rode up, leaving a white gap between the belt and the skirt. She was forever feeling behind her for the skirtband to tuck it in under the belt, but two minutes later the belt had ridden up again. I used to get so lost just looking at her that I scarcely heard what she was saying.

I swore to myself not to let her meet Claudet, because she

so obviously admired him. But when, toward the end of April, the sailing news stated that he was leaving Boston for Le Havre within the next eight days, I figured it was safe. I wrote him a formal request to interview him with one of my colleagues who would be qualified to ask him all the interesting questions I myself had been unable to. His reply was a polite letter setting the time and place for Wednesday afternoon, the day before he would sail. I enclosed a copy of my letter to him along with his reply and sent it to Julie without a comment. This time it was she who sought the meeting. She sent *me* a telegram: to meet her at the bakery!

Under that worn hat her light eyes were shining. Her face had color. She liked and admired me for what I had done.

"What should I wear?" she'd ask excitedly. "What should I say? Please don't tell him I'm only a student! On the other hand, if you pretend that I'm a real newspaperwoman, I won't know what to do! Is there a special kind of notebook to carry?"

It was wonderful to watch her. Regardless of the cold-blooded intentions I thought I had, I wanted only for her to be happy, even though all the excitement and gaiety was for someone else.

The question was where to meet so we could go together to Claudet's. I took a long breath and gave her the address of my roominghouse on Brimmer Street. Claudet had moved from Cambridge into Boston and was at the Hotel Vendome on Commonwealth Avenue, not too far from me. She was so excited that she agreed without even a quick questioning glance of alarm. We would be together for only a moment before it would be time to set out again. The hard-boiled seducer I wanted to be assured my panic-stricken self that he wanted only to give her a sense of safety and familiarity in my room against some future time.

The particular Wednesday turned out to be one of those days when life plays its most vicious trick: the granting of one's wildest dreams under circumstances that turn them into disasters. The Satanic game began early in the morning with a note on my desk from the Boston *Transcript*. I had submitted a copy of the first article to it several days earlier. Now, said the note, the paper was accepting it! Good news? Great! But explain it to Julie without revealing that I had been stringing her along all this time! As far as she knew, the *Globe* had bought the series long ago.

Then, ten minutes before Julie was due to arrive, a student came hurrying up to my room from Professor Claudet to say that there could be no interview that afternoon: the professor had too many last-minute chores. I was frantic with disappointment. Only five minutes, I said, as if I were talking to Claudet himself. The student was bewildered: that was his message. The professor had been on his way out of the hotel, getting into a carriage, when he gave it. At least, I thought in panic, if I had some proof in Claudet's own handwriting that he had canceled the appointment, but there was no note. I was on the point of asking the student himself to write one, but I let him go.

Again, the situation was made to order. Julie was coming to my room, and now there was no longer any reason for us to go out. We could stay in and we would be alone together —but for what? I shuddered.

She came up finally, so beautifully dressed that I was completely intimidated. Her skirt swept the floor. Her hat was a giant disc of feathers that slanted across her head. Her corset made her look as if she were defying the winds. To me, Julie stood there looking like a duchess about to enter a reception, knowing she was going to hear at least ten different proposals of marriage as she swept through and prepared to laugh off each one of them.

"My God!" was all I could say.

She loved my admiration. She paraded around the room in a parody of elegance, hardly able to contain her delight. She had done something to her hair, to the way she carried her head; and she knew how lovely she was.

"Borrowed finery!" she said as she pirouetted before me. "Whoever thought I'd turn out to look like this?"

"I did!"

She shrugged me off and stood before my mirror.

"You couldn't have! Only girls would have known; and they hate me." She slowly turned her head from side to side, holding it imperiously—her eyes cold with objective self-appraisal. "I must say I return the compliment—"

"They don't like you?" I asked in astonishment.

"From the moment I arrived, they've looked at me as something the cat dragged in," she said absently. "And they bore me to death with their squeaking, giggling foolishness—" She cut herself off to concentrate on primping the collar of her dress. "But as soon as I said I needed clothes for a man, and who the man was, they forgot about our war and pitched in and dressed me themselves. *Voilà!*" she said, spinning around from the mirror to face me. "Are we late?"

"We're not going," I said. "He just sent a message canceling."

She looked at me, and beauty slipped from her face. Minutes must have gone by before she said a word.

"Is this a joke?" she asked.

I said that he had sent a student. She asked to see the note and held out a gloved hand. A few minutes ago, that hand had been elegant and soft. Now it was demanding and cold. Grant's hand at Richmond must have looked more gracious to Lee when it sought his sword. I said again that he had sent a student. There was no note.

"If this was simply a trick to get me here, you were wasting your time!" she said sharply. "And it was a pretty contemptible trick, if you want to know!"

"But you saw Claudet's note—in his own hand."

"How do I know it was? You could have written it yourself! If it weren't for the money you've already paid me, I wouldn't believe you about the articles either. You're the most obvious liar I ever met! You strut around like a two-bit dandy, thinking you're God's gift to women, and all the while you're just as countrified as I am! What a fool you've made me look! Those girls will never stop laughing at me now! Why, I could be expelled from college for being here like this without a chaperone. And don't look at me with those sick eyes! I mean every word I say! Good-by!"

She started for the door. I put out a hand to stop her, but she threw me off. She was unbelievably strong, as if she had grown up playing with boys, competing with them in all their games, and even beating some of those who were in love with her.

"Julie. I *am* in love with you, but I didn't lie about Claudet. I lied only about the articles—"

That stopped her. Until then she was almost out of the door, her face was red and white with anger and hard with irritation. Now she checked herself, returned, closed the door behind her. If ever she was dangerous, this was the moment. I was terrified.

"You lied about the articles?" she said slowly as if she were asking me to understand very clearly that I was confessing to a hanging crime.

I told her that I had lied only because I had so much confidence that eventually it would all turn out to be true. And it had. The *Transcript* had taken the first, it would take the rest, so the lie was justified.

"And the money?" she asked.

Eventually, it would all be earned; I was positive of it.

"Eventually?" she echoed the word and continued to look at me. "Does that mean I *don't* have to give it back?"

Now it was my turn to lose my temper.

"Damn you and the money together!" I shouted, "I never asked for it back! I'd never *dream* of asking for it! You came into that trolley this winter looking like the Poor Little Match Girl and I fell for you on the spot. I *had* to get you some money! And if you want to know," I went on, getting still angrier, "I *borrowed* that money, Miss Julie Porter, and *I'm* going to pay it back. Those articles *will* be sold!"

She had calmed down as I shouted at her. I stopped. She could no longer meet my eyes. She turned away to remove the lancelike pin from her hat so she could take the hat off; then she began to laugh. The laugh rolled on and on until she was laughing so hard that she couldn't speak. God only knows where that laugh came from; it was open, free, and wild. Tears streamed down her face. There was a word she was trying to say, but her lips simply couldn't frame it.

"Poor Monty!" she finally said. "Poor, poor Monty!" But she shook her head, and again she was speechless with that wild laugh.

"How hard you must have worked! How many lies you must have told! How much anguish . . . !"

"I did it because I love you!"

"And those stories about the editor . . . !"

"Because I love you!"

"And those telegrams, every one so urgent!"

"Because I love you!"

She was so weak with laughter that she could only shake her head as she spoke. "And the lies you must have had to tell to get the money!"

"Because I love you, Julie. My God, how I love you!"

She sighed with exhaustion and opened her tear-reddened eyes. They looked soft and liquid; and for the first time I saw tenderness for me.

"Monty! Monty!" she sighed. "What are you doing to yourself! You know I don't love you."

"But I love you, Julie."

"I guess you do," she said again in that same voice: tired and tender. "I guess you really do!"

I was about to tell her to put on her hat and I'd take her home at once, to prove how much I respected her; but instead she placed a hand negligently around my neck and rumpled the back of my head. She closed her eyes and pressed my head slightly towards her. The invitation and opportunity were all I needed and it was hours before we left.

I should have walked out with her into that fine May afternoon with the strut of a man who had seen and then finally possessed what he wanted most in the world. I was happy, of course, in a way, but what I discovered when we were alone left me frightened and even sort of horrified. I actually ached with the love I felt for her—but I also ached with what I could not ignore. She walked beside me along Beacon Street, radiant, unaware of how crushed I felt, her false shyness and innocence just as deceiving as the first time I had seen her on the trolley car four months earlier.

The cane I had bought had been for swaggering through a very different kind of situation, and for a man with very different sensibilities.

4

IN MY ANGUISH, I HAD TO MAKE MYSELF BIGGER THAN I was, and so as we walked along in the May afternoon, I suggested that we make one last attempt to interview Claudet on the ship next morning before it sailed. It had the right effect: the idea made her flush with excitement, and she said she would try to get away from college but she wouldn't know until the last minute.

Next day I rode the trolley all the way out to Harvard Square, standing with only an upturned collar as shelter from a spring rain, but I didn't care. I even told myself that it didn't matter that there had been someone in her life before me. It wasn't worth the heartache. I made myself keep thinking only of how we had been together the day before and how she would look up at me when she came along. All that counted was how she felt about *me*.

She came hurrying from Garden Street beneath an umbrella that hid her face. The umbrella went down and there she was—with no sign of the magnificence she had borrowed the day before, with no sign that she even missed it, or that there was anything the slightest bit unusual between us. Had she forgotten that yesterday had ever happened? Her only concern was that she had to be back by three o'clock.

I nodded dumbly, but I was more hurt than I could say. We boarded the trolley for Boston. I sat very close to her just to be touching her, but she misunderstood: she thought I needed room, and she moved away. I slipped my hand under her arm and pulled her back close to me. She frowned until she turned and looked up into my face. Suddenly she smiled, and touched my hand. I was happy all over again. But then she took a book out of her bag—a mathematical treatise—and begged me to excuse her while she read. For the entire ride, she sat absorbed in her book, while I sat longing for her look.

Near the docks, traffic made a fearful din as we hurried along the street: the hawking barks of the venders, the cobblestone rumble of wagon wheels and handcarts, the clop-clop of hoofs. Arching over the wharfside street were the bowsprits of docked old windjammers. Masts, spars, tall smoking funnels, the smell of brine, all of it made me feel the air of adventure and far places. Julie's face glittered with pleasure. At length we found the *Anjou* and went up the steep gangplank past bearded officers into dark mahogany saloons and public rooms. I went on ahead along the corridor and knocked on Claudet's stateroom door. He was in his shirt-sleeves and wore arm garters. Looking past him, I got a glimpse of dark polished wood, a dim lamp in gimbals, and cramped brown quarters.

He looked at me through the partly opened door, frowning at my interruption. He was already unpacking. I reminded him of who I was and why I had come.

He started to close the door. "This is not the time. I have already said everything there is to be said in my lectures. Such ideas are not for newspapers. Excuse me, but it is impossible!"

I pleaded. Flattery was meaningless to him, and so I simply told him that unless he granted an interview, no more than five minutes I swore, my job would be in jeopardy. He looked at me with annoyed resignation, then opened the door. When he saw Julie he frowned abruptly.

"Wait for me in the saloon. I shall be there in five minutes."

It's thirty years ago, but that day I remember as the day I learned the meaning of the word "outsider." Claudet, casual and elegant, and Julie, who was neither, sat and talked across a tea table in the main saloon of the *Anjou*, both of them oblivious of themselves and everyone else about them. Around us, fashionably dressed women in furs and scarves moved about, their dresses trailing along the carpets. Their occasional glances at Julie immediately appraised her as a nonpassenger—someone's poor young cousin. The men, in their tweed capes and tweed deer-stalker caps took more interest in her—at least their second look was interested— caught by her cameolike stillness as she sat enrapt by the man talking to her. Officers hurried through the crowd, ignoring everyone. The air was full of leavetaking, with bells clanging every so often, and the distant screams of seagulls from outside.

I had begun the conversation with Claudet conventionally enough, but Julie cut in to ask him to amplify one of the points of a lecture with such knowledgeability that he looked at her sharply for a moment and then spoke directly to her on the level of her question. The conversation was full of feeling on both sides, yet not one word did I understand. I was proud of her, but apprehensive. Then the technicalities ceased, and, with a curious little slant of her head and a look of total unself-consciousness I hadn't seen before, she asked: "But how did the idea *come* to you? What were you doing? Were you walking, or working, or just sitting and staring? And did it come all at once or—as it might have—half formed, and even wrong?"

Again he gave her the inquiring glance of discovery and amusement. The man who had grown up in the entranced forest had found a human being with a quality like his own.

"You are right, mademoiselle. I *was* wrong at first. I was on a train." He rested his elbows on the arms of his chair and leaned forward on them, making himself comfortable. "I had been visiting my parents in Normandy, and I was returning to Paris. The carriage was swaying, and I also swayed." He imitated the motion and laughed. He was different from the distant man I had met alone. The jolting of the train, he said, became in fantasy the shaking of a test tube. Is this the way if felt to be a droplet in an emulsification? He immediately visualized an ideal system of droplets in a surrounding media. What *were* the forces on an emulsified domain? He went on, speaking rapidly, fancifully, laughing, but recreating all the ideas that had led to the final flowing eruption of the idea— away from the emulsified cell to the idea of solution, from solutions to the idea of osmotic potential which came to him, he said with a joking flourish, just as the train puffed to a halt in the Gare St. Lazare and he got down from the carriage.

She watched him, sitting there in the ship's saloon with the erect and modest carriage of a primly brought-up young lady, but there was a mysteriously undefinable gleam in her eyes. Then it dawned on me that she was looking at him, I swear, the way a hungry child stares into a restaurant like Delmonico's or Locke-Ober's. Had Claudet so caught her fancy that I was finished after no more than twenty-four hours' possession? I existed neither for her nor for him. They had absorbed each other.

"And then?" she asked.

"And then it remained only to see if I was correct. I went home. I took pencil and paper. I worked everything out in mathematical detail."

"And it came out right!"

He smiled. "It came out all wrong! All wrong! It was necessary that I start again. And again I was wrong! I made five more starts; five different sets of assumptions. All of them wrong."

"Then when were you right?"

He leaned his head back and again he laughed. His teeth were very regular and even.

"I had been right the first time; my mathematics had been wrong! I am very weak on function theory," he said apologetically, the way you or I might offer regrets for dancing poorly.

"But you used Liouville's theorem with such elegance!" she objected, defending him from himself, and once again he looked at her, startled by admiration. She flushed defensively. "I learned function theory before I came to the Annex."

."In a lower school?" He couldn't believe her.

"It was not in any school. I learned from someone who

had a passion for mathematics," she said. "The kind of unrequited, suicidal passion you read about in old-fashioned novels." For that moment she was seeing neither Claudet nor anyone present in the ship's saloon.

I seized the opportunity to bring myself back into the interview.

"Tell me, Professor Claudet, do you feel confident that the day will come when all of man's questions about the universe will be answered?"

Why do layman's questions about science always sound so fatuous? They both looked at me emptily, a little embarrassed for me, then at each other with a mute exchange of helplessness. At last, more out of deference to her, I imagine, than out of respect for me, he replied gently, "I, too, was brought up to believe that reason must eventually rule supreme, but I am no longer so sure that it is true."

Her interest was piqued now, and she frowned, because if anyone ever believed in the sanctity and omniscience of science—it was Julie.

"One of the most brilliant men I know," he said slowly, "perhaps also the most disturbing—has been trying to convince me that while every question that man can think of asking nature will eventually be answered, there will still always be mystery. Why? Because, he says, all the questions which could be asked of nature are not askable by man."

"Why not?" Julie asked after a moment.

He shrugged. "That is precisely his point: because man will never *think* of asking. Because human perception is dim. Because human intelligence is so very limited. The history of science tells us how slow and tortuous is the crawl and creep towards even the dimmest understanding of nature. Ask yourself how many ideas in science which you learn today were taught identically a hundred years ago."

"Because we have made progress!" she retorted.

He laughed.

"My friend would reply that in tens of thousands of years, man has learned not one thing about nature that stands the test of time! What man calls 'progress' is the changing of his mind! Certainly we make closer and closer approximations to the reality of nature, but who can say we still do not have infinitely far to go? The more we try to find out about nature, the more mystery we seem to find."

"Well, let's grant that we do," Julie said, puzzled by what

he was saying. "Does that mean that the excitement is only in the discovery? In that case what difference would it make if we threw out tomorrow what we think is correct today?" She thought for a moment. "We would have something new and better in its place, and the fun of doing it all over again tomorrow and every day after that. Perhaps your friend is right."

He laughed again. "You sound more like a huntress than a guardian of knowledge!"

She didn't know whether to be pleased or hurt. She flushed uncertainly and reverted to the work he had described at Harvard. Once more the conversation was beyond me. Never in my life, neither before nor since have I felt as lonely as I did then. And helpless. Nothing but the arrival of sailing time could free me from invisibility.

Finally we stood on the pier as the steamer was backed out into Boston harbor by the tugs. She walked thoughtfully beside me to the trolley stop. I suffered as I thought of how she must be thinking of this man who was older than I, more interesting than I, more talented, more educated, more handsome—more of everything I could have asked for. I could think of nothing to say against him, nor did I really want to. I was sick at heart because I admired him myself. I couldn't stand her silence. "Well, what do you think?"

She shook her head. "What a wonderful way to live!" she sighed.

I couldn't help but rub salt in my own wound. "He doesn't have a wife."

Again she gave me that startled look of incomprehension. Once more I had been wide of the mark. I went light with relief as I felt myself stumble on a truth: it wasn't at all that she wanted to *share* his life. She didn't want the man, she wanted far more: she wanted to replace him entirely: to *be* what he was and *have* what he had. I understood it at once, and like a fool, I thought that my own interests were safe. I was actually happy!

5

SHE USED TO REST HER CHIN ON HER CLENCHED FISTS, with her elbows on the table in my room, so that her discontented, dreaming face was the keystone of an arch. Her rich hair was carelessly gathered in back. Little by little as we'd talk it would come loose; more and more of it falling in locks on her neck. She would poke at it blindly, only creating more disarray. Her gray eyes were staring at something a million miles away—in a world where I had no existence.

Even when she tried to bring me into her world, the results were not what she wanted. Once, when we had been very close and warm, she reached out languidly from my couch where she was lying and took a book from the shelf behind her.

"Is it a novel?" she asked.

I reached across her and took the book. It was *Vanity Fair*.

Her head was resting against my shoulder. She closed her eyes.

"Read to me," she said.

"What part?"

"Any part. Didn't your family used to read out loud in the evenings?"

I opened the book at random and began to read. I was self-conscious, but I kept at it. For a page or so, she was motionless, then she became restless and took the book from me.

"Never mind, Monty," she said, gently. "If there was reading in your home, you weren't the one who did it."

"We didn't used to read out loud."

"*We* always did," she said. She put the book back. "And Papa was the best. It would have helped if you were a good reader too." She sighed. "Oh well—!" and her voice trailed off, a little bored.

Many things bored her, including the Annex itself: it was no challenge to her. The girls disliked her. She didn't know why, she simply disliked them in turn. The truth, as I found later, was that she disturbed and frightened her classmates. They envied her brilliance, but even more, they envied the magnificent body, the carriage, that allowed her to walk through each situation as if it were scarcely worth noticing. She was quiet and self-contained; but she had a temper that made one girl say afterward: "She could have killed me!" and mean it literally.

At Radcliffe, in those days, the theatrical productions of the Idlers Club were the center of the college's social life. All the girls were involved. Julie simply walked away with a book under her arm. At that time, too, there was a big movement of athletics, but I doubt if Julie ever put on a pair of the blue serge bloomers that was the standard costume for many of the girls. She didn't own a tennis racket, nor did she play golf, which was just becoming so fashionable that girls who never played were beginning to wear golf skirts and golf capes. Julie thought them ridiculous: the plaid was worn on the *inner* side, where no one could see it while a drab, solid, oatmealish color was shown to the world.

The wonderful hearty laugh that I found so overwhelming had a very different effect on women: they sensed something in it that was beyond them—it was too full-blooded, too vital, too wild. The very qualities that allowed young women to worship her two generations later on as some kind of priestess, were the qualities that made her own contemporaries draw away from her. It's too hard to live with someone larger than life.

What did she believe in those days? In most of those things that were ardently supported by young people who considered themselves "progressive," a very fashionable word then. When you come to think of it, what they believed then in 1900, they believed with such ardor that their ideas were forced on the country and even became the commonplaces of twenty years later. For example, Julie was passionate about the position of women, about their right to vote, their right to work, their right—to be more precise about her private version—to study chemistry and to do research in it as freely as men. Whenever she spoke about the place of women in society, her color would heighten, her eyes would take on fire, her voice harden. She could say *"Men!"* with such chilled contempt that I couldn't help bridling with defensive rage. I always wanted to make love to her in the little time we had together, but whenever she was on the warpath, I kept my hands to myself.

She was passionate in general about social justice—for the Pullman strikers, for the steelworkers, for the Grange, for the factory workers. She hated the Russian Czar, the German Kaiser, and the King of the Belgians. At different times she was strongly for socialism and then for anarchy, except that she didn't believe in assassination, even though—to continue her catalogue—men like Carnegie, Rockefeller, and other bloated capitalists deserved fates worse than death.

By and large, what she thought about these things, a sizable fraction of her classmates all over the country also believed more or less—these were the ideas that were bandied about on Saturday night when they went out to each others' rooms or to beer gardens, but they also danced and sang to the piano or to mandolins, ate chafing-dish suppers, and generally had a good time. In Cambridge, of course, we also went to concerts and to lectures.

The only thing unusual about Julie was that whenever she spoke about such things, she no longer seemed to speak with her own voice. Seafaring phrases tinged her arguments. And we argued, all right; because what my intuitive ear was hearing so enraged me that the point we were arguing about was simply a disguise for my jealousy.

"Why don't you try having your own ideas!" I said angrily once as we were walking along the Charles. She carried a parasol which she twirled. It obviously bored her. I was angry because I wasn't going to see her the following day— she had special permission to work in the laboratory—but I didn't dare show my rage for fear she'd call me an antifeminist.

"They *are* my ideas," she replied stubbornly. She let the spinning parasol rest on her shoulders like a gun, even though the afternoon sun was on her face. Her very boredom angered me.

"They are not! You picked them up from somebody else!"

Her answer was sharp but I was still listening only to my own intuition.

"It's a man," I went on. "I can tell! You even use his voice when you talk about them!"

She stopped dead and looked at me very steadily. Even the twirling parasol was still. A retort almost whipped at me, then she checked herself, and started walking again.

"And he was a sailor!" I said. "You sound like a sailor's little parrot!"

Once more she stopped. The retort with which she had been about to lash me before, flickered again. She was white with fury, but I didn't know how to back down. What I didn't know then was that she was also sorry for me. That was why she tried to control herself. Just the same, I remember her icy challenge to me to take issue with her if I dared. "I *did* use to know someone who taught me a great deal," she said defiantly. "He was a good, kind, honest, human being— the finest, most generous man I ever knew or will know!"

I said nothing.

"And he *did* follow the sea," she said.

Even then the expression was old-fashioned. I told myself to let the matter drop. I figured that any man old enough to talk that way had been too old to be any threat to me. She was staring at me, refusing to go another step until I backed down. Then I saw that tears were running unchecked down her cheeks. For what? Anger? Love? Love for whom?

The shy little Julie I had picked up in the trolley car on that winter day was turning out to be far more than I had bargained for, far more than I knew how to handle. I gave in to her and let my gaze fall, withdrawing the challenge; but at the same time I made up my mind that when she went home for summer vacation, I would break with her.

6

AT THE END OF THE TERM, I TOOK HER TO THE WHARF for the Vineyard steamer. We were as embarrassed as we were sad. I thought that perhaps she too had decided to let the summer end things between us; but also like me she didn't have the courage to say so openly.

I waved as the steamer pulled out. The water was still and glittering; the horizon a glare of hot June haze. I was sad but also relieved. I'd had a tiger on my hands, and I was lucky to be getting off so easily. Just the same when I left and went to work I was so lonely that I didn't even feel the heat.

Within a week after she had gone, the *Transcript* offered

me thirty-five a week to specialize in science for them—almost twice what I was getting at the *Globe*. I didn't dare accept, but I didn't dare turn it down. I played safe: I accepted on condition that I start in September. That would give me three months to read myself blind, to cram my head with as much general scientific background information as it would take. I was determined to hold the job without Julie. I owed it to my self-respect to earn my own money. Never again would I go through the humiliation of another interview between Julie and some other Claudet.

That summer was a succession of hot lamplit evenings. I used to hurry to the public library every night past pale limp ghosts—men in their underwear and women in cotton dresses —sitting on their front steps with fans and newspapers waving slowly in the darkness against the heat. More than the heat, though, I remember the excitement of reading as if I were driven by demons.

The books I read that summer are forgotten today, but they seemed then to have been written in fire. I guess at best they were on a high school level. I understood everything with an intoxicating clarity. My mind was suddenly without a roof or walls, as if a beach wind had burst open and torn away all the doors and windows to a shut-up cottage. I found myself reading as if my eyes and brains were Julie's. The hunger to learn that was driving me was the hunger to learn that I had seen in her. Just by having been with her and listening to her, I had caught a wild contagion; and yet I knew with a sort of pain that at twenty-five I was already too old and too uneducated to be anything more than an outsider looking in with love and longing for something I could never have myself.

I thought of Julie all the time. Perhaps the reading I was doing was a roundabout way of being with her, because I longed for her. Pleasantly, her letters surprised me with their warmth. During the six months we had known each other, I took it for granted that if I ever relaxed pursuit of her for one moment, she would walk away, completely unconcerned, even unaware that I was no longer around. Yet here she was, writing that she missed me.

Later I learned that she was as surprised as I was by her feelings. On the steamer, she had waved good-by to me just as sadly as I had waved to her, then she turned away and thought of half a dozen good reasons why I wasn't the man for her. She was as right about me as I was about her, but resolution was no stronger for her than it had been for me.

As much as I didn't want to love her, I loved her. I wrote, and asked if I could come for a couple of days.

She wrote back with a wonderful warmth. She had found a room for me down the street, but I was to have all my meals with her and her father. She sent an exact schedule: what time the steamer left the Boston pier; what the stage driver's name was, and where she'd be standing on the general-store steps to meet me when the stage drove in to West Tisbury.

Yet with all that, on the day my steamer came into the crowded Vineyard Haven harbor jammed with coastal traffic —schooners, barges, tugs, and freighters—I made her out on the wharf waving and jumping up and down excitedly. She was wearing her hair down again, with a bow at her neck the way she had done in the back parlor that winter. She looked fifteen, but her long white dress showed off her marvelous figure. She called to me that she had taken the two-hour stage ride Down Island just to meet me and ride back with me. She hugged my arm as I got off the gangplank. We were both grinning with delight at seeing each other again.

As we walked to the stage, everybody we passed nodded to her or smiled with friendliness. If there *had* been a number of men before me in her life—something I kept pushing out of my mind as fast as it kept pushing itself back in—nobody seemed to know about it. Certainly no one glanced after her with that loose-lipped, malicious grin usually reserved—at least in my town—for the girl who gets talked about too much in the local store. Just the opposite—they treated her with pride and affection.

"Julie, notice you got your hair down again," the stage driver said, flicking a whip at the ambling horses, on the way Up Island. We were passing green woods and sunlit pastures. "When it's up, I have to treat you like a young lady. Down, you're my little old Julie again. One of these days you're gonna have to make up your mind!"

She laughed. "It's more fun this way, Burt."

"More fun for you maybe." He winked at me across her. "But less fun for us tryin' to keep up with you!"

Later we sat on the porch of her father's little house in West Tisbury. It was night, and warm even there on the Vineyard. You could smell the green night breath of the trees, honeysuckle, and horse droppings in the road. On the dozen houses along Music Street where they lived there were little Japanese lanterns on the porches.

"When you wrote me *what* you were reading, *how* much it meant to you, I felt close to you all over again!" she said.

We were in a green wicker porch swing hung on chains that groaned on the forward rise and sighed on the falling return. "I guess I must care more than I like to think," she said.

I squeezed her hand and said nothing. I let the darkness blow slowly back and forth against our motion. Breaking with her then was as impossible for me as it had been for her, no matter what either of us wanted to think. I was determined, though, to be able to handle the *Transcript* job by myself. On the other hand, the last thing I wanted to do was to take a position with Julie and then have to back down from it.

There are some women who give you the feeling that if you should fall down, they'd help you up, brush you off, hold you until you're ready to take off on your own again. Not Julie. At least not to me. She put me on my mettle. Fall down in front of her, and she'd probably throw back her head and laugh.

She made me wary, no matter how crazy I was about her, no matter if I was holding my arm around her. She had given me too many surprises already.

Music Street was a quiet, tree-lined little lane only a few hundred yards long that ran from the South Road to the Middle Road. Julie's father lived in a small frame cottage painted green, about the middle of the street. It was boxlike: a kitchen and a parlor-dining room on the ground floor and two small bedrooms above. I wondered where they had found room for all the brothers and sisters she had mentioned. The answer came—without my asking—from her father.

Professor Porter, as everyone called him, was a weary man, unpressed, too refined for life. He would have been elegantly shabby if it hadn't been for Julie taking care of him. He was about middle height, with thin gray hair, thin gray skin pulled tight over a narrow face—with a thousand lines instead of wrinkles, a beaked, aristocratic-looking nose, and bloodshot, moist, haunted gray eyes. He walked with a stoop and a cane and paused frequently to rest and catch his breath. In the late afternoons, with the sun still shining on him, Julie would tenderly put a large cashmere shawl around his shoulders. At least a half dozen times he said to me absently: "I bought this for my wife in London in '59—more than forty years ago. A shop called Jellicoe's, near the Strand. It outlasted her, and it'll outlast me, just as Mr. Jellicoe said." Julie never could put on the shawl to suit him. Invariably he'd adjust it himself, complaining: "Amelia always knew just how to do it. A pity you never got the hang of it from her."

The only time Julie was the girl I thought I had seen in the trolley—gentle, soft, giving love and needing help—was when she was with her father. She was full of tenderness for him. She listened to his opinions—often rambling and inconsequential—with submissive respect. She never argued with him. He was a man of vast erudition. Probably he was brilliant. He recited Victor Hugo in French and Heine in German as easily as he quoted Shakespeare or Tennyson or Pope. He had a sharp tongue for her mistakes, and she accepted his rebukes without any attempt to justify herself even when she was in the right. To me, he seemed a pedantic tyrant, who spoke in pompous old-fashioned sonorities, but I didn't dare offer her any sympathy—she would have chewed me up for criticizing him.

Julie was unable to talk about the brothers and sisters she had lost. Her father had no such trouble talking about his children; and his grief was as real as hers. He walked along the South Road with me one sunny morning and pointed out a large rambling house set back from the edge of Tea Lane.

"This is the house I really think of as home, sir," he said to me, leaning on his stick and trying to catch his breath. "My wife at the piano and the children around her." Tears ran down his cheeks, and he made no effort to wipe them away. "No man was more fortunate in his children than I, yet they're all gone!" As if Julie didn't exist for him. "My boy Ronny may have been high-spirited, but it was only to be expected." I imagine he believed I knew all about Ronny, and only the worst. "Ronny had it in him to be one of the greatest writers. As a journalist, young man, you would have been the first to appreciate him. He had wit, an observing eye, a gift for a phrase. I think of him as all laughter, sunshine, and impatience. And my eldest, my Amelia"—he paused to shake his head, unaware that I was embarrassed by his literaryness —"I've taught many boys, but never have I seen anyone as receptive to knowledge. She soaked up information as if she had been starved for it. She had it in her to be anything she pleased: a Maria Mitchell, a Harriet Beecher Stowe. If she had lived, with that voice of hers, today she'd be a bigger star than my cousin Priscilla. You probably know my cousin Priscilla Porter by her stage name—Portilea."

I was enormously impressed. In those days, an opera star was even more fabulous a creature than movie queens today. "Portilea is Julie's cousin? Julie never mentioned it!"

He didn't even hear my remark about Julie.

"Priscilla *does* have talent," he said grudgingly conceding that the world was within its rights to be giving her some attention, but certainly it oughtn't to be overdone. Julie's reticence meant nothing to him. It was the lost Amelia he was thinking about—"Amelia simply had the bigger talent."

I remarked that at least he still had Julie.

He looked up at me quickly, but I didn't understand his expression. He nodded and started to walk on.

"Julie, yes," he said reflectively. "The ultimate irony, I suppose!"

Dukes Academy, where he had been headmaster, stood at the corner of Music Lane and the State Road—a tall, high, square, white-shingled building. Around it were grounds and playing fields. The school was closed for the summer, and the boys were gone. He passed it at least once a day with me, but I never saw him glance at it nor do I remember that he ever made any remark about it. His children who were dead still lived with him, but his own lifetime of work—what he himself had made of himself—was locked away in silence. He was a bitterly disappointed man. In an objective way, I could feel sorry for him: a man who had lived for and in his children, and the only one of them who had been spared to him was the one he didn't want. Yet, while I felt pity for him, I felt much more for Julie—to love a father so much, to want so passionately and so futilely to make up to him for his losses, when her very existence was his reminder of how much was gone. Even I knew he didn't love her. It was clear to everyone but her.

Seeing her that week on the Vineyard, I could never be more than momentarily angry with her again.

7

THAT HOT SUMMER ENDED WITH A BRUTALLY TORRID September, and it was in a heat where horses were collapsing on the streets that Julie returned to Cambridge. Everyone looked harassed and cross, but she more than most. Her appetite for science had outrun what the school had to offer, and here she was—at the beginning of her third year—faced by the prospect of the meager laboratory instruction that frustrated her to the point of fury. She spent three busy weeks, intriguing and begging until at last she set up the exciting possibility of working with her chemistry professor in his own laboratory twice a week to perform experiments under his guidance. The work would have to be done in his private lab, because under no condition could she attend the courses he gave the Harvard men.

For another three weeks the decision hung in balance. She told me—rather happily—that she was probably going to be too busy to see me as often as we had done until then. Perhaps, she said, she might even move to another boardinghouse nearer to the laboratory. As for the laboratory itself, her voice fell to reverence whenever she spoke of it.

I saw the laboratory a long time afterward: a narrow, tall-ceilinged room with dirty walls and dingy paint, all of it scarcely bigger than a good-sized pantry. Along one wall stood a worktable—a sort of waist-high wooden shelf. Racks of chemicals were hung over this table, and at one end of it stood a convoluted apparatus of glass spheres and tubes being heated by a Bunsen burner. In the apparatus a dark brown muddy mixture was slowly bubbling with a sound like rheumy coughing. There was also a stone sink, several gas jets, and some electrical outlets. It was a drab, dusty place, poorly lit, and with a sulphurous odor, but to Julie, who had understood all along what Chase was doing, it had been suffused by a sort of stained-glass glow.

When I got to know more about scientific research, I realized that even this little room that Chase had to work in was fairly rare in America for those times. There was hardly any place in the entire country for a scientist to work except in a deserted shed or a cellar. People always liked to talk about the "wonders of science," but science then wasn't really part of anyone's life or thinking.

I was introduced to Professor Chase myself when I took Julie to a Friday night concert of the choral society about the middle of November. We all met for a moment in the crush of people at the entrance and then went inside. The old hall hadn't had electricity installed yet. In the orange yellow gaslight, Julie's face had a false vitality. The program was half finished when she leaned over and whispered into my ear: "I can't sit here any more! Let's go!"

She walked out, leaving me to follow or to stay. I was after her in a moment. In the white light of a street arc Professor Chase had taken her arm for a moment and informed her that the board had made its decision: she was to have no advanced laboratory work with him. Tears streamed unheeded down her cheeks—not tears of sadness, but tears of rage. She said no more and kept on striding away. I followed.

She walked from Harvard Square to Brattle Street where the horsecar still ran. Shortly it would disappear forever and be replaced by an electric trolley over on Mt. Auburn Street, but there in the distance that night, like a little train of lights going to fairyland, one of them seemed to be merging with the trees between us and Longfellow's house. Finally it went away. The street was then dark under the bare branches overhead—dark except for the lights of the large houses set back on spacious lawns, and the few isolated street lamps hissing away the night. She had said nothing all this time, only walking swiftly, rubbing her hands with a nervous wringing motion. Once, I said, "Darling—" a word I really don't know how to say.

She said, "Oh *don't!*" with utter revulsion, twisted away from me, and hurried on in the darkness.

She kept crossing and recrossing the street in a way that made no sense. I hurried after her, knowing that she might be better by herself, but unable to leave her. Finally, as she was about to cross the street again, I took her arm to stop her.

"There's a big puddle over there. I saw it by the street light when the carriage went by."

"I don't care!" she said, snatching her arm from me. "And it's that street light I can't stand. *All* the street lights. I can't bear to see myself, not even my own shadow! A woman!" she said with passionate contempt. "Who ever wanted to be a woman? They've made me hate myself for being a woman!"

She shook with sobs and there in the middle of the street, she covered her face with her hands.

"Julie—" I said, praying she wouldn't slap me in the face for my sex.

"I'm as good as any man in the college, yet any idiot who wears trousers can walk into that laboratory, and I—" she said touching her breast, "I—I who need it the way I need to breathe, *I* can't! My God," she said, clenching her fists, her teeth, her lips, "I shake with the way I hate!"

She was like a sibyl, a priestess, a Fury—then just as suddenly she gave way to real tears.

Professor Chase had been vetoed by all sides. The Harvard anti-coeducational faction said that it was bad enough that Radcliffe girls after graduation could come and attend certain classes with the male graduate students. No matter how promising this young Porter person might be, let her wait until she got her degree. The Radcliffe faction in addition took the prim position that it was unwise and indiscreet for a young girl to work unchaperoned hour after hour in the private laboratory of even a professor of Harvard. If she were older, they said, of course, it might be different . . . There was still a third faction which I discovered. Years later, I went to interview Professor Chase toward the end of his life, when he, too, was finally awarded the Nobel Prize. Ironically enough, this was ten years after Julie had received the award with Claudet. It was then that Chase showed me the dingy little laboratory which once had meant so much to her. No, he didn't hear from her these days. He was glad though that she had the recognition that was coming to her. Had he seen it in her as a student? He smiled a little crookedly and took a while to answer me. He had been more sure of her achieving eminence than he had ever been of his own chances, he said.

"She was right to do what she eventually did," he said. "Even if the powers that be had given it to me and allowed me to take her on, I still couldn't have done it."

"Why not?"

He looked at me over his glasses, a white-haired man with liver-spotted, arthritic hands.

"My wife wouldn't have stood for it. She took one look at that young lady across the room in Fay House and said, 'Absolutely *no*,' because at that point Julie was laughing out loud at something, and if you know Julie then you know that laugh. Years later, when Julie became so famous, and the King of Sweden made that fine speech to her, I handed the newspaper to my wife and said: 'Now what have you got to say about that girl?' My wife put on her glasses and read it all without a word; then she handed it back to me. 'Well?' I demanded, 'That's the Swedish King talking.' 'It doesn't signify,' she said. 'Just you wait until the Swedish Queen hears her laugh! She'll take that medal back fast enough!' "

Julie's disappointment came at the very moment when I was having trouble of my own. In my two months at the *Transcript* I had been trying to write about science by myself. It was still beyond me. I had to spend hours looking up the meanings of the sort of words Julie had at her fingertips. "Apples, peaches, pears, kinetic energy, trivalency, buttercups . . ." For Julie each word on that list had equal clarity, equal familiarity. For me, every article I wrote was pure torture.

There had been no actual complaint yet from my editor. There had been, however, pointed reference, first, to my slowness, and then to the fact that "here and there, the clarity isn't up to your standards." My "standard of clarity" had been set in the pieces which I had written with Julie. The message was clear: give up the job, or give in and ask Julie's help.

Saturday afternoons, we usually met toward the end of the day in the quiet of the History Reference Reading Room in the new Boston Public Library in Copley Square. It was—and still is—a big-windowed alcove with forty or fifty seats and there are never more than five or six people there. We used to have endless privacy and quiet while exposed to public view. After the library we would walk invariably to Chandler's Soda Parlor—a place of colored glass lampshades, mirrored walls, colored marble, white tile floor, furniture of twisted iron wire and the sweet smell of vanilla in the air. She used to have a strawberry sundae, and I'd take a chocolate cooler. Then we'd walk down toward the river and over to Brimmer Street for an hour or so together up in my room.

After she got her bad news, she was like someone bereaved. She was grieving for a dream. That particular Saturday I spoke just as we came out of the library. I said I knew how badly she still felt, but I needed her help. She appeared to be listening to me, her head bent against the first snow of the year. Heavy white flakes settled on everything with a slight frying hiss, and turned to rain. On her face though, it looked like tears.

She was silent for a while. Then she sounded tired. First she said she'd have no time. Then she said she'd help me just as a friend without pay, but only when she was free. No, I insisted, because I wanted to tie her to me—it had to be a regular business arrangement. She sighed and agreed to think it over.

She brought the matter up, though, just as we were leaving Chandler's—the one part of the day that I wanted to be absolutely quiet. We always used to walk to my room together from Chandler's with a silence between us that grew warmer and closer as we crossed the avenues and streets, mounted the stairs, flight after flight, and opened my door. As it shut behind us we used to turn into an embrace—with our hats, gloves, and coats still on, her purse still in her hand, the books falling to the floor about us—as if we had been waiting all week for this kiss—this almost more than what was to come afterward.

I treasured the silence after Chandler's because it gave me the illusion that she was feeling exactly what I was. Of course the silence offered her a chance to think a thousand private thoughts of her own that were never disclosed to me.

"Since you insist you want to be able to come to me any time for help on your articles, the only fair and sensible way would be to give me a regular weekly salary," she said.

I told myself that there was no reason why I couldn't give her a regular five dollars out of my thirty-five a week.

"Fifteen dollars a week would be about fair," she went on calmly. My heart stopped. That would leave only twenty for me—exactly what I had been making at the *Globe*. It would have meant Good-by, Sweet Raise.

Frankly, I didn't know how to handle her. Here we were—about to make love. There she was—playing the Yankee Trader! Damn near half my salary! How could she!

"I'll think it over," I said; but the mood was spoiled for me. There is something bittersweet, ugly, or perhaps only pathetic in the way two angry people momentarily stifle their rage to make love to each other. No sooner were we out of bed and beginning to dress again than she was right back to it. She still said fifteen.

"How about seven?" I asked, furious with her and with myself.

"Ten," she said stubbornly. She was holding her corset to

her body and presenting her back to me for lacing. "I went over my figures, and I'm going to need at least ten dollars a week."

Over *what* figures? What did she mean, *need?*

How do you tie a woman's corset when you're arguing money? I wanted to throttle her with the laces and at the same time I wanted to bend down and kiss the curve of her naked back. God, how I loved her! Yet I was still damned if I'd give her ten.

"Ten," she said again, and now I could hear the dangerous stiffening. "If I were a man, you'd give me ten dollars!"

"Don't try singing that song to me!" I said. "I'm not the one who kept you from getting into Professor Chase's lab. I'm not the one who keeps you from having the vote. I'm not—"

"Ten!" she said quietly, wriggling within the corset to keep the fit right. I knew it was hopeless. So ten it was, and in the end I *was* damned for it.

8

AT LEAST MY WORK GOT DONE NOW. AS FOR THE money, I swallowed hard and didn't let myself think about it. The day would come when I wouldn't need her help. Then another idea became increasingly insistent—the day would come when whatever money I gave her would all remain in the family. My old dream of marrying the richest girl in Boston society was being replaced by a willingness to settle for the poorest girl in Cambridge. I began to have daydreams of the well-known journalists—Montgomery and Julie Crocker. We would travel all over the world. We would have staterooms like Claudet's on international steamships. We would be booked on grand Pullman cars and interview the great men of science—Roentgen, Koch, Mendeleyev, Thompson, Rayleigh, Michelson. The *Transcript* was only the beginning. I became wild with impatience for the wonderful future waiting for us. The daydreams snapped me into action. I mailed copies of my best pieces to magazines like the *Century, McClure's,* the *Atlantic* and a half-dozen others as samples. I offered to do more extended articles.

Julie was sitting in our usual place in the History Reference Reading Room when I brought my good news to her. After Claudet had gone, she became a steady reader of the French research journal *Comptes Rendus,* to which she had taken her own subscription. She always carried the current issue in her bag to read on trolleys, horsecars, in waiting rooms, in the library there, and even in soda fountains if I too had something to read, or even sometimes if I didn't. With the magazine went a worn little pocket French-English dictionary with a blue canvas cover and a title in black ornate old-fashioned type. The dictionary lay in her lap, always ready for her frowning use. On the flyleaf, in slanting calligraphy was a man's name: *Asher Pease, Valparaiso, 1878.*

I asked: "Who is Asher Pease?"

"A man," she replied steadily, still reading, and took the book from me.

"A man you know?"

"A man you don't know," she said.

"There's a Valparaiso in Indiana."

She still didn't glance up. "This was bought in a bookstore in the other Valparaiso."

"Chile?"

"Chile," she said and went on reading.

In the back of the book, there were other notations—some were heavily mathematical, and some were cartographic, like meridians of longitude and latitude with dates from twenty years earlier. She didn't want to talk about it, and I was too proud to press it.

That day, she sat there in the library so engrossed in her journal that she didn't even see me come up to her. I silently lay the letter from *Scribner's* on the magazine page she was reading. She frowned at first, then as she read, the frown subsided.

"How much would they pay for something like that?" she asked.

"Not one word of congratulations? Not one hurrah? Just: *how much?* What a Yankee you are!"

She laughed a little.

"Ah, you know I need the money! Of course, *hurrah!* But how much?"

"I don't know. Maybe fifty, seventy-five, or even a hundred. What counts is that it can be the beginning of something important."

She patted my hand. She really was glad for me.

"Not for me alone—for us," I said, but instead of her face lighting up, she looked wary, almost alarmed. "I don't understand you," I said. "There's hardly a girl in your class who wouldn't give anything to be in your shoes—to have your chance at an interesting career—"

"But I'm not a writer! I don't want to be a writer! The way *you* want to write is the way *I* want to do what interests me. Why is that so difficult to understand!" she cried.

"But Julie what I also understand is that what you want most to do, you *can't!* That's the sad fact. If you *do* want a career that touches on science, here's as good a one as you'll find. And while it may not pay like banking, there's a better living in it than being an old professor somewhere."

She unpinned her hat, sighed, and laid the hat down next to her. From two tables away, a bald reader with ginger whiskers looked up and frowned at her forwardness: ladies did not remove their hats. She even ran her fingers through her hair.

"And I also meant it another way when I said *us*," I went on.

She looked at me, her light eyes awaiting an explanation. I had to laugh.

"Well?" I asked.

"Well, what?"

"'What do you say when a man asks you to marry him?"

Her eyes grew very large. The idea of marriage—at least, marriage to me—was so fantastic to her that she was stunned by it.

"But we never said anything about getting married." She was almost stammering.

"I thought you'd want to," I managed to say. "I thought we loved each other. I thought it would be nice to be together— to make every day a Saturday afternoon."

"Monty," she said with great earnestness. "I swear I never thought about us that way. I thought we were just being happy together in a way that didn't need talking about." I let that go by without looking at it, but I knew that a sixteen-inch shell loaded with implication had just passed. "And anyhow," she added, "I can't get married as long as I'm a student."

I kept trying to face the fact that I was being turned down. It was unbelievable—like dying. "We'd wait, if that were the only problem. But it isn't."

"No," she said honestly. "It isn't. I just don't think of my-self as settling down a married lady."

"Who's settling down?" I demanded. I was angry. "I'm talk-ing about getting married so we can travel together, and go to London, Paris, San Francisco. There are a million places to go and write about where important scientists are, and it's all in-teresting. *That's* the kind of life I'm talking about. *And* mak-ing love in the bargain. Every day—if we want!"

She smiled a little and flushed.

"What about it?" I insisted.

She shrugged and evaded me as she put the pin through the hat.

"No," I said, refusing to get up. "I'm not going anyplace or do anything with you unless I'm your fiancé. I *was* going to marry a great Boston heiress, then I talked myself into conde-scending to you. After that, you can't turn me down!"

She looked at me with her hand on my shoulder. "You're really a very nice man," she said, laughing. "I'll never think anything else."

"Are you saying good-by?"

"I'm telling you what I think, that's all."

"If you don't want to be a fiancée, can we be a little bit en-gaged?" I asked. I had come all the way from pride to plead-ing.

"Will that satisfy you?"

"For the time being."

"All right, you can be my semi-fiancé."

That was enough of a victory for one day, it seemed. We left the library walking hand in hand. In my room, she was softer than she had ever been with me. I had touched her quite deeply.

The commission from *Scribner's* was for a piece on the Harvard Observatory, and on what Pickering thought of the chances of the sun being an inhabited body surrounded by a glowing atmosphere. Today, of course, it sounds funny and naïve, but there was a time sixty or seventy years ago when responsible scientists thought it a serious possibility. Pickering, one of the early astrophysicists, was knocking it into a cocked hat. I went to the Observatory armed with questions Julie had carefully written out sitting at the table, and I took down his answers as close to verbatim as I could. Julie explained his answers to me, continually tucking in that shirtwaist that al-ways escaped her belt; I explained her explanation; and that was the piece. I sent it in, and two weeks later I got a check for a hundred and twenty dollars. I gave her forty, feeling like the Man Who Broke the Bank at Monte Carlo. She threw her arms about me and kissed me with delight. The following month, I got another assignment: to go out to Chicago for a piece on A. A. Michelson and his experiments on the velocity of light.

For me, every week of that winter seemed to be leading directly toward everything I had ever wanted—even though it was all coming in ways I had never foreseen for myself. But while I was becoming happier, Julie was becoming more and more subdued. Whatever satisfaction there was in producing the articles was all mine. She brightened only when I passed money on to her. I wondered whether her father appreciated how much pleasure she took in earning his support.

As for her silences, and her long periods of frowning preoccupation, I thought she was going at last through the pain of realistically accepting her position as a woman. I knew she was suffering, but I felt that at least on the far side of the suffering would be something better and more peaceful for both of us.

In those days, most women accepted the legal deprivation ordained by custom—and went about getting what they really wanted through all the indirect paths that have always been open to them. A certain amount of dissimulation, or what were called "womanly wiles," had to be second nature. But Julie couldn't bend—there was a passion in her that either had to be killed or it would in turn kill her. Sometimes in bed, she would turn away from me and sob heartbrokenly. I thought that I was living through its death, and like an expectant heir, my face was draped with appropriate grief, but my heart was impatient for the moment of liberation. The truth is that I wanted Julie to be a nice, quiet wife, a submissive helpmate to her husband, and I longed for an end, once and for all, to her tears, to her depthless yearning, to her silent heartache. What I had to offer was far better, far more practical than her harebrained ideas. Sooner or later, she would have to see the truth.

The question was, what could I do to speed up the process? How could I help her over her own hurdle? I decided that she ought to meet my parents. After prolonged arguments—in her boardinghouse, on the street, at my place—interminable, they seemed, she agreed to visit my home.

In those years the call of adventure was not the hum of an

airplane engine but the distant wail of a steam whistle—for Julie it was the hoarse blast of a ship backing out into a harbor full of masts, spars, and full funnels—for me it was the long cry of a locomotive in the country night. That winter, though, I was able to hear the whistle from within the train itself. After almost two years in the city, I was coming home: a man with a career. My name was printed in newspapers and magazines for hundreds of thousands of strangers to see—and I had a girl walking into the train beside me holding my arm.

I was as proud of her sitting next to me—of her looks, of the way her new veil made her face soft and mysterious—as I was of what I had made of myself. We sat there side by side —I with my newspaper and she reading her *Comptes Rendus* with the little blue dictionary of Asher Pease of Valparaiso in her lap.

The wooden car jiggled and jumped and we swayed and bumped in the plush seats that smelled of oranges, cold coffee, and tobacco spit. She was oblivious to it all.

In that car though, I smelled the intake and outgo of living things as Julie read. I smelled Julie's hair, her skin, the dry-goods odor of her clothes. And I thought how contented and reassured she would be on our ride back at the end of the visit.

"She's very pretty, Monty," my mother said to me when I had finally pressed her for an opinion. "But she don't seem much good around the house. I mean to say, she tries well enough, but it's as if her mind is someplace else."

"I guess it must be on her studies."

My mother looked dubious.

I said, "She'll learn."

Again that look from my mother. "If she hasn't by now, she won't. I don't think she can cook either." My mother, once started, never did know when to stop.

"And her clothes. They're all right, I mean, but the way she *dresses* herself, Monty. Somehow the buttons never come out even, and the belt is always off to one side or the other. Probably she never had a mother to show her things, poor girl. She has a nice character though. It's just that her mind is always someplace else. Was she the only girl you met down there in Boston?"

I sighed and said: "No, but she was the one I liked best."

My father too had misgivings. He was polite but ill at ease

with Julie. We lived on the homestead that every man in my family down to my grandfather had farmed. My father used hired help. He himself ran the grain and feed store which my mother had inherited from her father.

He was embarrassed by Julie. She was the first girl I had ever brought home. Moreover she was a college girl—a Harvard girl, as a matter of fact. Not only had no men in our family ever been to college, but no girl in our town, and only a handful of men. My father thought it perfectly all right to be running a business which he got from his wife, because he took it for granted that my mother couldn't possibly make a go of the business by herself. On the other hand, he worried when I told him how much Julie helped me because she knew so much.

"What I don't understand is what she needs *you* for," he said bluntly.

"She can't write the way I can," I answered. He wasn't convinced. After all, to him reporting wasn't like making up stories—it was simply a matter of putting down one word after another about something that had actually happened. It wasn't anything he'd think of doing himself, but if he had to, he guessed he could. And any Harvard College girl ought to be able to do that as well if not better than a young fellow with only a diploma from our town's Howard Webster High School.

Still, he conceded Julie was a pretty girl and neither flirtatious, flighty, nor full of ideas about clothes and parties all the time. "And I like it that she comes from a town that must be something like ours, and not from the city," he added diplomatically to make up for anything unpleasant he might have said. I told my parents that Julie's cousin was Portilea, the famous opera singer. Instead of being impressed, they were dismayed—how did she come to have an Italian-sounding relative?

Julie wasn't happy either, except when we'd get out of the house by ourselves and take long walks across the fields.

The roads were rivers of mud, but she laughed as she strode through them. She was herself the personification of the coming spring. She touched the bark that was beginning to glisten for the budding that was still weeks away. She stopped to take deep breaths of the air, tender and sweet with the scent of rain and the moisture the sun drew up from the wet dead leaves and earth.

She seemed full of fun, too, when we visited friends with whom I had gone to school. Most of them were married now. She enjoyed the dance at Grange Hill; she enjoyed the Community Supper at the First Congregational Church, where sure enough the Reverend Doctor Basehart told Julie that *he* knew Dukes Academy on Martha's Vineyard very well. He said he had heard it spoken of as one of the finest boys' schools in the country! "That was when my father was Headmaster there," Julie said with calm pride.

I consoled myself with the thought that, by and large, as such visits go—certainly when we were by ourselves—it was not too bad. The embarrassment and strained feelings with my parents should have been expected. Julie wasn't like the other girls in our town.

At the end of the week my parents began to feel enough at ease with her to ask questions. They were hushed for a moment only when told that Julie's mother had died.

"Still and all," said my father weighing the whole situation, "your father must have made a good thing of it there in that school if he could afford to send you away to college. Darn few men can afford to do that. I know I couldn't send Monty, and I run a business."

"My father didn't send me," she said quietly. Her tone warned me to cut into the inquisition.

"Julie goes to college on money she inherited," I said.

"From your mother?" my mother asked.

"No," said Julie in that same distant voice. She sat there with a bone-hard quality that made pity pointless. I rose to end the talk.

"But certainly from a relative," my mother went on, anxious now to put bounds to the vast area which Julie's cold silence was leaving open. "Some uncle or aunt?"

"No," Julie said again. She made no move to join me. She sat as she was—at the kitchen table, her elbow resting on it. She looked reflectively at my parents. I was terrified that she might very quietly tell them to go to hell. But then she let her hand fall and the storm passed. "From the man I was going to marry," she said. "My fiancé died and left whatever he had to me so that I could get a college education."

My parents stared at her, then at each other, then together they turned to me. Why hadn't I told them? I stood looking down at Julie.

"That would be Asher Pease?" I asked her. "The man in the French dictionary?"

"Yes." She was still talking quietly, but she was glad now that she had finally got it all said.

"You didn't know about this?" my father asked me.

"No, Pa, I didn't. I figured where she got the money wasn't any of my business." His lips tightened because he felt I was reproving him. I was sorry, but I did want to keep the record straight so I went on: "But now that I do know about it, I think it was a darn nice thing to do!"

My parents said nothing; they didn't agree. I didn't feel so great about it myself, but from the way Julie looked at me, I had pleased her; and at the time, that was enough for me.

9

IT WAS GOOD THAT WE WERE LEAVING. THE FOLLOWING day, Julie said that she was sorry my parents were so disappointed in her, but I assured her that they liked her well enough and that next time we would all be easier.

She just sighed, turned away, and went on with the little packing there was to do. What the sigh meant, I didn't know. As we got aboard the train, my good-by to my parents was more formal than I liked. My parents' good-by was warmer than was natural. All around, it was a strain. I wished we had never come.

On the train back to Boston, I kept waiting for her finally to tell me all about Asher Pease. I didn't really want to hear about him—it would have been a form of torture. Again and again, I was on the point of blurting out my question, but I had said out loud that it was none of my business, and my pride wouldn't let me take it back. Just the same now I hated the visit home; I hated what I had learned.

The trip to my parents' had a curious result: for different reasons, to each of us, our Saturday afternoons no longer seemed stolen moments of carefree romance. We no longer came up my stairs on fire for each other. Our breathlessness at my door was simply from the exertion of climbing three flights. I was the one who was pleased. It wasn't as exciting as

it had been in the beginning, but it was—at least for me—
more recognizable—as if in all the years I had lain awake in
our town, hearing the train whistle its way to distant fame,
thinking that I was yearning for the day when it would be my
turn to get aboard the 6:02 and ride away to New York, Rio,
or Nome—I was at the same time slowly being infused with
something very different—so that after a while my blood-
stream carried white cells, red cells, and domesticity cells. The
atmosphere in which I really breathed most freely had to contain oxygen gas, nitrogen gas, and domesticity gas. Without
being aware of it when it happened, I was so thoroughly and
pervasively conditioned to the domestic state that any girl
with whom I might have a passing afternoon's adventure, I
had to make into a mistress; any mistress I had to make into a
wife. I could talk from night to morning about adventure, but
as soon as I stopped to catch my breath, the fake was apparent.

Julie's new quiet was not due to a growing contentment like
mine but to a growing distance she was putting between
us, as if she were slipping away from me into herself. She
looked haunted. I turned from my quiet and went into a pan-
icky pursuit of her.

What I wanted simply was *her*—tied to me inescapably.
Once and for all I wanted to stop tormenting myself about the
meaning of every word she casually dropped; I wanted to stop
watching every nuance of every change in her expression for
hints of anger or displeasure. I wanted to stop worrying about
whom she had known before me. For the next couple of
months, I was in a state of continual tension. My nerves were
so exhausted that I was screaming inwardly for an end to it. If
I had been a different man, or less caught by her, I would
have asked for "an end—one way or another," but I could
allow myself to think only of one kind of end—to get married
at once, secretly if necessary.

"I'd be expelled," she said, as if the college had an intelligence system that ferreted out every student's doings. I said
angrily at last that the college still hadn't found out about our
Saturday afternoons on Brimmer Street.

"That's entirely different!" she said with a purely feminine
illogic that forever—for me—outbalances all her later accomplishments in science. I will always see a blond, pale-eyed girl,
her pompadoured hair on the verge of disarray, shrugging her
shoulders with more femininity than could be distilled from a

thousand domesticated housewives, and saying, "But that's entirely different!" when whatever it was, was not different at all.

When I took her to the wharf in early June, for the steamer to the Vineyard at the start of her second summer vacation, I was dead set on pushing aside her objections. I asked if I could come down to the island in two weeks. She seemed agreeable enough.

"If we can't talk of getting married right now," I went on, "at least let's tell our folks what we plan to do."

"Oh, why is the *telling* so important?" she said wearily. "What difference does it make as long as *we* know!"

"It's important to me!" I said. "Maybe it's my way to show off because I'm so proud of you. If *that's* an insult, go ahead and get mad!"

The whistle was blowing and the deck hands were beginning to handle the warping lines fore and aft.

She looked up at me helplessly.

"Oh, Monty, how I wish for your sake I were all the things you like to think I am! How I wish you really could know *me!* Monty, look at me, will you," she said desperately. "Look at me, and just once really *see* me!"

I saw the tight-waisted, full-sleeved white blouse; the perspiring face with pitying lips and frowning forehead—the different expressions of all the different women she was—and I could say only: "I see Julie."

She reached up, touched my face, then glanced quickly about and gave me a swift, light kiss. When she turned away, she was crying. She cried as she went up the gangplank. I was touched by her tears because I understood them as love for me, and so I stood there while the *Island Queen* pulled away from the wharf, and looked up at Julie on the swayback deck above the dirty gold lettering on the dirty white hull. She turned to wave to me, and I waved to her.

After she left, I wrote every day. Only one letter from her came to me that week and it gave me no reason to expect anything. Then three days before I was to come down to visit her, I got the wire saying: DO NOT COME STOP HAVE COMPLETELY CHANGED MIND ABOUT FUTURE STOP AM WRITING FULL DETAILS STOP PLEASE FORGIVE STOP KINDEST REGARDS STOP JULIE.

I read it over a hundred times, feeling as if I were slowly bleeding to death. I wired back to her in West Tisbury: COMING JUST THE SAME STOP LOVE STOP MONTY.

I felt a terrifying urgency: everything would be smoothed over if only I could get to her on time. If her letter came before I left, I made up my mind to hand it back to her unopened when I got there. If I opened the letter, or if I failed to reach her in time, there could be only disaster.

I hoped to see her waiting on the Vineyard Haven wharf. She wasn't there.

I hoped she'd be waiting at the stage depot. She wasn't there.

I hoped that on the jingling drive Up Island I'd meet her hurrying down in a buggy because she'd been detained. But in the seven-mile ride we passed no one at all.

Burt, the stage driver, had looked at me with what I thought was surprise, but he said nothing beyond: "How're ye keepin'?" I could still tell myself that I was only imagining his reluctance to talk to me, but I couldn't deny her father's amazement when I burst into the house. He got up from his chair at the kitchen table.

"I thought she had written you!" he said. "She gave me a letter to mail to you, and I mailed it."

"Where's Julie?"

"Oh, my dear boy!" he said with genuine pity, and sat down. He waved me to a chair, and I sat on its edge. "Julie left here the day before yesterday. She took the steamer to Fall River, and from there to New York. If she made all her connections, as I have every reason to believe, she should already have sailed from New York."

"But to where, and with what?"

"For Paris, to study."

I started to cry. I couldn't help myself. But I still didn't understand.

"How could she? We were going to be married!"

He rubbed his hands with his acute agony at having to see my misery. "She told me about that, but she also told me that she couldn't go through with it. She knew that sooner or later she'd bolt. Ever since Asher died, she has lived without looking back. She is just beginning to come out of it. She *is* genuinely fond of you, but she couldn't face you any more. The girl she showed you was not who she really is inside. Nor could that true Julie face another year at Cambridge, not when what she has always wanted so desperately was available if only she moved quickly and decisively. I suppose it was a choice between what you wanted for her and what

Asher had always wanted for her—and Asher—say what you please about him—wanted for her what she wanted too. She loved him very much, I regret to say! So much, that she couldn't bear to talk about him after he died. But I'm afraid her last talks were with her cousin—Priscilla—not with me—"

"Portilea?"

"Portilea—Priscilla, I think of her—she's staying in Edgartown, and Julie went over to see her. She always does in time of trouble."

"But where will she study? And again—with what?"

"At the Sorbonne, my boy," he said gently. "It was always her dream. Women there are given the same opportunities that men are, they attend the same lectures and, most important, have access to the same laboratories."

"The Sorbonne? But—*how*, man, *how*? How'll she live? Who'll support her? Who paid her passage?"

He looked at me with astonishment.

"Why, *you*, of course!" he said. "The money you helped her earn made it all possible. She'll have only a little left over after she's paid for her ticket, but if she's very careful, she should be able to get by for a while, and by then, who knows?"

"But she needed that money for *you!*"

He frowned. "But I have my salary from the Academy. I may no longer be Headmaster, but I've continued as instructor. No daughter need support me. Every penny Julie earned, she saved."

"With this in view?" When I looked back, I saw that she really never had said it was for him. It had been my own explanation. "Did she plan this from the very beginning?"

He sat for several minutes before answering, a very tired old man. "I'll tell you a terrible truth, young man: *I* don't know. I didn't know my only living child's innermost thoughts! She came so much later than the others: she seemed to be so much less. I was sure I didn't need her. Perhaps something I said or did made her finally feel it. Well, I was wrong. I see now that I never appreciated Julie! I never understood her! God help me, maybe I'll never see her again!"

He never did.

I walked to the crossroad and rented a livery in which I drove over a rolling plain to Edgartown, while the tears fell without stopping. When I got near Portilea's house on Water

Street, I could tell which one it was by the enormous sparkling automobile that waited by the walk. I scarcely glanced at it as I went by, but afterward I realized that I had seen it with a piercing clarity because of what that damned arrogant car stood for: it had a gleaming Delft blue tonneau with a long-beaked engine snout, bright red spokes on the pneumatic-tired wheels and deeply quilted red leather seats perched high fore and aft—shining brass serpentine horn, brass square lanterns. The Delft blue mudguards were like the outstretched wings of a pouncing eagle—altogether a ten-thousand-dollar fantasy.

It was French, you see—because in those days only France had enough wealth, luxury, and aristocracy to build such machines for casual toys. To me at that moment, the car represented the France which had the glitter and the culture to draw girls like Julie from all over the world. God, how I hated the French brilliance, swagger and superiority, to which at that very moment, she was sailing away from me! Years passed before I could make my private peace with France.

For all my driving to Edgartown, Portilea could not see me. The great lady was resting, I was told. I went back to Boston.

Julie's letter came a few days later. It said nothing that made any difference. She was gone, that was enough. So she had been miserable? What of it? I was miserable now. She promised to write me from Paris. She never wrote. Perhaps she was ashamed of having appeared so heartless and didn't want to face her own cruelty. Or perhaps she hadn't been heartless at all and had acted only out of self-preservation, fighting for what she had to have or die. What she accomplished later with her life is one answer, but it doesn't sufficiently explain why she never wrote. We *had* been fond of each other. I could waste a lifetime trying to guess at the answer. She said in that last letter: "You do need the kind of girl you think I am. Unfortunately, I'm not that girl, Monty. I feel compressed and suffocated when I try to be her to please you. For the few years I was in Cambridge, I was a stranger even to myself. I never told you about Asher and I can no more talk about him than I can about my brothers and sisters, so you must realize that there is a whole side of me that I have never showed you. If, at times, I seemed cruel or capricious, it was because the side of me that was locked away was not free to correct actions which I knew I was always going to regret. You must please try to forgive me, Monty. I seem clear only to myself but I have neither the words to describe all of me nor the faith that I'll ever find anyone who'd understand the words I might use. I'm alone. I suppose I always will be."

In spite of all my big plans for travel, I have been to Paris only twice so far, but I never looked her up. Perhaps I will the next time I go.

Or perhaps the time after.

PART THREE— HAL PRESCOTT: II

1

So MUCH FOR MONTY'S STORY. YEARS LATER, HIS WIDOW acknowledged my condolence note, but I had written from my home and signed it Hal Prescott, while she on the other hand addressed her reply to Dr. Harold Prescott and sent it to the Institute. Why? Certainly the gesture was calculated—she was far too self-aware a woman not to know what she was doing. On a modest scale, she was the Boston heiress Monty had always wanted, but I think she harbored a deep resentment against everything he had lived and felt before he married her. Perhaps because of Julie, she identified me with that time of his life even though I had met him so much later. To have held the grudge all those years! Monty himself had said that he was one of those unlucky men who are destroyed by having their wildest dreams granted.

And it's true. Take the way he died.

I remember that I had been thinking of him again just about when it happened. When I got home after the war—I'm of the age where *the* war now means Hitler's war—I began making little pilgrimages back to places I had known as a boy and I was in Fortuno's, on Beaver Street, for the first time since I had been taken there by my father about 1905. Then it had been one of the restaurants where all the Wall Street people used to go—huge noisy plump men with glistening mustaches, tall starched collars and deep laughing booming voices —at least so they seemed to me at eight when I walked, ran, and stumbled behind my father into the main dining room clinging to his hand, as he strode in to show off his son to his fellow brokers. In those days, it was full of the glitter of curving glass fixtures, the sparkle of glass globes, the glint of glass flowers against polished dark wood and expanses of white linen and heavy silver—almost too massive, I remember, for a boy of eight to handle.

I had come here by accident, at a moment when three hundred lives were poised with noisy pleasure at the peaks of their trajectories. Then, as I had grown up, the same men had slowly withered within their wrinkling skins. The pulse of their activity had gradually slowed; their hair, teeth, their eyes, and at last they themselves had died. Some forty years later, when I ate by myself, the glass was dull, the woodwork drab, the silence oppressive. Of all the nerve-bundles that had quivered there that long ago noonday to the glitter, aromas, fragrances, and bursts of sound, only I and a few elderly diners were there to count the empty places and to go through the menu which remained the same, even to the old-fashioned printing that still promised oysters of five varieties, four kinds of herring, seven soups, an infinity of roasts, game, fish—for page after page—and a list of desserts which included pies, puddings, fruits, *Pêche Melba*, *Poire Hélène*, and—I almost choked—*Glace Portilea!*

I called the nearest waiter and pointed it out to him: *Portilea*. He started to list the ingredients, but I cut him short— how long had it been on the menu?

"Ever since the old days," he said. "Long before I came here. Portilea was once a famous opera star, I think. Sang Wagner, Beethoven, and all like that."

It probably had been there on the menu the day forty years before, when I came there as a boy. I had the sense once more of having collided somewhere out of time with Julie. Then, in a brutal coincidence, either that day or the next, the newspaper carried the story of Monty's plane disaster—twenty correspondents and photographers were being flown out to the Pacific to cover one of the atomic bomb tests. Monty had reached a point in his life—he must have been about seventy —when he shouldn't have taken such an arduous trip under any circumstances, but I heard that he had become increasingly jealous of his unofficial title as dean of the science reporters; and so the man who had always wanted to travel to the distant places had finally got his wish and died of it.

I went soberly back to Fortuno's for no reason I could discern except that the sight of Portilea's name in print brought back the youths of so many lives: Julie's, Monty's, Portilea's, mine—all so widely spaced in time, and it had a bittersweet sadness. I even ordered a portion of the mysterious Glace Portilea—ordinary ice cream with a chocolate sauce and, of all things, bananas! Bananas, so help me! If Portilea had still been alive, I would have asked her why, but she too was gone, and the bananas in Glace Portilea will have to go on being unexplained. But I can guess.

Ice cream, chocolate sauce, and bananas all together! Why? Because she must have been a glutton at heart. When I finally met her—which I did in 1942—she was an enormous woman, even in those days of rationing. Absolutely shapeless, without a trace of a former glamour, beauty, or elegance. Where was the woman who had been the toast of Shanley's, Delmonico's, Mouquin's, or Maxim's? She was a Mrs. George Hennepin of Cadogan Place, London, a widow with rooms to let, whose hair was thin, dyed a violent shade of red found naturally in no hair on this planet. Her make-up was also fantastic, but while she was ridiculous to look at, and infinitely vain, nobody laughed, because her wit could be sharp, even cruel, and her laugh still had a vitality that made me think of Julie.

In February 1942, I had been bombed out twice when my British opposite number decided that he himself would find me lodgings—and my new landlady set out to impress me with the high tone of the place. She listed the titles and connections of past and present neighbors among whom was no less than a cousin of the legendary French lady scientist—Julie Claudet! Once this neighbor was even pointed out as she waddled slowly around the little park leading an ancient Skye terrier who also waddled. To me, Mrs. George Hennepin was simply another name, and I never would have spoken to her except that she herself stopped me one day.

She looked me up and down with disapproval and shook her head.

"I much preferred our uniform in the other war, Colonel," she said as if she were giving me fair warning. "Far more military. Look at you, young man! My chauffeurs used to be better turned out! I understand you know—or knew—my cousin Julie."

I said I hadn't seen Julie in almost twenty years.

"And I haven't seen her in forty," she snapped. "Where is she these days?"

As far as anyone knew, Julie was still in France—occupied France—not Vichy. At that time we were working up transfusion calculations for the coming invasion, and our people had made contact with her to bring her out; but she had insisted on remaining with the French. When our people told her that she could be very useful to us just then, she told them tartly that she was already being useful to her own people. Her refusal was final. All those conversations were strictly government business, and so I told Mrs. Hennepin only that I didn't know where Julie was.

"Probably still in Paris," she said. "She's got enough of her life there, God knows! And to think that I was the one who sent her there!"

"You?"

"Yes indeed. Just as I was the one who told her to go to Radcliffe. She was in school there at the same time as Helen Keller, Gertrude Stein, and Josephine Hull. Once upon a time, Colonel, whenever it was a matter of Julie making a decision about where and when to go, that girl came to Yours Truly, and cousin Priscilla always gave the right answer!"

"Priscilla Norton?" I said. "You? Portilea?"

Her whole face went slack with astonishment, the painted eyes and mouth all absolutely round, open, and disbelieving.

"You mean you only just recognized me?" she said.

2

I SAW PORTILEA SEVERAL TIMES AFTER THAT AS SHE walked in the little park. I nodded, but I never stopped. We were in the middle of a war, and even more to the point, I was in the middle of a life still surging forward, and so I had no inclination to stand and call up memories that had thorns of humiliation.

Gradually though, my feelings changed because of my work. Our calculations of the transfusion and plasma requirements for a massive invasion were based on very high casualty rates for the first wave, and I took it for granted that I would accompany it. The odds against survival were overwhelming, and I slowly came to accept the fact that I—who had never been particularly lucky—would not come through. I was in the same fix as everyone with me, and so there was nothing to do but to go on working without thinking, but I was secretly sad inside, grieved to be leaving my children, because they and my work were really my only sources of pleasure.

I say I stopped thinking about it. What I mean is that I got used to it. In my spare time, I took to composing my own obituary in fantasy; and then—like an explosion—it dawned on me that no obituary of mine would ever mention Julie! But she was so deeply a part of who and what I was that any account of my life that didn't include Julie was unbearable. It made me angry just to think about it. It wasn't her fame that I wanted to be bracketed with; it was that I was who I had become because I had once loved an exasperating, unreachable, fantastically stimulating woman who had briefly given me her attention and had pummeled, slapped, shocked, and kissed me into some semblance of shape, and then, when it was clear that I was so much less than she expected or demanded, had given me up without a second thought. Or *did* she think of me afterward? And those tears which she had said were for someone else? *Had* any of them been for me? The goal of our armies was Paris—eventually. The odds were 9.87 to 1 that I personally would never make it. But *if* I did, and if I went to see her, would she remember me? Was there something she could tell me after all these years that would once and for all put a stop to the rankling pain that more and more seemed to be darkening the windows of my heart—a sense of failure that hovered just barely out of sight and out of feeling? Then I had to remind myself of the numbers: I wasn't going to get to Paris.

I had met Portilea during a temporary lull, while the Germans were preparing the next phase of the London bombardment. When the bombing began again, almost every night was half a hell, and what sleeping time I didn't spend in the official shelter, I spent underground with my neighbors of Cadogan Place; and by then I wanted passionately to talk to someone about Julie and perhaps get some clue to what she really had meant in my life. If I was who I was because of Julie, I had better find out who Julie was. Instead of simply nodding to this fat old cousin, I actually sought her out.

Portilea's air-raid costume was on the bizarre side. Once in the dark I saw her silhouetted against a searchlight beam, bundled up in ragged coat upon tattered coat, worn sweater upon patched sweater, and pantalooned in the bargain. Her outline against the light looked like some huge bell toddling along on two clappers. She herself remarked that she felt like one of those geological diagrams of a slice through the earth's surface.

"You know," she said. "Like in those illustrated magazines, with the different layers labeled with names like Post-Devo-

nian or Pre-Camembert or whatever. Take this mink—" The
long outer coat was indubitably fur, but there wasn't much
more you could say: it was worn, matted, and going bald.
"Call it High Portilea—bought in its youth—Berlin 1908—
when I was thirty-seven and my voice at its peak. Fur-bearing
suitors were still clustering in bunches—like grapes. This bed-
jacket"—she showed a strip of wreckage of pink boa-edged
silk from beneath a man's faded hacking coat—"call this Early
Farewell Tour—Brussels 1923, the beginning of three years of
concerts, and bought in anticipation of an affair with a beautiful young Swede. It never occurred to him what I had in mind,
or if it did, he was more interested in younger women. This
scarf"—it was a dingy white lacy wool worn over her head
and then molded smartly to a close fit by being wound around
her neck and throat; if she had been younger, it would have
made her beautiful—"takes us back to an earlier era. St. Pe-
tersburg 1902—Middle of Fame—scarves like this I'm told,
you can pull through the eye of a needle or a wedding ring—I
forget which. Young *Gospodin* Scarfski was very tall and sensitive and he used to cry with emotion. And this"—she
pointed to the trouser legs that protruded baggily from beneath the long flannel once-yellow nightgown that hung unevenly below the ancient mink—"call that Late Rescue—they
were my husband's, my *last* husband, that is. George was a vi-
olinist—a first fiddle—with the Metropolitan Opera in New
York when I first sang there in '06. Later he went home to
play in the London Philharmonic. I sang with them in 1910.
Of course I never noticed him in all that time down there in
the pit. Don't you think that wonderful man looked me up
when I found myself down and out giving lessons in Brighton,
of all places? Showed up one day in 1936, a fine-looking wid-
ower of sixty-three, and he picked *me*—a bedraggled sixty-five
—when he could have had a woman half my age. Poor, wonderful George—so kind, so sweet, so boring and modest—but
I was the most grateful, most appreciative wife any man ever
had, because to George I was still the star—the diva, the
prima, the beauty. I have always been and will always be,
Colonel, the bitch of the world, but never to or about George.
He gave my life a beautiful flavor just when I needed it most.
That appalling racket above us? It's all, of course, a dreadful
nuisance but nothing more. I had a marvelous life when I was
young and even for some time after. I made the mistake of
continuing to fall in love far too long and lost my money at it.

Then just enough of the horrors of being old and alone to make me appreciate George. Say, do you know what would be an absolute scream? If somewhere there was a seventy-eight-year-old trombonist, someone who played at La Scala in 1897 when I first sang there—and he too remembers me as I was, and will look me up after this war is over so that I can get out of this damnable climate and live happily ever after in Florence for another fifteen or twenty years! Except how boring to be so indestructible!"

Time, though, is a ghastly comedian, full of cruelty, as all murderers have to be. The mature Julie I had known was someone Portilea didn't know at all. Neither had Monty Crocker. On the other hand, the Julie she did know was a stranger to me—a girl, really—a prediction perhaps of the woman, I was to know, but different—just as the country itself and even the very time in which they were living were so different from what was to come.

To understand that difference, you had to take the cities and towns you knew and shrink them to half their size. Over the empty places that were left—sand flats, meadows, and riverbanks—birds soared and cried. You had to let our six-lane highways melt and disappear into the earth and in their places see a few meandering narrow dirt roads with grass and daisies growing in the center crown. The buses, trucks, and trailers you hear roaring to the horizon had to disappear there like ghosts. Overhead, the twinkling winglights of the Paris-bound Pan-American airliner become stars going nowhere. When silence settled down, you could have seen the passengers and cargoes they might have been carrying being blown at a few miles an hour or towed along the coastal waterways in schooners, sea-going barges, and tall-funneled side-wheelers.

In the 1880s that Portilea recalled so easily, the little port towns of America were still the only open windows to everything that was far away, even a little coastal port like Holmes Hole—

Yet for all the slowness, smallness, and vast distances, it was a time of change in the world in which she and Julie were girls, because the island's life was whaling and the whaling grounds were no longer the South Pacific but the Arctic. A whale's flesh was no longer to be hacked, boiled, and fried down to oil for parlor lamps; the whale's skeleton was the new money crop, because a hundred million ladies from Moscow to Melbourne were coming to feel that they could

not decently appear on the unpaved streets of that gaslit world
without one of the fashionable new whalebone corsets.

All this was the talk Priscilla Porter grew up with, because
her father ran a ship's chandlery on Water Street. The entire
island of Martha's Vineyard was suffused with whaling, fishing
and shipping talk; not only the port of Holmes Hole, but even
West Tisbury, eighty miles away, where Julie was born and
grew up. Priscilla remembered it all very vividly, as vividly as
she remembered Julie, for just as Julie had remained a perma-
nent bruise in my life, Portilea—simply as Cousin Priscilla—
had a score of her own to settle. She claimed that she didn't
like Julie, and she was downright explicit about it.

"She was too much like me," she complained. "In most
ways we couldn't have been more different; but in all the ways
that counted we were blood cousins all right. In the beginning
I was really fond of her. I understood her drive, and she understood mine. I'll say this for her: she never stood in judgment on me the way lots of others did because of the way I
got my start. But then her own start wasn't very different,
when you come down to it. In those days, that was the way it
had to be. A girl got nowhere without some man to stand up
for her to clear the way, to push her along a little until she got
the feel of things herself, and to put up the money. A few
fathers did it for their daughters, but damn few; and still fewer
brothers. No, for us then it was this way: a man had to love a
woman to distraction, the woman had to love just as distractedly something in herself—the face she saw in the mirror, or
the voice she felt in her throat, or the talent in her heart. It
had to be fire on both sides. You and he both had to burn
with it. It wasn't for people with pale souls."

Actually, there were only three occasions when her adult
life crossed Julie's, and each time Julie, trapped in some dilemma, was the one to seek the meeting. At least, as you will
see, that was the way Priscilla Porter told it to me. Approxi-
mately, it went like this:

PART FOUR—
PRISSY

1

My family didn't see much of the west tisbury Porters (she told me). They were different from the rest of us. In the first place, their father, Cousin Ralph—only the immediate family dared call him that, everyone else said Professor; and only his wife was ever heard to call him plain Ralph—was really what we called an Off-Islander, having been born when his mother was visiting her own Off-Island relatives in Brockton. He grew up mostly on the Cape. Then, too, he had gone to Harvard College. Of course, back in the days before the Civil War, boys went to Harvard when they were only about fourteen or fifteen and could be pretty wild. They carried pistols, some of them, and some fought with sabers. They got even wilder later during the war years.

Some very high-toned people would go to Europe after four years of Harvard or Yale to study still more, but only a handful of men on the Vineyard ever got to college at all—any college—and Harvard was more than grand enough for our stomachs. When I first knew Cousin Ralph, his wild days were over twenty years behind him, and as Headmaster of our Academy he was a very dignified and learned man.

Cousin Ralph was different, too, because even being schoolmaster on the Vineyard was an odd thing for a man to be—most of our men were whalemen if they weren't divers, fishermen, or salvage men, which was a fancy name for wreckers. In the Vineyard, in those days, only when a man was sickly or had too much of the sea would he settle down and run a store, like my father. All our men had the sea in them one way or another, but the only time Ralph Porter had been to sea was just before the war—he fought at Shiloh—when he took his young wife to London to see the sights there—another thing that made him different. Our people were certainly used to being in foreign places—whalemen got to St. Helena, Buenos Aires, Valparaiso, San Francisco, Hawaii, the Fijis, and anyplace you might care to mention, and sometimes they even took their wives—but they were traveling by way of business you might say. Cousin Ralph Porter and his wife Claire were outright tourists on the ship—passengers. That was another thing we never heard of.

Of course, having somebody as educated as Ralph Porter did give the island a bit of tone. When prominent men of letters like Professor Lowell, and James Whittier visited our island, you could always be sure that one of the men in tall hats and tailcoats with ribbons in their lapels—the welcoming committee, was Uncle Ralph. When I was little, I was sort of terrified of him because he was said to be so terribly educated. He was always kind to me though, and I even liked him after a fashion because of the way his children were always so gay, and the way he would joke and play with them. Not just romping games, but word games and riddles and rhymes and puzzles that took brains. What's more, they all had minds that were so fast and nimble that they were shooting the answers back and forth before you could even begin to think. I always felt foolish, slow, and stupid when they were around. There were five of them, two girls and three boys. The older ones were about my age and Julie, the youngest, trailed us by eight years. Bright as she must have been, she didn't stand out because what she knew precociously was still very little compared with what the others were doing—reciting, inventing, composing, learning. They nicknamed her "The Starer" because with bedlam going on around her she could squat down and stare at a blade of grass, or a daisy, or a toad, transfixed by only God knows what! They all attended the classes of the Academy, but the two girls had to sit silently, absorbing, but never reciting. Ronny was the eldest and the leader. In school, under his father's eye, he was a well-behaved boy; but outside he was a wild one. The others streamed after him like a pack of brilliant wolves chasing ideas, jokes, and songs instead of sheep. People tend to think that in those days, boys and girls behaved differently from the way their grandchildren did, but as far as I can see, the boys I grew up with were as free with their hands as tight bodices and slapped faces let them be. They were always wrestling with us in the haylofts and in the open meadows, and we wrestled back if no grownups were looking. I secretly adored my cousin Ronny. The only time he made me cry was when his hand flashed in and out of my dress—not because I really objected but because he did it as if

it were a joke. He humiliated me. If he had only asked when
we were alone, and asked me with that sort of strangled,
pleading look boys get, I would have let him, I liked it as
much as he did, but everything was a joke to Ronny. Too
much so.

His younger brothers Joey and Dan were not identical twins
although they had been born at the same time, and they were
miniature Ronnys. The oldest girl, Amelia, was just my age,
with a singing voice like mine, but half an octave lower.
Maybe she would have been a contralto. I thought my own
voice was shrill compared with hers only because I admired
everything about her. We used to sing together in the choir
and at public programs when important visitors came to the
island. We had long white dresses made alike by our mothers
for our "appearances," and I was secretly flattered when people took us for the "Porter sisters." Both of us, too, had
strong, thick necks of which we were ashamed, although later
I was assured this was the mark of the singer.

But I was sort of an outsider to them as was everyone
else. They lived in a fierce and simple world divided into only
two camps: the Porters and the Un-Porters, and they were the
Porters. Then an Edgartown cousin who hated their clan-
nishness pointed out that we were all as much Porter as they
were. Ronny was caught for only an instant. He conceded the
point but then divided the Porters into Upper Porters and
Lower Porters, at which the Edgartown cousin immediately
pounced and claimed that all Porters except the West Tisbury
Porters were Upper. "Of course!" said Ronny in a flash. "All
apes feel at home up in trees!" Then he glanced at me, for this
was after the hand-in-the-bosom incident, and he was sorry he
had made me cry. "Prissy, you can be a Lower, with us, if you
like. You're human!"

"That's right," said Amelia. "Prissy is more than a cousin."

"Porterer than Porter!" Joey said. He chanted: "Disports
none Porterier than thou!"

"Portilea, Portilau," sang Dan as an amen, and that's where
my name came from because as long as Amelia lived she was
secretly Portilau and I was secretly Portilea in a private game
of names we used to play at choir rehearsals.

Through all this, Julie was on the sidelines—wide-eyed and
bewildered, far younger than we, being only about five or six
at the time when I was thirteen. When she wasn't the last of a
streaming line of Porters running across the back fields, or

squatting to stare down at one of her mysteries, she was sitting close to her mother who hated to have her very far beyond her touch. Julie was so used to her mother's illness that she never looked up at the racking cough that got worse and worse. It was consumption. Doctors called it a disease of the cities, and said that Cousin Claire had brought it with her from Boston. Somewhere along the line I discovered that the reason Cousin Ralph was teaching at Dukes Academy and not at a real college was so poor Cousin Claire could have the benefit of our air. We were very proud of the Vineyard when we heard this, and nothing surprised us more than that her condition kept getting worse rather than better.

When I knew her, Cousin Claire was already as frail and pale as paper, with a gentle sadness so deep that a smile passing over her face only served to highlight the longing she felt to go on living with her children especially her beloved little Julie. Maybe she was thirty-seven or thirty-eight, no more, but to me she was elderly and dying. These days, except for war, death is remote except for old people, and everyone forgets how brief a time ago that death was everywhere, waiting every hour, in every home, for every age. People lived with it as an ever-present threat, like an unwanted relative you couldn't send away but had to bear with; not only their own deaths, but the death of loved ones sleeping this very minute in the very next room down the hall just outside that door.

When Julie was six, almost seven, she came out of her mother's room one evening with a peculiar shocked and guilty look on her face—half tearful, half pouting—"Mommy's playing a mean game; she won't talk to me even when I push her!" Then a moment later she burst into tears and put her head in Amelia's lap. "Mommy's dead, I bet!"

It was guessed that since the little girl had been so much with her mother, she very probably had caught the infection. No one told her, and she played unconcernedly, but for months, everyone watched her as if the Angel of Death was walking behind her with hands outstretched over her head. It was a horrible shock then, when the one who turned out to start coughing in the night was Joey. In two years it was over, and with the two deaths the Lower Porters became a subdued clan. Julie was the quietest. She rarely smiled. Everyone was too preoccupied to notice that at the age of eight she was doing the assignments of the eleven-year-olds. Ronny remarked that she sucked in information the way she breathed and with about as much effort. I saw her myself concentrating on some book she was reading so intensely that she seemed hardly to know there was a real world going on about her. She and Ronny were particularly crazy about each other, but he couldn't help fooling around with her—even when it was still thought she was marked for death. When she read like that, he'd pick her up and swing her on his lap to show us that she'd still go on reading. She didn't even hear us laughing at her absorption.

Ronny, who was so full of vitality that he always seemed to be dancing or telling the next to the last line of a joke, was gone in less than six months from his first showing of blood, which only Amelia had known about. It was stunning to hear the silence of the house after he was gone. I stopped going. Danny was now the only son, but he could imitate Ronny only while Ronny lived. Afterward, he had neither the heart, nor the model, nor much will.

When he was sixteen, he slipped away from home leaving a note I never saw but which I heard went something like: "Dear Pa and Girls: I can't just sit around here and wait. I'm going to places which Mommy, Joey, and Ronny never saw— places that won't keep reminding me of them all the time. When I'm located, I'll write." As far as I know, no one ever heard of him after that.

Amelia was seventeen, and Julie was a pale, large-eyed twelve, a wraith of a girl who always walked soberly by her sister's side. They were inseparable and looked as if they were besieged; and I still couldn't make myself go to their echoing empty house. I used to ask Amelia to visit us, but she would simply sit with a listless silence. Her hair was dull, her eyes were haunted. She still sang, but her voice now had a heart-breaking quality—half a wail, half a lament—as if every note had its own slurred grace note of tears. Whatever had been between us was gone—it was little Julie's understanding look she now instinctively sought.

I can never—and never could—be funny or mean about Amelia. First I had looked at her as someone who belonged to a select group far above me; now it was the other way around. The boys were coming to our house all the time, and Pa said they were "shoaling up on him so thick he had to beat 'em off with oars."

My own taste ran not to boys but to Terry Daggett, who was what I considered an older man—about twenty-nine or thirty. He was running his own salvage schooner and had more nerve than anyone else in his business, going out in all kinds of weather and making all kinds of money. Pa didn't exactly see him as a son-in-law, but neither did Terry, who was as wild as everyone said he was, but honest. He finally confided to me that he already had two wives—a respectable woman he hated in Framingham, and a girl in Port-au-Prince whom he no longer loved, he said, now that he had met me. He had sweats of fright about being arrested for bigamy, but he said he'd see to it that I got everything I wanted because I was really the girl he was willing to die for. I told him there was no need for him to die: I knew just what I wanted—to go to Boston Institute of Music. He said done and done, and although Pa shouted himself blue in the face, in the end Pa did give in. Pa hated to spend his own money even more than he hated the idea of a grandchild without proper sailing papers. So everything was taken care of, and I was finally getting off the island, which had been growing far too small for my ambitions.

Because things were going so beautifully for me, I felt that before I left I ought to go visit Amelia. My, that big house was quiet and empty, but she smiled to see me so dressed up, and her eyes lit a little. Julie had gone out when I came in, whispering that she was glad I had come for Amelia's sake. Amelia talked about me to her all the time, she said.

"Amelia, why don't you come with me!" I said on impulse, because I felt a gush of real love for her. "We'll be together. We'll each sleep on one half the bed, and eat half the food and each take the lesson alternate days!"

She laughed a little, like a tired woman, and shook her head. "Even if I had the voice, I couldn't go just now," she said. "I have to wait at least one more year and be really sure that Julie is going to be all right."

For me, landing in a lively city like Boston was like stepping into a champagne bath. It was almost three years before I went back to the Vineyard. Our town's name had been changed from Holmes Hole to Vineyard Haven, but the place looked the same to me, only a little smaller. On Oak Street, near the school, I saw a tall, healthy-looking, bright-eyed girl who appeared familiar, and on a third look, it turned out to be little Julie; but what a changed Julie! She was wearing a woman's dress, and she had the figure for it, all right; but her hair was down in a long braid with a large blue bow just below her neck. I threw my arms around her, and asked her what she was doing in town all alone. She said she was living there now, temporarily teaching school until a regularly licensed teacher could be sent down. I laughed at the idea—pleased that little Julie could be so grown up at fifteen and asked how Amelia was. Julie went white. Her eyes glared at me so furiously that I was frightened. Then without a word, she turned and walked away. It was two years before she got over her anger with me for not knowing that Amelia was dead. Finally, though, she came to me for advice—the first of the three times I told you about.

In the meantime Terry Daggett slipped his cable one night and sailed away owing money to everybody and his brother. I was stuck high and dry in Boston, but Professor Burns at the Institute now had a deep faith in my voice. He was positive that he could get rid of the slight break I had in my upper register—almost a screech—and he got me a scholarship to continue my studies. I began to sing at club socials and church affairs for a few dollars here and there. I also sang in two choirs on Sunday, but I had no complaint since all this was making me eminently respectable and allowing me to earn my own living in the open for all to see. People just forgot Terry, and anyhow they were talking about Julie now, not knowing what to make of her goings-on.

Now that I was home, I heard how Julie came to be living in Vineyard Haven alone. A short time before, Cousin Ralph had been a little strange, talking to himself and forgetting where he was. In the mornings, Julie had to help him dress and then walk down the road with him to the Academy. She had to go and bring him home at night. She was a large pale girl then, the neighbors told me, with haunted eyes and deep brown rings beneath them. She used to walk along South Road like a tired old woman. It was one thing though to get poor Cousin Ralph to school, but another thing to have him perform his duties when he got there. Julie tried to perform them for him and did fairly well. In short order, though, the Board of Trustees had to appoint another Headmaster, but out of pity they kept Cousin Ralph on as instructor at half his salary. Little by little, under Julie's care, he came back, but he was more like some lone survivor of a shipwreck in which he had lost everything—family, love, goods, mind—a dazed relic wandering for the rest of his life up and down an empty shore.

Along about then, the vacancy occurred Down Island, in Tisbury Township School in Vineyard Haven. Someone suggested Julie Porter until a regular teacher could be found. During her father's worst time, everyone knew that she had taken over the youngest classes for him and so she had some experience; besides—and this was a great attraction for the Board of Selectmen—she would probably accept half the salary the former teacher had been getting. Julie accepted, all right, and I can guess at both her guilt at going and her secret relief to be out of that house where the memory of tragedy was in every breath she took, in every tick of the clock, in every click of a closing door, in the long silences in between.

Cousin Ralph escorted her to Rebecca Standish's boarding-house up on Spring Street where Rebecca and Cousin Ralph made an arrangement: Julie was to pay a reduced rate and help with chores like making beds and waiting on table. Her room was a little one—I was in it myself—on the northeast corner of the top floor with a single high round window that looked out over the harbor if you stood on the lower rung of the chair. In a storm, the room could be cold and damp for the five days the wind held.

The first night there, Julie told me, she cried herself to sleep; she was only fifteen, but after that there wasn't much time to cry. Mornings she was up early to make the beds of the first risers and serve them breakfast. Then off to school to teach until four o'clock, and back to Spring Street to make the rest of the beds and serve the supper. School was held on Saturday until one o'clock, when she'd take the stage Up Island with provisions for her father, arriving there around three-thirty. She'd clean up the house—he had moved to Music Street—and prepare meals for him for the next few days. She'd wash and mend for him until Sunday evening when it was time to take the stage back Down Island to Vineyard Haven so she could start all over again on Monday morning. She was always so tired, she didn't even have time to think.

Rebecca Standish's place was ordinary enough, and the boarders who were living there when I visited Julie could have been neither more nor less interesting than those who had been there when she first came two years earlier, except, of course, for Asher Pease.

I had known him myself for some time, at least to nod to on Main Street even before I left to go to Boston. To me, he was simply one of the characters around town. He used to stride past everyone with his hands in his pockets, his shoulders hunched, a ferocious but absent-minded scowl on his face. Where he was going, nobody knew. He was tall, and rather on the slender side. He was what they used to call "dark-complected," and he wore his black hair very long. It had isolated gray strands, but right along the center, from a point on his brow straight back there was a thick streak of white. He rarely spoke to anyone. Some people said he was shy, others said he drank; but then, lots of men drank in those days. I thought of him as an older man, but my father once referred to him as "a young feller." Looking back, I guess his age then at about thirty-six or -seven. Nobody knew where he came from. Nobody knew how much money he had to live on. He didn't work. We thought he was rich. Once he had been an active skipper in the Sag Harbor whaling fleet, but he had never sailed on a Vineyard vessel, nor had any Vine-yarder ever sailed under him. Nobody knew why he was on the Vineyard. He got mail from various places in the country and sometimes heavy books came from bookstores in Boston —learned books. Most nights he wrote late with the books open on his table; but nobody knew what he wrote, or what became of the pages. What I knew about him—a man I really didn't know—everybody else in town also knew—which was nothing.

Julie was probably the only one in town who could look at the titles of Captain Pease's books and have any idea of what they said. She wasn't sure herself until she looked into them as she cleaned his room, and she discovered that they were all about mathematics—very difficult and advanced kind of mathematics. Until she told me this, I never knew myself that mathematics consisted of more than addition, subtraction, multiplication, and division—what we called "figuring." Of course I knew about geometry and algebra, but the way I had been taught, they, too, were only fancy ways to solve surveying problems. That there existed exalted realms of mathematics of which I had never heard, with names I couldn't pronounce, much less pretend to understand what they referred to, filled me with a kind of horrified awe.

Nevertheless one such book, the simplest, she said—calculus—she found she could read a paragraph at a time—very slowly, a few lines a day, for the first several pages, at least. She did this only out of curiosity because the captain didn't happen to be in the room. One day she was standing with the calculus book in her hand, her broom against her side, engrossed in these strange hieroglyphics, when she heard a sound behind her. Captain Pease had come into the room, had seen her, then quietly closed the door. She said that he was looking at her with pale murder.

"How dare you look through my things!" he said softly.

"But I was only reading."

"Reading?"

He snatched the book from her. "Really? And precisely what did you read?"

She was frightened by his dark cold fury. She felt that the more exact the detail she could repeat, the more thoroughly she would convince him that she had been doing only what she said—what else she could have been doing, she had no idea. He listened to her, then began to frown a little, taken aback.

"That's what you read, all right. But do you know what it means?"

She told him. His anger disappeared but the scowl remained. He walked to the window, clamped one of his long cheroots between his teeth, and put his hands behind his coat-tails.

"Well damn my eyes!" he said over and over, as if he had been taken in a swindle. He took another look at her. "A female with a brain! Who the devil are you?"

"I'm the schoolteacher in town."

"You're a liar. You're the cleaning girl."

"I'm also the schoolteacher."

"Then why is your hair down? How old are you?"

"I'm sixteen."

He took a long breath. "What other books did you look at?"

"None."

"Don't you ever say 'sir'?"

"No, but I could if you insist."

He took one more long angry look at her, and then nodded toward the door. "Get out," he said.

After that, his suspicious eyes were always on her as she waited on him for supper and breakfast. Nor did he stop scowling. A few days later, when she went into his room to clean up, he was sitting in the brown plush armchair with his arms folded, obviously waiting for her. He nodded towards the bed. The book lay there.

"That's for you," he said. He always spoke as if he were giving orders to a foremast hand. "Read it."

"I can't now."

"I don't mean now. Take it to your room. You do have a room here, don't you?"

"Yes."

"And not 'Yes, sir'?"

"I'm sorry."

"If for no other reason, I'm enough older than you to rate the courtesy."

"I see."

"I see, *sir!*"

"I see, sir."

He shrugged in disgust. "You don't even know how to say it properly. Don't do it any more. Sit down."

"I—I'm busy."

"Sit down!" She sat on the edge of a chair. "All right, I know all about you. Your name is Julie Porter. Your father used to be Headmaster at that boy's Academy Up Island, and your whole family was damn near wiped out." Then he said uncomfortably, "Maybe I shouldn't have put it that way. I didn't mean to make you cry."

"I'm not crying, sir." He frightened her, but now he was also making her angry.

"I told you not to say *sir!*"

"No, sir."

"Oh, damn it!" he shouted. "Stop it! I didn't mean it. Take the book. Finish up and get out!"

It never occurred to her that she didn't have to take the book or read it simply because he had told her to. Any order he gave had to be obeyed. That seemed the natural order of things. As exhausted as she was every night, she worked over a page or two before going to sleep, holding on to the words as she slipped off, terrified that he might appear at any moment day or night and demand that she recite it to him exactly as it had appeared on the page. Yet he was nowhere to be seen when she went to his room to clean, and nowhere to be seen on the lanes as she came and went from school. And while she was terrified of him, for a reason she didn't understand, she was disappointed not to find him.

Then suddenly there he was again, waiting for her in the brown plush chair, his arms folded, scowling, demanding to know how much she had read and what was it all about.

Perched on the edge of a chair, she recited for him, as submissive to him as any of her eight-year-old students were to her. He listened to her in silence, chewing his lip. Then he put a pad of foolscap in front of her, took from his pocket a jack-knife with which he could have killed a man, and whittled a point on a stub of pencil. He quickly scrawled out some problems and handed the paper to her for her solution. She worked out an answer in a few minutes and handed the paper back to him. He sat and looked at it for a while. The scowl was now no more than a worried look, but his voice came out as brusque as ever.

"All right, go on with your cleaning." She got up, not knowing whether to be relieved or disappointed. She worked quickly and clumsily in order to get out of the room as fast as possible, and at last she fled ashamed, and wet with sweat.

She began to work hard at the book. Suddenly it became enthralling. She tried to explain it to me with the same words I would have used to describe my own feelings at hearing one of the Schubert *lieder* for the first time—a sense of recognition of something I had always been in love with—even though I never knew it existed.

If you love music, then simply by hearing one note follow another in marvelously unexpected combinations, the winding thread of sound can evoke in you a hundred different emotions. It was like that for Julie, except that instead of finding her pleasure in the realm of sound it was in the world of ideas. As soon as I substituted my own musical terms for the mathematical words she was using, Pease stopped seeming a tyrannical ogre, and became someone stunned by the discovery of a marvelous talent waiting to be formed. Julie though was far too unaware of herself to realize what was happening even when he gave her another book to read—another mathematical treatise—and again checked her progress. She was put off by his forbidding manner. She didn't know whether he was pleased with her or not. She was afraid to ask.

One night sounds thundered from his room as if piles of books and even pieces of furniture were tumbling about. Julie was about to run down to him, but Mrs. Standish pushed her aside as she flew past her along the hall and down the stairs. For the moment Mrs. Standish opened his door, Julie could hear him roar at her with uncontrolled rage. Then the door closed behind her. The voices became muted and finally quiet.

It was hours before Julie's heart stopped pounding, and still longer before she ceased worrying about him.

The next morning, Mrs. Standish told her not to do his room. Captain Pease didn't feel well, she said. Julie asked if it wouldn't be wise to call the doctor, and Mrs. Standish gave her a grim answer. "Captain Pease doesn't need a doctor."

Within a few days, Julie was permitted into his room again. He was exhausted, pale, bitter-tongued, unable to meet her glance. Before she left though he handed her a third book—mathematics applied to physics—but since she knew nothing about physics, she was unable to make anything of it. She kept away from him for fear of revealing her failure.

Just the same, when she came into his room some weeks later she found him sitting in the brown plush chair, waiting for her.

"Well, what did you read?" he demanded.

"Nothing."

"Why not?"

"I don't understand any of it." Her voice was coming out very small. This was the moment she had been dreading.

"You don't know any physics?"

"No."

"Why didn't you say so?"

"I was afraid."

"Of *me?*" It seemed to be the most incredible thing he had ever heard, but she nodded. "Why?" he demanded.

"You'd see that I'm stupid."

He looked at her disgustedly. "How could I ever think you were stupid, child? If I had one tenth the mind you have, would I be here in this Godforsaken place: beached, wrecked, a rotten drunk? I would have gone to the German universities, I would have studied, I would have—" He shook his head and never finished. He got up and went to his pile of books and pulled out a volume. "Put aside the book I gave you and read this. Then we'll go back to the one you've got and together we'll sail through it."

Now he was full of talk every time he saw her. All his life, he told her, he had wanted to be an educated man. His own father had been killed in a skirmish at Fredericksburg, and he had been raised by his mother and an uncle in the whaling trade who sent him to sea early. He had his master's papers by the time he was twenty-five. During that time, of course, he had had to study the mathematics of navigation. Bowditch's navigation led him to Bowditch's celestial mechanics and had introduced him to higher mathematics in general, and here he found his love. Even I as a girl knew about Nathaniel Bowditch. His book was like a Bible to my brothers and to every other American boy who wanted to go to sea. All port towns of New England knew Bowditch as the mathematically-minded skipper in the China trade who was able to discover and correct the errors of the great French scientist LaPlace. We grew up being told that he was another Franklin. Until Pease began to study, he himself didn't know any more than I did that mathematics extended beyond the complicated "figurin'" required to fix a latitude and longitude.

"But mathematics comes slowly to me, not like it does to you," he told Julie. "You read something once or twice and I can see it fixed in your mind. I read it ten, a dozen times, then I have to write it down in my own words—"

"Is *that* what you write at night?" she asked.

"I write out the proofs and derivations that I follow in the books. Unless I write it in my own hand, I don't understand it. I write as I read, and I learn as I write."

"And once you've written it?"

"Why, I burn it," he spoke as if surprised that anyone else might do things differently.

By the time he was thirty he had accumulated enough money to retire from the sea and do what he wanted, which would have been just fine, he told her, except for one legacy from his life at sea. In a storm in the Java Strait, a falling spar had thrown him to the deck and crushed his chest. After that he suffered from recurring seizures of pain so intense that there was relief only in morphine or whiskey, both of which had been prescribed by physicians. Even I can remember doctors who claimed that morphine wasn't habit-forming, and of the two, it was more highly recommended: it worked faster and was considered more refined, but morphine frightened him, and he preferred to get along on whiskey when the pain attacked.

At thirty, then, he presented himself at Cambridge and took the entrance examinations for Harvard. He passed well enough, but he was given a merciless personal questioning because he was older than the other entering students by over a dozen years and because he was considered to be a man who had frequented the taverns and cribs of both coasts of North and South America. However, he kept his temper and convinced his inquisitors that he was a serious man, and that his grasp of mathematics was impressive.

Within a month, he told Julie, he was disgusted. He had no interest in any subject outside mathematics, no patience with the boyishness of his classmates, nothing but contempt for instructors who didn't know how to keep ship's discipline. One day he walked out of class in disgust and never went back. He made an arrangement with one of the professors of mathematics to come to his room and give him private instruction.

After two years of that, he left abruptly and appeared on the Vineyard where we were used to our men being different from ordinary landsmen. Too many of our boys spent most of their early years at sea without a proper boyhood, and too many years of their early manhood at sea without any proper refinement. They were either foremast hands who were ferociously equal or officers accustomed to being obeyed without a word. Asher Pease was even more untamed than most, yet longing for something that was more abstract than music, and more delicate than poetry. Only Julie knew how lonely he was not to have one single mind with which he could share his innermost interests.

"He was like Robinson Crusoe, starved for the sound of a human voice," Julie said. "He found me and taught me to speak. He gave me far more than I ever gave him."

As a child, she used to squat down to stare at a blade of grass or at a daisy, fascinated by the lines of its design and the pattern of its color; now at sixteen she was sitting up nights at her table by candlelight to pore over the chemistry, physics, astronomy, and mathematics books that he gave her.

"It was happiness for me to learn!" she said. "My mind was always spinning! I only half understood most of what I was reading, but even that delighted him. It allowed him to straighten out my ideas for me."

Until Mrs. Standish became convinced that what was passing between her star boarder and her excited young charge was only an outlandish kind of teaching and that the conversations which so absorbed them were only a kind of doctor's talk, she insisted that all their meetings take place where she could hear and see everything. But neither they nor the other boarders wanted them to be in the parlor because they were so downright unsociable, so oblivious to everyone else. And their lingo was a nuisance. Captain Mather couldn't talk about Chancellorsville when they were around. Mr. Sparks couldn't damn President Cleveland, and Mr. and Mrs. Bird couldn't enjoy their stereopticon slides. Captain Pease and Julie were put off by themselves with their books in the cold of the empty dining room next to the parlor while Mrs. Standish seated herself in the parlor with her crocheting, near enough to the open door to keep her eyes on them. They worked away by the oil lamp with pencil and paper, Julie flushed and chewing her lip in concentration, and Captain Pease alternately upbraiding her for her slowness or holding her wide-eyed with a rapturous account of some experiment that promised to solve a problem of fifty years' standing.

Mrs. Standish got tired of her chaperoning long before her charges did because they were so absorbed in what they were doing that they never noticed her. They were then permitted to hold what Mrs. Standish called "their little lessons" in the captain's room, as long as the door was left open. But it was a drafty house particularly when the Northeasters blew. The lamp flame danced uncertainly as they bent over their exercises, and they shivered with cold. At length, Captain Pease slammed the door shut and poked up the fire. Mrs. Standish immediately flung the door open, to see them seated opposite each other—Julie haltingly reciting a theorem she really didn't understand, and he holding his hands to his head in agony at her stupidity.

"The door, Captain," said Mrs. Standish.

"Damn the door, ma'am!" he shouted at her for the whole house to hear. "Now you can either come in or go out. If you come in, you take part in what we're doing. If you stay out, you can leave us alone!"

Mrs. Standish went out and closed the door.

After that, no one bothered them any more. Mr. and Mrs. Bird told everyone in town that it was unnatural for a girl to know things that weren't meant for women to know. Captain Mather said that there wasn't an ounce of harm in it, the girl didn't understand a single word of it; she was just saying those things back to Captain Pease to please him, her own father being such a poor stick of a man. The rest of the town said what they wanted.

He took to calling for her at school to walk home with her across the fields. They still had no idea that people were talking about them because as soon as they met, they fell at once into the conversation they had left off only a few hours before. He was making up for all his years of isolation, and she was finding in him all the companionship she once had in three brothers, a sister, a father, and a mother. Those two probably enjoyed each other more in that one brief year than most couples do in a lifetime together. They came to be such a familiar sight that people practically stopped noticing them, even those who were scandalized.

"I saw how gentle a person he really was," Julie said. "All that roaring and those tirades were only a manner of speaking for him, or else they were his way of hiding that he was in pain. As soon as I found that out, I ached for him. I couldn't stand to see his agony once the fit was on him and —God forgive me—I used to beg him to use the morphine the way the doctors had told him. He said that morphine was only another form of opium and in his time he had seen too many opium users. Whiskey was the only other thing that helped him. I urged him to take it whenever I could see the pain getting too bad. I used to feed it to him until he got wild drunk, but I never minded. Never! I was even glad for him!"

Sometime during the spring of the year, Julie and he became lovers. She never said anything about how or when, but if I know my town, I know what the spell of our great wide empty beaches can be on one of those blue days of sudden warmth when the air is gold and melting, when the water sparkles in the sun and falls on the beach in limp little waves, when the dune grass droops in absolute stillness, and the terns and gulls search the air for zephyrs to soar upon. There's a silence that goes high into the cloudless sky and stretches for miles and empty miles along the beach. Any man and woman walking together in that silence are wide open to themselves and to each other.

He became full of plans. He would walk up and down in his room, the books momentarily forgotten, clapping his hands and rubbing them together with relish because now life was a feast he couldn't wait to start on.

"I'll get some money together, then we'll get married, and we'll sail away from the Vineyard once and for all to do what I always wanted! A year in Paris preparing for the entrance examination, then a year or two at the Sorbonne, a year at Göttingen, another in Vienna—with the greatest mathematicians and physicists—"

"And chemists too?" she asked.

Once one of my professors at the Conservatory was dreaming aloud of the repertoire I would one day have. I listened with delight to the list of composers he was promising me but there was one name not being mentioned. At last I said: "And not Brahms?" And in his startled look was amusement and regret that I should have this questionable desire for one of the moderns. But on the other hand, it was reassuring proof that I was only a girl with a taste less austere than his and that no matter how far I went, I would always need his guidance.

It must have been with the same affectionate indulgence that Asher Pease said, "All right, for you it will be chemistry."

He went over his needs very carefully with Julie. The steamship fare to Europe, second class, would cost forty dollars apiece. To live modestly in Europe while studying should come to about two and a half dollars a day for both. A hundred dollars a month would see them through handsomely. His original capital when he first retired, he told her, had been thirty-four thousand dollars—his share from three voyages, but the income had fallen off drastically.

He went to the bank to account for the present state of his investments and came back with the knowledge that he was a poor man.

Along with other whaling captains, he had invested his money in enterprises he really knew nothing about. The result was that he had been living on his capital for the past three years; but even that had dwindled to less than six hundred dollars.

"But I don't have to go to Europe," Julie said. "I'm content to go on living here. I'm happy with you."

"I don't want you to be content!" he said sharply. "I'm not. Don't you want an education? Don't you want to study? Don't you want to go to college?"

"I'll find a way to go," she said calmly.

"And it's not the most important thing to you?" he demanded.

"You are the most important thing to me," she said.

He was so moved by her reply that he could only scowl his thanks to her, and clasp her shoulder.

Two days later he went away without saying anything to anyone but Mrs. Standish, and then only that he wouldn't be in for supper. He took the mid-morning packet for New Bedford. The wharf hands at Holmes Hole told Julie that they remembered him standing by the forward rail leaning down on his elbows. A deck hand aboard the packet told Julie that he remembered him getting off the steamer at New Bedford without a parcel, package, or valise as if he were going to the city for a day of business or shopping.

All the next day, Julie kept track of every New Bedford packet as each one docked. The third day, too, there was no sign of him, nor any word. She cleaned his room and told herself there was nothing to worry about. The next day was Saturday. She waited until the very last moment before taking the stage Up Island to her father's; then she rode off, almost with relief because now there would be no more waiting! When she'd return on Sunday night, he'd be sure to be home. On Sunday night, when she got back his room was still empty. Mrs. Bird brought a letter for her on Monday, her watery eyes bright with excitement.

"That letter's come from over a thousand miles, Julie, all the way from Chicago!" she said.

Julie tore open the envelope. The letter itself was dated from New Bedford. He had the stilted style of someone who had never in his entire lifetime written one personal letter—only business correspondence and terse entries in a ship's log. He wrote her that on his arrival in New Bedford he had been offered a command which he had to accept or refuse on the spot—a 1200-ton bark-rigged steel-hulled steamship, the first of its kind for Arctic whaling. The master had died, and the ship was waiting in San Francisco for a new captain. He had accepted the command and had gone directly from the shipper's office to make a western connection. He wrote Julie that he was to get five hundred dollars cash when he reached San Francisco and stepped aboard the ship, another forty-five hundred dollars cash on completion of the voyage, and, in addition to these cash payments, a lay of twenty out of one hundred and sixty shares of the profits of the voyage. This would—with luck—take care of them for the rest of their lives. But even if the voyage were poor, he pointed out, there should still be enough to carry them for five or six years of the life they had planned together.

To Julie, it was a relief to hear from him, a joy to see the proofs of his love, a heartache to be told of the long separation to come, and a shiver of terror at the realization that he might be too old—close to forty—to be going back to the rigors of whaling—to the bad food, bad air, bad water, and harsh work in a killing climate. But since what he was doing, he was doing for her, she owed it to him to put on a good face and go on with her life. By this time, she needed no outside incentive nor any guide to send her to his books. She continued the routine of her daily tasks but every night by candlelight, she went page by page into the enthralling life he had opened for her.

About that time I happened to be home for a few days, enjoying my first taste of success. I had joined the Boston Opera Company the season before and I had sung three small roles, then Barberina in *The Marriage of Figaro,* and finally Marguerite! Now simply by walking down Main Street with my head high I could take more revenge than Monte Cristo ever dreamed. On my last day home, I came from the post office to find Julie waiting for me. She was about eighteen then, but she got up slowly as if she were sick. Her face was white and drawn, but when she spoke I saw she was suffering from heartbreak, not disease.

"I need your advice, Prissy."

For a moment she was silent, then with such sudden power and depth that I was shocked by the intensity of her passion she cried: "How I hate death! It's vile! It's cruel!" and told me what had happened to her. After Asher left, she went on, she got one more letter from him from San Francisco and nothing more. But he had warned her to expect no word from him unless he should pass a ship homeward bound. The first weeks that went by were a terrible heartache she refused to allow herself to feel; it had to be borne, but at the end of four months she gave in to her terrified concern. By that time though he had been dead three weeks of pneumonia. He had been away from the harsh life too long to stand the rigors. His body had been wrapped in canvas and buried seventy fathoms deep in the icy water somewhere north of Cape Barrow. All that he got from his great gamble was the five hundred dollars' arrival money. That had been sent in its entirety to the Martha's Vineyard National Bank with instructions that it was to be delivered to Miss Julie Porter for her education in the event of his demise.

I kept quiet until she could get control of herself. She had loved him with gratitude, with devotion, with self-sacrifice, but still not the way I knew a woman ought to love. Perhaps she wasn't old enough yet to have felt it.

"Do you *want* an education?" I asked.

"More than anything in the world, but can I leave Papa?"

"What does he say?"

"He says to go, but he's so hurt he can hardly speak to me."

"Why?"

"Perhaps because I had never told him about Asher. Papa hardly knew him, but he never liked him. I think he thinks it ugly that Asher was so much older than I. Except that he really wasn't. You know, sometimes Asher could be like a boy," she said, and as she went on speaking about him, her voice grew warm with all that naïve, passionate, childish love she had felt for him, and it was love, all right. It was all still inside her, even though the man who had called it up was gone, and I wondered myself what would become of that love. Love is born, lives, and dies in its own scale of time that has nothing to do with the scale of time lived in by the people who feel it or evoke it. I didn't, don't, and never will understand the nature of love. It simply awes me, and so I was more impressed by the depth of her feeling than I was by her problem, because to me there is no question about what a girl ought to do if she has at least an ounce of talent, an inch of backbone, and a running start of a few dollars for her to give herself a chance.

"I *know* you feel that way, Prissy," said Julie. "That's why I came to you. But what Asher left me isn't enough by itself. Even if I had the nerve to go to Paris, I don't know enough yet to pass the entrance examination for the Sorbonne. I'd be using up Asher's money to prepare for those examinations when I could be doing that here. On the other hand, I could get into an American college right now—just as I am." She thought for a moment, and her face was tender. "Maybe it would please Papa if I went to the Harvard Annex for girls."

She was sure she could pass Harvard's entrance examination. But Harvard Annex for Girls—Radcliffe—charged two hundred dollars a year for tuition, which meant that Asher had left her just about enough for only the first two of the four years, but nothing for her living expenses.

Just the same, her mention of Harvard which had a solid New England sound impressed me more than talk of the Sorbonne, since at that time Paris made me think only of *La Vie de Bohème* and Svengali.

"Julie, you can earn whatever you need at Harvard for tuition and for living once you get up there," I said. "Advertise in the Boston papers for pupils for tutoring, the way I gave music lessons. You'll see how well you'll do! A girl with spunk in her can show the world if she wants to!" I put my arm about her shoulders and gave her an encouraging little shake. "All you have to do is to *want* to!"

"I *do* want to, Prissy. Not only for Amelia and Asher, but for myself too. I'll go."

I left the island shortly after. Within the next three years, only wonderful things happened to me. At the end of that time, *en passant*, I came back to the Vineyard in a dress by Worth, with a French maid sitting beside me in my new French automobile driven by my French chauffeur. During the same three years, Julie had been working quietly in Cambridge. I had come home, full of success, to see my mother and to look at myself in the mirror of my old bedroom. Julie came home full of frustration, and when she came to my house in Edgartown that summer—the second time our lives crossed—she was so desperate and so trapped that I had to help her escape. Radcliffe, she told me, had been one long disappointment: there had been no laboratory work for her. Apparently she was as stifled by that as I would have been if I had spent that much time studying only musical theory without one opportunity to open my mouth and sing.

Until that day I had always thought of science as doing complicated sums in one's head or amassing bits of odd information which no one cares about like the fact that the brain lobes of the rabbit are connected to the wrong sides of the body so that rabbits get all confused about which way to run when threatened, or that water is made up of hydrogen and oxygen. But apparently there is something very much more to being a scientist—Julie gave a sense of a need to touch and to feel, to invent, and manipulate. Julie was the first to make me feel that such a hunger existed.

At Radcliffe Julie had been having an affair of some sort with a young newspaperman for whom she obviously felt only pity. But I could see too that she was also beset by irritation because he wanted very much to marry her, and she was afraid that he would bully or badger her into it.

"What I can't make him understand," she said helplessly, "is that I don't have any real feeling these days; that I'm still numb inside."

"Doesn't he know about Asher?"

"He knows there was a man, but not really how I felt

about him. Even I don't know any more what I felt about
Asher, and I can't make myself talk about it. Nor does he
know about Amelia and Ronny and Mama and how it was
with the boys. He sees only my outside face, the color of my
eyes and hair. He touches my hand and looks at me with love
but I can't tell him what's inside me, and he can't even begin
to guess." She laughed a little sadly, "He wants me to be a
newspaperwoman, can you imagine? I've helped him with
some articles about science and so now I've got enough
money to get to Paris and live for a year at the Sorbonne. I
met a young professor from there last winter, and from what
he told me about the laboratories for students—men *and*
women, I know the Sorbonne is what I want. Of course I
could also use that money for my last year at Radcliffe. But
if I stay in America, Prissy, I'll stop breathing. I know I
will."

"Because of this young man?"

"Because I'm finally ready for the Sorbonne. I have a feeling Professor Claudet will help me. If I don't go now, I never
will. Yet it's so far away, Prissy, and how will I live? And
what about Papa?"

"Your father would be proud."

She said nothing for a long time. Her eyes were tired and
resigned as she said "Papa will never be proud of me. Of us
all, I'm the last one he would have picked to go on living
with him. I come home these days because I need him: not
because he needs me. I *do* need him, Prissy!" She was silent
for a moment, staring straight ahead, and then she cried out
with all the torment that was in her: "I can't stand it that
Asher's somewhere under the ocean! I can't breathe when I
think of Amelia buried in her last white dress! I can't live
with Ronny gone—with the boys gone—with Mama gone! In
Cambridge, half the time, that's what I'm screaming inside
even though I sit there studying, reading, or listening to a
concert! The rest of the time I live only skin deep, pretending
that most of my life never happened. There's nobody there I
can talk to who knows what it feels like. With Asher I didn't
have to talk—we had something else. Now that he's gone, it's
even more impossible to talk. That's why I come home—it's
easier to be with someone else who's been through it!" Again
her voice fell quiet and she confessed: "But it's torture for
me to be with Papa. If there *is* a good reason why I was the
only one allowed to go on living—whatever it is or turns out

to be—Papa's attitude forever says it's not enough. That's what I suppose I *do* get from what you call 'this young man.' At least *he* loves me and wants me. I see it every time I look into his face; he wants *me* and no one else." She sighed. "But I'm only using him, Prissy, and that's not good—either for him or for me!"

I put my arm about her shoulders the way I had done the other time. "I'm for you, Julie," I said. "And I always will be. You know that."

Her smile was slightly wry as she patted my hand. "You're good, Prissy, but this hand was really for Amelia, not for me. I understand. I'm glad you still remember her. Let's have *that* together, Prissy. All right? But let's be honest about it."

"It was for Amelia," I admitted because I couldn't lie to Julie. I could admire her candor, but it put me off. She was too harsh, too cruel on herself. "Maybe it's because I see you as Amelia now as well as yourself. Perhaps you're all of them."

"They're *with* me, Prissy, but not *in* me. I'm all alone in there."

"No, you're not," I said sharply, to put an end to that kind of talk. "You've got me. And once you get to Paris, you'll make out. I'm coming to Paris too—right after you—sometime toward winter. I want to find you all settled someplace and hard at work under that young professor of yours. Them's orders, girl! And as for that young man—"

"Ah, how do I break it to him?" Again I could see how tormented she was by how much she felt she owed him but could never make herself pay. "What do I say?"

"You don't break it to him. Let a letter do it. There's only one word for what you do."

"What's that?"

"Skedaddle! And you do it tomorrow!"

I didn't get to Paris that winter. Theresa Gottschalk came down with pneumonia, and so I went to Milan and sang Marguerite and her other roles. From there I went to Vienna where I finished the season. Instead of returning home that summer or going to Paris, I was fool enough to let Arthur Schipper talk me into going to Capri with him. By mid-July we were so bored with each other that we were yawning in each other's faces. During our last days there, the only times we touched each other were when I sat in front of the mirror in our bedroom doing my hair, and he crouched behind me to watch himself tying his tie. From Capri, finally, I went to Paris.

In all that time, I had neither heard from Julie nor thought of her.

In Paris, I was immediately drawn back again into the "American colony," which at that time had a fantastically varied membership: there were the Southerners who had dug up their gold and fled the collapse of the Confederacy thirty-five years earlier; there were the Northerners who had grabbed their boodle and fled the collapse of Tweed's group in New York twenty-five years earlier; there were the loud and lucky western miners who were spending the gold, silver, copper, and lead from every strike—California, Virginia City, Leadville, the Yukon—all these men, their wives, their children, and their children's children, and an assortment of other Americans who over the years had been arriving in a steady rain—all of them with money from one source or another, most of them chagrined that neither money, looks, nor sheer brass could get them accepted by the French world of the Faubourg St. Germain. The other worlds that existed in Paris—the semi-French, semi-foreign worlds of writers, musicians, scholars, and artists were not exactly "worthwhile" except to "bohemian" Americans like Annie Mead, who, if she hadn't been an American society lady, might have sung professionally herself in a small way. When I knew her she had a house with a lovely garden surrounded by high walls in Passy on the Rue de la Pompe. It was very grand and modern. That very year electric lights had been installed in every room.

Both she and her brother Lyman had been brought up in Paris, and he—with his pointed beard, boulevard clothes, and monocle—looked a thousand times more Parisian than American. He had only disdain for his French classmates at the *lycée* who had called him *le covboi de Nevada*. Annie and Lyman adopted all the musical Americans who passed through, and that included me. Their friends lived on the fashionable boulevards radiating from the Arc de Triomphe or nearby. Lyman and Annie found an apartment for me on the Avenue de l'Alma right near the American Church of the Trinity. Here the new buildings—blocks of flats and *hôtels particuliers* were creamy white with gilded wrought-iron balconies. It was the Paris of the Exposition—the fairy-tale Paris of *la belle Epoque.*

Even the weather was a thing of beauty—a reprise of summer, that week of my arrival: full of the odors of the Paris boulevards on hot afternoons: the tar aroma of hot asphalt, the ammoniacal pungency of horse dung, and the sweetness of violets, all of them—sweet, bitter, brutal—intertwined like floating gauzy scarves, and drifting together past my nostrils. Occasionally among the carriages, automobiles hummed by, trailing their plumes of cloying vapor colored the transparent blue of evening. Permeating every scent and every mixture of scent was the hot green odor of sun-baked leaves drifting down in great swaths from the boulevard trees.

On my way to rehearsals every morning at the Opéra, I moved through the sparkle and jingle of smart harness, the glitter of speeding carriage wheels, the brisk trot of hoofs. I would pass the great, green, galleonlike buses: the three-horse doubled-decked *impériales*. Wherever I looked, every street seemed to have its gardenlike burst of umbrella color—the cafés, each of which I yearned to visit. My guidebook said that a lady could lunch alone at any of the first-class cafés in Paris. In contradiction, Annie Mead had warned me that no smart Frenchwoman ever would, and therefore I also was not to. However other smart women boasted that they had their own cafés. By the time I came home from rehearsal, it was dark, and the city glowed with some electric lights but mostly with gaslight whose poles carried advertising signs—pipes bent in the shape of letters and perforated for gas, so that the words glowed in the night with the soft brilliance of gas flame. The hotels and even the cafés I had passed in the daytime also had their own gas letter signs glowing above their entrances. In the street throngs were tall-hatted men with naked-shouldered women, and in the night air was a suggestion of an excitement that was tantalizingly not for me, because I was too busy learning two new roles and had no time for anything else except, whenever possible, the Friday afternoon receptions at the American embassy. Here, a large portion of the American colony in Paris would come every week. When I asked someone about a young American girl who was studying here, I was told that over a thousand Americans—young men and women—were studying art in Paris that year. Nowhere did I run into anyone who knew of Julie or had heard of her.

Yet she was in Paris, all right. Within a week after my first performance there came a note through the Opéra, asking if she could see me. She enclosed an address to which I could write. I didn't wait, but found a closed cab—ladies alone could not ride in an open cab—crossed the river and went along the new Boulevard St. Germain, then up a slanting, narrow, cobbled side street to a tall, narrow, stucco house with patched peeling walls of many shades of gray. A second-hand clothing store was on the ground floor and secondhand men's shoes hung in the window in a cluster—like a bunch of black leather bananas. A couple of dozen badly crushed tall silk hats were also piled together for sale in the window looking like the debris swept up after a street fight of maddened millionaires. The building had slumped within its frame and had a woebegone, tragedy-stunned look, with dried brown tears of rust dripping from the shutter hinges. I told my driver to wait for me. After all, I was paying a franc and a half an hour. He relaxed his reins. The horse sighed, shifted its weight, twitched its ears, and shuddered its skin at a fly.

I picked up the hem of my skirt and went gingerly through a short tunnel to the apartment of the concierge, who looked at me with a frown wondering whether I was a *grande cocotte* or a society lady. She told me that Mlle. Porter lived on the fourth floor rear and was at home.

The stairs were narrow and uneven, and the air smelled of cooking. There was a monotonous buzz of voices changing from landing to landing just as the smells changed from cabbage to frying fish to hot olive oil. I knocked on Julie's door and heard no sound within. Then suddenly the door was opened by Julie herself, frowning with irritation, her eyes strained, her hair half down and hairpins coming out, her lips smudged with ink, and her face paler and thinner than I had ever seen. When she saw me, her mouth opened in astonishment. The pen clattered to the bare floor, and we both stood away from it for a moment so that our skirts would escape the spatter of ink. Then we fell into each other's arms. I could feel that she was all skin and bones. Her hair, her clothes, even her skin, had a stale smell. Over her shoulders I could see the absolute poverty of her tiny room: a sagging, unmade iron bed with a single thin blanket, a battered table by the one window piled high with open books at which she had obviously been at work, a single wooden chair drawn up to it. There was a shelf along one of the cracked plaster walls with two cracked dishes: one cup and one chipped saucer, and no cabinet that might have held other crockery or other food.

There was not even a carpet on the floor, but only books—piles and piles of books.

"Prissy! Am I glad to see you!" Her breath had the odor of hunger.

"I'll bet you are!" I said pushing in. "You look terrible, Julie! You're starving! You need a bath! Look at your hair! Where are your clothes?" I was delighted to see her, but I was in a rage because she had taken so little care of herself. I pulled aside a faded red cloth that hung from the wall. Behind it, hanging shapelessly from three nails, was her entire wardrobe—the same clothes she must have had at Radcliffe and even then they had already been old and worn. Obviously she had no friends: a woman with one cup is a woman who has no visitors.

"Get yourself together," I told her. "I have a carriage downstairs. You're coming to my place for a week. I'm going to fatten you up, wash you, and see that you get some rest. You poor girl, you've been through hell!"

She looked at me with astonishment. "What are you talking about, Prissy? I can't leave my work. I have to prepare for tomorrow, and what hell have I been through?"

"But look at you!"

"Why, I've been having a marvelous time!"

"Do you know anybody?"

She had to think. "I've been too busy."

"Too busy to eat! When did you eat last, and what did you eat?"

"I don't know. Some prunes, I think, and there was a carrot."

That was too much. "Listen, Julie, hook up that dress, button up those shoes, and put on a hat! You're coming with me, or I'll take a switch to you! Now, *git!*"

That kind of bullying talk from the time and place where we had both been small made her smile and become docile. I took her back across the river, and home. I made her soak in the bath until she was completely relaxed and then sat her down to a good, solid meal. But she fell asleep before she finished. She was exhausted. She spent most of the next few days sleeping and eating. From one day to the next, her color brightened and her skin took on a brighter texture. Her hair began to shine, but she was bored, for while I was helping her physically, I was really depriving her of her laboratory work, her books, her lectures. What had appeared as shocking poverty to me had been a state of bliss for her: undisturbed immersion in her studies.

The previous year, she confessed, had been a total disaster, but she refused to go into details. The man she had come to work with—Claudet—had been abroad when she arrived and would remain away for at least a year or so teaching in Prague. She could have cried with her vexation and panic, but there was nothing to do about it. She set herself, for one thing, to learn French. Then her money began to run out. She left the comparative comfort of the English-speaking pension for a tiny French room in a small French house on the same street, but closer to the Boulevard St. Michel—a house with no water except in the hall, and only a charcoal stove for heating and cooking. Her money was down to where she was living on fifty cents a day for room and board —just about half of what anyone would consider a bearable minimum.

Just the same, she spoke of her work with fervor and said she was glad that Claudet had not been in Paris: she would have made too poor a showing for him. Now she was better prepared for his return. I asked about other young men, but she shrugged me off as if I had interrupted her with an irrelevancy. She was brushing her hair through all of this and I watched her. She puzzled me. Was she waiting for Claudet because she was in love with him? Or because she was so impressed with him as a scientist? There was no doubt that she was happy with her work and her professors. She kept speaking of the largeness of their conceptions and especially of the laboratories where she was learning the techniques of experiment under their guidance. She was using equipment far more advanced than anything she had dared dream of in Radcliffe and—what was important—she was working side by side with men students and on equal terms with them. Yet for all her enthusiasm, I could detect a difference in the way she spoke of Claudet—he was not only admirable to her as a man, but as a man concerned with chemistry as advanced to most chemists as chemistry itself was beyond the range of the layman.

She kept talking of the excitement of her work and I kept thinking of her poverty. I thought I had taken in a pitiful bird with a broken wing to nurse back to health; and here was my bird telling me I had interrupted its freedom and that it was impatient to fly away! She couldn't stay with me: she was saying, because it would take about an hour and a half to go from my flat to the university. That would mean three hours to travel every day. There simply wasn't that much time to waste.

I marveled at her dedication, but I had to smile too. I recognized all the ardor and self-immersion that I myself had felt only a few years earlier. The one difference between us, though, was that I had never allowed my work to push men entirely out of my life the way she seemed to have done. If she wasn't in love with Claudet, then I didn't understand her; but I did have to admire her. She put the brush down and shook her hair free in the sunlight. She had an ethereal quality which I was forced to respect, even though experience had told me that it would end disastrously for someone. I went to my private purse, the one I have never shown any man, and took out a hundred dollars.

"You're going to change the way you live," I said. "You're going to raise your budget from fifteen dollars a month to forty. This is a loan. Before this hundred is used up, I'll see to it that you've got more."

"But, Prissy, I can't borrow when I don't know how I'll be able to pay back."

"Yes, you can," I said, forcing the money on her. "And as for the rest, I'll arrange for you to be earning it."

It made me burn with fury to think of all the elegant American ladies in Paris, with their morning drives in the Bois with coachmen fore and footmen aft, their ritual of shopping only in the afternoon and without descending from their carriage, their golf at Enghien, their racing at Auteuil, their yearning to be part of Parisian society, their hypocritical concern for French charity organizations to give them French social position, while here was Julie right in their midst and more deserving of help than a dozen charities.

I made up my mind that the ambassador himself must sponsor her. She was the only American girl working for an advanced degree in the school of science. It was a matter of national prestige, I told the ambassador at his Friday reception. He patted my hand in a fatherly manner and said that American prestige in Paris was being very well upheld by my Desdemona at the moment. He recommended that I take up Julie with my own sponsors, Annie Mead and Lyman.

"But they're interested only in musical people."

"Tell them your young protégée sings the music of the spheres."

I had misgivings, but he appeared to be right. Others in the American colony were sponsoring artists, sculptors, musicians, composers, writers, jockeys, even horses—but nobody had an honest-to-God scientist; it was different enough to be interesting. Annie and Lyman said they would like to meet her, but of course they would have to discuss the matter with Marcel Raubard.

"Who is Marcel Raubard?" I asked.

They glanced at each other, amused by my ignorance. Surely I had heard of Professor Raubard; at the moment it was one of the major names in science. I said that I didn't even know the minor names—I was simply an ignorant singer going from town to town earning a living as I went.

"How pathetic you make it sound!" said Lyman drily. He had a habit of caressing his pointed black beard from beneath with a little fluffing gesture of his forefinger. His dark hair lay flat on his head, parted in the center, with short bangs on his forehead. His monocle and a bored supercilious air were supposed to suggest aristocratic disdain combined with cold-blooded dangerousness. He knew the jargon of music, and all of the important names, but nothing about music itself. In the same way I was sure he knew nothing about science. However, he was paying my rent at the moment. He had helped with my Opéra contract and the Paris critics, and he still hadn't asked for anything in return.

"Annie is going to have an evening party, and you shall meet Marcel Raubard," said Lyman. He had deliberately not said *soirée*, and his sister glanced at him for it. "Actually, earlier that same day he's going to give his first lecture of the season at the Collège de France, and we'll be there."

"At a scientific lecture?" I asked in downright astonishment, and again there was that exchange of smiles. All their lives, I suppose, they had smiled at each other that way. In Paris, they explained, the opening lecture of a celebrated *savant* could be considered by people of fashion to be as important an occasion as a first night at the theater or a sensational court trial.

"And you just sit there?" I asked.

"It's good for the soul," Annie said lightly. "After all, how many people attend the opera at home without understanding a single word?"

"Or church?" Lyman asked, picking up her thought and making her nod and smile. "Or for that matter, anything!"

Which sent Annie into a gale of laughter.

Two days later, I asked Julie about Raubard, and sure enough, she too told me that he was a brilliant scientist. I said fine, I was starting a campaign to interest him in her career.

"You mustn't interfere!" she said in a panic. "Why, he wouldn't waste two minutes on me!"

"You felt this other French professor would help you."

"But Georges Claudet is such a different man! He's younger—as a matter of fact he was also Raubard's student —but Claudet is sensitive, gentle. He listens. Raubard is—" She was helpless to describe him. "Terrifying! Simply terrifying!"

"No man ever terrified me," I said. "You've decided me. I'm going to his lecture, and I'll tame him for you."

She looked at me with a little smile. "I'll be there too, but I'm afraid he'll swallow you with one gulp. You'll see!"

I went with Lyman and Annie. Many other carriages besides ours were pulling up to the Place Marcelin-Berthelot, and dozens of people were already crowding every entrance. The lecture was being held in a steeply graded amphitheater-shaped room. When we followed the crush in, there was only an empty blackboard and a bare table on the little stage down front. The Meads and the other exquisitely dressed people, who obviously couldn't have had the vaguest idea of what was to be said had managed to get seats well forward, and there they sat, nodding at each other and gossiping among themselves as if they were waiting for a play to begin, while up behind us were crowded the young scientists and students for whom the course was really intended. Many appeared to be poor; they all had the same hungry look—not for food, but for some rarer sustenance, too delicate to be put into words. Yet they were youthfully noisy, impertinent to each other, and, in a sense, as bohemian as artists except that they lacked the artist's patina of dirtiness, their faces were more intelligent, more sensitive, more refined, and they seemed more dedicated behind their fun.

Somewhere among them, yet apart from them, was Julie. I strained back to see her through my opera glasses.

Suddenly there was quiet in the overheated, overpacked room. The student joking and the fashionable gabble stopped in mid-sound. What had stunned everyone to silence was that a side door had opened and a tall, heavy-shouldered man with a lumbering walk was in the room, looking neither left nor right, his dark-bearded head held forward and expressionless as he made straight for the table.

He was dressed in formal black and white evening clothes —the traditional costume for lecturing professors, but as he stopped, turned, and looked at us, he had a somewhat brutal air—so like a preoccupied pirate that he made even his starched bosom, his white tie and tails look a little raffish.

He was a formidable-looking man, all right, and his light eyes—seeming all the lighter and colder because of the darkness of the skin about them—gazed out at those of us who were in the front rows—even at his hostess for the coming evening—as if our presence there were contemptible. A lock of his long dark hair fell across his forehead, where it lay for a moment, then abruptly he tossed it back, raised his head, and began talking to the people above and behind us with such direct, rapid-fire rhythm that his words seemed like bullets from a Gatling gun—"Recent calorimetric studies of phase-law relationships—" or something equally incomprehensible, so that I and the other sight-seers—the lorgnetted, monocled, silk and satined, cravatted *voyeurs*—were at once left stranded like fools on the shore, while he, his students, and his confreres, sailed away together in their common understanding.

And why not, I wondered, as one professional observing another! He was right, and we were wrong to have come, although there wasn't a trace of embarrassment to be seen on the faces of either my companions or their friends. The fact is probably that they were as overawed as I was. Raubard's voice was harsh, almost crude, but so decisive and sure that even though I understood not one word, I was afraid to be bored: at any moment he might take a gesture of my head or an expression on my face for disagreement, and become so infuriated by even this slight sign of opposition that he'd come to a dead stop and rasp out at me his cold demand that I stand up then and there and retract my objection.

His voice poured along in that half-disdainful, overpowering growl, not even interrupting himself when he turned to write mathematical symbols and diagrams of his apparatus on the blackboard at a furious clip. The chalk kept breaking under the impact of his heavy hand so that as the lecture went on, a fine layer of chalk dust and chalk streaks began to cover his hands, his tail coat, his trousers, and even his black hair when he'd push it back impatiently from his forehead. Yet there was nothing ridiculous about his gradual transformation into a snowman.

At the end, he stopped abruptly and walked out of the same door through which he had entered. After a moment of silence, there was prolonged applause from behind us. I looked around to see the entire amphitheater standing for an ovation. Far away, up in the last row I thought I saw Julie standing with the others, and I tried to wave to her, but the crush of people in opposing streams kept me from getting any closer. She had been right, I wanted to tell her; he had terrified me, but deliciously.

"You see?" said Annie, applauding with the rest. "Now you see what a *coup* it is to be having him for dinner on the same evening as such a success! He's the only professor of the Collège de France who will visit Americans, and we're one of the few Americans he'll visit."

"He has to," Lyman explained drily. "He's married to one of us—a fourth cousin or so. If it weren't for her, we wouldn't know him either."

My impression that evening of the American-born Madame Raubard—when she was five her family had fled from New Orleans after its fall to our armies—was that of a dark, intense woman about forty, with a discontented mouth, an irritated frown, and dark eyes that glittered, whether with wit, rage, or insanity, I couldn't tell. But she was continually harpooning glances across the room at her husband to see what he was up to. For his part, he never seemed to look at her. Like the other men, he carried his hat with him in the French fashion, setting it down on the floor next to his chair, but since he stood mostly, in his restlessness, the hat was a drum for his tapping fingers. Even in the informality of a drawing room, his voice was harsh and impatient. He had all the little French amenities—his *mais oui, monsieur,* or *merci, madame* were as swift and as effortless as anyone else's, yet the gruffness of his voice and manner managed to negate six centuries of *courtoisie* at will. People spoke to him deferentially, but he could short a boring question with a curt: "Nonsense!" or an even more curt: *"C'est idiot!"* You couldn't even win his favor by ridiculing someone with whom he himself disagreed because he was liable to snap: "Yet he *is* brilliant! Always remember that!" And all the time, he'd be turning around and around lowering like some huge animal chained by manacles to a stake so he could be examined by the multitude, and whose light, impatient eyes kept roving angrily over everyone's head. For what? I wondered: Then I knew—for a pretty woman to look at. They came to rest on me, and paused so markedly that I could feel his gaze like a warm hand resting with impertinent familiarity on my hip. I tried to ignore what had happened and took the offensive at once. Of Julie, he said in impatient French: "I never heard of her." She was described to him. "I never saw her." I said she had enrolled for his lecture the previous year. "Then she never came," he said, refusing utterly to be drawn into any discussion outside ourselves and then he looked down at me with his hard stare: amused, direct, and bored all at the same time as he went on, still in French: "Now, you, mademoiselle, I would have remembered!"

"Nevertheless, she remembers you, monsieur."

"Does she?" he asked lightly. "And will *you?*"

"I will ask myself that very question, monsieur, from time to time in the years to come." I walked away because now I was angry with him even though I had also been strongly attracted.

When we went into dinner, though, I found I was sitting next to him. We bowed mockingly. But the spark of interest between us had been noticed by others.

From across the table Lyman was watching us. From her end of the table, Madame Raubard was watching us.

In me was that light-headed feeling of being posed on the verge of a dangerous delight. I didn't care who watched me or who approved or disapproved. I had the sense that my big, dark-bearded table companion also had a pulse running faster than our neighbors. He too had that secret smile, that veiled anticipation of satisfaction, that heightened color.

During the supper he was asked a hundred questions of the sort that non-scientists ask scientists on such occasions. His replies were civil enough—but bored, and had an undercurrent of mockery. Only when someone tried to nail him down with a question about the future, did he reply with any feeling: "How can you expect a serious man to talk, know, or even discern a future? Even the most intelligent man can no more imagine the how, the what, and the who of human society in a hundred years than Napoleon himself would have been able to predict that people like us, dressed as we are, could be gathered in just such a house, lit by an electricity controlled beyond his dreams, in a part of Paris that scarcely existed! And if what will be in the next hundred years is inconceivable to man's limited imagination, think how impossible for humanity to envision the next millennia—which itself is only a flick of time on any cosmic scale. Why, it's almost half an illusion to play with the reality of our own moment —even if one treats it as an instant in a process of continual change. The very chemistry I spend my life at is a study of an ephemeral world. Yes! The substances of the planet, including everything on the face of the earth, exist as they do only as a result of the temperatures of the earth and the sun —both of which are constantly changing."

"But certainly the laws of nature are valid everywhere and for all time!"

"Are they?" Raubard asked skeptically. "One would certainly like to think so, but who knows? Will we ever know?"

His questioner was slightly shocked but persistent. "Surely," the man said. "Surely you believe though that a day will come when science will eventually discern all the secrets of nature!"

"I believe that our science will find answers to all the questions about nature that we can think of asking. But the questions we will think of asking at any moment will go on always being only a fraction of all the questions that could be asked. What I mean to say is that we can know everything we think we ought to know about the universe and still know practically nothing. It's not the universe which is infinite, but mystery!"

Madame Raubard, at the end of the table, laughed in the silence that followed. Her English was American southern— her French was Parisian. "Marcel had few toys as a child, and so he plays with ideas. He loves to startle with contradiction. Now he has left poor Miss Porter's mouth open with astonishment. It is astonishment, isn't it?"

It certainly was; but at what was going on under the table, not at what he was saying above it. During the short exchange, I had felt a foot press firmly against mine. Was it an accident? His eyes were cast down as if listening to the questions. I moved my foot slightly. Without the slightest change in his expression, I felt myself pursued. In another moment, again there was that impertinent pressure against my slipper.

Impertinent but delicious. In the depths of my body I was delighted, but I pretended to myself that I was intensely irritated by his audacity. Did he think I was that easy? Why, he wasn't even deigning to look at me! Lyman, across the table, continued to stare at me with baleful warning. I moved my foot again, and again I was pursued. I still insisted that I was angry but I was not too amused and pleased to keep up the game of indignation.

Here was this man who was making his bigness felt in waves. Massiveness of mind and personality seemed to exude from him like the giant swaths of cool air that came flooding down into alpine valleys in the summer, forcing you always to be aware of their source: the glacier-peaked mountain soaring up just overhead. Even sitting next to him, my head came only a little above his shoulders. I could look down sideways and see his hands resting on the table before him: square, large, clean hands with strong black hairs curling on the back of his wrist and on the backs of his fingers. They made me think of animal softness and animal violence. His heavy shoulders spread well beyond the width of the chair, reaching almost to my ears, and I was afraid that once I caught his odor it might easily be the cold, deathly scent of chemicals; but then a gesture of his arm and a wave of his hand brought me only a warm waft of the pungency of his tobacco, his perspiration, and something even richer, more masculine, that made me think of body-heated dark red leather.

In a rhythm that had nothing to do with the uninterrupted flow of his voice, my foot was pressed with demanding insistence. It was not enough apparently that I submit to his touch, I was to respond to it with an acknowledgment. I refused. I moved my foot away. His voice went calmly on talking about the table, but the pressure was repeated. I was to be given no peace, no quarter. At last, very slightly, I replied; electrifying myself with the implied promise. He acknowledged nothing, neither by a glance, nor even by a slight change of color. The pressure against my foot was maintained, though, and there was a warm flow of feeling between us through the contact.

Then he finished what he was saying and swung himself around in his chair away from me to cross his legs, and it was at that moment that Madame Raubard caught my astonishment: because even though he had moved away, the pressure on my foot continued! It wasn't he at all, it never had been!

It was only when I glanced across the table and saw Lyman's red face, glinting monocle, and compressed lips that I realized that *his* was the foot that had been touching mine all along. He was asking at last for the rent to be paid. The idea was now repulsive. I wanted someone else. Then I suddenly sensed that it had been Lyman's pleasure to wait for just such a moment. But there was no need to panic, I told myself. He wasn't my only sponsor. If I were adroit enough, I could maneuver his sister to stand between us; but I needed just one glance down the table to where she was sitting, and the sparkle of amusement in her eyes told me that she too had been watching and that she enjoyed her brother's games at least as much as he did. I wondered what would happen if I should ever turn poor Julie over to this couple's tender sponsorship.

In a way though, the joke was on Lyman. The only feelings his touch had called up in me were for Raubard. But as long as I paid my rent, I figured, there seemed no reason why I couldn't eventually use my premises, as it were, for my own pleasure. And so the rent was paid, but intimacy with Lyman left us both untouched. We behaved exactly the same to each other as before. He still stared at me through that glacial monocle; he went on fluffing that little black beard, sardonically curious as to what I was going to do because, of course, what had attracted him was my feeling for Raubard.

"We mustn't forget that little student friend of yours," he said, screwing the monocle into his eye as he stood by my window. "It's been weeks since you spoke of her, and then you said she was in trouble. Didn't I see you wave to her at the lecture?"

"I thought you weren't interested, since Raubard didn't seem to know her."

"I'm not interested in everything Raubard is interested in. If Annie and I like the girl, there's no reason why we can't make our own decisions. Raubard can approve her afterward."

He turned to see how I'd take his implied offer, but I showed no pleasure. I even invented excuses to avoid any meetings between him and Julie at that time, but for all my plans, Lyman came in one day when Julie was with me. His elegance made her at once uncomfortable—she was not used to such men, and she got up to go. I saw him examine her poor clothes, her carelessly arranged pompadour, her worn shoes from which a few buttons were missing, her chemical stained fingers and contrast it all with her face, for she was pale again from self-neglect and her skin had that transparency that made her look delicate, pure, and remote. He put on a quiet charm I had never seen him use and he begged her to sit with us. He said that he had heard of her through me and that he was extremely interested in her and her studies. He was very gentle with her. She let herself be reassured. She was even charming in her smiling reticence. She said she didn't want to bore him with an account of her work—which she knew was of interest only to herself—but he countered by dropping the names of Raubard, Berthollet, Pasteur, Becquerel, and the Curies, all of whom he said he had met at one time or another. She was impressed, all right, and asked if he had also met Georges Claudet. He said gravely that he knew the name, lying of course, but his voice had the right tone of deference.

She walked right into the trap and in another moment was talking with unrestrained ardor to Lyman about what she found fascinating and—naïvely—what she thought was also fascinating to him. I swear he didn't understand one tenth of what she was saying, but he nodded, smiled, looked surprised and delighted, simply by taking his cue from her voice, her face, and her hands, which had suddenly become feminine and vivaciously eloquent because she was talking not so much about herself as about ideas and her own feelings about them.

Within half an hour though, embarrassment caught her. She rose quickly to leave, apologizing for talking so much. Her eyes moved from Lyman to me and back again, silently beseeching us to forgive her for having remained so long. I was really moved to see how her intelligence in abstract things would always be so helplessly at the mercy of this total lack of insight into people who surrounded her. It made her seem even more unworldly, even more vulnerable. We were both silent for a while after she fled.

"She's charming," he said at last. He took his monocle out of his eye, which made his face look naked, then put it back more firmly. "We'll give her the money."

"Without asking Annie?"

"Without asking Annie."

"And how soon will it be before you'll be pressing her foot under the table?"

He turned so red that the monocle glinted against the darkness. I thought he was going to strike me. Then his rage passed with such speed that my heart was still beating in fear of him while he was already smiling.

"Are *you* complaining of my treatment of you?" he asked. "You know very well that if you hadn't wanted to press back, you needn't have." I had no answer to that, but he knew what my answer would have been because a moment later he said: "We must have Raubard meet our protégée."

"I'm not at all sure that she's going to be '*our* protégée.'"

He gave his French shrug, but his glance warned me not to interfere. I silently determined to do all the interfering I could, but not until after I took the opportunity to meet Raubard again.

Lyman arranged for Annie to give a second *soirée*. She sent out invitations to almost twenty people including Julie. Two days before the dinner, I had Julie come to my flat to show her how to wear one of my own dresses—a magnificent dinner gown I had bought in Vienna—and what to do with her hair. Ordinarily, I suppose, she wouldn't have bothered, but she couldn't resist the chance of meeting Raubard even though the prospect still terrified her: she was afraid that she'd look like a fool the moment he'd talk to her. My maid and I stripped her in order to do a thorough job, and my maid kept murmuring her admiration for Julie's body. I too remember silently thanking my stars that no man in whom I was interested would ever have the chance to look at those magnificent breasts, the almost flat gently curving belly, the small rounded hips—all firm, strong, delicately white, and all of which she was totally unaware.

My maid did her hair while I pinned the green and gold dress for her to make her own alterations. We both finished at the same time and stood back together to look at a transformed Julie. She stood rather stiffly, balancing the elaborate coiffure and afraid to disarrange the pinned-up dress; but the very pose gave her such style and elegance that she could have worn a tiara. Her naked arms and shoulders looked as if they had never been revealed before.

Two nights later when she came into Annie's drawing room, I could see that our preparations had been in vain. She had been unable to repeat what the maid had done to her hair; perhaps she hadn't even tried; it had a hastily thrown together look. Nor had she taken in the dress where I had pinned it for her.

"I just didn't have the time," she whispered in answer to my fierce stare. "I got caught up in the laboratory on an experiment and I didn't notice the time. But it *feels* very comfortable. Doesn't it look all right?"

"It makes me think there's a very naked girl somewhere inside there; and as for the *corsage* it gives you—well, don't lean forward!" She flushed to her eyes with embarrassment, but she couldn't help laughing at herself. "Poor Prissy, you're always trying too hard to help me; and all I do is disgrace you!"

"But at least you could have worn a corset!" I hissed.

She looked even more stricken. "I have only one, but there were so many knots in the laces that I couldn't tie it."

"And in the entire city of Paris you couldn't find a new string?" I was riding my rage like a witch on a broomstick.

"I didn't have time," she pleaded again. "I was absolutely unnerved by the thought of meeting Professor Raubard." She glanced around for him. "I was afraid to come without having finished the experiment. I kept thinking he might ask me how far I've gone in physical chemistry, and I wanted to be able to say that I *started* work on the theory of solutions. That seemed more important."

"Well, it wasn't! I'll have to get you some sort of light scarf."

I found something gauzy of white silk. It was as transparent as mist and she would have been better off without its suggestiveness, but now she refused to give it up. She clung to it as if it were as opaque as black velvet. I was so irritated with her that I stopped caring. I was anxious myself to speak to Raubard before Lyman arrived, and once I introduced her around, I left her to fend for herself.

Raubard's face took on interest at seeing me, and we both laughed a little at meeting again.

"This time I have my protégée with me," I said. "Now you'll be forced to remember her. She is over there, across the room."

He wouldn't even take the trouble to turn his head.

"Very well, I shall remember her," he growled humorously. "But you *did* remember me."

"I did indeed. May I present her?"

He still ignored her existence and looked over my head at Lyman, who had just come into the room, searching at once among the faces.

"—Even though we were interrupted and will be again?" Raubard went on, and I felt myself flush. He knew all about me and Lyman.

"But interruptions of that sort need be only as temporary as you wish, depending on *what* you wish," I said, putting him squarely on notice.

He looked down at me searchingly. "English is a strange language. Sometimes people say *you* when in French we would say *one*. Were you speaking of me specifically or were you making a generalization?"

"That very ambiguity is what allows me to say what I please and at the same time appear to preserve the proprieties. Don't take it away."

"Ah, don't fence with me," he advised softly. "There are enough mysteries in my work."

He stopped because Lyman came up to us then. A sly satisfaction on his face puzzled me until later. I had risked an argument with Annie, pleading with her to have dinner in the conventional manner with place cards, even though it had become all the rage in her circles for the guests to take their own places around the table informally as they came into the dining room. However, I was determined to have Raubard sitting between me and Julie, to force her presence on him; and of course to give me access to him myself. Annie had given in angrily, but my victory was meaningless because Lyman had now moved the cards so that *he* would sit between Julie and me, and had put Raubard far away from me, on the far right of Julie. It was clear that Lyman had decided that Julie was an exotic bird whom he was determined to charm and taste at least once. Ordinarily, I would have been delighted at the prospect of relief, but Julie was under my protection and I wasn't going to give her up to him so easily even to buy my freedom. Moreover, for me to talk to Raubard meant that I would have to call to him across Lyman and Julie.

I was furious. I was blunt and short with Lyman unless he was talking to Julie. Then I would interrupt and make the talk general around the table. Finally, Lyman turned to me with a question glinting behind the monocle.

"I wish to God I knew what you were up to," he murmured. "Do you or don't you want me to help this girl?"

I was afraid, too, that Julie would irritate Raubard. I had heard him say he hated to be reminded of his laboratory when he was out of it, while she on the other hand spoke with warmth about nothing else. Of course, I was seeing him only by reflection, as it were: through the calm of his wife across the table. For once, she seemed completely at ease. She could even look at me without anger.

I took Julie home in my carriage. She said very little. She had been overwhelmed, I thought, by the splendor and elegance. I asked about Raubard, but she shook her head.

"He was much kinder than I expected him to be, but I bored him. I could feel it. He's far too brilliant to waste his time on me."

As I rode back to my own flat afterward, I realized that I ought to be pleased that things had worked out as they had. Madame Raubard had not been alarmed, Lyman thought he had won a victory, and Marcel knew all he needed to know about my availability; the rest was up to him.

I had no doubt that in a few days I would receive either a note from him, or what was more likely, a personal visit without any advance warning. I thought about him all the time. I waited. I'd hurry home to be there in case he'd come.

But nothing of the sort happened. After Annie's second *soirée*, he seemed to have disappeared. He ceased coming to receptions and dinners given by the American colony. His wife came alone—thin-lipped with or without his presence— to explain that he was preoccupied by a new series of experiments, and after a while I realized that I was waiting in vain. Julie also dropped out of sight. Summer came and I escaped Paris by going back to Capri. When I returned, I was stricken with guilt as I remembered Julie. I wrote. She answered my notes: grateful for my interest, but told me I wasn't to worry. Actually, I didn't. I think at that point I was becoming tired of her. Lyman was impatient though. He continually asked me how and where to send her the money she needed. I said I'd write her myself. Then Lyman stopped asking. There was a curious glint of amusement in his eyes, even malicious amusement, and his ardor died. Days went by without my seeing him. Thank God, I thought, he's found someone else.

Then came a long delayed note from Julie in answer to my

last letter to her: thanking me again but saying very definitely that she now no longer needed any help and *that* at last was what caught my interest.

I went to her room. She was not at home. I went again. She was out. I went a third time and I was lucky. She let me in slowly, pleased to see me, but obviously displeased that I had picked that particular moment to come. The room was changed. A new oil lamp flooded it with light. I noticed a larger bed. Heavy curtains covered the windows. Her one cracked dish and one saucer had been added to: there were now two of each and they were no longer cracked. Another table stood in the room; the first still covered with books and papers, but this second table was set for two people—with two tall, unlit candles—a fantastic luxury for her.

"Why haven't I seen you?" I asked.

She smiled, but was clearly exhausted.

"Because I work sixteen hours a day. I've finally found work in a girl's school. Isn't that wonderful? I work only a few days a week for one hundred francs a month. It's very much more than I need—but it does take time!"

I was delighted at her pleasure in the pitiful pay: twenty dollars a month! "So that explains the new luxury! But I see you have time to celebrate."

She looked even more embarrassed. Then she impulsively put her arms about my shoulders and squeezed her thanks. "I can't, Prissy, but you have been so wonderful to me, and I don't know how to thank you. I'm happy! You know," she said, walking me slowly to the door, her arm still around me, "I don't think I've ever been happy in exactly this way before. This is something that's in my blood, in my mind, in my stomach, my knees! I feel at last as if I have everything in life that's good!"

I had to laugh at her. "A job gives you all that? A girl your age? Julie! There's a man. I'm not blind. Your Professor Claudet has come back to Paris!"

"Claudet?" She looked at me in astonishment. "I told you —he won't be back until next year."

The door opened almost in my face. A man backed into the room in a black cape, and a black broad-brimmed low-crowned hat, his arms laden with parcels. He turned around, and there facing me stood Marcel Raubard, his dark face filled with good humor fixed by the shock of surprise. He glanced at Julie to see what this meant, then back at me, still good-humored, but completely at a loss.

I also didn't know what to say. I had absolutely no claim on him; he was another woman's husband, and yet I felt pain and humiliation. Any sign of feeling would make me look like a fool. I couldn't force myself to smile. Nor could I play the amused co-conspirator. Nor could I be the indignant patron of an innocent young protégée led astray. All I wanted to do was to be out of the room.

He was the first to recover. He simply decided to ignore me for the moment and stepped over to the table where he put down his parcels and slipped off his hat and cape, obviously very much at home in the little room. And Julie set about untying the strings and unwrapping the papers as if she too were already so used to being with him that no words were needed to discuss the ways and means of doing what they had done together a dozen times before. He was the one who remembered to invite me to join them. I had the feeling that he was enjoying the situation. I hated him.

"I was just going," I managed to say; but instead of taking myself off, as I had promised, I stayed and tried to salvage something by reminding him that he and I still shared a world. "Your friends', the Von Hocheims', reception begins in an hour and a half, and I must dress for it. Shall I be seeing you at the embassy?"

"You will not see me there," he growled. I could feel myself irritating him with my appearance, my very stance—for the first time I saw how much he hated the world in which we had met: but I couldn't stop myself. I wrapped my fur piece around my neck with what I knew was a theatrical sweep, but since I did it better than most, at least in my own eyes I was saving my pride.

"You're fortunate you don't have to go," I said. "Still I think it would do Julie a world of good to know such people —for her career, of course!"

Julie smiled, but Raubard snapped: "Julie has no need of such people. That world is not hers!"

"You met her in that world," I reminded him. "Perhaps she could meet other men as fascinating. I have an interest in Julie, as you know—"

"I know indeed," he said abruptly. "And I thank you for that interest; but it's no longer needed."

That was too much. I said in English—as deliberately as I

could: "Thanks from a stranger for my interest in my own cousin would be about as close to impertinence as one could come!"

"Perhaps, madame," he said with an icy indolence. "I know you had in mind a number of arrangements as a result of that 'interest,' but I'm not at all sorry to have thwarted so many plans."

"Plans? What sort of plans, sir? Whose plans? Plans for what?"

"Your plans. Lyman Mead's plans. Oh, I know your Mr. Mead very well and for a long time!" He was in a cold, irrational rage with his jealousy, I could see it, and yet I couldn't keep myself from snapping back at him.

"Meaning?"

"Meaning that when Julie told me some months ago at the Meads' that there was some talk of her being helped by them, I knew exactly what Mr. Lyman Mead had in mind and so did you."

"I was helping her, sir!"

"So she told me, and so you thought; but I ask myself only whether you were helping her get them, or helping them get her!"

"Are you calling me a procuress?"

"Or perhaps you were simply ransoming yourself by arranging for Mr. Mead to be so interested elsewhere that you could slip off unnoticed whenever you pleased. If this is the way cousins treat cousins in America, it's all one to me; but it strikes me as a shame to play such games with someone like Julie—"

"Instead, sir, you prefer to play them with her yourself! And rather than use your own money for your young ladies —as Lyman at least does—you use the funds of young girls' schools for your little employments! One hundred francs a month! My God, what a penny-pinching cavalier!"

"Prissy! Marcel! Both of you! Stop that at once!" said Julie, her face completely white and horrified. "How can you two say those things?"

"You heard what he said to me, Julie! He must have said those things to you before. You permitted him to?"

"Prissy, I never paid any mind. What do I care what he had to say about Lyman Mead?"

"And what he had to say about me?"

"Prissy, he doesn't know you the way I do. Nothing he says can change my feeling for you."

"But you *did* permit him to talk about me that way!"

I couldn't stop myself. I hated their closeness and the way she took her possession of him for granted. Even more, I hated his jealousy over her.

"I'm afraid I didn't pay much attention, Prissy," she said. What stung me was that she was beginning to sound a little weary of the whole business. "I was too involved in the work."

"Well, *I* was never so involved in *my* work that I didn't have time for *you*. Good-by, Julie, I can see that you don't have any need of me ever again!"

I slammed out and hurried down the stairs, holding my skirts to keep from tripping over them, alert to every sound behind me. I wanted her to have turned on him and say, "See what you've done now!" and then run out after me, begging my forgiveness, but I heard nothing. No doors slammed. No voices were raised in argument. When I was near the second floor, I thought I could hear a man laughing, and I told myself it was Raubard. By the time I reached the street I was sick with rage and humiliation.

I thought surely the following day I would hear from her, but again there was silence. Either she had no idea how hurt I was, or she knew and didn't care. I simply couldn't believe that the girl on whom I lavished so much care and concern could repay me with such callousness. The days went by, and no note, no letter—nothing but silence.

A week later, though, she came to me.

"Prissy, you can't go on being angry with me."

"I expect an apology."

She shrugged. "Of course, Marcel can be childish—"

Marcel! How calmly she took her right to call him that!

"I don't want any apologies on his behalf. I want an apology from *you!*"

"Very well, it's *my* apology, but let's have an end to this, once and for all!"

"That's not an apology!"

She stood there helplessly, but with growing irritation. "Then what *do* you want?"

"I want you to break with that man—" By that time, I don't think I did really, but I couldn't stand the way she was humoring me. However, she took me very seriously, and her face went white.

"I love him, Prissy," she said. "He's more than brilliant. He's difficult, perhaps, but—"

"But he's someone else's husband."

She was still trying to be reasonable, but it was getting harder and harder for her to control her temper. "There are things in this life you don't know about, Prissy, and it would be wrong for me to discuss his business—"

"His business is pinching girls—pressing women's feet under tables—!"

"You're determined to fight with me," she said. "I came to make peace with you, and I still want to, if you'll allow me—"

"I told you—I want you to break with that horrible, odious, loathsome man. You told me you were in love with this other scientist—this Claudet. Why can't you be satisfied to wait for him?"

"I never said I was in love with Professor Claudet!" she said indignantly. "I only said I wanted to work with him more than with anyone else in the world. That's not love; and that was before I ever dreamed it possible to work with Marcel. I don't understand you, Prissy. You're absolutely bent on making everything impossible."

"And I don't understand you unless that Marcel Raubard is some kind of Svengali to your Trilby. Look at you! He's got you so hypnotized that you do nothing but think his thoughts, wish his wishes, and love him at his bidding. He has made you the vehicle of his genius!" I quoted Du Maurier dramatically. "But he's also cut you off from the one person who *was* close to you. Get your wits together one of these days, girl, and look at yourself! That's my advice to you!"

Now it was her turn to look at me speechlessly and walk out, slamming the door behind her. I was both sorry and glad. But if I didn't understand her, I understood him even less. The fact is that I understood nothing that happened after Annie Mead's second dinner party, and I didn't want to understand.

I left Paris that winter without seeing Julie again, and when I returned, I made no effort to see her. Nor did she try to reach me.

I didn't hear of her again for about five or six years when

from her photograph in *Le Temps,* I learned that she was the celebrated Madame Claudet whose name had been appearing in the newspapers for some time. So she *had* married the man she once swore she didn't love! Had she in the meantime come to love him? Or had something else happened in her life? Years later I was in London when I read of her husband's death, and I almost wrote to her. I wanted to, but I couldn't make myself write, "My dear Julie—"

I put down the pen, tore up the paper, and knew I'd have to wait until she finally came to me with the sort of apology I was determined to have from her; but I have never seen her again.

However, I did see Raubard once more—this was about fifteen or sixteen years after that night at Julie's. He must have been in his middle sixties, but what a shock it was to see him! He went by me slack-jawed, staring blindly ahead, walking with a slow, inch-by-inch shuffle, his limp body almost erect but with his knees bent like a bear's as if he were about to squat on his haunches at any moment. His mouth was open and he was panting. He was led along like a shuffling bear by his wife, who wore her hair exactly as she had the last time I had seen her, but now the hair was white. The small sourpretty face was also the same and yet changed. The skin had withered, whitened, and hung in tiny folds at the corners of her mouth and beneath the once-angry eyes. Now those eyes were serene, and—what struck me as more horrible than anything—inwardly pleased.

This must have been early 1917—before America entered the war, and it was a charity affair. As one of the Republic's Immortals, he was on hand to lend dignity to the proceedings. I was to sing on the program. Madame Raubard's gaze swept the dais as she—an angel of loyalty and devotion—led her stroke-blasted husband toward his seat. Her eyes found me—recognized me—held me for one brutal instant, and paused imperceptibly, as if to show me the man her husband had become. The little gesture—almost a music hall magician's *voilà!*—was a conversation only between us. She said nothing to her husband, and I doubt if he saw me or knew who I was when he heard me sing.

Later he was led, still shuffling slowly and blindly, off the platform before any of us left, because we all waited in deference to him. In the intervening years, of course, his genius had fully flowered to the point where he was considered another Bernard or Berthollet, and we watched the wreck of a human being move away, aware, all of us, that in spite of what we saw, there went the remains of a mind that would live on for hundreds of years.

Leaving the platform, she glanced back just once—whether to find me again or not, I wouldn't swear—but I really think she did. I had the feeling that if there was a single source for all the mystery and the misery that followed from Annie Mead's dinner party, she somehow might very well be that evil center, and yet I remembered the utter calm of her face that night as she sat there across the table and watched it all begin. She had fooled me completely, but so had Julie.

No one could be angry at Raubard after the sight of him shuffling along toward his death; but I still went on feeling the way I did about Julie—she should have known better. I was still the only family she had left; the only one who knew how she had lain awake in the house on West Tisbury to listen to the night coughing of everyone she loved as they were taken away from her, one by one. I was the only one to know everything there was to know about her. She owed me love, that girl did, because I loved her—even if what I loved in her was someone else—Amelia. At least, I always thought it was Amelia until this moment when I finally say it out loud. Now I see it was Julie herself—Julie herself, Julie, all along!

PART FIVE—
HAL PRESCOTT: III

PRISSY'S ACCOUNT OF JULIE AS SHE WAS IN THOSE early days in Paris remained fixed in my mind. I glanced away for another quarter of my own lifetime; but when I looked back, there was Julie at precisely the moment where Prissy had left her. Yet everything was changed. Certainly for me. Life had turned dark with a growing sense I had of my own failure even though I had a drawer full of honors, prizes, and citations. I knew that when a scientist passes sixty, it's his decorations that are getting the honorary degrees, and so they didn't help. In my heart, I felt I had fulfilled nothing of what my life had once promised, and I was impelled to find out why. My wish for an answer became a real hunger to know, and so there I was, in the Institute on Rue d'Ulm once again, back in Julie's old office with the same plate on the door: DIRECTEUR. But I had come too late: someone else was sitting in the chair. Fortunately for me, though, it was someone who had known Julie longer and more intimately than anyone else. But even so, something had missed between them. They had seen into each other's hearts and were at the same time blind to each other. They had worked together and thought differently—not only because they were different people, but because they were of different generations, and no bridge has ever been built across time.

The talk about Julie began in roundabout fashion with my remark about the rash of changes in the face of Paris. My complaint about the contemporary architectural style provoked a shrug and a little wave of dismissal: "It's all the same —*contemporain* of today, *moderne* of thirty years ago, or *l'art nouveau* when I was very little," I was told. "The only thing that changes is the way the artist distorts reality. Today it is the naïve wish to imitate the functional simplicity of laboratory apparatus—as if the essence of a laboratory were only the simple-looking apparatus itself and not the complexity of what is happening *within* the tubes, pipes, and chambers. *L'art nouveau* with which I grew up was just as foolish in another way. Rainspouts were carved to look like slender tree trunks with curling leaves of ivy twisting about; everything was supposed to be something else, or something growing, or something flowing.

"Even in the illustrations in the magazines and books, from 1905 to 1910, hair was not allowed to be plain human hair. The ladies looked as if syrup or *mélasse* were dripping from their heads.

"I can still remember in particular an old *affiche* for Sarah Bernhardt, I think it was, making one of her usual farewell appearances in *Médée*—a figure of a standing woman staring at you straight out of the overdecorated picture—with her arms clasped dramatically before her, a dagger in one of her hands, and at her feet: the bodies of two dead children—all drawn with that flowing line as if they had been poured. What struck me then and what still remains with me now was the expression on the woman's face. I asked my mother who the lady was. She said an ancient princess. I said, *Maman*, who are the little children? She said they were the lady's. I asked if the children were really dead or only sleeping. She said unfortunately they were dead, that the lady had killed them herself. So I asked, Why does she look so surprised? Because the very point of the picture, the expression on Bernhardt's face as she looked out at you, was one of wide-eyed, doltish surprise—not as if she had just performed some ghastly act of devastation and horror, but as if she had heard an unexpected little *tinkle* from off stage. I could not then put it into words, but I tell you that if that particular woman had killed those children, she had done it by accident with her hatpin while dressing herself to go meet her lover for a *thé dansant!*

"But I remember my mother stopping and going up to the faded poster to examine the picture more closely. Then she turned and looked down at me with an expression that I will never forget. She appeared to be suddenly breathless with pain, and I could not imagine what I had done to cause her such unhappiness. This was after my father had died, you understand, and my mother was so busy at her work that I could see her only on Saturday afternoons and Sundays. Each moment with her was precious to me, and here I was, spoiling it all by my foolishness. But she wasn't angry at all when she spoke, only very gentle. She said: 'You're right, she *does* look surprised! Ah well, perhaps she didn't know what she was doing.' Then she added something I couldn't understand until years later. She said this: 'Perhaps she didn't know how *not* to do what she did!' We walked a little farther, but my mother was more disturbed than I had realized, because whatever plans we had had were canceled at once. My mother stopped a passing fiacre, and we stepped into it and drove off to the Grands Magasins du Louvre where she bought me what seemed the most huge brown English toy bear I had ever seen. I slept with it for years after. But that is a long way from where we started. What were we talking about?"

I said there had been no real digression—we were there to talk about Madame Julie Claudet, that I had come to Paris specifically to talk about her.

There was a long silence and a frank examination of me that started by being sardonic and then, after our gazes had held for a while, became kind. "Well, it's true, you *do* have a right to ask," I was told gently, and then came the other surprise: "She was always waiting for you to come, you know. She could not understand why you never did. She followed your work. I had the sense that sometimes she even was taking a certain pride in you—a little of the way she took in me." My face must have showed what I was feeling, and to help me there was an abrupt change of tone. "You must understand that what I knew about her, I knew mostly from the outside even though I loved her very much. I know also what I have been told by other people who loved her and by people who hated her—there were those too. And so, in the end, I too am only guessing, the way everyone has to guess about another person, although my guess is made from a point closer to whatever truth there is than anyone else's—so close to it that it hurts. That is why I can tell this only if I do it as if my face were averted, as it were; with no expression in my voice, almost as if it were not even coming from me. I will have to speak of myself as if I were someone else, and it will take time. You have that much time?"

What I was about to say would have sounded florid, so I simply nodded, and this is the way, more or less, it was told to me; this is how Julie, whom I had last seen through Prissy's eyes, came to life again, moved, suffered, and grew; but very differently from the way Prissy had ever imagined.

PART SIX—
JULIE

1

THOSE FIRST FEW MONTHS IN PARIS, SHE HAD A LITTLE room on Rue Gît-le-Coeur, that dark, quaiside, narrow fifteenth-century alley next to the Place St. Michel. Each day the world was new all over again for her. She was twenty-three and so pelted by impressions that between each sunrise and each midnight there stretched a year of minute-by-minute discoveries. Each unexpected sight and sound—the twanging melody of a European hurdy-gurdy in the court below, or the sight of the old-fashioned white linen caps worn by the *vendeuses* in the narrow little street hawking milk, rolls, herrings—by the women working in the *crémeries* and the cafés on Rue St. André-des-Arts, by the *blanchisseuses* coming and going to the the Quai St. Michel to work on the laundry barges on the Seine—the different calls of the chestnut seller, the umbrella mender, the knife grinder, the hoarse call of the blind man, the gorgeous uniforms everywhere, red-trousered soldiers walking, talking, strutting, riding, trotting, cantering along the avenues and the boulevards, their tightly buttoned tunics a shade of blue depending on the branch of service, and each one glinting with metal, and looped with braid—everything caught her eye and ear, each demanding that she dwell on it to the exclusion of all the others, the way she used to when she squatted down as a little girl and stared at the buttercup or the daisy, memorizing the patterns of petal and color so that she could know once and for all what would be repeated for-ever from daisy to daisy, from buttercup to buttercup, all over the field, in every field of the world.

For weeks she was able to buy only those foods she knew how to pronounce. She wandered through the city by day, ig-noring the men who ogled her, followed her, and called to her. At night she sat home alone to study the language. When lectures began, she was overwhelmed by the difference be-tween the meager French her ear could identify and the silken sounds that rolled so glibly and with such fluency from the lips of her professors and the high-speed argot from the students who seemed to fill the entire Latin Quarter to the exclusion of anyone over thirty. It was a world of youth, and in that world she was like a child aware that all around her the people were communicating with each other with rapid clumps and spears of sound which she was always on the verge of understanding, while understanding itself was as elusive as light reflected from a ripple of water. The sounds that came from her own mouth seemed to her to be formless and unintelligible.

She tried to soften the disaster by reading up each night the material which she thought would be covered in lecture on the following day, but even the most complete familiarity with Avogadro's hypothesis or Van't Hoff's precepts on stereochemistry, for example, was no preparation for the elegantly discursive French of Adrien Talbert or, in particular, the taut reasoning, picked off on his fingers, by Charles Durand who would then turn and write out the three determining equations for chemical equilibrium which he had just deduced with such lucidity for everyone but her. Her notebook remained a blank, day after day, and panic was an increasing weight in her throat.

But through all this time, in her dreams, fragments of French expressions heard during the day flitted through her mind like blown leaves fluttering against the wall of a house where they were caught for good, and an accumulation of French phrases gradually became available to her and then part of her own speech.

She worked absolutely alone and lived alone, immersing herself in her work. She never let herself think of her mother, or of Ronny leading them all laughing across a field, or of Amelia stunned to silence, or Asher exuberant and young again with plans to be doing exactly what she was now doing, or Monty's eternal rueful bewilderment with his inability to understand what had stood right before him.

Half the time she forgot to eat and was lightheaded with hunger. She was white, ethereal, and almost unworldly. The young men around her who took her at her face value—as an untouchable saint—she didn't even see. The others, who mistook an American girl's freedom and informality for flirtatiousness, angered her. She was warned of what might happen by some of the other girl students who conducted themselves with the demureness and constraint of well-brought-up young European ladies.

"But what do I do?" Julie asked helplessly.

"It's the way you walk, the way you hold yourself, the way you sit, the way you look at a man—"

She was exasperated. "But I look at a man the way I look at a woman!"

"But you're not supposed to look at a man—not unless you know him well. Not straight into his eyes the way you do. You look as if you're flirting; and you laugh out loud with anyone you please."

"With anyone who says something amusing, yes. Is that wrong?"

The girls—one French and one Belgian—looked at each other and shook their heads.

"Don't you see?" she was asked despairingly. "Don't you see that we have to be particularly careful? Simply because we are doing something so advanced—we have to prove to the world that it is possible to be educated among men and still remain ladylike!"

She burst out laughing at them, but fingers were shaken at her.

"You'll see," she was told. "We know how the men here think, and you don't."

She found out when she went on a picnic with a group of students from the organic chemistry lab. A dozen of them, chattering like birds, rode the train out of Paris as far as Fontainebleau, where they dined in a restaurant under the trees and got a little drunk on wine and began to pair off. The young French geologist who worked next to her in the chemistry laboratory as her partner and had asked her along, walked with her through the woods until they were alone and suddenly caught her around the waist in the midst of a conversation. It had been a pleasant day up to then and Julie would normally have had no violent objections under the circumstances to being kissed, but the unexpectedness of the onslaught made her react as if a bee had flown into her face, and the young man was embarrassed and chagrined by his awkwardness and his failure. He put his arm around her neck, almost choking her as he bent her backward.

"You American girls!" he was saying. "We know you!"

"Don't be foolish," was all she could say, embarrassed by her own ineptness at the situation. He spoke no English, and he was only laughing at her as he pushed her down on the ground. Expertly, he held her jaws so that he could slip his tongue in and out of her mouth, and when she tried to writhe, he pinned her legs with a strength she didn't expect, forcing them apart with speed and expertise. Until that moment, she had never really believed that a woman could be raped without acquiescing to some extent, but now she knew with terror that it was more than possible. Back and back, she was bent. She froze in her groin as the knowledge paralyzed her, and she hated him so much that as his hot winey breath blew in her face, she wished he would die.

Then suddenly she was free. By some miracle, at the last moment he had tried to alter his grip on her exactly when she was straining in her supreme effort to free herself. She rolled wildly away from him and got to her feet where she stood dazed and panting. He sat there foolishly, looking up at her. They glared at each other. She was poised for flight or to scream as soon as her muscles could decide of their own accord what to do, and in that instant his twenty-two years of bourgeois training overcame the rapist in him. The insanity in his eyes died. Once again he became the docile student who had been working next to her all these months, the uninspired apprentice who had continually turned to her apparatus to see what she was doing so that he could follow her. He held out his hand to her.

"Help me up," he said, "I think I hurt my back."

In spite of herself, she had to laugh at him. "You're unbelievable!"

He spread his hands with a disarming shrug. "What do you want? Three times a week I'm with you—I touch you. I smell you. I look at your eyes, your hands—you're a beautiful girl. You are very very approachable. Our girls behave differently. What should I think?"

She didn't give him away when they rejoined the others, but after that she had neither time nor inclination for the men students. She was so impatient with their overtures—even those who were best-intentioned—that she was almost cruel, but in her absorption she never noticed it.

Then, without warning, she received news of her father's death. The letter was from her father's cousin, Priscilla's mother, and it was clear that no one was with him at the end. Probably no one had been with him for some time. He had died alone. She was crushed with guilt. She too was now alone. Nowhere was there any place to go any more to which she could attach the word "home." The little house on Music Street, wrote her cousin, was being sold by the bank to liquidate her father's debts. She was so oppressed by her feeling for him that she would sometimes cry out in physical anguish at the memory of it. Surprisingly, she had no tears, only a depthless sadness. She sensed uneasily that far down within her, some violent chain of action was being started—the way a tree begins to fall only long minutes after the killing cut has been made. She was frightened wondering if there hadn't been one thing which she might have done differently that would have kept Amelia alive, or Asher from going away, or herself from leaving her father. Half the time she felt on the verge of tears, but her eyes remained dry. She wrote to Monty another letter of explanation but tore it up the following day just as she had torn up all the previous ones as inadequate.

Then she discovered from an *affiche* on a kiosk that her cousin Priscilla was to sing in Paris. Prissy was someone Julie usually held warily at arm's length, because Prissy's violence of attachment or aversion could be tigerish and dangerous, but once again she made herself think only of Prissy's other side and that it had been Prissy's mother who had written of her father's death. Prissy could also be impulsive and warm, her advice was straight; and more than anything now, she and Julie shared the very roots whose tug so sharply reminded Julie where her heart was tied.

She wrote to Prissy, in care of the Opéra, hoping for no more than perhaps some roundabout news of her father's last year. In answer, though, Prissy herself came swirling into Julie's life, skirts rustling, feathers and boas fluttering with the largeness of her movements, horses, grooms, and coachmen bowing in her wake, a constant chatter of famous names glittering in the air about her like coins being scattered by a softhearted drunk as he reeled through an orphanage on Christmas Eve.

"You poor, poor baby!" she cried, folding Julie into her arms, and Julie's loneliness was lessened.

2

PRISSY HAD A FRIEND, A MAN; AND THIS FRIEND WAS A fool, but a fool of a certain kind. In appearance, he was the perfect *boulevardier:* clothes, hair, beard, glance, posture—all *à la page*—and yet it was half a disguise because really he was American. An ordinary American's mustache would have been long and had a romantic droop on either side of his mouth. This man's mustache was sharpened to stiletto points and waxed as erect as a butterfly's antenna. An American needing eyeglasses would have worn nippers, pince-nez, or even spectacles; this man sported a monocle. Lyman had a spurious charm that seemed to Julie to be almost greasy in its insincerity. He flaunted the names of men who were gods in her eyes, but he showed in less than three minutes' conversation that he hadn't the vaguest idea of what these men did or even why, through hard work and steadily applied brilliance, they should have achieved eminence. They were simply names to him. Perhaps he had met them in salons, but for him to pretend that he was familiar with their world was laughable. Julie met him in Prissy's flat and felt sorry for her. There had to be a certain dinginess in Prissy's soul for her to be able to accept this man on any terms.

What was most distasteful about him was not his fatuousness but the way he had of looking at a woman: as if he were seeing her not as she was, but either naked or mysteriously veiled in tantalizingly diaphanous garments. It put a certain dreamy glaze over his eyes because he was also transforming himself from the tail-coated fop into a king casually commandeering the soul of the slave who stood before him. Little flickers of cruelty and sheepish smiles chased successively across his face. His fingers just barely kept from reaching out to touch her wrist, her thigh, her knee. How could someone like Prissy bear him? How could she look at him so seriously —almost as if she were afraid of him?

Out of pity for Prissy, Julie tried to engage the man in conversation for at least a few moments. Then her revulsion proved too much, and she rose and fled. But her pity had all been wasted. Prissy understood nothing and followed her to the door, saying: "You mustn't be so shy, Julie dear! Lyman isn't all that overwhelming."

"Shy!" My God! thought Julie, and wondered in her turn what it was that drove Prissy. To Julie, anyone with a talent —any talent—was one of the world's elect, and someone with Prissy's voice and mastery no more needed a Lyman than she needed another pair of ears.

"But a woman always needs a man," Prissy insisted at another time in answer to another question. "Any man, because the truth is that this is a man's world."

"No, it's not," said Julie flatly. "It doesn't have to be."

"Well, it is! And that's why I've decided that Marcel Raubard is the man to help you!"

Julie turned to face her, dumb with astonishment at her cousin's stupidity. "Do you know who Marcel Raubard is, Prissy?"

"I do," she said calmly. "I've already met him, as I told you. And I'll tell you again: I'm going to make him help you."

"Prissy," Julie said helplessly. "People don't *make* Marcel Raubard do anything. Nobody could *make* him go on practicing medicine when he decided to give it up for research; and nobody could make him do comfortable research when he decided to do what he did. I beg of you, you'll only infuriate him if you try to interfere."

"And yet I'm bound to do it!" said Prissy stubbornly.

Julie met Marcel Raubard at a *soirée* to which the unexpected invitation read: *"Mademoiselle Mead sera chez elle—"* and gave the date. The note added: *"On dansera."* Mademoiselle was Lyman's sister and also one of Prissy's friends. Raubard appeared to be the terrifying rude man she had expected as she watched him from across the room, screened by the women's plumes, fans, naked shoulders, and glitter of moving jewels.

She had heard him often enough at lectures where he had spoken with harsh, gravel-throated certainty; and even here where she couldn't hear him, she could see his peremptory gestures and the sardonic flicks of his dark-bearded head as he made passing conversation with the group of homage-payers who clustered about him. Then, to her utter surprise when she found his eyes full on her, she caught a sadness behind the appearance of mockery, as if deep within him, streams of energy were being consumed by pain, wordlessly endured. In that brief glance, he was himself startled that she could see so swiftly and lucidly into what he wanted most to disguise. He held her for a moment, questioning her mutely, then he frowned and turned away. But after that he looked back again and again and even a third time demanding: "Did you really see it? What did you really see?"

She had the sense that he was stalking her through the crowd with his eyes. There was no place she could hide in this strange new terrain where richly dressed people were waited on by liveried servants, all of them moving slowly around huge rooms. The electric chandeliers would have been brilliant even with candlelight. All the voices about her had the velvet purr of assurance, yet no one impressed her except Raubard. He was the one man there who had pitted his mind against the vastness of the universe. The others here had their jewels, carriages, châteaux, and *hôtels particuliers* either because of passive inheritance or because their adroitly directed rapacity and guile had extorted goods or favors from people less adroit, less rapacious. She was embarrassed for Raubard, that a man of his gifts and attainments had to be here with people worth so much less than he. Why did he come?

She was alarmed to find that she was seated next to him at table; and she scarcely noticed that on her left was Prissy's friend Lyman; but Raubard did nothing to frighten her.

"You are the American student?" he asked in French.

He had leaned his head toward her slightly, looking down past her, not at her. It gave him a conspiratorial air.

"Yes."

"And you have studied in America?"

"Yes."

"Did you, by chance, ever attend any of the lectures of Willard Gibbs?"

"He lectures at Yale where I couldn't have heard him," she explained. "Women students aren't permitted there."

His "Ah!" was an acknowledgment of something conventionally pitiful, as if he had forgotten that she was crippled, or had asked about the health of a relative and had to be told that the funeral had been held last week. "Yes, of course! We, at last, are beginning to do things differently. But, Gibbs is your greatest scientist, you understand. We would like to bring him here, but he insists that he is too old to come, and so I intend to go there to work with him for a time before it is too late, *if* it can be arranged and *if* I can bring myself to go," he added drily.

She was silent for a moment. "You don't like the United States?"

"It is a matter of temperament, mademoiselle," he said gravely, but his mocking intent was clear. "I have many American friends here in Paris, and I find them on the whole sympathetic, but America itself—" Then as if he had gone too far, he defended himself: "After all, *you* left America to come to Paris—"

"I don't think of myself as having come to Paris—as *Paris,*" she said in a voice so low he had to lean still closer to hear. "I think of myself as coming to where I could work."

He smiled slightly, still without looking at her.

"For you Paris has no name then?"

"It doesn't need a name. To me, it is the place where work is being done by Le Châtelier, by Berthelot, by Duray, by you—"

His eyes veiled instantly. He was repelled and wary of what seemed to be obvious flattery. Then he saw that she was perfectly innocent in her honesty. His guard dropped as quickly as it had come up, and he looked at her searchingly. In that same moment he was too open to her; and it made him uncomfortable. He frowned and turned away to his partner on the other side.

His wife happened to glance up just then as he turned, and an expression of satisfaction spread slowly over her face, as if she had just become aware that what she was chewing so delicately was, after all, delicious.

It was the moment when one by one all the people at table were turning to the partner they had so far ignored, and in a moment, from her left, Lyman came leaning toward her.

"I hope he hasn't been bullying you too much," he said. "I had one ear cocked in your direction all the time and if it had seemed for one moment that you were in trouble, I was ready to come to your aid."

She assured him that she had never been in any danger.

"No, I can see that you can quite take care of yourself," he remarked. "And it is exactly because of that quality that I want to be of help to you. It is not only the Lord who helps those who help themselves."

"He has you to help Him do His helping?" Julie asked.

Lyman gave a startled little laugh, and his monocle dropped to the limit of its cord.

"Why, you're the very devil!" he said. "And yet you look so damned ethereal! What a combination!" He played with the eyeglass. "No, I do *not* consider myself the Lord's assistant, though my sister and I are bound to do what we can to give you a hand one way or another. We must get together and discuss your situation—in practical terms."

"Thank you," was all she said.

"So we can know exactly what you need, who you should know, where you should live. I don't mind telling you that we can make all the difference in your career," he said, putting in the monocle.

"That's very kind of you."

"Well, we do it because we get our own satisfaction out of it too, you know." His eyes were smoky with his vision in which she had probably been commanded to anoint the royal body with oil and honey and then to lick it all off with her tongue. "That's what makes it all so worth while," he said after a moment.

He was about to go on, but Julie's cousin called him peremptorily from the other side, irritated by the attention which he was paying Julie. Apparently she was a very possessive woman. The last thing in the world Julie wanted was any ill-feeling from her cousin. Probably she had been very obtuse! While Prissy had said that she would do her best to get Raubard to help she had very pointedly said nothing about Lyman. The message could have been—*leave Lyman alone!* That a woman as brilliantly attractive as Prissy could think herself seriously threatened by someone like Julie made her instantly pathetic in Julie's eyes and defenseless. At that moment, the tables were turned, and it was Julie who felt the protector.

She ate the exquisite food in silence for a while, relieved at last to be ignored.

"You cannot be serious about Paris," said Raubard leaning toward her again so that once more his scent and bulky warmth enveloped her. She still could not fully grasp the gentleness with which he was treating her in such violent contrast to his acerbity to everyone else. It was as if he considered her too fragile for the smash and crash of ordinary human contact. Instead of searing her with sarcasm, he said quietly:

"Paris has too much besides its science to offer to be ignored. There is art here, there is theater, there is thought, there is music, color—"

"There is everything," she agreed. "When I'm tired, or when I've worked too much, I walk down the boulevard to the Île de la Cité to visit the flower market, just to walk around the stalls and breathe the air and see the marvelous colors and the beautiful shapes. I love flowers, and there are no flowers anywhere like those I see in Paris. I rarely buy anything, but the flower sellers all know by now how I feel about flowers, and so they are all very kind."

He glanced his surprise, but he nodded silently.

"And then I find myself fascinated by the patterns of the cobblestones in the street," she said. "They are not laid out in lines and files as with us but in arcs that never begin and never end, each one opening out into others. So when it rains, here, the reflections from the wet pavement form marvelous patterns—"

Now he looked at her very sadly. "Yes, that is also Paris," he said gravely. "In addition to the Louvre, to the Académie, to the Sorbonne, we also have cobblestones—"

"And the Seine—"

"Ah, mademoiselle, only the quais are Paris; the water is not ours. It passes through."

"Now you're laughing at me!"

"I only defend Paris," he said smiling a little.

"But simply because I didn't praise everything in it. I *did* give all the praise I have for what I came for, while you didn't have one kind word for my entire country. Do you realize how you shrugged it away—almost a hundred million people spread over three thousand miles?"

"You are right," he said, still with that unexpected gentleness. "But you must understand that the America you know and the America I married are very different countries." He didn't even glance at his wife across the table, but for the moment that he thought about her, his nostrils were pinched, and his lips were thin with whatever was so taut within the hugeness of his body. When he looked at Julie again, what was gentle in him was gone, and his dark lips had a cruel shrewd little smile. "I am forty-three, you know," he said suddenly switching to French.

She said nothing.

"And who put you next to me?" he asked. "Or is it our

hostess's brother whom you are really sitting next to?" And he nodded slightly beyond her toward Lyman.

"I'm sitting between you," she replied, adopting French after him.

"No," he said lightly, and the smile persisted. "Nothing is ever that simple! Are you here to be 'helped'?" He gave the word a curl.

She sighed. "Whatever I'm here for, I'm sorry I'm here."

"Because of something I have said?"

"I told you," she said, looking down at her plate. It was difficult for her to talk, but still more difficult for her not to be honest. "I admire you enormously," she said with genuine distress.

"You mean my work?"

"Of course."

His smile disappeared. For a moment his face had that haunted vulnerability. Then the mockery returned, but only to his mouth.

"I was only an *écolier* in '71, but I am glad to say that I did take part in the fighting, and I want you to know that there was never a bullet used by either side in the Commune as lethal as your 'of course' just then! *My work!* My God!"

"I don't understand."

"I told you," he sounded almost bored. "I am a man of forty-three."

3

JULIE WAS USUALLY THE LAST TO LEAVE THE STUDENT laboratory—not because she worked more slowly than the others, but because she was almost twice as fast. Whenever possible, she used the long laboratory afternoon to recheck her own accuracy, to re-enjoy the pleasure of the precise manipulations, to watch once more how the fall of the one crucial drop of reagent could start a precipitation cloud forming within a clear liquid, or the way the fog of an unfocused microscope field came slowly into clarity on a microcrystallization.

From the beginning, she had the exquisite touch and the

deftness of the born experimentalist. Her eye was sensitive to almost a millimeter's difference; her fingers learned to have a fluid adjustability.

Whatever it was within her, she sensed it most sharply when she was almost alone in the huge high-windowed room. Then the dingy frosted glass panes glowed yellow-gray from the western autumnal sky. The laboratory air was tinged with brimstone incense—the odors of the analytical reagents. The very atmosphere itself was danger-filled, but the power on the bottle-lined shelves—acids, corrosive hydroxides, lethal sulfides—was power to be respected, even cherished, not feared.

This was the time of day she loved best even though she was so tired from having stood for hours at the stone-topped worktable that a three-minute rest as she perched on a high-legged lab stool could seem pure ecstasy.

She was seated that way one early evening when through the doorway she saw Raubard standing in the corridor, a heavy, cape-like, dark coat over his shoulders, a black low-crowned hat pulled down over one eye, and his cigarette a drooping white line across his black beard. He looked at her somberly for a moment; then with only the curtest nod to acknowledge that they had ever met, he looked beyond her for someone else—someone who was apparently not in the room at all because he turned and went away without coming in.

A week later, she saw him again—in the same hat and cape—this time standing on the Place de la Sorbonne, watching the entrance to the Faculté des Sciences from across the street. He stood on the corner in front of the Select Hotel and looked straight at her so that their eyes held for more than a moment. Again his head moved in that short curt nod as he took the cigarette that had been hanging in the corner of his mouth, threw it away, bouncing over the cobblestones. He turned his back on her and walked quickly away up the Rue Victor-Cousin toward the Rue Cujas.

She saw him still a third time outside the lecture hall as she passed Mahieu's, the crowded *tabac* on the corner of the Boulevard St. Michel and the Place de la Sorbonne. Again, he seemed to have the air of waiting there in the early dusk, totally oblivious to the noisy crowd of students who were milling around him. He nodded this time too, even touching the brim of his hat before he turned away. She crossed the boulevard and went down the time-haunted slope of Rue Monsieur le Prince, where her hurrying footsteps echoed.

The unevenly plastered walls of the ancient low buildings faced each other point-blank across the narrow street which hadn't changed much since Comte had walked home here past them fifty years earlier, since Cadoudal with an epaulette gone, breeches torn, boots clattering, had come running down this same hill to be trapped by the police on that corner down there after his attempt on Napoleon's life. Blaise Pascal used to stand at exactly that same window up there. Old ghosts were at home here in the shadows, and Julie walked along at home with the ghosts until one of them tapped her on the shoulder. She whirled to find herself facing a cloaked figure. It was Raubard, unaware that he had frightened her by his sudden appearance. He began to speak the moment she faced him, while she was deaf with the blood throbbing in her head.

"I understand that you could use some work." He spoke very rapidly. "There's an opening for a chemistry tutor in a girl's school. There aren't enough pupils to justify the salary of a regular teacher with a degree. It would be almost like taking private pupils two days a week. Professor Duray has recommended you for the position. I have passed on the recommendation to Mademoiselle Lafosse, the headmistress."

He had to say it all over again. He used exactly the same words and the same toneless intonation, as if he had already gone over it in his mind so many times that he had memorized a pattern. He stopped abruptly, wet his lips slowly, looking down at her with a perplexed frown, as if he were trying to understand something outside himself.

This time she understood part of what he was saying, but while the words were clear, it made no sense to her that he —of all people—was telling her—of all people—about a job. At last, the depth of her own paralysis began to dawn on him.

"You understand what I'm saying?" he asked. "This is a job for someone who still doesn't have a license. They are even prepared to accept a foreigner."

She nodded, then shook her head.

"You told me at dinner that you needed work."

Again she shook her head. Then she said, "I do, but I didn't tell you."

"Does it matter who told me?"

"No. I'm sorry. Of course not."

"And so I bore it in mind, mademoiselle, that's all."

"You mean—" She found difficulty saying it. "You mean there's a job for *me?*"

"You don't want it?"

"Oh, I do, indeed! Except—"

"Except what?" he demanded impatiently. He was frowning very deeply now, and she could see that she was irritating him with her stupidity.

"Except nothing."

"Then go tomorrow to this office at three o'clock."

He handed her a piece of paper. It had been rolled into a little cylinder so many times and so tightly that it felt like a cigarette. She started to unroll it and read it in the feeble light. He said abruptly: "That's all, mademoiselle," and walked away so quickly back toward the Boulevard St. Michel that she gave up trying to follow him to thank him.

The next day she went to the address he had given her. It was a small but very select academy on the other side of Paris on the Boulevard de Courcelles near the Parc Monceau. The headmistress was a spinster in her sixties who maintained nevertheless that her school had modern ideas. It was therefore decided that the older girls at least could be introduced to some of the concepts of science.

"So, you have finally returned to Paris, mademoiselle," she said, and Julie replied that she had never been outside the city. It was the lady's turn to be surprised. "But my neighbor Professor Raubard told me weeks ago that he wanted you to have the position when I asked him for a recommendation. He said, though, that he was unable to find you."

"I see," Julie said slowly, and looked down at her hands clasped in her lap.

"You have rather a strong accent, mademoiselle," observed Mlle. Lafosse.

"Yes, mademoiselle," said Julie.

"You are English?"

"No, mademoiselle, American."

The lady's face fell, but then she shrugged. "However, your recommendation is so impressive that I can't ignore it," she said and described to Julie her duties. Julie didn't hear one word she said. "You may start next Thursday," Julie was told.

Five days after that, there was a knock on her door. She opened, to see to her surprise the concierge standing there, a peppery little woman, who had a perpetual frown as she sat busily knitting or peeling vegetables by the window of her dismal little loge. Julie couldn't imagine why she was there. She had come to Julie before only for the rent, but her rent was paid.

"This monsieur wants to see you," the concierge said nodding suspiciously into the darkness behind her. "Is it all right?"

Raubard stood there, with the same tormented expression she had caught at the dinner party, but he was saying nothing, waiting for her to declare her acceptance or rejection.

"Yes, of course," Julie said to the concierge, and then remembered to add, still amazed at the woman's concern for her, "Thank you, madame." The woman turned away down the dark narrow stairs.

After a moment, Julie stood aside, and held the door open for her guest. Raubard came into the candlelight. He almost touched the garret ceiling, and his shadow on the wall was monstrous as he slipped the hat off. He looked around the small room.

"I understand that you accepted the position," he said. "Have you started yet?"

"Yes."

"Do you think it will suit?"

"Oh yes, monsieur, I'll work very hard at it," she promised, yet when he turned, she saw that he hadn't meant to ask that at all. He looked vexed, and this frightened her: he might hold her responsible for his discomfort. She quickly offered him the chair which she took away from the book-and-paper-covered table. He shook his head quickly—too quickly.

"Thank you, mademoiselle, but no," he said, "I must go. I simply stopped to see if everything was going well."

"And come up four flights? It was very kind of you." If he had wanted to, he could have beckoned a finger at her at the college at the end of any of his two lectures a week and have her come down the amphitheater aisle to his lectern where he could have put the same question to her. Yet at the lectures, he never even nodded to her nor to any of his other students. He came in and went out, blind and deaf to everyone and everything but his own thoughts. Now, in her room, he was thoroughly ill at ease. He kept turning this way and that, as if he were impatient to get away, remaining only at her insistence.

"I was just going by," he said. "I simply stopped to see if everything was going well." He had forgotten that he already said that.

"Thank you, monsieur, you are very kind to me. And I must thank my cousin too."

"Your cousin? What cousin?"

"Madame Portilea. You said she told you about me. Didn't she give you my address?"

"No, mademoiselle, she did not," he said coldly. "And I did not help you because of her, but because Professor Duray gave me your name when I asked who was his most talented pupil. I had been asked to recommend someone. I told you that. I do not have a reputation for doing favors," he went on.

"Yes, monsieur."

"And your cousin would never have given me your address. It was not meant for me. Nor would I have asked for it."

"Yes, monsieur," she said again, although her mind was saying very rationally that he must have asked someone—and the thought came to her as a complete surprise—or he had followed her home! It was incomprehensible, yet it fitted with the accidental meetings that had been happening so frequently. The idea that a man so remote, with such vast intelligence, and so godlike, might think of her as a woman left her speechless: her mouth hung open. He swung the hat back onto his head, pulling it down sharply over one brow.

"That is all, mademoiselle," he said, as if it were he who was dismissing her. He took another glance around him. "I hope the salary will make your studies easier." She nodded her thanks, but he went on in a very different voice—softer, reflective, "Although why I should be surprised by what I see here, I can't imagine! I didn't even have this much in the room I had as a student down the hill on the Rue Danton in a house even older than this. But I was happy there," he added more softly. "And Paris was smaller, brighter, gayer, more cruel in some ways, and more kind in others, and I never thought the day would come when it would be possible to be a Member of the Academy and at the same time so damned moonstruck—!" His voice had taken on an edge. He stopped abruptly and walked out of the door, growling, "Good-by, mademoiselle!" and slammed the door behind him.

Her heart was pounding so hard that it ached. She had to sit down. Her lips were dry, her body was on fire. Two days later, at his lecture, he came into the amphitheater, lectured for an hour and a half, then walked out without once glancing at her. She hadn't expected him to, yet she walked across Rue St. Jacques away from the college slowly, dazed, blind to the carriages, cyclists, and drays. The pain in her chest from her pounding heart was almost suffocating. Late that same afternoon, when she was at work in her room, she heard the heavy tread coming up the stairs and the pencil fell limply from her fingers onto the paper covered with notes. Again her lips went dry. By the time the knock came on her door, her heart had started that unbearable pounding. She could do nothing more than rise, trying to catch her breath. She called for him to come in. She had to call twice because her voice was faint in her dry throat. He opened the door himself, frowning as he stood there. He let the door close slowly behind him, and took off his hat. Then he put his fingers to the top button of his coat. They paused there, asking her permission. Even before he put it into words, she nodded.

Finally she found her voice, and it was suddenly crucial to tell him the most essential truth about herself—because nothing between them could be trivial. She didn't even know what she wanted to say until she heard herself blurting: "You have to know how important it is for me to be here—in Paris—for me to be a scientist." The words flooded out of her without making the sense she intended.

He frowned and stopped with his coat half off. "Are you making a condition?" he demanded. His voice was very harsh, but really it was heartbroken. "I make no conditions on you. Say one word and I'll turn around and go away. Send me away if you want. Nothing will change for you, I promise you that."

She shook her head. "No, it was no condition. It was that I wanted you to know about me."

"I already do. The way you know about me."

"I do!" she said with relief. She put her hand to her heart. "It hurts me here so!" she said in a small voice. "Please— make it stop!"

4

ACTUALLY SHE KNEW NOTHING ABOUT HIM EXCEPT THE mountainous presence; huge, hard beneath smooth white skin, and so strong that she could be lifted, set down, carried as if she were a leaf in his big dry hands. It was he who embraced her. Her reach was as inadequate to clasp him as to encompass a tree a century old. His hair, the down on his arms and chest, his Mephistophelean beard were soft, even though each strand was thick and looked like a wire. His entire being was like that: tough and hard to the eye, relaxed to her touch, until alarm or anger turned the muscles beneath the skin to metal.

What she felt for him had no name, nor any resemblance to anything she had ever felt before: it was too primitive, too atavistic, too convulsive and overwhelming in its pleasure; too suffused with an enthrallment that was mystic, almost religious. There was no feeling that she had made a choice from possible alternatives. Some vast, supreme fate had selected her from all the world and ordained what was to happen to her, and she could only submit, glad and grateful. When he was pleased, she was rewarded. When he wasn't, she suffered the agony of inadequacy. She was a priestess serving the divine being who materialized and disappeared at will, not the mistress of a man who came up her stairs a few times a week at dusk on his way home.

He wanted her to move to more suitable quarters, but she refused. He wanted to give her money to buy things for herself, but she said she had her salary. He came then with gifts she couldn't refuse without looking foolish; a secondhand chair so at least they could both sit at the same time. He took some well-scoured, slightly battered pots out from under his cape, silently conjuring them while the smoke from the cigarette that dangled from his red lips curled up into whorls around his arched eyebrows. She laughed. He made magic passes with his empty hands to prove they were empty, then reached back into the cape and pulled out what looked like a square of some blue material. She took one end, but it seemed endless. Yard after yard came out and finally in her hands was more than enough for curtains for the windows and to cover the open shelves.

"All right," she said, laughing. "But no more!"

The next time the magician conjured a quilt of down from somewhere because he had noticed that she had been using her overcoat as an extra blanket. At times, though, sometimes in the midst of laughter, on sudden impulse she took his big hand and kissed it, rubbing her cheek against his palm. Then he would slowly and gently stroke her hair with his other hand; but when she'd look up at him, his face would be deep with pain.

Yet he could make her laugh, and he laughed himself. The more they saw each other, and the tenderer he became, the more he also became what he was everywhere else: sharp, amusingly bitter with an anti-romanticism that was infused with a passionate hatred for love.

The very word made him clasp his head in pantomime of revulsion. Once he stood that way for a moment, and then his voice came out in almost a shout of rage. He claimed that love was nothing but a license given to two decent people to destroy each other! He had twenty different ways of saying to her: "You don't love me!" and not one of them was accusation. Any kind of sentimentality could bring a string of sulfurous aphorisms to his sensuous red lips, thinned to anger.

He was married to the daughter of a brilliant member of the French Academy of Medicine—an American political refugee who had served with the Confederate Army as a young man, and had been naturalized a Frenchman by the Emperor himself.

There was something either tragic or frightening between Raubard and his wife, and Julie was reluctant to hear what it was, as reluctant as he was to talk about it.

"Can't you leave her?"

"I have children!" he shouted at her, as if her failure to understand were as brutal an attack on him as all the things he had just listed. "I love my children! I leave her every day in my work, and that's all the escape I want."

"All?" asked Julie because she had suddenly surmised something else.

"No, not all," he said with sudden quiet. His dark gaze was level on her through the cigarette smoke. He took the cigarette out of his mouth deliberately so that he could say what he had to say with unimpeded clarity. "Within the past few years, I've begun to have other women—and not one until you meant anything to me. That's why you terrify me."

"I terrify *you?*" she burst out at the enormity of the statement. "You appall *me!*"

"Oh no!" he cried, and the harshness in his eyes and voice drained away like sand in rain, leaving what was always beneath the brittle cover: the deeply sensitive man, full of affection; so twisted by life that the disguise behind which he hid was the reverse of everything he could be naturally.

He came at different times of the day, though never on the days of his lectures. If she weren't home, he let himself in with a key they had made for him, took paper out of his pocket on which he made some notes or calculations, and was soon busy at his work as if he were in his own study. If she came in after he had gone, his cigarette smoke still hung in the air, some of his discarded papers were crumpled in the fireplace along with the burnt cigarette stubs. Sometimes he brought cheese from the *crémerie* or something from the *charcuterie;* the remains of the food stood in crumbs on a plate on the shelf. Sometimes he was still there when she came in from her own teaching or exhausted from the hours of delicate laboratory work. She'd lean back against the door, enjoying the sight of him in her room before she closed her eyes to rest for a moment. Then she'd take out a few hairpins, shake her head and let the hair come tumbling down below her shoulders. When she opened her eyes again, he was looking at her from her chair at the desk—his hand still poised over the paper, but there was tenderness in his eyes, desire, a plea, even though the red lips had a slight irony in their smile. His glance would slide sideways to the bed, and then return to his work because his slight nod in the bed's direction had given his order, which was, very simply, "Take your clothes off." When she was ready, the pen's scratching would stop, and he would join her.

It was the only time she could speak to him with tenderness. Even when his sarcasm came flicking at her, it was impossible for her to be angry with him. Beyond his curled lip and growling voice, his eyes held something that watched her anxiously and pleaded for the fullest depth of her feeling for him. In the act of love, his lips were clamped in an angry tight line as if to keep himself from uttering the impulsive endearments that kept springing from his heart. Afterward he would hold her to him almost with desperation, his eyes pressed tight, murmuring, "My God, My God, My God!" and his devotion to her, however he attempted to disguise it, enveloped her like summer sunshine.

From Friday to Sunday she never saw him. He disappeared into some other existence, some other self, which she thought of as majestic, almost imperial, until once and only once, by accident, she saw his Sunday self with his family.

It was on a Sunday morning, a warm day in May, and the sky above the city was a childish blue with white sheeplike clouds. Young couples on bicycles, some riding side by side, some in tandem, flicked and sparkled along the boulevards among the carriages, fiacres, and automobiles—all heading toward the open country. Picnicking families converged on the Gare St. Lazare to take the trains out to the forests of St. Germain and St. Cloud—students, artisans, shopkeepers—swarms of straw-hatted parents, sailor-suited children, all laden with bundles, baskets, sand pails and shovels—all converging from every direction into a broad, funneling stream into the station entrances.

Something familiar caught Julie's eyes, and there she saw him: his wife slightly ahead of him, and three hurrying children—two girls with sailor hats and blouses and flounced serge skirts that came to their black-stockinged knees; and a boy, also black-stockinged to above his knees and also wearing a black straw hat held in place with a black elastic band. They were all carrying their little packages, but the heaviest load by far hung in two huge baskets, which Raubard, sweating and bowed at his shoulders, sagging at his knees, carried in either hand, so heavy, and so large that his arms stuck out on either side. His shuffle was almost bearlike. His broad-brimmed white hat was on the back of his head, his face was red with exertion, and a handkerchief was stuffed into his collar to catch the sweat that made his face shine in the sun. He looked as conventional as all the other fathers; droop-shouldered and wooden-faced with the loads they were docilely carrying for their families. He was just an ordinary man, looking a little heavy in the waist, more than a little tired of his life, weary even of his own weight and hopelessness. He was different from the others only because of his eyes of pain and because of the knowledge she had of his piercing mind and what he had already done with it.

She never told him that she had seen him that day; but the

sight of him so hot, so laden, trapped, unprotected, so ordinary, so hopelessly heartbroken, made her love for him all the more tender and protective.

5

FROM THE TIME THEY BEGAN TO BE TOGETHER, THE clock stopped and the calendar froze until August, when he left to join his family in Brittany for six long weeks. There was a unique colony on the channel coast, the small fishing village called "Port Science" by those who knew that the summer colonists walking around in the long bathing suits, sandals, and white duck were the physicists, chemists, biologists, and mathematicians who made up the Institute of France and Nobel laureates. To Julie, his departure was something to be taken fatalistically—the way she would have expected a god to return from time to time to Olympus. It was a cool summer fortunately, and she used the time to prepare for the heavy year to come because she was going to present herself as a candidate for a *licence ès sciences*.

When he returned in the fall it was as if he had never been away, but now time overwhelmed her. Between her work as tutor, her own studies, her few hours with Marcel, and her preparations for the coming examinations, there were hardly enough minutes left over to sleep. She was always rushing, always tired, but always happy.

A couple of notes from her cousin around the end of September went unanswered at first because Prissy had become unreal and beyond communication. At last, though, Julie replied. She remembered all that Prissy had offered to do for her and indirectly actually *had* done. But Marcel picked up one of the notes Julie had left lying around. He was about to toss it aside when he saw the name and address of the sender.

"What are you doing with this woman?" he demanded, shaking the note.

"What woman?" Then she saw what he was holding. "That's Prissy! She's my cousin."

"Have nothing to do with her!"

"What are you talking about?" she asked in stupefaction.

"I insist that you have nothing to do with her!" he repeated angrily. "She's a danger to you. What she stands for—what she is!" He ripped the letter in half, then ripped it again. "That's how she should be treated! I tell you that woman is dreadful!"

"What are you doing to me?" Julie cried. She bent to her knees to pick the pieces from the floor. She rose clutching them. "This is all that's left of my family! You've got cousins, brothers, sisters, aunts, uncles, children. This city, this whole country, is your home. But I'm all alone except for this! Only one person in this city, on this entire continent, knows the country road on which I was born, or what my parents looked like. Except for you and her, nobody knows me even *now,* and you won't speak my own language to me. I have to talk to you with an accent—with the grammar of an illiterate!"

His face had been stricken with a sudden understanding of her isolation, but as soon as she began to speak of his language, he looked bewildered.

"But we speak French!" he said helplessly, as if to be speaking even bad French ought to be more of a pleasure for her than the English of the poets. "And you *do* have me. And this woman is dangerous for you!"

"Dangerous!"

"Yes, dangerous! Don't you know who she is?" He spat out a word that was clearly supposed to be shattering in its brutality, but Julie only stared at him in her innocence. "Why, you don't even speak the French of an illiterate!" He mocked her. "She was fattening you up for that odious man—"

"What man—?"

"That half man," he went on, his hand cupped and fingers touching—a wagging white tulip of utter contempt, "that man who pursues other men by touching the women they touch, by kissing the mouths they kiss—that's the man who had his toad's eyes on you, and eventually she was going to get you for him!"

Julie hooted with laughter. "You don't know Prissy!"

"And you don't know Paris. And you don't know those people over there on the other side of the river! My wife's dear friends! I loathe them. I loathe their rich money, their rich clothes, their rich houses, their rich way of buying buying buying stones, trees, horses, pictures, or people; *and* their bad French—"

Again Julie laughed. "Their worst sin," she said in English. "You can't stand bad French!"

"It hurts my ears," he admitted, but he was beginning to smile a little. "The French ear—" he cut off his lecture and waved it away. "This is something we understand only among ourselves."

"Then let's spare your French ears," she went on in English. "From now on, *you* be the one who speaks with the accent. We'll speak *my* language for a change."

"You're joking!" he said in French. He had become pale, quiet.

"Not at all!"

"I *won't* speak English to you! And I must ask you not to speak English to me!"

"But why?"

"Because it is the language which my wife speaks to me!"

She felt such a queasiness in her heart that she thought she was going to vomit.

"And I am not good enough to speak the same language as your wife?"

Blood darkened his face, and he shouted at her: "You're *too* good! I *hate* English! I hate the cold sneering sound she gives it! To me English is the language of a half-demented woman! Speak French to me, for God's sake! The little mistakes you make aren't mistakes, they're as much a part of you as your fingers, or the catch in your voice, or the way you walk. I love your French!"

The argument over Prissy had been sidetracked, not ended; because when Prissy finally did come of her own accord to see why Julie never came any more, Marcel happened in a moment later. They went at each other like dry wood and flame, and Prissy walked out. Julie started after her, but he caught her arm and held her. "Let her go! That woman sees men only as animals," he said bitterly. "She makes them know it. The result is they *do* become animals—to her!"

"You were horrible to her!" Julie said trying to break away from him. "You had no right to talk to her that way in my home!"

"Your home?" Ironically, he slowly turned his head to look at "her home." Then he bowed: "Excuse me, mademoiselle, if I defended this château against the wrong dragon! Did I soil your magnificent tapestries with blood? I thought I was fighting an ogre, not your fairy godmother in disguise!"

Julie stood there, slowly rubbing her arms. Her face was white; one foot was tapping impatiently.

"Mister, when you want to be," she said in plain American, drawling it out in true dockside Vineyard style, "you can be a real Jim-dandy six-pronged son of a nickel-plate bitch!"

"What?" he said. "What?"

She shook her head. "You may hate the English language," she went on implacably in English, "but there are whole mountain ranges of it you have never heard. Never!" she added.

She belatedly pursued Prissy to her own flat across the river, but Prissy was in a lurid rage. There was no peace to be made. Only when Julie left did it occur to her that Prissy's bitterness was that of a jealous woman. Julie walked back to the left bank across the elegant new Alexandre bridge, her head bent against a bleak October wind. The sky was dark and violent except for the western horizon, where the setting sun made an orange clarity. Against that distant light, the entire city: chimney pots, church spires, and bridges stood out in a spiny black silhouette of scissored sharpness. All about her—even her mind—was a brutal vividness. She asked: if Prissy's violence against Marcel was really the underside of her desire for him, then what was Marcel's rage against Prissy? Was he angry with her because she was the woman of another man? Julie felt small and drab between them. There they were: each one wanting the other, and neither seeing that it was mutual. Julie couldn't bear the humiliating idea that she was benefiting only by a foolish misunderstanding. It was as horrible as the idea of Marcel with another woman. Both visions tortured her. As she walked along the quai and then toward St. Germain des Prés, she became colder and harder within herself. She was in an icy fury when she finally let herself into her room. Marcel was seated at her table, working under the green-shaded light of the new oil lamp. His pen was scratching over paper, diagraming some apparatus that continued to displease him.

She watched him angrily without a word. He didn't look up at her. Finally, she took off her hat and shook her hair loose.

"I went to see my cousin Prissy," she announced.

He said nothing, the scratching continued, but he had hardened.

She let fly with her bombshell.

"And any time you want her, you can have her. She's mad for you."

The pen scratching went on without interruption.

"Did you hear me?" she said.

"Yes."

"And?" she demanded sharply.

He put his pen down slowly.

"I know all about that cousin of yours," he said. "And I don't want her. I want you." He picked up the pen again, crossed out his sketch and began all over again.

6

MANY TIMES THIS WAS TO HAPPEN: INTO A GLASS BEAKER the size of a water tumbler, full almost to the brim with transparent liquid, Julie released a single drop of a second liquid from a pipette's stem. The liquid sphere, two millimeters across, dropped through the air and broke the surface into ripples, and then the ripples died away.

In the late afternoon of the laboratory day, minutes ticked away. Then imperceptibly, a milky mist began to suffuse through the clear liquid, seeming to come from everywhere within it at once. The mist thickened to opacity and the beaker's liquid became like milk.

The chronograph ticked away more minutes, then just beneath the upper surface of the liquid a faint line of transparency reappeared, so thin it might have been a trick of light. The cloud of white within the beaker descended with the timeless patience of the inorganic world where nothing dies and nothing lives; where there is only endless change.

Julie was fascinated by the precipitation: but its simplicity was like the simplicity of a daisy—the more intently one examined it, the more one found that could fascinate, the more there was to puzzle about.

To Julie, the emergence of solid within liquid was almost as much a wonder as Creation itself. Intuitively she sensed a connection, but the more she thought about it, the more it eluded her. Always in the back of her mind, as she hurried up the Rue Monsieur le Prince and crossed the Place de la

Sorbonne, or hurried within the university itself through the echoing corridors of the Galerie Dumas, or the Galerie Bernard which led to the physics and chemistry rooms, there was a picture as stark as the first day of the world—a black liquid void without end—and diffused throughout this inconceivable volume were tiny white points and grains, each one having the inexplicable power of seeking what it needed from the surrounding medium to reproduce and augment itself.

Her obsession was primitive and naïve. She didn't even realize that she was circling into the very field that was Marcel's specialty—the dynamic nature of chemical equilibrium. He had such a profound grasp of the molecular dynamics of any chemical reaction that he could almost see how the reacting molecules darted endlessly within the confines of the volume of a flask, colliding with each other by chance, combining momentarily only on collision and, when sufficiently energized by other collisions, separating again; so that at no particular time could one say that any irreversible change had taken place. The world of chemistry as Raubard saw it was mobile, tentative, loaded with change.

"You don't pay attention to my lectures!" he said to her irritably. It was winter and the table lamp was lit. His face, half in and half out of the shadow, looked masked. "You should have known that all along I have been talking about just such things. They're the physical embodiment of the ideas. Does it mean that, to you, ideas have no life?"

She was no longer afraid to argue with him about what could exist between a man and a woman as lovers, but she never argued with him as a student. Then she was docile, silent, and pale. More than anyone else, she was aware of how little she knew compared to him. His prestige was overpowering. He had very little patience as a teacher. His standards were far too high to tolerate the sort of mistakes one made while learning—even when they indicated increasing mastery. He had no temperament for disciples. Only colleagues interested him. He had been that way ever since he had been twenty-two and an eleven-page paper of his had created a sensation when he read it at the International Chemical Congress at Brussels.

"You're wasting your time in the analytical laboratory," he told her one day. When he was restless, he paced the small room, pausing abruptly every now and then at the little window which was so high that only he was tall enough to look through it down at the roofs of Paris. All she ever saw was sky. He stood there for a moment, frowning, as if the Louvre, which he could see in the distance, displeased him. "It's no longer a challenge to you," he said, turning to her suddenly. She was at the stove preparing tea. "What you don't know about techniques now, you can look up whenever you need something. I've watched you—"

"When?" She went on pouring the tea into cups because she didn't really believe him. "You never come into the laboratory."

"I've stood outside in the corridor. I saw how well you use your hands now. It's time you learned to use your mind as well. The chemistry of test tubes is meaningless unless it corroborates or amplifies an idea. Ideas! Ideas are everything!"

She put the teapot down.

"Georges Claudet is coming back to Paris next month," she said. She made it sound like a challenge. "Would he permit me to do something in his laboratory?"

Raubard had been about to sit in his accustomed place at the table, but the apparent *non sequitur* stopped him. "To do what? You're not ready yet."

"But you just said I was."

"I said nothing of the sort! I said it was time to learn to use your mind for something original."

He himself published only a fraction of the actual research work he performed. His notebooks were treasurehouses of highly original experimental results that he didn't think worth reporting. He regarded experimental work deductively rather than in an inductive light. Most of all, though, he was spoiled by the success of that first paper. He had been only a twenty-two-year-old medical student at a time when thermodynamics was as rarefied and as little understood as relativity was to be half a century later, but he had the temerity to argue that the carbon atom be thought of as having the configuration of a tetrahedron, not, as Van't Hoff and Le Bel argued, from considerations of space; but on the basis of energy considerations. He was one of the first to realize what Willard Gibbs was doing, just as Gibbs was one of the first to realize that Raubard was destined to be the man who would take up from where he himself would one day leave off.

Since then, though, Raubard had been unwilling to publish anything less grand than a real *aperçu*. This would have been pure arrogance if it hadn't been justified. By his middle forties, he had three such major insights to his credit, any one of which alone would have satisfied another man as a crowning contribution to a lifetime of work. Raubard continued to experiment incessantly—but always by himself. His one assistant was not even a chemist, but a semi-illiterate mechanic who helped him build apparatus and kept his tiny laboratory in order. Not even Julie dared dream of working with him.

"Ideas!" he said to her continually that winter. "Where are your ideas?"

"I can't think in the abstract," she said wretchedly. "It has to start with something real. I told you, it has to come from my hands."

"Ah, an excuse! Nothing more!" He was impatient. "Besides Claudet has nothing for you at present," he told her finally. It was already spring and they were just returning from a walk in the Luxembourg Gardens. "You see, I did ask him for you, but as I predicted, he says you're not ready."

"But how can he say that?" She had been leading the way up the poorly lit staircase, but she was so surprised by what he said that she stopped in the half-darkness and turned. "He doesn't even know me!"

"Yes, he does. Keep going! He remembers you from Boston." He followed her up the rest of the way to her landing, watching her curiously. "You made an unusual impression on him. Women usually don't."

"But perhaps I can explain to him—"

Marcel put her aside as she seemed to take a moment too long to open the door. "Explain nothing. Don't see him. Believe me. I know Claudet. He was my own pupil. No one can seem more quiet, more gentle; but no one can be more stubborn, more implacable. Besides, he's right," Raubard went on reasonably as the door opened for him. He let her precede him. "I wouldn't take you on myself. You're absolutely green, and besides you're a woman—"

She went pale as she turned on him, blocking the doorway. "I came to France precisely *because* I'm a woman. Claudet himself told me—!" She was stuttering with her fury. "How dare he! How dare *you*—!"

"Shh!" He put his forefinger to her lips, then again moved her gently aside so that he too could enter the dusk-lit room. "What's all the excitement for? Do you want to call out the neighbors? Turn on some light, for God's sake! Look at you!"

"Don't treat me that way!"

"How *should* I treat you?"

"Like a woman whose mind you respected!"

"Oh my God!" he said, putting his hands to his head. "I don't want any damned hysterics from *you*, of all people!"

"And I don't want any male chauvinism from *you*, of all people!"

"What's come over you?" he asked. "Why such rage?"

"Because of the way you spoke. You said Claudet was right—"

"To hell with Claudet! I refuse to fight with you about him! I refuse to fight with you about anything!" he shouted. He walked up and down in the tiny room. At last he was the one who set the lamp glowing, and the light seemed to promise peace. He took her hands in his. "I need you too much. I need your calmness, your good sense, your sympathy, your youth—"

"And not as a woman?" she asked.

"Oh my God!" he shouted again in an eruption of temper. "The argument began because I *said* you were a woman. Then you get angry because you want to be considered as a mind—whatever that is! Now when I speak of *all* the things you mean to me, you demand that I think of you again as a woman! Never in the world was there ever such damnable inconsistency! You want everything!"

She stood there by the table, subdued by the fury she had aroused in him, yet behind her lowered eyes she was secretly pleased that in spite of all his refusals, he had actually approached Georges Claudet on her behalf. He continued to shout at her, but she no longer listened too intently. She felt only very tender and grateful to him, not hearing him because she had long since lost her terror of his storming tongue, retaining only a taut wariness that was even exhilarating in a way.

"I want no more talk about laboratories," he was saying. "Not until you show that you can come up with an idea of your own worth working on. I don't care how little it is, just let it be valid!"

She glared at him and silently determined to vindicate herself.

In spite of what he had said, she sensed that she was far more an experimentalist than a theoretician. She immediately cast around for an opening through her other professors, not telling Marcel of her attempts. In the meantime she set to work on theory under his guidance. He was a scathing perfectionist of a teacher, but she was grateful to him for the change he was creating in her; she could feel it within herself as an increasing mastery of her work. She was calmly determined all that spring as the examinations approached and she was calmly determined when she took them in July. A week later she stood in the rear of the amphitheater filled with other students—all of them accompanied by parents and friends—to learn the names of those who had passed. They were to be read off in order of merit. She was the only one there who was alone, but she was used to the half-ache of loneliness. Her name was second out of forty-three. She had her degree—now she was ready to take a post. But where it could come from, she didn't know. Her classmates murmured congratulations as she moved among them to the door—but she could no longer bear to remain here where everything seemed finished for her.

7

SHE WAS LEAVING THE BUILDING WHEN THE *préparateur* of her laboratory stopped her after having pursued her down the corridor. He had been sent by the professor to fetch her. She felt a pang of alarm: was there going to be a change in her standing? The young instructor laughed: No, he had good news—there was a temporary opening in the department's research laboratory, and the old man had sent out word that he wanted the most promising experimentalist from the graduating class.

"But I was second," she said.

"You were second only in the written examination; you were first under me," he replied. The student who had placed first in the examination was really a theoretician, inept with his hands. "If he walked through a lab with his hands in his pocket, he'd still break every piece of apparatus in the room. No, even if you're a girl, you're the one. I had my eye on you from the first day."

He took her up the spiral staircase and knocked on the

heavy wooden door to the private study just above the chemistry amphitheater. When the command came to enter, he pushed the door open and then left her to the old man's mercy. *"Bonne chance!"* he whispered.

Felix Salomon-Delachet was then well past seventy-five, a veteran from the days of Liebig, Dumas, and Berthollet, half a century earlier. He was stiff, bald, and half blind, but his ideas were as active as ever. He believed so devoutly in the old-fashioned tradition of the professor's aloofness from his students that generals were said to be less unbending to the conscripts doing military service than Salomon-Delachet had been to them when they had been his apprentice scientists. He peered up at her coldly from his old-fashioned black leather chair.

"Mademoiselle!" he barked. He remained seated. She stood.

"Yes, *M. le professeur!*"

"You have read, mademoiselle, that chemical reaction involves a change of energy with every change of substance?" His high-pitched voice was dry and pedantic as he led her through the catechism.

"Yes, *M. le professeur!*"

"Yet you are also aware that there are exceptions which have still not been explained by the new molecular theory?"

"Yes, *M. le professeur!*" she answered mechanically, but puzzled by the elementary questions.

"And that one of these exceptions is the realm of the dilute electrolytic solutions?"

Her response was slower this time. She was becoming wary. At any moment, he might leap from the obvious to the complex.

"Sit down, mademoiselle," he said brusquely. He pointed to a straight-backed, uncomfortable-looking chair. She sat with her hands in her lap, her gaze straight on him. "I have some analytical work to be done, and I am told that you are careful and precise. I already have four *préparateurs particuliers* working on different phases of this problem, and I have a seven-month opening for a fifth worker. You are a woman, it is true, but then, times change. Are you interested in a laboratory post or are you preparing to compete in next month's *agrégation* for a teaching position?"

"Research, monsieur le professeur."

"Very well. The research post is yours. There will be certain problems because you are not a man, but once you establish yourself as a good worker you will find the others ready to overlook your difference. This is the research: when dilute solutions of sodium nitrate and potassium chloride are mixed, the two compounds become four compounds, but no heat of formation is produced. I want to know: *why not?*"

She looked at him blankly, not knowing what to reply.

"That's all," he said. "That's the problem; *why not?* One mixes the two solutions and no heat is produced. Two compounds become four compounds. Chemical reaction has obviously taken place—but where is the heat that the theory requires? Or is the theory wrong? That is all, mademoiselle." His tone told her to get up, and she did. He seemed unaware of her mystification. "Report to Room 317. I expect you to justify your recommendations. Bring me interesting results."

He swung his chair around, leaving her nothing to do but withdraw. She went out of the stuffy little office in half a trance, went to Room 317 to be informed by a card tacked to the door that all enquirers were to return the following morning, then just as dazedly kept on going out the other side of the building through the entrance on the Rue St. Jacques, then down the hill, and across the cobbled street which gleamed in a soft July rain, to the Rue des Ecoles. There a side entrance to the Collège de France led upstairs to Marcel's study. This was where he worked, experimented, and received visits from his students, but this was the first time she had ever gone to him there. She knocked lightly on the door and then turned the knob. The knob was wrenched out of her hand by being turned violently from the inside. Marcel appeared himself in the doorway, too obviously blocking her way, his face red and strained.

"Mademoiselle, I am occupied at the moment," he said very formally. Behind him, she could see a narrow section of the room. "Please return in an hour or so." As he closed the door, a green velvet shoulder moved swiftly behind his back, hurrying to peer past him into the corridor before the door closed to see the visitor being called "mademoiselle."

Julie turned away dumbly. There had been something proprietary in the movement of that green velvet—it had felt free to pry.

She stood once again in the rain on the Rue des Ecoles, paused on the wet stone, and then hurried off. She didn't want to see who would be coming out. She sat inside a little bistro past the Balzar, and through the bleared glass watched the traffic on the Boulevard St. Michel—the streaming horses, the carriages beneath the hunched coachmen closed in with leather panels, the pedestrians under their umbrellas. An omnibus passed, and its upper deck too was covered with black umbrellas. Then, almost abruptly, the sun came out. She ordered a cup of tea which she touched only with her hands to warm them against the crockery and sat in a dumb agony. What was she waiting for? Why should she go back? If he had someone else, why couldn't she leave him alone, for God's sake? She rose impulsively and left the café to go home, but then she turned back again. She couldn't leave him without giving a chance to explain what had to be—*had to be*—a perfectly innocuous situation.

When the clock told her that an hour and a half had passed, she went slowly up the steps again, her heart pounding against the chance of a second rebuff, her face white and set. This time he answered her knock by opening the door listlessly and turning away as she walked past him into the room that contained his life work, his innermost secrets. She looked about at the roll-top desk, the deeply cushioned swivel chair, the black leather sofa with the headrest worn and perpetually indented. There were no surprises except for a faint trace of lavender which scented the room.

"She saw you," he said. He leaned against the desk looking down at his clasped hands. "It was the one thing I didn't want to happen."

"Who saw me?" Julie asked. It surprised her how she could sound so calm. Any instant now, he was going to tell her something that would break her heart.

He glanced at her with a slight frown. "Emma," he said, and when she still looked at him stupidly, "my wife," he explained. "She's known for a long time that there was someone else, but she didn't know who. Now she knows."

Julie still waited.

"She is going to hurt you," Marcel said. "I don't know how, but she'll find a way. She's very patient."

Julie began to breathe again, very slowly.

"Was *that* who it was?" she demanded. "Was that *all?*"

He shook his head. "When Emma hurts you, it isn't trivial. She'll smash your life."

She shook her head.

"She'll smash your life, I said," he insisted. "Emma isn't an object for anyone's pity."

"Perhaps, but I can't face her."

"She stayed somewhere outside after she left just to watch you come in—just to be sure. I don't know where, but she saw you."

"And she's waiting for me to come out?"

"She won't bother. She knows what she wants to know."

"You know all her actions so well!" Julie said slowly. "This, I gather, has happened many times."

"Enough times," he said stolidly. "I never denied that, Julie."

"And it'll happen again?"

"Can *you* predict tomorrow?" he asked.

"Some things," she said. "Tomorrow I'll still love you."

He looked at her steadily. "For me too, tomorrow will still be the same." Nothing could make him use the word *love*. "But now that the damage is done, what in the name of God did you come here for?"

She said wryly: "And I thought I was coming with good news! I got what I've been yearning for all these years."

She told him about Salomon-Delachet, but there was no pleasure in his face.

"It's a start of sorts," he conceded. "It's a good enough problem, and a dozen laboratories have gone to work on it. But the electrolytes really do not violate the laws of osmotic pressure, freezing point, boiling point, heat of formation. They can only *seem* to be the anarchists of the molecular world. Believe me, my dear, the answers will be found just over the next hill."

"Then perhaps I'll be one of the ones who help find them," she said doggedly. She couldn't bear to have her great prize treated so lightly.

He turned away in impatience. "Why be content to be only 'one of the ones'? In science, the big advances are made by those who work alone. *Alone*, mind you! Only animals move in herds," he said bitterly. "And herds do only animal things. To be absolutely individual, ah, that's the big thing!"

"But I feel more of an individual at this moment than I ever did before," she said. "Someone is willing to entrust a piece of research to *me!* It's recognition."

"And *I* never recognized you?"

"You said I wasn't ready! You judge me by terrible standards. But I'll show you!"

"I recognize what is potential in you, what you will have when you *are* ready!" He was tired of the argument suddenly. "Will you have to give up the tutoring to find the time for this? Will Salomon-Delachet give you any money?"

"A small stipend, perhaps. I'll find out tomorrow. But I don't care! I want only this chance to show you what I can do."

"Of course I'll make up any difference for you," he went on. "I can't let you go back to starving."

"I'll live on what I earn!" she said strongly. "You don't even hear what I'm saying. I'm talking about work and you talk about money!" His face turned dark. He took her arms and shook her. "How dare you refuse me!" he demanded. "You'll take my money; you'll take my care; you'll take everything I give you!"

She glared back at him, then burst out laughing. She put her arms about him and held herself close, her face pressed against his chest, his hugeness, although he kept glancing at the office door.

"Oh my God, how I love you!" she said. "I love you! I love you!"

"And the money?" he demanded.

"We'll see!" she said, "we'll see!" She had no intention of giving in. She was also reluctant to give up the deliciousness of his offer of such care. But more than anything, she wouldn't surrender her determination to prove herself. "And *you*'ll see, too! *You*, more than anyone!"

8

EACH MORNING AT EIGHT JULIE WAS AT THE RUE CUJAS entrance of the Sorbonne when the door leading to the laboratories of her section was unlocked. It was an entrance used only by research workers. The others—all of them men—some no older than she, came and went to their laboratories with easy assurance. Their polite "Good morning, mademoiselle," "Good night, mademoiselle" were offered to her with a bow, with a handshake if they met on the staircase; but she was never included in the little talks or gatherings in the laboratories up and down the landings. The hum of masculine conversation could always be heard somewhere outside her door. Sometimes it was a burst of low laughter over a remark made earlier in a café or the night before at a gathering in someone's home. Sometimes it was the staccato passion of scientific argument.

Above her and below her, they all knew each other, they were all members of an unofficial family. She was the outsider in every sense. Which was worst—being a woman, or a foreigner, or a researcher who had still not proven herself worthy of admission to their guild—she couldn't tell.

At midday, the men all came trooping down the stairs again, the deep voices alive again with chatter and banter, most of them going home to dinner, others to the *brasseries* or bistros in groups of two, three, and four; but no one thought to include her.

Marcel himself went every day to the *brasserie* Balzar on the Rue des Ecoles at a special table reserved for himself and colleagues from the Collège de France, the Sorbonne and even some from the Ecole de Physique et Chimie. Each man on entering took the nearest empty place to the others. The talk was vivid and wide. Debates ranged over physics and chemistry and then went on to theater, painting, the personalities of opera stars, philosophy, and always politics—always Left, and always L'Affaire, since there was no one in Paris then who each day of his life didn't either hear, speak, or read the name *Dreyfus*.

It was good, strong, masculine company, and Marcel loved the companionship. He always came away from each dinner full of stories, ideas, and anecdotes for Julie. Sometimes in her room he would invent belated retorts that he would use tomorrow; but he never asked her to join. For that matter he never thought to ask her what she did at her noonday meal. What she did was to remain by herself, eating something she bought on the way in the morning in a *charcuterie* on the Rue de Vaugirard.

She told herself that she had asked only for the opportunity to work and not for the company of men, and so she worked; insisting that she wasn't lonely at all. She preferred to cook something on her burner. She would see Marcel at the end of the day in her room to which he now always climbed for an hour or so before taking the omnibus across Paris for home and supper with his family. When he left, she would heat up something for herself to eat, again eating alone. Afterward she would settle down to further study for the work which had been assigned to her.

The research went badly from the very beginning. She had been warned that she would probably get a null result, and that was exactly what she got, no matter how carefully she did the work.

In spite of the complicated apparatus, the essential nature of the experiment couldn't have been simpler: she started with two glass flasks, each of which contained a different dilute solution. Thermometers measured the temperature of each solution at the beginning of the operation. The liquids then flowed simultaneously into another flask where a third thermometer registered the temperature of the mixture. What was expected, according to the newest molecular theory, was also simple: the temperature of the mixture was expected to be higher than the temperatures of the reactants with which she began, because new chemical compounds had supposedly been formed. Yet whether she mixed her two solutions rapidly or slowly; whether she began her experiment at elevated temperatures, or close to the freezing point; whether she used a thermocouple to detect the temperature rise, or even a Beckmann thermometer capable of measuring a thousandth of a degree; and regardless of how much or how little insulation she wrapped around the entire system, the temperature change was always zero. The pages of her research ledger became covered —one after the other—with notes and descriptions and diagrams, the calculations always produced the same answer: "Temperature difference—0." Either she was a failure or the theory was a failure, but the theory couldn't be—because as a final step of each test, she poured the mixture into an open dish over a burner, and evaporated the water until all that was left was a white powdery residue. Analysis showed four salts— nitrates and chlorides of sodium and potassium—chemical formation had taken place all right. But where was the heat of formation?

She used all her ingenuity to escape from the morass of the zero result. The apparatus recommended by Salomon-Delachet was gradually transformed. Step by step, the arrangement of glass flasks, tubing, stopcocks, and calorimeters became uniquely her own. With each change she learned some new technique. What was so tantalizing was the renewal of hope every time that finally the phenomenon would show itself. Even though the other *préparateurs particuliers* were also getting zero results, she nevertheless felt the failure to be entirely her own.

The continued zero result was maddening. There were times when she could have smashed the thermometers. The heat rise had to be somewhere within the spherical glass flask where the mixing took place. The only possible explanation was that it was being masked by something still unknown.

Every time she thought of her boast to Marcel, she flushed with shame, but he never referred to it again. He was philosophic about her failure and sympathetic, but not particularly interested. He never said: "I told you so," but he found a dozen ways to tell her that it was too bad she was wasting herself on an unimportant work. She refused to listen to discouragement; but she was no longer so cocksure about all the big things she was going to show. She stopped her dogged repetition and withdrew to think. She walked out of the laboratory and down to the river. Without knowing why, she was drawn to the wooden footbridge across the Seine—the Pont des Arts. It became her private avenue to stroll slowly back and forth from one bank to the other. She went there day after day, only half aware of the soothing familiarity of the damp gusts of air that buffeted her, of the liquid splash against the piers beneath her as she leaned on the rail and stared unseeingly east at the green promontory of the Île de la Cité, or west to the Louvre and the quais that stretched along the river to the glitter of the afternoon sun. They were the sounds and scents of Vineyard Haven harbor, and they calmed her while day after day she held her mind to the problem like a fist clenched about a stone, exhausting herself physically with the effort of concentration. At last on a certain sun-hazy day, the fingers of her mind unfolded; the stone had become a faceted jewel—a possible answer to her question.

She went at once to Marcel's study not to "show" him, but humbly to ask his advice. "Suppose the zero result implies exactly what it says? Suppose there is no error?"

"What do you mean?" he asked slowly.

"I mean that the lack of any temperature change could mean that there is really no chemical reaction at all."

"But you know that one does take place," he said with impatience.

"Yes, but not *when* it takes place," she said. "Everyone assumes that the reaction occurs when the solutions are being mixed—"

"Well, yes," he said slowly.

"I'm saying that the zero result at the moment of mixture may very well mean that the reaction isn't taking place at that time at all! Perhaps at some later time—at a time when I'm not looking for it. And if it should occur at exactly the moment when I'm already adding enormous amounts of heat to evaporate the water, the whole effect could be masked."

"Epatant!" he breathed with pride. His eyes had widened and he was laughing, his hands outstretched toward her. "Why not? It fits!"

"And so instead of looking for a temperature rise at the moment of mixture," she said, "I ought to search for something at the moment of precipitation."

He put his hands on her shoulders with mock solemnity. He leaned down and kissed her, first on one cheek and then on the other, while she was laughing with delight at her accomplishment.

"Now you are ready," he announced. "Now finally you are ready! You must design a method at once to try it out. Maybe you *will* show me, after all!"

9

SHE REPORTED HER IDEA TO SALOMON-DELACHET WHO listened as if he were bored. He didn't look at her once.

"Ingenious," he said mildly. "But you realize, of course, that to detect the effect you describe will be almost impossible. Unless you also have some original ideas on calorimetry?"

"I think that with some revisions of the present apparatus—" she said, but he cut her off.

"I assure you that a far more drastic approach is necessary," he said at once. "What you are telling me is that you haven't yet given it enough thought. Unless you have a really new idea, please don't bother."

"Still," she said stubbornly. "If you will only let me explain—"

"No," he replied. He turned his back and spoke to her over his shoulder as he worked. "It would be only a waste of time. I tell you that any variation of what you have at present simply will not work. Try it, and you will see. But don't spend more than a month at it!"

"But—!"

"That's my last word on it! Not a day more than a month. That's all. You may go, mademoiselle!"

He turned out to be right—her method of adding heat to evaporate the water totally masked any internal energy that might have been produced by an exothermic reaction. While she worked at it, Salomon-Delachet discussed her concepts with his other assistants. A really brilliant vacuum method was suggested by one of the senior researchers—an Alsatian named Elsberger.

His laboratory was on the top floor, and Julie went up to see him. He was a man in his early thirties with a prissy, pedantic air. His laboratory was immaculate. It was not enough for him that apparatus was clean inside where it counted, exterior—brass knobs and nickle trim—had to glisten too. His plain bony face glistened. So did his eyeglasses.

"Oh yes!" He had a tiny nervous laugh that sounded like a snicker. "You're the young lady with the interesting idea! Well, we shall soon see!" He pointed to a gleaming constellation of spherical glass chambers interconnected by glass and rubber tubing. There was a high-speed vacuum pump, a mercury manometer and a McCleod gauge. "I'm going to adapt that setup for vacuum evaporation. In another week or so, it'll be ready to go. Then I'll be able to tell." He laughed again. He might have been coughing. "Yes, yes, then I'll be able to tell you whether there's anything to it."

She watched him for a few minutes. He worked with frowning concentration and forgot she was there. He obviously had wide experience in vacuum technique. She left. She continued doggedly with her method, enmeshed in exasperating failure by her own stubbornness.

She continued to go upstairs to watch Elsberger longingly as he made rapid progress in getting his apparatus ready. From his first test, it was clear that she had been right in her explanation of the true nature of the phenomenon. He got a positive indication almost immediately.

"There's no question but that you were going in the right direction," he said grudgingly, for now that the experiment promised success, his attitude toward her became cold and almost secretive. He was increasingly reluctant to share credit with her. "Your version of the process was far too primitive and naïve. But I'm getting it into acceptable shape." She tried to tell herself that it was science that was going to benefit if her insight were correct, not any one individual; but she was sick with envy for his superior experimental insight. She found it harder and harder to visit his laboratory and watch him work; while he treated her more and more openly as an enemy. Finally she stopped going altogether.

To her surprise, the other researchers knew what was going on. Staircase conversations stopped as she came past and she found herself being included in the talk. She was asked into laboratories as she went by: she had become a member of the staff.

"For ten years that cold fish Elsberger's been waiting for an idea that could be worthy of his exquisite technique. He was never able to come up with one of his own. Now you've given him this marvelous present," she was told. "He'll make his reputation out of this; unless you come up first with a good result of your own."

"I won't," she said simply. "I can't. His method is better than mine."

She continued to work, but as the weeks went by, she felt gloomier, more futile. On one of her worst days, one of the staff men came into the lab and silently handed her a copy of the December issue of the *Zeitschrift für Physikalische Chemie*. He stood there, stroking his mustache and watching her.

"What does that look mean?" Julie asked. "You're frightening me to death!"

"Wegmann's article. Read it and see!"

"Who is Wegmann?" she asked. She found the article: "Electrolytic Compounds and Heats of Formation," by A. K. Wegmann, University of Göttingen. She read it slowly. There was the whole idea set forth with great mathematical elegance and with far more profundity than she could ever have managed. Accompanying the report was the complete experimental proof based on a vacuum method even more powerful than Elsberger's. There was no question: Salomon-Delachet's entire staff had been anticipated by the German by at least a year and a half.

"That's that!" said her visitor with satisfaction. "At least Elsberger won't be walking off with the credit."

"That's not much comfort," Julie said.

She felt the defeat very sharply. She put on her coat, pinned on her hat, and escaped the laboratory, oppressed by her smallness next to what seemed like the towering talent of the man who had anticipated her. Elsberger upstairs may have aroused her admiration and envy for his technique, but he had never made her feel outclassed. Compared to the far more experienced German scientist, though, she felt like a bungler: better than anyone else she knew how much more profound his insight had been than hers. She couldn't bear to look at her own apparatus any more. She hated its ineffectiveness.

She went to Raubard's study, hardly knocking on the door, telling him at once what had happened and how she felt. For a while, they discussed it. He was sympathetic, but not overly so.

Something remote in his tone, something that said his mind was busy with other things, made her realize with a pulse of panic that she had been absorbed by her own work for so long that she was out of touch with him.

"There's some kind of change," she said abruptly. "What is it?"

"Nothing really," he replied with a little shrug. But then after a moment, he told her: he was getting ready to leave her.

10

"I'M GOING TO AMERICA," HE SAID, AND HANDED HER A letter to read. Regularly every four or five weeks for years now, he had been receiving a letter in English with this same spidery, impeccable handwriting from the United States, postmarked New Haven. Sometimes the letter was a three-page mathematical monograph with "My dear Raubard" at the head of the first page and "Very truly yours, Willard Gibbs" on the last page. Sometimes, too, the letter was only a brief note—"Nothing new with me this month. Lectured. Much snow. What do you think of Bjerkeman's paper in *Phil Mag?* Is Ostwald serious about November? Write. Best. Gibbs."

This time, the letter he handed her read: "My physician, a real hard-bitten Down-Easter, has served me warning, now that I'm coming back from the second attack. He puts it rather cruelly this way: I may have a third attack, but I won't ever have a fourth. That's Yankee humor for you. He is giving me this macabre notice, he says, because if there's anything I want to be sure will be taken care of, I'd better take care of it right now. Which brings us to you and what we have been talking about ever since my first attack four years ago. It means that the time has come. You'd better get here just as soon as you can. I've already arranged for your position here. You will be Visiting Professor in Theoretical Chemistry."

Marcel had often brought Gibbs's letters to Julie's place. Many of them, he had answered at her table. The Sorbonne-Yale correspondence between the two men amounted to a decade-long conversation on current thought about molecular behavior and chemical kinetics. Gibbs lived a quiet bachelor life with his sister and her family in a modest frame house in New Haven, but his true value was appreciated only by scientific contemporaries who themselves would be remembered fifty years later. His personal correspondents were, like Marcel, the most thoughtful and productive minds in world science. It was his fate to be known and appreciated during his own lifetime only abroad and belatedly. Raubard was intellectually closest to him, the man destined to take up where he would leave off, and so in Gibbs's eyes, as well as in the eyes of world science, Raubard was the heir apparent. At the time of his first attack, he had invited Raubard to come and spend at least a year working with him in close collaboration before it was too late. Raubard had accepted in principle at the time; but Gibbs never mentioned it again until now. Julie handed the letter back to Marcel.

"When do you go?" she asked quietly.

"As soon as I finish up my course of lectures."

"For how long?" She continued to keep her voice low and drained of feeling.

"As long as necessary."

"Have you told your wife?"

He sighed. "Not yet. She didn't know that I had agreed to go in the first place until that day you saw her here in the study. That's why she was in such a rage."

"And will she go with you?"

His lips twisted slightly. "You don't understand," he said. "It's true that I accepted Gibbs's invitation in the first place because there was the obvious obligation to the work. But there was a more personal reason—Emma would never join me in the United States. Whatever she feels for me—love, hate, rage—what she feels against her old country is stronger. Before I met you, it seemed to me that my only chance to get away from her and to breathe for a while was to go to America. It never occurred to me when I agreed to go to Gibbs that I would be finding the same thing here in a room on Rue Monsieur le Prince. Because of you, I'm able to go home to that house every day now and live the few hours I have to be there. I don't care—Emma's hatred no longer seems so important. The following morning, I'm back here in my laboratory and after that I go to you."

He had long ago come to terms with his marriage as a hell from which there would never be any escape. He had made the mistake of marrying a beautiful young woman who had loved him with a half-demented intensity while he in turn had not loved her. With an imperiousness she had retained from a plantation girlhood, she told him that she wanted him. Her American openness shocked him momentarily but he was just as open with her: he told her honestly that he didn't return her feeling. Since she couldn't command his love, she derided his scruples. She told him that he knew too little about life to know what love really was. She insisted, with the calm complacency of an American girl, that once they were married, everything would turn out all right. She carried with her the romantic aura of a rich foreigner, an émigrée follower of a lost cause. Her father—a surgeon—was a man of eminence in the profession to which young Marcel had apprenticed himself. Marcel's fellow students told him that he was insane to hesitate. His own father, a physician in Neufchâtel en Bray—heard of what was going on and wrote sternly that a young man who wished to have a Parisian medical career needed all the friends he could get; a rich wife was even better than a friend.

At twenty-one, Marcel had known only the lucky side of his life. Anything he had ever wanted, and more, had come his way. His medical studies never required any effort from him, and yet he stood at the head of his class. He was almost bored. Only chemistry fascinated him, and even there he leisurely performed a theoretical research one summer that turned out to be an eleven-page classic. When he met Emma, he was a tall, heavy-shouldered, dark-haired boy, with a lowering walk and a face that already glinted with facets of poetry, passion, and ruthlessness. That a beautiful girl wanted to marry him seemed no great miracle to him. His assent was that amused shrug which says, "Why not?"

Friction developed at once between his unswervable insistence on going his own way and her possessiveness. She actually felt that she owned him. To her, marriage was an act of submission on Marcel's part: he owed it to her to be as docile to her wishes as her father was. Marcel didn't even bother to repudiate the debt, he simply ignored it. They had been married several years when he announced one evening, almost as an afterthought, that he was no longer going to the Hospital but to the Sorbonne to work in Le Châtelier's research group. Her face turned white. "And your patients?" she asked.

"I've already sent them on," he said lightly.

"Without consulting me?" she cried. "Or Papa?"

"What difference could it make? This is what I want to do, and that's enough."

Her face grew even whiter, and her eyes became large as she stared at him. Her mouth opened as if by some impersonal mechanism, and only moments later, out of the red roundness came the screaming. "No! No! No! . . ." endlessly, and on a single note. She stopped only when he took a carafe of water and threw its contents in her face, but he was shaking. He couldn't imagine what had possessed her. Her father was called from across the park, and the screaming began again. They would starve, she cried. Marcel was throwing away a future. Her father pleaded with Marcel to reconsider his decision—it had always been her wish that her husband should follow her father. Marcel couldn't believe that they were serious; he was obdurate. They sent to Neufchâtel en Bray for old Dr. Raubard, who was saddened to learn of his son's decision; but this time he rather weakly attempted to take his son's part. After all, he argued, what Marcel wanted to do was in one of France's great traditions. Whether it was or not made no difference to Marcel. The bull-shouldered young man strode angrily up and down the green and gold velvet parlor of his wife's home while his wife and the two older physicians—the two fathers—hammered away at him and at each other. At last Marcel brought his hand down on the top of a marble table with such force that the crystal chandeliers were set tinkling.

"Not one more word!" he said facing them. "I'm going to do as I wish—what I feel I *must* do! That's all! It remains to decide only this: do I continue to live here while I work, or do I move out just as I am—in the time it takes me to walk to the front door—?" He pointed his finger at his wife. "You decide. One more word—even one sound—and I go!" He kept his finger leveled at her like a revolver. She stood mute. Her eyes were red with tears and brilliant with hatred. Even her sobbing was shocked into silence. Slowly, reluctantly, he lowered his finger and accepted his victory.

She took her revenge in a thousand ways over the years.

He had two daughters whom he adored and a son, the youngest of the children. The boy had his mother's frail physique, his father's mind, and a large-eyed white face of heart-breaking delicacy. Marcel was haunted by the fear that the boy would never survive to maturity. The fear was so strong that he couldn't even imagine the boy as a grown man; yet the boy read and looked forward to the day when he would be as great a *savant* as his father. He selected astronomy as his field, and with his father began to build a telescope of salvaged lenses and rolled black paper. The boy adored the father who could help him work such a miracle, but one day the telescope was found mysteriously smashed. The mother was all innocence—she knew nothing about it. The servants had been careless—she said airily. Nothing more. The boy wept because he had loved the instrument and the labor that had gone into it. Marcel's face was dark with rage. The very next day—miraculously—she produced a new telescope—a magnificent one—bought from an instrument-maker in Amsterdam. The mother presented it charmingly to the boy as "Mama's telescope." Each time he referred to it thereafter that way, she brightened and glanced triumphantly at her husband.

In the same mysterious way, research notes, papers, and theoretical calculations which he made at home and left on the desk in his study were sometimes swept out, burnt by mistake, or simply disappeared. All this in a house in which nothing was ever out of place.

There was nothing mysterious, though, in the way Madame Raubard demurely kept reminding the girls—each time they asked for something—that there was no money for such things because Papa had decided it was more important for him to do as he pleased rather than provide a comfortable living for his family. If there was any prestige in having become one of the outstanding scientists of Europe, if there was any honor in having been made a Professor at the Collège de France, no hint of it ever came from her. It was not the diminution of their income that had been the unforgivable insult: it had been his refusal to become her creature. The war went on between them relentlessly. When he couldn't ignore her, he bore the attacks of her simmering rage; when he could stand no more, he let his anger explode out at her, then she retreated at once with lowered eyes, waited a week or two, and then deftly, quietly, she was back once again at the attack, and he would slam himself away from her into the parlor of gold and green velvet—a room that was bitter cold five days of the week with a fire in the fireplace only on Wednesdays —his wife's receiving day—and on Sundays. It was Marcel's refuge the rest of the time. Here he could be alone in the heavily ornamented and betasseled ice-house of silence, hunched against the cold, for which he was grateful, because no one dared follow him in there.

Still he was faithful to her for more than fifteen years. His work continued to be as brilliant as ever, but only his oldest and closest friends remained devoted to him. His tongue, cold and sharp, made it difficult for others to approach him even though he longed for serenity of heart and mind, for an end to the ceaseless pressure on him, the daily insult, the perpetual waiting for the spring of malice, the need to relieve his own rage by some mindless spurt of revenge. Even the brief, passionless affairs he threw himself into gave him no relief. Only now that Julie had become part of his life was there some lessening of his bitter aloofness, but the heritage from his life before her was this commitment to Gibbs and to himself to go to New Haven if he ever were called. He decided to remain in Paris until June and join Gibbs in New Haven at the end of the American academic year.

Julie listened to all the plans being made and said nothing, even though they meant the end of her life. Marcel would be gone for a long time from the way he spoke, nor was there anything in his thoughtful, almost absent-minded tone to indicate that he'd have a moment's regret over his separation from her. He seemed to think that she viewed the whole thing as calmly as he did. She tried to keep up that appearance for him, and covered her agony. Once, though, as she rested in his arms in her room, she indicated that she expected him to return to her when he came back to Paris. At that he turned his head swiftly, with a frown.

"What are you talking about? You know by that time you'll have someone else!"

"You're not serious!" she said with shock as she raised herself on an elbow to look at him.

"Well, *you* certainly can't be," he retorted.

"But I love you!" she said slowly.

"My God, love!" he sighed turning away.

"Yes, love!" she said with sudden fury. "And you know it! I don't ask for your love! I don't even ask you to accept mine. All I ask is that you *know* about it."

"I know about it," he said sharply. "But don't expect me to believe that it will keep you faithful for a year."

"And what should I expect you to believe? That I'm a whore?"

"I don't want a scene with you!" he shouted at her suddenly. "You're the one woman who ever made sense to me, but now you too are going out of your mind!"

She swung herself off of the bed. "You'd drive any woman out of her mind!"

"You're blackmailing me!"

"Because I use the word *love?*" She began to dress with quick, angry movements.

"Because you want me to use the word *love*. It revolts me!"

"You're insane!" she said coldly.

"Stop that!" he shouted at her, leveling his forefinger at her exactly as he once had at his wife. The words snapped out like bullets from the imaginary pistol he could have used on every member of his wife's sex—as if they were all co-conspirators against him, all of them sly, all of them suffused with great malice. "I told you, I want no scene with you! You will go on being the woman I respect! There'll be no more tricks, no tones of voice, no reproofs, no sulks! I'm going to America! For years it's been known that I'm going.

When the time comes for me to leave, I want the same *Au revoir, Marcel* I get every day from you! Not one word more! Not one sigh!"

From behind her silence, she looked at him with sudden depthless pity for the terror she perceived. He had an absolute horror of being caught by any feeling of tenderness.

So she too gave him the silence he demanded at pistolpoint, just as his wife had. But where Mme. Raubard had gone mute out of terror of losing her victim, Julie held her tongue out of compassion. She knew that his ranting was really his plea for protection against further heartbreak. He could bear no further hurt, and she could not bear to cause him any.

This time, though, when he lowered his hand, he did so guiltily and with shame that of all people it should be Julie who bore the brunt of his latest outburst of temper. Still, he couldn't make himself say, "Forgive me!"

He dressed himself slowly, frowning to himself all the while but being elaborately polite to her each time the confined space of the room made him brush her with his huge movements. At last, he put his arm about her shoulders and gave her a surly bearlike hug and shake. "You made me so angry, I almost forgot your going-away gift."

"A gift for me?"

"It'll be ready tomorrow, but you must come for it. To my study at the college."

"Is it that big?"

He burst out laughing, his anger completely forgotten. "It's nothing you can carry, I promise you that. But you can talk to it, and it'll answer you. You'll see! I'm giving you what you came to Paris for."

When she walked into Marcel's study the following day, he was not alone: Georges Claudet was standing by the window, and he turned as she came in. The afternoon sunlight from the Rue St. Jacques outside gave Claudet's outline a golden aura. Next to Marcel, he looked delicate, slight, almost dandyish. His smile, as he bowed, was formal and cool. An ironic amusement was tinged with sadness. "I hope Mademoiselle remembers our last conversation as well as I do."

"She does, she does," Raubard said brusquely as he held out his hands to her in greeting. "Come in, everything is finally arranged."

She was consumed with curiosity about the gift, but she

hoped that Marcel would not present it to her in Claudet's presence. She would have preferred to withdraw in modest silence until the two men whom she admired had finished their business and Claudet had left, but Claudet seemed to be intent on her, waiting for her to say something to him. She was embarrassed by his continued regard.

"Well?" asked Raubard impatiently of them both.

"I'm satisfied, as you know," Claudet replied, his gaze still on Julie. His smile was unchanged. He completely ignored the older man's brusqueness. "It is Mademoiselle who looks undecided."

"Undecided about what?" Julie asked, looking from one to the other.

"The gift! The gift!" said Raubard. He was like an excited boy. He put an arm about Claudet's shoulder, and said to Julie: "You have a new post. You are to be *his* assistant. He has agreed. *He* is my gift to you. *You* are my gift to him."

"I have agreed," Claudet echoed his former teacher, but now the sadness in his little smile was dominant. "It remains only to decide how, when, where, and at what, you are to be my assistant."

Raubard impatiently dismissed the qualifications. "The *how* is simple—*préparateur particulier*—out of my own budget; the *when* is now; the *where* is the only problem, but certainly somewhere in Paris there must be laboratory space!"

Claudet seemed much younger than he had at Harvard, because she had known Marcel in the meantime.

"But does the arrangement suit you?" he insisted, demanding her acquiescence as if Marcel weren't there. In their last meeting, he had treated her in her role of interviewer-student with some amusement and condescension. Now there was much more acceptance of her. "Are you willing to leave your post with Salomon-Delachet?"

"I'm overwhelmed!" Julie replied. "I don't know what to say."

"There's nothing to say," Raubard cut her off. "We must celebrate at once. Let's go to the Balzar, the three of us. We'll each have a dozen oysters before the season ends. Today the *spécialité* is *blanquette de veau*, and I'm dying of hunger."

In the café, Marcel herded them toward a small table where they could be by themselves. He introduced Julie with a proprietary hand on her arm as "the girl I told you about in Salomon-Delachet's laboratory; you know, the girl with the brilliant insight into precipitation of highly ionizing salts—"

With a sinking heart Julie wondered if she were there at that time only because Marcel had found someone behind whom he could hide her, but she had underestimated him. At the table, he put her in the corner seat. He himself moved in next to her on the banquette. She was his. He waved Claudet to the seat opposite.

"And when are you leaving?" Claudet asked.

"The first," Marcel said, motioning to the waiter. "Next week."

"Next week?" Julie said, turning to him in alarm. "You never said it was that soon!"

"I didn't know myself until today," he replied negligently as he took the menu.

She couldn't make herself believe that their separation was that unimportant to him, and she assured the constant ache in her heart that before he left there would surely be a sign of his true feeling. When Asher had gone, it had been bad enough, but his death had a finality about it. Here, Marcel hadn't even left yet, and she was dumbly suffering more than ever before, probably because the ghosts of all the previous losses were whispering to her, reminding her of what it was to live with a raw hole in her heart. Still, she continued to hide it all from him. Three days before his departure, they were seated in a café and he turned peremptorily and asked her what was wrong. She shook her head and said only that she was concerned about the work she was finishing up for Salomon-Delachet. Yet she was stunned by his apparent insensitivity.

The last afternoon in her room started like all their other afternoons. For at least an hour, there was nothing to show that he felt it to be any different. Then suddenly, within himself, the massive collapse took place. Pretensions, prides, and disguises crumbled and poured down in an internal avalanche, leaving him shock-eyed and limp with helplessness: it was clear to him at last that he was leaving her.

His gaze on her, piercing her to what she really meant to him, was incredulous at the intensity of what he felt. Then he closed his eyes as if the sudden clarity were too blinding. He took her to him in an embrace so close that it pained her, yet tears of relief came to her eyes at last.

"You will come back, won't you?" she whispered up to him, and after a moment she felt him nod against her head.

"Oh my God, yes! Yes! Yes! How could I not?"

They sat close to each other in silence with his hand on hers and her head against his shoulder. Occasionally, he'd touch her face with his fingers, her eyes, lips, her brows, the curve of her nostrils. For an hour they clasped each other that way, then suddenly he stood up and kissed her so hard that his lips crushed hers against her teeth. It was a kiss of desperation.

"That's all!" he said harshly. "And now I have to go!"

With neither *au revoir* nor *adieu,* he turned and strode out of the room. She didn't move from where she sat, but listened to the sound of his feet racing heavily down the stairs. She remained there even after the other noises of the houses covered his flight.

11

TWO MONTHS LATER, IN A CITY OPULENT WITH SUMmer, she was sitting alone at a table on the terrace of the Café Cluny. She was early for an appointment with Georges Claudet, but the afternoon heat and her own unhappiness made her indifferent both to the length of her wait and to the turning heads of men who passed and saw her sitting alone. She could have looked interesting only to someone who was lured by eyes that were smoky with pain.

The shady side of the Place St. Michel was hot enough for her to fan her wet face with her handkerchief. Only one letter had come from Marcel in the time he was gone. It wasn't the letter's matter-of-factness that depressed her or even that there hadn't been other letters; it was his presence that she yearned for. She had long ceased to hear the harshness of his tone or even the occasional barbs in his remarks. She knew only the warmth and hunger in him that had made him come to her every day and mount the four flights of stairs to sit with her in her small room, to find comfort in her nearness, her odor, her touch. How important could a momentary gruffness have been when his eyes followed every movement she made, when his face glinted with pleasure every time she handed him a teacup or poured him a glass of wine?

She had come to Paris to work, she kept telling herself sternly after he had gone; and now she had all the work she could handle. Why didn't it absorb her? She replied that she was only cleaning up her assignment for Salomon-Delachet before starting with Claudet, so how could she expect to find it interesting? *I must be spoiled,* she decided, *I'm getting so used to the idea of working in a lab that I've forgotten what it once was like to yearn for even a glimpse of one.*

Nevertheless, she wrote to Claudet to remind him of her existence. She hadn't heard a word from him since Marcel's departure, and she began to worry. Had Claudet forgotten her? Or hadn't there been any agreement in the first place? Days went by without any reply from him. Finally he sent her a note that struck her as odd: instead of inviting her to call on him at the college, he appointed a time at a café. It seemed rather a frivolous attitude, she thought at first; but she already knew him as too serious a man to think that for long. Then it dawned on her that she wasn't accustomed to meeting a man who was free to be seen with her. And at last it came clear that the college was closed for the summer. The meeting was set for five o'clock, but she felt so lost, that she arrived half an hour early.

Apparently, the Cluny was a favorite of the people she had worked and studied with. She saw familiar faces among the tables; chemists, physicists, and mathematicians. Some were talking affably, some in heated argument. One of her own colleagues from Salomon-Delachet's staff looked up and nodded as she went by. She continued walking down to the Seine, where she looked at some books along the quai, then ten minutes later she glanced at the little watch pinned to her blouse. She returned to the café. Again, her fellow staff member nodded as she passed. This time he rose and came through the tables to ask her to sit with them until Claudet appeared. She was too shy to accept, but she felt a sort of surprise that she had at last become eligible to join the life that had been going on among other people like herself. An edge to her loneliness was removed, but she took a seat alone at an empty table.

At ten minutes to five Claudet arrived; his face too was damp with the heat.

"I thought surely I would be here before you," he said.

"It's not important," she replied. "I was too impatient to wait."

His gaze was full of silent insight. The question he was supposed to ask—why she was so impatient—hung in the air. Instead he signaled a waiter.

"From what Raubard told me, you were very close to something interesting."

"Close, but not close enough," she replied.

He refused her self-deprecation. "There are men here who were supposed to know more than you—and they didn't come as close as you did. Of everyone here in Paris, *you* were the first to have the idea. Doesn't that give you any satisfaction?"

She shook her head. "That particular satisfaction passed like that," she said snapping her fingers. "The real pleasure was in the moment the idea came to me. My God, what an ecstasy! But then, once I started to work it out in the laboratory, I lost the impetus: it was clear I was on the wrong track. From then on, every day was an eternity of frustration. I can't tell you how happy I was in a certain way to read that article by Wegmann! Everything was finished. There was nothing more for me to worry about!"

He laughed softly. "Just the same, you're lucky to have turned out to be one of the people to whom ideas come."

"It was the only one, I'm afraid," she said with a slight smile.

"It will happen again," he said calmly. "And again."

For the first time, the look of sadness on her face lifted slightly.

"That pleases you?" he asked.

"Yes," she said frankly. "I hope with all my heart that it's true."

"You'll see that it is," he said. "I take it you'd like to start work as soon as possible?"

"That's why I wrote you. I must have work."

"I hadn't forgotten you. If it's a matter of money, I can arrange to have an advance paid to you before the term begins."

"It's not the money at all," she said swiftly. "I want to be doing something so interesting that I don't care about anything else. No one will work harder or with more concentration than I!—I promise you!"

He smiled in sympathy. "Is it chemistry you want, or forgetfulness? Science isn't a clinic for mending broken hearts

—it can use dedication, not self-immolation. One needs a clear mind, not tear-stained eyes. Am I going to be sorry I've taken you as assistant?"

"You'll never be sorry."

"Oh, come! I'll need a better smile than that!"

"Put me to work, and I'll get you that smile."

He laughed quietly. "Now that you put me to the test, I have to confess that it's not going to be that simple. Painters and sculptors find studios in Paris far more easily than scientists find space to do research. A few francs for paper, canvas, or clay, and the artist is at work. In science, life is more complicated. I have no laboratory at all. My college is too new. We barely have room for the student instruction laboratories. You and I are beggars for a few square feet of space where we can have access to running water, access to gas, and the crudest kind of equipment. Of course, the rich ones pay for their laboratories out of their own pocket, but I'm not rich. Are you?"

For the first time in weeks, she laughed a little. "I can barely pay the rent for the room I live in."

"Nobody here has any money," he said affably. "Nobody ever will have. It's only in the bohemia of the artist or poet where recognition and overnight success can move someone from a studio on Montmartre over to the Parc Monceau world of horses, carriages, *hôtels particuliers,* and villas in the country. Our bohemia may be smaller and perhaps more exclusive, but it's definitely poorer. And the sort of recognition we get won't make anyone rich."

"Do you really believe," she asked, slightly flushed, "that I am in Paris studying chemistry in order to get horses, carriages, villas, *hôtels particuliers?*"

"No." He was unperturbed by her rebuke. "I don't think so. On the other hand, I'm not accustomed to women in our field, nor am I accustomed to Americans."

"And is your impression of both so poor," she went on, "that you feel justified in saying such things to me?"

"I apologize. I was trying to find out what you stand for."

"I don't know that I stand for anything," she said slowly. "Except that I want to work—right now."

"So do I. And I hope to have some place by next week."

"And you'll write to me if you do?"

"I shall tell you in person. Right here, same day, same time. Does that suit you?"

She didn't hesitate for a moment. "Perfectly."

"Because if I have no success as a beggar," he went on equably, "we shall put *you* out on the streets and see what success *you* have at it!"

12

THE SUMMER PASSED THROUGH PARIS LIKE A SLOW FEVER. Even in September, when the weather began to turn cool, Georges Claudet had still not found a satisfactory form for his newest theoretical calculations. His meetings with Julie at the Cluny for informal conversation became a regular weekly arrangement—the same time every Wednesday—even at the same table whenever possible. Any mention of a specific experiment irritated him because he didn't want to tie himself down yet to one particular mode of thinking. He wanted to talk driftingly, impersonally, and he enjoyed nothing better than to uncover some facet of thinking that could make him change his mind about something of which he had until then a firm opinion.

Julie became more and more impatient with him even though her admiration for him continued to grow. She had finished with Salomon-Delachet and classes hadn't yet started for her pupils. There was no call on her time that wasn't self-imposed. She set herself a regimen of reading chemical theory and advanced physics to prepare herself for Claudet's work, but she lacked flexibility in higher mathematics. She looked back ruefully to Asher's naïve enthusiasm for her gifts, but it was clear to her now that while mathematics was a language she could learn to speak with competence, it was not a language in which she would ever write her own poetry.

Marcel's letters during that time were rare, friendly, and cool. She paid little attention to his observations on American life: he didn't understand the essence of what he was seeing in America any more than most Europeans did. She searched only for his feelings for her. Much of what he wrote about his work was beyond her, but she saved his letters against a day when she would know enough to understand.

She was suffused with frustration. Time was slipping by.

She still hadn't started work that might lead to the doctorate she was now determined to win. She had reached a point where she could have returned to the United States with her Sorbonne degree to a position in any of the best women's colleges, teaching chemistry, but it never once occurred to her that her scientific or European education was finished. More than that, she was determined to take a French doctorate, the most difficult one in the world to obtain. In France, the doctorate was awarded only for an original research of the first importance. The German degree was issued so routinely that the very sound of "Herr Doktor" had an almost comic-opera overtone in academic circles of serious intention. What she would do with her French Ph.D. once she got it, she didn't stop to think; with her it was a matter of feeling, a desire that was unencompassable in words.

By September, Georges Claudet was still not completely satisfied with his own formulation. She worked up enough courage to suggest a small research that she would like to try herself if she had the laboratory facilities.

"But I haven't arranged for a place to work yet," he said. "In this very café, there must be at least a dozen others—chemists, physicists, physiologists, in the same situation as you are—just as full of ideas and energy, but no laboratory to work in."

In the end, she took the problem to the principal of her own school. Fortunately, she didn't go into elaborate details, so that the principal got the impression that all she needed was some space to put a workbench and permission to use the glass beakers of the demonstration equipment. It was understood that Julie would replace anything she broke. A corridor on the top floor, Julie pointed out, had a bay in it about eight feet deep. Students passed that way only twice during the school day, and Julie promised that she would stop working during those times. She mentioned too that the work would be under the supervision of Professor Claudet of the recently formed Collège des Sciences and that he himself would be coming to check progress from time to time. The principal asked to think the matter over for a few days, but basically she was pleased at the opportunity to impress on the parents of her pupils that the school was now attracting some of the most outstanding researchers of the Republic.

Julie herself laid the foundation for all the trouble to come when she omitted to mention that she was connecting twelve feet of rubber hose to the gas outlet down the corridor for her Bunsen burners, or that twenty feet of copper tubing were going to have to run back to the faucet in the lavatory to give her water. Julie arranged all these connections after school hours when the girls were gone and the other instructors were busy correcting assignments. She worked alone at the top of the building. No one interfered.

Georges Claudet came to help her. They met the principal once on the stairway, and Julie introduced them to each other. He was examined with sharply appraising eyes that estimated the price of everything he wore and the value of everything he was before a cool nod of the head allowed him to pass. Around the end of October, he brought her a possibility:

"I can probably get a commission for you from the Bureau of Mines for a perfectly straightforward, dull, unrewarding problem that will bore you to death but pay you 500 francs: they want someone to work up a method of separation of a rare-earth double sulfate—a rhodium salt. Why they want it, I can't imagine, but who cares? At this point it's an opportunity for developing technique. And you should be finished by the time I'm ready to start."

Claudet had a remarkable sunniness of disposition that made it a quiet delight to be with him. He was kind, he had insight, he smiled often, and his way of treating what was beneath his standards was simply to ignore it. An entire population of unimaginative scientists, bad writers, untalented artists, inept musicians might never have been born as far as he was concerned. A patient shrug, and the slightest of smiles was his way of saying that the work or the man was not worth another moment of his time. Those who wished to be among his friends had to perform at their highest excellence. He was a stimulating companion, his friendship was always being sought. Through him at the Cluny and at the Balzar, Julie began to make many friends, poor young scientists—all of them as ambitious as she was, all of them existing on a few francs a day, all of them hungry for a place or a chance to work.

Her almost correct guess in the precipitation experiment had been distorted by word of mouth until it appeared that she *had* been correct and that only laboratory politics had sentenced her to a botched experimental procedure that was bound to fail while someone else stole the credit. She found that she had become a sort of café heroine, pointed out by the habitués to their guests.

When she tried to correct the story, her honesty irritated her listeners. She gave up. Georges was amused.

"You have only one choice," he advised her. "Live up to the reputation. *Be* brilliant!"

13

ONE EVENING EARLY IN NOVEMBER, JULIE WAS ALONE in her room, changing into her one dress to meet Georges. He was taking her to a concert. Their occasional afternoon meetings had become, without either of them remarking it, evening meetings as well, for concerts, theater, music hall, and modest *soirées*.

For Julie, with Marcel gone, this new life of work and friendship was a godsend. She felt Marcel's absence almost every moment of every day as pain. She was continually calculating the time difference between Paris and New Haven, as if to know the time where he was brought him closer to her. When she arose every morning, she knew it was the middle of the night for Marcel. In the Paris afternoon, a particular intensification took place for her no matter what she was doing: Marcel was rising to join the waking day.

Without Claudet and her experiment, Raubard's absence would have been too painful to bear. She rode across Paris every evening to see if a letter had come during the day. On the rare occasions when something actually was waiting, her heart rose with delight at the very sight of the envelope at her door. All she asked was to know that he continued to think about her.

On this particular day, there was no letter. The long ride home on three buses had been an empty ritual. At such times, she wanted to turn at once and leave her room; but she went through the routine of changing into her dress. As the knock sounded, with her dress half-hooked, she went to the door.

An exquisitely dressed woman of forty stood there. Her fashionable violet parasol matched her violet dress and sweeping hat. She had a long neckpiece of monkey fur. Her entire bearing was one of pride and challenge. She looked Julie up and down with a slight smile, and then said in English with the drawl of the American South: "I see that you are still in Paris, Miss Porter. I came across Paris just to see if you were here."

Julie was bewildered.

"Where else would I be?"

"In New Haven, with my husband," Madame Raubard said calmly. "May I come in?"

Julie stood aside to let her pass. She had seen the woman's face only once before. She felt pity for her, but there was something distinctly unpleasant in her bearing.

"I'm afraid you must come directly to the point," Julie said. "I'm to meet a friend, and I'm late as it is."

Once again Madame Raubard smiled with that cool disparagement. "I have already come to the point. Some woman is with my husband in America. I thought it was you. Obviously, it isn't. Who it is, I don't know. I imagine that you know even less than I do."

Julie said nothing, numbed by the woman's animosity as much as she was by what she was saying. Madame Raubard waited for Julie's response, refusing to release her.

"You look sick," said Madame Raubard. "Poor girl! But then if Marcel could be unfaithful to me with you, you must not be surprised if in your turn, he would betray you too. Still, I pity you. At least he remains my husband. You, he leaves nothing."

"I don't understand what you want, Madame Raubard," Julie said faintly. "I beg you to go. If you thought that I might have gone to America with your husband, I can understand why you might have wanted to come to see whether I were in Paris. But now that it's plain that I'm here, there is no reason for you to remain."

"I have no intention of remaining," Madame Raubard said with a little smile. "As you say, I have accomplished what I came to do."

To tell me about Marcel and another woman, Julie almost said. Then she decided not to believe the story. The woman was lying.

"He traveled on the ship to New York with a young woman," Madame Raubard went on. "He was with her constantly, so I was informed. He did not share a stateroom with her, although he spent most of his time in hers. In New York, he lived openly with her in the Hotel McAlpin as Professor and Madame Raubard. In New Haven, of course, he lives alone, but I know that she is there too. Actually, I even know her address. You must agree I had every reason to believe that it was you." She laughed a little. "It never occurred to me that he had time to begin still another affair while he was getting ready to leave Paris. On the other hand, why should you be any more successful with him than the others were? My husband is the sort of man he is," she said with a charming air of resignation that bordered on pride. "Nothing will ever change him. It would be pure hypocrisy to pretend sympathy for you, but I assure you that I *am* somewhat relieved that you appear to have found consolation in advance of this news; if indeed it is of any concern to you any more."

"Just go, Madame Raubard, just go, please!" Julie begged. She sounded faint with despair. At last, satisfied, the elegant woman adjusted her furs and with a flicker of a smile, left.

Julie closed the door after her, and stood there. Darkness fell. She lit no candle. She felt weak with pain—as if every nerve in her body were raw with exposure. After a while, she began to weep. She left the door, went to the table, and buried her face in her arms.

She didn't hear the second knock on her door. The door opened slowly—the darkness within flowing out into darkness of the landing. Georges Claudet, hat in hand, touched her shoulder before she knew he was there. Her eyes gleamed up at him in the darkness.

"I waited and waited," he said in a low voice. "Then I began to worry. Are you ill?"

She turned away and shook her head.

"Did you have bad news from home?" he asked again.

Again she shook her head: he knew that she was alone.

"A letter from Raubard?" he persisted, and even though she shook her head a third time, her manner told him that he was close to the truth. He sat down across the table from her and put his hand on hers. He made no move to put an end to the darkness. She tightened her hand on his in gratitude. They sat that way for a while. Then he gave her his handkerchief so that she could blow her nose. The homeliness of the sound was a bond between them.

14

SHE THREW HERSELF INTO WORK TO BE RID OF THE acrid memory of Madame Raubard's visit and her malice. Julie tried to tell herself to be sensible. She had never cared before how Marcel had spent his nights, she had simply shut her mind to whatever he did out of her sight.

She stood stonily at her worktable, but instead of seeing the apparatus before her, she saw Marcel leaning over a woman with indistinguishable features, kissing that new face as he used to kiss hers. If a man's body could ache with hunger for a woman, then her own body was aching just as unashamedly. A hundred times a day, as she stood there in the girls' school, with the girls sometimes trooping by her laughing and giggling, she saw herself naked on her own bed with Marcel above her, entering her. She couldn't drive the image away even by striking her head with her fists. In the end she wrote to him, describing his wife's visit. She simply stated what had happened without accusing him or demanding denials. At best she would have to wait three weeks for an answer from him.

Her nights of waiting were as bad as her days. Within a week, she looked so haggard and ill that Georges said: "This will have to stop. You're killing yourself. You must leave Paris."

"How? With what?"

"You must go to my parents' house. We live in a little town—Breuilly near Pont-l'Evêque—the countryside is beautiful, and my parents—well, you will see for yourself. They are the way people would be if a God really existed."

"But I couldn't go," Julie protested. "I don't know them, and they don't know me. And what am I to do there?"

"Invite some friend to go with you. Isn't there some young woman with whom you studied?"

"I have no friend but you."

"But wouldn't you feel compromised if I were there too?"

In spite of herself, she had to smile, but the smile was sad. "I? Compromised? Are you serious?"

233

He flushed slightly. "I asked only how you felt about it. Certainly, in Breuilly no one would think so. Everyone there knows my parents. You will come back a different woman," he said. "My father will change your life!"

Georges arranged to leave college for a week. On a windy October day of sun and fast-moving soft white clouds, they packed a bottle of wine and a parcel of lunch and rode in the second-class carriage as far as Pont-l'Evêque, where they got out and took a stage drawn by two bony horses over a muddy rutted road. The canvas curtains flapped in the gusty October air. Rain had fallen recently, and the way was slow, especially uphill. On a particularly steep slope, they had to walk to spare the animals. At another point, the leather harness snapped and the driver got down and made the repair with a string as if it were a matter of course. He was a heavy man about Georges's age and spoke to him familiarly. Arsène's one acknowledgment of Georges's position in French science was the question: "How are things in Paris?" Julie he called mademoiselle, and said: "I thought maybe she was from Marseilles." Mostly, though, Arsène gave Georges the gossip of the region. "He takes too much on himself, your father. He refuses to listen to anyone, and yet we all try to make him slow down." The day, the stage driver, the rutted road, the countryside about them, all reminded her so poignantly of West Tisbury that a sense of relief suffused her. She swayed with the stage, feeling the countryside as it passed—the trees, grass, leaves, sky, clouds, and shadows. Within her was a familiar song whose melody was the wind and the murmur of green things stirring. In this wild, sweet world, only one other human being existed with her: Georges. Marcel belonged to the more brutal species, along with his wife and all the shouting, cursing, sweating, urgent, grasping people who bruised each other with blows, cries, and maliciously broken promises. Here she was free of them all.

No further bad news could reach her here. She felt safe, protected by a friend. The French voices became a murmured blur of sound. What she felt for Georges had a haunting familiarity; she had known it all before—affection, veneration, gratitude—and then a name flashed into her mind: *Ronny!* because this was what her brother used to call up in her. She had the same sense about him that she had during the shipboard interview—a longing, not to possess him, but to be transmuted into him.

Georges's parents were really what he had said they were. His father had been the local schoolmaster for forty years, and everyone roundabout between the ages of fifteen and forty-five had once had to stand before him to recite lessons. His meticulous clothing was old and had gone out of style twenty years before; his wire-framed spectacles were bent, battered, and patched. His wooden shoes were his sole concession to the countryside. He wore them for tramping along the muddy ways and across the fields. He, M. le curé, and M. le maire formed the triumvirate that ran the town's lives. M. le curé, the priest represented the Right, the mayor considered himself the red-white-and-blue-sashed embodiment of the Third Republic, and M. Claudet was the proud disciple of the spirit of the Commune. Everyone's troubles were his business.

At the supper table, two candles kept the family from darkness. The fragile old man, who had never traveled more than twenty miles from the village, sat at the head, accustomed to his authority. His only son, whose name was already spoken with respect in five languages showed him the same deference and respect that he had as a boy.

"It's a tragedy that one of the great savants of our time can't see that the human mind is the most exalted creation we know," he said of Marcel, for whom he had reverence even though he regretted Marcel's beliefs. "I pity him for his blindness. For me, the training of the mind is the noblest of professions! All my life, I've been exalted by my calling. Certainly, it's true, the intellect has still not evolved to its utmost capacity. Until it has, we have to bear with the tragic events caused by man's misjudgments. But the future must certainly be the earthly paradise built out of man's ultimate wisdom and goodness! It pains me so to see that you no longer share this vision, my son. How sad it must be to live without the feeling that one is working toward a future of joy!"

The older Claudet spoke with tender compassion. He was intensely aware of his son and loved him warmly. What Julie had wanted from her own father, this man was giving freely to the only person in the world she now loved as a friend; and in gratitude she loved the old man.

"Perhaps my father is right," Georges said to her, as they walked together the following morning. The day was windless and gray with a low, hard ceiling of cloud that made every sound flat, clear, and small. A road passed out of Breuilly that Georges said he had never taken before beyond a certain farmhouse. They soon passed it. On one side of the road was a peat bog, on the other a stand of thin trees black with a rain that had ceased about dawn. She was suffused by a gentle sadness, but she wasn't depressed. She felt an unending tenderness for the delicate man with her. It moved her to see how unaware he was of his superiority to his father in knowledge, accomplishment, and potential. Then she saw that it was neither naïveté nor childishness in Georges. It had to mean that he possessed an intuitive recognition that there was more to a man's worth than his stock of information, or his learning, or his material possession. It was in this indefinable realm that Georges must realize he was still a lesser man than his father.

She put the question directly. "What does he believe about himself?" she asked Georges. "If there were such a thing as a philosophic algebra, every man would have to solve two simultaneous equations for himself. The first equation would define his place in the infinite cosmos of atoms, space, and prime forces. The second would state his place in the finite cosmos of men and society. Either religion or physics takes care of the first, but the second equation is what we're talking about now. There is something your father believes about who he is, and what he does—both in the town, and at home with you and your mother, that makes him a superior person. I feel it as well as you do. I love him. He is simple, even childlike at times, and yet only a fool would condescend to him. What is it that he has?"

"I don't know yet," Georges said simply. "I know that it's there. I feel it. But I can't name it; I can't measure it."

"Can you duplicate it within yourself?" she asked.

"I try."

"And I think you achieve it," she said. "Tell me this then: when you do it, what do you tell yourself to do?"

He burst out laughing after a moment. "I used to tell myself: 'Behave like Father.' Now it has become a habit."

"Is it only mimicry?"

"No," he said. "If there were a guiding precept, I think it would run something like this: make yourself completely open to what another person is feeling and have pity for it. But you see, Julie, I can achieve it only when what some other person feels is something I can respect. When I can't respect it, the person ceases to exist for me. That is where my father is superior to me. I cannot imagine a limit to his compassion."

"And what is Marcel's feeling about your father?"

"You have to understand that Marcel is a man who is crippled by despair. His inner self is black with it—the way the heart of a dying tree is black with what is killing it. If someone in a Paris café were to say the things to him that my father does, Marcel would demolish him with a savagery you have still to see. But when my father says them, Marcel never answers. Not out of forebearance; but because my father is spotless of despair. It's a superiority Marcel cannot question. My God, how I pity that man!"

She sighed and shook her head. "If you know Marcel so well, you must know about every part of his life."

"As well as you can know another man," he said cautiously.

"You know then about the women."

Georges said nothing—his expression went blank except for his eyes.

"And about me too?"

This time his answer was direct but gentle. "About you too."

She told him about Madame Raubard's visit. "Was what she told me true?"

"How can I know? I've heard absolutely nothing to make me think it true. You have to ask him, not me."

"I did. I've already written to him. But still, I'm asking you."

"Julie, don't torment yourself. You are here to forget about such things." He turned away from her and pointed through the dripping trees. "Look at that little lake over there. I remember where we are now. All along I've been having the feeling that I saw all this before—"

Julie would not permit the evasion any more than the sunless day permitted a shadow. "Georges," she said, calling him back, "you know Marcel. Is what his wife said possible?"

He turned to her now with a directness that held no pity.

"It *is* possible," he said. His gaze was without compromise. "You know that as well as I."

15

RESEARCH JOURNALS, UNIVERSITY SEMINAR ROOMS, AND cafés frequented by scientists were filled that year with a clatter of gossip. All over Europe, test tubes, distillation flasks, and hypodermic syringe barrels were producing new surprises in every field of chemistry. It was a year of excitement for young chemists. For older men it was a time of trouble and heartache. Theories resting on a lifetime of work were suddenly proven wrong. Reputations that had been secure were headed for oblivion.

In the Boulevard St. Michel, on the Rue St. Jacques, in the Place de la Sorbonne, however, were all the young men who were avid for the future to begin. To them, the entrenched ideas were so recently learned that they seemed as new as the very newest. There was no dramatic choice for them between old and new. Because it was easy for the young to be objective, they appeared ruthless to their elders.

Actually the young men were in love with a way of life. What the money world's myopia failed to see was that the seemingly quiet realm of the scientist was a place of passionate pursuit of fantastic goals—a world with a ravening appetite to probe, to discover, to know.

One cool spring evening at the Café Cluny, with six chairs squeezed in a circle around a table barely large enough to hold the glasses and saucers, two chemists, a physicist, and a mathematician were passionately arguing with Georges. Gaslight flickered in the dark wind that swirled up from the Seine. Julie listened idly. Within a few months she had become used to being the only woman in a radius of six or eight tables—alone among forty men; until a man's chance word or even an inflection of his voice or a glance would remind her that she was like a little girl seated on the grass while all around her lay coiled the recumbent body of a giant sun-dozing lion, content for the moment to let her live and share the light and the glorious day. At any moment the animal might turn its great slow blinking eyes to look at her, its tail might twitch once or twice; and before that great maned head turned leisurely away again she would be obliterated. Her position in Parisian science was so tenuous that she didn't dare think about it.

With half her mind, she eavesdropped on the conversations about her. On one side, there was excited talk on the possibility of radioactivity in the sun. On the other side a biochemist was describing how the serum of human blood was physically incompatible with the sera of blood from other species. Behind her an opinionated organic chemist was claiming that Kekulé's insight into the structure of the benzene ring was as great an achievement as Mendeleyev's recognition of the periodicity on atomic structure. The talk bubbled with controversy. But by now she knew who everyone was, and that only a few of them were talking from first-hand, experimental knowledge.

But whatever they lacked in cash, research equipment, or access to some cubbyhole laboratory, they more than made up in spirit, inventiveness, and intellectual daring.

A chance remark at another table evoked an overwhelming picture in her mind: in a black velvet void, she saw a huge drop of water shining with diamond brilliance. She felt exaltation. She was seeing the drop both from within and without at the same time with the omniscience of dreams. Something profound seemed about to be revealed to her. The drop throbbed and pulsated before her eyes—powered by the shimmer of individual molecules—a motion of exquisite delicacy that was timeless, deathless, endlessly vital. The elements of life charged the water globule: energy, dissolved acids, salts, minute suspensions and fragile jellies, each linked to all the others by stabbing threads of electric current and tendrils of magnetism.

The vision for her was apocalyptic: she had a rushing sense of water as the medium, the atmosphere, the very essence of organic life, permeating even the subcells of every living thing on earth. Water could no longer be seen as inert to what took place within it, the way air was to the flight of birds. Water, modified and altered in a million variations by whatever it held in suspension and solution, was itself the substance of an entire chemistry. She sat there in the café with a sense of dedication that stunned her—the need to explore the universe within the drop of water as far as she could go.

The others at her own table continued to talk, unaware of

what had happened to her or what her silence meant. For the rest of the gaslit evening she had nothing to say and no one noticed, not even Georges.

16

SHE WAS SITTING MOTIONLESS IN THE MORNING SUN-light in her room when the tap came at the door. She didn't look up from the letter in her hand even though she had stopped reading it. The rap came again, more sharply, but she was still too listless to reply or even to raise her eyes.

With the next knock, the door was pushed open. Georges entered and glanced at what was in her hand.

"From Marcel?" he asked. She slid the letter into the envelope. "No," she said.

"I can come back later if you want."

"No," she said quietly. She put calm into her voice. "It's only a family matter. Besides, if you came, it must be important."

"It is," he said. He sat down opposite her. "I'm ready for you to begin work."

She gave him her face and filled it with attention, but her mind kept wandering back into its cave of pain. She tried again and again to concentrate on what Georges was saying, yet it flowed past her like an autumn wind. Only a few whirling leaves of words tumbled out of it: "Colloids . . . ultramicroscope . . . gold sol . . . Zsigmondy." Out in the void where she hung suspended, she silently asked herself: What in the world was an ultramicroscope? Zsigmondy was a name she vaguely remembered from research journals: either the *Zeitschrift für Physikalische Chemie, Annelen,* or the *Chemische Physik* or anyone of a half dozen others. She only knew that he was concerned with those liquid systems which refused to obey any of the laws that governed true solutions. Julie didn't know what Georges was talking about—not so much out of ignorance as because her concentration had been shattered into uncollectable pieces of grief.

Georges was so absorbed that he didn't detect her fraud for almost half an hour, then abruptly he stopped.

"You heard nothing I said!"

"But I did!"

He picked up the envelope on the table and glanced at its postmark. "It *is* from Marcel," he said coldly. "You allowed me to go on!"

"Read it yourself," she said almost without interest. He instantly dropped the letter back on the table. "No, seriously, it's all about Gibbs," she went on. "Not a word about me, about himself, or the things his wife came here to tell me."

"Perhaps he thinks it too ridiculous to treat seriously."

"I don't think you really believe that, Georges," she said quietly. "You believe what I do: that this is his answer."

Georges seemed to be observing the patterns of pressure along his tightly clasped fingers. Then he straightened up at last and as if she hadn't spoken at all; he said stonily: "Here is what you must read for the background to the work. These three articles gave me the information I needed to go ahead. When you've finished, we'll talk again."

He took the journals from his portfolio and left them. Then without meeting her gaze, he rose swiftly, shook her limp hand, and left. She knew him well enough to know that he was offended, but not why. She made no move to go after him.

17

SHE WANTED A SPECIFIC ANSWER FROM MARCEL TO HER letter, and at the same time she dreaded one. The days continued to go by without a word. Now it was Claudet who was pressing her to work where she had once pressed him. He didn't once refer to Marcel's unresponsive letter. Until now he had been content to sit in his study, or the café, talking, speculating, making seemingly endless calculations that were unsolvable. The German research though had made everything fall into place for him. He became hurried, taut, abrupt. The little working space which Julie had found in her school was suddenly precious to him, but it was impossible to remove even temporarily the apparatus she was using for the commissioned experiments. Its structure was such that once it came down, it would be down for good.

"Then finish it up as fast as you can," he said.

"I *am* working that fast right now."

"It's not fast enough," he said. "I'll help you."

She had never seen him at a worktable. She couldn't imagine him with his sleeves rolled up.

He arrived one afternoon after school hours—with a neatly packed paper parcel under one arm. He scarcely nodded to her, removed his coat and vest, turned back his cuffs, opened the parcel, slipped on the lab smock it contained, buttoned it all the way up, and gently put her aside as he stepped to the table. He looked at her apparatus, at her placing of the reagent bottles, at the empty flasks, whistled softly to himself, riffled through the last few pages of her notebook, which lay open on the table, asked her a couple of questions, and then finally nodded his head. He then swiftly rearranged the positions of all the bottles and test tubes until he was satisfied. He turned back to the most recent entry in the notebook and put his finger on a solubility determination.

"We start from here."

The elegance he had in repose, he had in motion. It suddenly came clear to her that he had rearranged the table like a surgeon—with everything placed nearest to hand. He did all the things every chemist was trained to do, but he did them with superlative deftness. In one continuous motion, he could unstopper a reagent bottle with his knuckles, and, gripping the stopper between them like the jewel of some monstrous ring, the same fingers and palm were free to grasp the bottle, lift, and pour out of it what was needed then replace and restopper it—all in one uninterrupted turning and flexing of a hand. He used his fingertips, palms, tongue, lips, and eyes. He sniffed a test tube's contents by wafting the vapor above it toward his nose with a few flutters of his fingers—one of the most basic precautions of the laboratory chemist against unexpectedly noxious fumes—but when he did it, he had the manner of a man in complete control of his quest. Working with no more than a tenth of what any chemist had a right to expect, he improvised with the means at hand so that not a moment was lost. When she could be of help, he told her what needed doing. Otherwise, she simply stood aside, kept out of his way, and gave herself an education by watching him.

During those few weeks there was still not a word from

Marcel. It occurred to her that perhaps her letter had never reached him. She wrote another.

Two months from the time he began, Georges completed her assignment for her. As soon as the date was noted in her ledger, he was off to the instrument makers for the parts he had designed for his ultramicroscope, leaving Julie to finish off the contract by writing up a fair copy of the report on the experiment for the Bureau. She discovered that Georges was paying for the instrument parts for his new research out of his own pocket. He had to borrow bus fare from her to ride across Paris to collect his salary. He was completely unembarrassed by his predicament.

Once she got the Bureau report out of the way, he pulled her into his frenzy. The fever of impatience to get the instrument assembled drove them both without mercy. Together, he and Julie arranged the optical train of lenses and slits for the impinging light beam. He even set up a carbon arc to give the sort of intense light source that was necessary for the ultramicroscope. The electric arc was dazzlingly bright but lacked steadiness. Georges then switched over to the high-voltage spark that was their undoing. The arc had had a comparatively quiet hiss; the spark's roar reverberated through the entire building. For the first time the principal took the trouble to come up to the top floor to see what in the world was going on.

She shrieked, then put her hands over her eyes to shield herself from the brutal glare.

"Fire!" she shouted. "My school! Fire!"

"It's only an electric spark," Georges called to her, but the clatter of ten thousand electric discharges a second drowned his voice. The terrified woman continued to scream. "Fire! Fire!"

Georges pulled the switch. Abruptly the roar and brilliance ceased.

"Madame, I beg you, it's nothing!" he said gently.

Timidly she peered between her fingers, spread her fingers still more, then finally lowered her hands, furious for having been frightened.

"Nothing?" she said. "You call that nothing?" She looked around sharply, determined to find something to justify her outrage. She found more than she expected—gasped, and pointed speechlessly to the unauthorized gas lines which snaked out from the main; at the unsanctioned copper water pipes that ran back to the lavatory, at the wires that ran to the precious electric cable from the school's own generator.

"What's that?" she cried. "And that? And that? You're robbing me!" Again she put her hands to her face in horror. "How dare you? Oh, how dare you! This is worse than the fire!"

"But, madame—" said Julie. "I told you that all I wanted to do—"

"You said nothing! All this costs money!" the distraught woman cried. "You misled me! You lied to me!"

"I never—!" said Julie with a white face, but Georges motioned her to silence.

"Madame," he said gently. "Mademoiselle Porter meant no harm. I know she acted with the best intentions. She certainly thought she had your permission. And certainly what she has used should be paid for—"

"Dishonest!" insisted the principal. "Dishonest!"

"Naïve," said Georges. "Naïve. And let's say that what has been consumed of water, gas, electric current comes to"—he took a number at random—"say ten francs?"

"Absolutely not!" she retorted with no clearer idea than he of what was involved. "At least twenty. But dishonest!"

"No, madame, naïve. But you're of course right about the twenty francs," he replied and counted it out though he barely could manage the sum. The principal took the money. Her face had not relented at all, but the rigid outrage of her body had gone. She faced Julie:

"As for you, mademoiselle, I'll allow myself to be convinced of your simplicity. You may continue to teach chemistry here, but all these wires and tubes must be out of here by tonight. Is that clear?"

"Perfectly, madame," said Julie quietly and the woman stalked out, leaving Julie and Georges in shattered silence—they were homeless once again.

18

IN THE BASEMENT DARKNESS, THE HORIZONTAL SHAFT OF light was as brilliant as newly minted gold. It extended only six inches. Within that distance the shape was changed by lenses and slits to the flat blade of light that slid like a sword into the telescope objective of the ultramicroscope and impaled the drop of liquid held there for examination.

Dust motes in the still stale basement air barely drifted through the bar of light, but the points of brilliance which Julie looked down on in the illuminated drop on the slide beneath her eyepiece darted microscopic distances with erratic swiftness. She had envisioned it all weeks earlier in the café before she had ever known what experiment Georges had in preparation. The uncanny repetition in reality of what she had once only imagined gave the experiment a dreamlike, *déjà vu* quality that almost drew her out of the dark mood with which she had come to the new laboratory earlier in the day.

She forced herself again to concentrate on counting the number of moving star points within the field of light. Some of them jumped and darted at lunatic speeds; others had only a quivering jiggle. Still others were almost completely motionless. Her eye couldn't distinguish the differences in size. Her count was sidetracked by the rhythm and scrape of a shovel across the basement floor scooping up coal for the furnace. She had to shut out the sound, and begin over—almost fiercely glad of the distraction from herself.

Georges had come upon this new working space in the basement of his own school. One day, he had seen that some leftover lumber stored opposite the coal bin could be stacked into one single ceiling-high pile, clearing several times as much floor space as Julie had had in her top floor window bay. The college gave Georges permission to rearrange the lumber on condition that he do it all on his own time, at his own expense, and as long as he didn't interfere with the school's routine. As for the school's water, gas, and electricity, they could be used by him in his experiments as long as the initial installations and connections made no claim on the institute's budget.

Georges's senior students had formed a volunteer labor squad. They cleared the lumber, stacked it, sawed and nailed together a wall of raw board to screen the laboratory space, while others ran water pipes, gas lines, and electric cables. On the day of completion, Georges and Julie played host and hostess in the laboratory at a mock-solemn celebration arranged by the students themselves: their leader, like a general at a review, called each of the volunteer workers out by name, and

as he listed the young man's contribution with pompous flour-
ishes, another student penciled his highly unflattering carica-
ture on the bare wood wall. The student who had been named
bowed, stepped forward, and wrote his signature under the
monstrous portrait with as much dignity as if he were signing
a treaty. When it was all finished, the leader dedicated the
eleven portraits to Georges: "No cathedral is complete without its gargoyles!"

After that the real work had gone forward with a surge.
From the beginning Georges hoped that the ultramicroscope
would enable him to prove once he had learned the delicate
tricks of the instrument, that there was no clear line to be
drawn between single molecules that were truly dissolved in a
liquid and the molecular aggregates that hung in fine suspension—the colloids. He was convinced, though, that the colloidal solutions—however transparent and clear they might appear to the naked eye—were not solutions at all but simply
suspensions. This would explain once and for all why they dis-
obeyed the classical rules. He and Julie, at that point of the
research that was to make their reputations and then smash
their lives, both thought only in the most austere terms of
physical chemistry.

Also, the reason they decided to work with colloidal solutions of gold was that the gold salt was so easily available in
photography supply shops. Not for one moment did Georges
or Julie anticipate where it was all going to lead.

The only times Julie's thoughts strayed were when she wondered about the mail that still didn't come from Marcel. She
got used to the few bad minutes every day of climbing her
stairs, waiting to see, once her eyes were level with the landing, whether or not there was a white envelope half protruding from beneath her door where the concierge would have
placed it.

She had even begun to dismiss what his wife had said, or at
least it seemed to have faded somewhat in the back of her
mind—until that very afternoon. She and Georges had met at
the instrument maker, and together they were riding back to
the college, holding the paper-wrapped lens mounts in their
laps. They were on the open upper deck of the omnibus. It
was a gray November day with a threatening sky and the wet
scent of rain in the air. Two lines of passengers, seated back
to back on the long bench that ran fore and aft, swayed with
the vehicle's motion behind the three plodding horses.

Very gradually she became aware of whom the voices behind her were talking. She turned involuntarily to Georges, but he sat as if he were deaf—with a stiff, angry face, staring straight ahead at the passing branches of the boulevard trees. The two young men at their backs were sharing the same story that Madame Raubard had come across Paris to tell her: they were laughing with admiration for Marcel's ability to make life obey his will regardless of the cost to others. The two gossipers got off somewhere near the Luxembourg, and she and Georges rode on in silence. Neither of them made a single reference to what they both had heard, even when they got off at the college. They separated without a word.

She kept the overheard conversation just beyond her attention while she concentrated rigidly on the job she was supposed to do—the determination of the particle density. It was a matter of straightforward counting. But she could concentrate stonily for only so long, and then she would hear herself going, ". . . fifty-eight . . . fifty-nine . . . fifty . . . fifty-one" and it was time to start all over again.

The darting points, too small to be seen by direct light, continued to sparkle at her from within the illuminated drop on the microscope slide the way the tiny glass shards can be seen glinting on a sunlit hillside miles away.

She had the count going well when she heard Georges come into the laboratory to see about his own evaporation experiment. A flash of yellow light in the corner of her eye told her he had lit the Bunsen burner. She heard the rattle of glass and porcelain.

At the end of her fifty count, she stopped for a moment and raised her head to rest her eyes. Georges was standing at the worktable with a beaker steaming in front of him. He kept the flame low and the rate of boiling down so that nothing would be lost through splatter.

"How does it go?" he asked. He kept his attention focused on what he was doing.

"All right," she replied. "And your lecture?"

"Not bad. Listen, Julie, about the omnibus—"

"There's nothing to talk about," she said cutting him off. "Marcel is the kind of man he is. He never pretended to be anything else. I either take things as they are, or I simply walk away."

"Yes, Julie," he said softly.

"Talk doesn't help."

"No, Julie."

"So I work and that's all."

She put her head back to the eyepiece, but she had to stop and rub away what blurred her eyes. He had caught the gesture but glanced back immediately to his work.

"I'll be all right," she said. "I'm all right this very moment. Ever since I came in, I've been thinking about it; and I've decided to walk away."

"Have you, Julie?"

"Yes," she said quietly. "I have to."

19

SHE WAS POURING THE DISTILLED WATER INTO THE 300-cc beaker when it occurred to her that a hurdy-gurdy was tinkling out a tune on the sidewalk above her head on the far side of the cement walls. She listened for a moment to the distant jingle of sound, trying to place the melody. Then she abruptly brought back her attention: the water had reached the halfway mark. For a few moments she was busy again, concentrated and frowning. She placed the beaker on an iron gauze over a Bunsen flame. With a pipette, she measured 1 cc. of gold-chloride solution and allowed its muddy turbidity to run into the heated water. She waited for the muddy water to boil and listened again. The hurdy-gurdy had moved to another spot farther away; but the song was the same. A stream of soft air touched her, and she looked up: the high basement window was open, and she saw soft blue sky. Suddenly realization hit her: it was spring, she thought with a shock. Another spring!

Then she remembered she had hurried to the laboratory through a spring morning; she had walked home late the night before through a spring darkness.

To be so absorbed as to miss the coming of spring! She thought of Vineyard beaches—the lap and curl of sunlit waves, the scent of bayberry bushes, the twitter of black and white sandpipers on empty beach and the golden twinkle of their yellow legs running from the white wash of foam.

The thermometer in the flask caught her eye: it had

climbed to within twenty degrees below boiling. Automatically now, her hand reached for the reagent bottle labeled N/5 $NACO_3$. She measured off 2½ cc. in a small graduated cylinder, which she held up before her eyes—it wasn't too crucial, even 3 cc. would do—and poured it into the steaming beaker. It splashed, bubbled once, and then was lost in the larger opaque mass.

The hurdy-gurdy was far away now—so faint she hardly heard it through the rumble of young men's feet overhead. She watched the beaker approaching boil.

Pin-point bubbles foamed at the bottom of the beaker. Her attention wandered again. Her stirring rod was ready in her hand. She didn't remember picking it up, but her fingers had known what to do. Now the true boil was reached—and she stirred vigorously. While the liquid was still spinning in its own vortex, she measured out again 3 cc. of the dilute formaldehyde solution, and, with her hand under tight control, she poured gradually, steadily, but really quite quickly, the odorous liquid into the churning spinning mass. The moment the last drop hit the boiling turbid surface, her other hand was already at the gas petcock and had snapped it off. She stood watching the liquid surface as it spun less and less swiftly. Clarity began to grow within the beaker as if the sun were dissipating a mist in ruby-colored air. At the end of a minute, no more, the solution was absolutely clear and a brilliant pure red. Only when the red liquid was strongly illuminated and observed from the side would the subvisible particles of gold twinkle in reflected light like microscopic motes of dust in a shaft of sunlight.

She let it remain there to cool and turned away to use the free few minutes for taking a reading on the first gold colloid she had ever prepared—almost eight months ago. It was their museum piece. She expertly took a drop of red liquid from the labeled bottle, put it on the specially ground slide, and slid it beneath the objective of the microscope. Her hands flipped switches, turned dials, while her eyes were already noting other details. The light of the ultramicroscope stabbed through its course and illuminated the drop.

Within it, the star points of light darted, vibrated, and drifted, exactly as they had on the first day the solution had been prepared months before. She made the notation in the data book. There was no diminution in energy, no sedimentation, no sign of any change of stability. Its source of energy seemed infinite. Then suddenly she had too much of the eternities of the inanimate. She had a warm longing, almost a bodily hunger, to see flowers, to pick grass and feel it in her hands, to see fields of daisies and rolling green horizons of hilltops and distant stands of woods.

If only Georges would give her enough time off to go down to the flower market, where she'd find that sweet smell of green things and the cool damp aroma of rich earth! He was the boss, *le patron*. The schedule of work was a heavy one though, and it was her own doing: Georges had been invited to read a paper at the Société de Chimie-Physique. When he had held back, she had been the one to urge him, to promise him the results of these additional experiments. Now he was counting on it. Perhaps Sunday afternoon, she consoled herself. She could make herself wait until then.

Georges was a fine man, she thought, but something in him must be missing. Was it humor? Was it the juices of life? When he came down at the end of his lecturing, instead of feeling softened by the spring day, he was irritable. What had she done wrong? He was looking at the data book and shaking his head. Abruptly, he slammed it shut.

"Go home. Pack a bag! We're going to the country!"

She was so shocked with delight, she kissed him.

"I'm not a machine, and neither are you!" she said. "Thank God!"

They were settled in the coach and the train had been speeding through the countryside for over an hour before he told her that Marcel was not returning to Paris for at least another year. She took the news silently. Georges had not ordered the trip because he shared her hunger for the springtime countryside, but to cushion the blow. What she felt, she herself couldn't name, but it was a bruise—big, diffuse, and distant. It had been six months since the overheard conversation on the bus convinced her that any future with Marcel would be too painful to bear. It would have been futile to blame him for being the man he had never denied being. His letters continued to drift in as haphazardly as ever. He never even asked why she now wrote rarely, and so impersonally. She had always assumed, though, that Marcel would have informed her himself that he wasn't coming home and now he hadn't bothered to do even that. If ever a last nail had been driven in a coffin, this was it.

20

DURING THE SUMMER MONTHS WHEN THE NEW EXPERI-
ments began, the basement laboratory was a cool and comfortable place to work. In August, though, the empty building
was locked up entirely. A heat wave moved up from the
south like an invasion of the sky, and the baked city shimmered in the brassy glare. Julie and Georges took the train
once again to his parents. A violent thunderstorm reverberated over Paris as they left, but inside the coach, Julie
swayed on the wooden bench with the comfortable sense that
she was on her way to familiar places where she was wel-
come and liked.

The heat was in Breuilly too—it lay all over France that
summer—but she and Georges took walks in the woods and
along the streams where the shaded air was cool. There were
long comfortable silences between them. Georges flicked the
pond surfaces with an idly swung twig that momentarily interrupted the buzz and swirl of gnats and water flies. Then he
would break his long silences and talk in a sudden rush about
a new phase of the work which had begun to interest him:
the means by which the colloid particle was able to maintain
itself in eternal suspension. He was sure that the answer was
to be found in some interaction between the electrified atmosphere that enveloped each particle and the surrounding
water. She listened with only half her attention. Her very soul
was indolent. Finally he laughed at her, stretched out on the
grass.

"You're too lazy to live. Let's take a walk to the ocean."

"The ocean!"

"It's only a few days' walk. I've got a knapsack. All we do
is go due north, and sooner or later we'll get there."

Cool shadows lay between the lines of plumed trees when
they started the following morning. They rode for a while in
an ox-cart that jolted along through the scent of sunlit meadows and sweet clover. At a crossroad they left the cart and
the shaded road and struck out across a sun-laden tilled field

that hummed with insect life. A windmill turned and groaned and fluttered in the green distance.

That evening they stopped at a farmhouse where a woman was drawing water from a well. Georges spoke to her for a few moments while a dog pranced and barked. Then Georges came back to where Julie was leaning on the fence on her elbows, enjoying the cool turn of the day.

"We'll stay here tonight," Georges said. "She has a room we can use."

"*A* room?"

"I suppose she thought we're married," he said negligently. "Don't worry, I'll find someplace to sleep."

They had a simple meal of thick soup and cheese with the family. After supper, it was still light. She and Georges took a wordless stroll along a deserted canal that was still as death. Not even a dragonfly whirred in the glassy quiet. By candle-light they went into the white-washed room they had been given. It had only one huge bed, not a chair or even a stool. Georges took off his shoes, stretched out on the floor with the knapsack as his pillow, and fell asleep at once. With his legs drawn up a little, and with his gentle slow breathing, he was the essence of innocence. She had to laugh at her predica-ment, but there was nothing to do but undress and get into the bed, conscious of his presence for the first time. She thought: a man is sleeping in my bedroom, but then she too fell asleep. When she awoke in floods of sunlight, he was al-ready out.

The next night, they slept at an inn in separate rooms. Through the thin wall that was between them, she thought again that she could hear that light weightless breathing of his. Once more she was aware of him as a man. In the after-noon they reached the Channel.

As they strolled along the flat empty beach, she felt dwarfed by the sky's silent immensity. She was thinking about Georges all the time now, grateful that he had never made a move to trespass. Instead, there he was, wandering down to the water's edge by himself. Could it be that he had no awareness of her as a woman? She was curious about what was in his mind now. She found herself looking at him with a different interest as he came back to her across the wide tidal flats of gleaming sand. His trousers were rolled up, his bare feet looked slender and fleet.

The fragment of a seashell in his hand fascinated him with

its lamination. But her attention was all on him now: his hands and wrists, she noted, were also delicate, yet full of strength. He held out the shell to her, and she found herself wondering what she would feel if he were to touch her. He went on talking—he had a child's curiosity and an encyclopedic knowledge—but she was examining his pale curving lips, the slight slant of his eyes, and the set of his ears flat against his head. Yet no, she thought, she could discern in herself no physical desire for him. Still, she began to wonder a moment later, what she would feel if he were ever to put his hand on hers. She looked up to find that he had stopped talking: he had asked her something. He was puzzled by her silence and the unusual inner thoughtfulness in her expression.

She searched herself to remember his words, then gave him the answer that allowed him to continue, but he had been made less sure of himself. On that dark silent level where people communicate without words, he sensed that she had asked him something, but it took time for the meaning to reach him. Because it was so diffuse, though, it seemed not a question from her but an idea of his own, and he was embarrassed and burdened by it. By the time they rode back to Paris to resume work, they were both silent; and Julie, also without knowing quite how or why it had all happened, had the heartbroken perception that a period of innocence had ended.

21

HE KEPT HIS FACE AVERTED ANGRILY FROM WHAT HE was feeling and in those weeks he focused his passion on the investigation of the submicroscopic atmospheres of electric charge surrounding the colloid particles. In the ultramicroscope, he could now make the darting star points twirl and spin with sudden attacks of insanity and then abruptly disappear as if swallowed up. Like a nightful of falling stars, the points of light plummeted to extinction as each in turn was caught and divested of its electrical atmosphere by invisible sodium ions.

The entire procedure required infinite delicacy to set up, observe, and to measure. As the work went along, Julie thought that Georges's increasing irritability came from the experiment itself.

Then abruptly he rose from the stool and stood facing her: "Understand that Marcel isn't like other men!" he said harshly, to her astonishment. "No one has the right to judge him who doesn't also judge his work! It's wrong of you—cruel and disloyal—to make me criticize him because of things he does in his life which are really no concern of mine! Or of anyone else's, for that matter! He's my teacher and my friend! No matter what he says or does, he has inner honesty! I admire him more than any other man I know!"

His face was red, his eyes blazed, his voice shook. She sat stupefied as he counted up Marcel's successive brilliances, each one of them enough to make a man's reputation.

"*That's* what *you* ought to feel for him—*that* respect, *that* forgiveness, *that* pity! *You* above everyone else. You're no ordinary woman. Otherwise I'd never have fallen in love with you the way I have! Yes!" he shouted at her. "Yes! I'm in love with you! God help me, I have been from almost the beginning!"

Then he turned away from her, and walked swiftly out of the laboratory, then out of the basement altogether.

She remained dumbly behind. Out of pure shock, she went on like an automaton. She was heartbroken: for the one person whom she had considered her friend—actually the one friend she had known in her life—she could feel only pity. She waited until after seven in the evening but he didn't return to the laboratory. She walked home with yellow gaslight flaring in the street lamps and in the café signs. One candle after the other burned down during the evening as she kept hoping that Georges would come. He stayed away from the laboratory the next day too. She wondered if upstairs he were staying away from his lectures as well, but she didn't embarrass him by going up in search of him through the college.

That evening again he didn't come to her room. She could no longer bear the thought of him in pain. She set out to look for him. She had never been to his room before, but she knew his address. When he opened his door to her knock and saw her, his expression changed to utter confusion and anger, but she went in nevertheless. She had the sense of a room not very much larger than her own.

"Have you been ill?" she asked as she came in.

"No," he said quietly. He turned the lamp up a little and the shadows were huge on the figured wallpaper. The room seemed a jungle of books. Everything was instantly familiar.

"Why have you stayed away?"

"Because I can't work with you."

"But *why?*"

"I told you why."

"You told me nothing."

"Nothing?" he demanded coldly. "I told you the most important fact in my life, of my existence!"

"That, yes," she agreed calmly. "But that needn't mean that you're unable to work with me."

"I can't pretend that I never said what I did say, or that I don't feel it."

"But you can't discharge me! It's more than the work. Look at you—you haven't slept—"

"Julie, I can't work with you any more," he said with agonized insistence. "I've betrayed my friendship for Marcel, I've betrayed the work, my relation with you—"

"Oh my God! How many scruples! What's come over you! You don't even sound like yourself!"

"Because that self doesn't exist any more."

"And all because you told me you love me?"

Her careless tone shocked him and made him turn pale. "Yes," he said, with quiet pride. "Because I no longer have a disguise for my feelings."

"What do you want?" she asked sick at heart with hopelessness. "I can't bear to see you in such pain!"

"I can never work with you again the way we worked before," he said. "To settle for less than I need would be humiliating to me and a nuisance to you. I couldn't bear to see myself through your eyes—"

"Stop!" Her voice was low but intense. "Stop it at once! Stop doing that to yourself. I asked you: what do you want so we can go on working together? I'm more than your assistant. I'm your partner—less than you, of course, but still your partner."

"Julie—for God's sake, go away! I could work with you now only if we were more than friends; more even than mistress and lover—only as husband and wife. That's impossible, yet nothing less would do!"

"All right!" she said, as surprised as he was at her words.

The radiant change in his heartbroken eyes was itself a reward. He didn't trust himself to take her hands, so she was the one who gave them to him. "I've been happy in my life only since I've known and been with you," she said.

He had no words, and he took her to him. At the first touch of her face against his, all emotion in her stopped like a bird stricken in mid-flight. Unnamable emptiness in her heart—utter loneliness—was the answer to the question she had asked herself so idly weeks ago: What would she feel if he touched her? Now, too late, she knew. She didn't—she probably wouldn't ever—love him. She was drenched with sadness and regret. Still, if she could give Georges comfort and pleasure, that would be small repayment for what he had already given her. She might not feel for him what she had for other men she had known, but what she did feel for him was unique.

He put his hands on her shoulders and gently held her away to look at her in a plea for her honesty.

"Julie, you don't love me," he said quietly. "I know how you felt about Marcel. Sooner or later, he'll come back to Paris. Then what?"

"If I could, I'd tell you I love you," she said. "I won't, not because I have compunctions, but because you're too wise to be fooled by a lie. You *must* believe, though, that I want to be your wife."

"I believe it because you say so; but still what about Marcel?"

"Whatever I feel for Marcel belongs to a life I don't want any more," she said. "Finally, I want someone of my own, my *own* partner, my *own* friend, my *own* person who completes me. I want the closest kind of life with you. I want to live with you, work with you, learn with you. And when Marcel comes back, what you and I will have together will be so strong that no one will be able to separate us."

"You can't know that now," he said, smiling sadly.

"I *do* know it!" she insisted. She took his hands again and looked at him with falsely candid eyes to hide her fear of his insight. She determined to dedicate herself heart and soul to him and that loneliness within her would remain a secret. Either life itself would wipe it out or she would make herself grow used to its burden.

22

She expected that Georges would move her at once into his room or that he would come to her. He surprised her by making no move at all. He surprised her still more by insisting on the necessity of breaking the news to Marcel. Julie was close to irritation with him about it.

"It's no business of his!" she said angrily. "You're humiliating me, Georges. I don't want his permission. I don't want his 'good riddance.' For the first time, I've found you unfeeling!"

"You're piqued," he said calmly. "But you must understand my own attitude in the matter."

"If you have one that's going to stand in the way, let's not marry," she retorted.

Georges went pale. In another moment he would flush—that was the way anger moved in him. "You talk that way only because I'm in love with you while you are not in love with me," he observed quietly—without a trace of complaint or accusation. She had the cruelest advantage in the world over him, but he was not afraid of her and she respected him for it. His self-possession called up the earliest feeling she had about him in Cambridge—that he had grown up in an enchanted forest, removed from other people, where the most savage animals were tame to his touch.

"You don't know Marcel the way I do," he said to her. "When he returns—as he will sooner or later—he'll be the man to whom we're most indebted as scientists. He'll be the one who gives us the most help, the best guidance, the deepest inspiration. Mark my words, Julie, our lives will never be extricated from his!"

"Then let it happen of its own accord," she said. "And if you want to write him, do it without telling me. I would have done it by myself—*after* we were married."

"Why *after?*"

"Because to do so before—from me—might seem that I'm giving him a chance to tell me not to. I wouldn't put *you* in that position!"

Georges smiled suddenly and put his hands on her shoulders. "Why do we quarrel?"

She kissed him lightly on the cheek, but within herself she was still wounded. She wasn't used to the coolness of his courting.

He set the day for the wedding two Sundays away. Julie suggested Breuilly because she knew his parents would be delighted. It meant that they would leave Paris shortly after noon on Saturday and arrive at Pont l'Evêque that evening. The ceremony would take place Sunday morning, and they could be back in Paris in time for Georges's lecture on Monday morning.

As soon as things were settled, Julie's anger changed; the idea of her marriage seemed infinitely dear to her.

Three days before the wedding she came down to the basement laboratory where Georges waited for her, cool and withdrawn. He said: "In spite of everything you said to me, you sent a cable to Marcel."

"I did not! What are you talking about?"

"Well, one of us told him, and it wasn't I," he said coldly. He handed her a letter in Marcel's handwriting. She glanced through the first few paragraphs which had to do with some theoretical calculations he had been working on with Gibbs. Toward the end there was this: "So you and Julie are to be married, or may even be married by the time you receive this. I'd wish you both the best of luck, but you know my feelings about marriage and I won't bore you by repeating them since obviously, you never took me seriously. I don't know who is the bigger fool—I, for thinking I could save you, or you for disregarding everything I said. Julie is a brilliant young woman but you will be a marvelously lucky young man if by marrying her you don't jeopardize your scientific collaboration. Retain that above all—even if you have to divorce her to keep her friendship!"

She handed back the letter. "I never wrote to him about us," she said. The envelope was on the table. The postmark was clearly stamped. "This was sent from New Haven only two days *after* we decided to marry," she pointed out. "Did you tell anyone about us?"

"Only my parents," he said. "They don't even know where he is."

"Well, someone found out. At least he knows. Now that you have his views on us, do you feel better?"

"I have his letter," Georges said quietly. "We'll all go on being friends."

"And that's what you wanted?"

"I want you for my wife. I want him for my friend."

She said nothing, and her silence could have been either acquiescence or foreboding. She herself wasn't sure what she felt.

23

JULIE HAD ALREADY KNOWN A NUMBER OF MEN, BUT she had never lived with one. Before her wedding she naïvely thought that the months she had worked with Georges left her little more to learn about him. From the beginning he kept astonishing her. The lightning of the unexpected struck all around her.

For one thing, he neither apologized for coming to the marriage a virgin, nor was he embarrassed by it; it was a fact about himself which he accepted like the color of his eyes. She couldn't believe it until he himself said simply: "I've never been with a woman before. You'll have to help me."

"You never loved a woman before me?"

"Once I did. A long time ago. I was twenty-one. She died. After that I never loved anyone else until I met you. I didn't even want to love anyone, for that matter."

"But you never desired a woman? You never needed one?"

He shook his head. "I told you," he said. "After she died, I never loved anyone but you."

It was not the answer to her question; but if he thought it was, that was an answer in itself.

He was the only man she had ever known who didn't carry with him afterechoes—the faded perfumes—of all the other women he had ever been with.

She was touched distantly by it, but it increased her lurking sense that he belonged in another, more rarefied life. He looked with open but unseeing eyes at passion, and he asked very little of her, but on the few occasions when he touched her, it was always the same: something in her came to a dead stop, and she was like a tensed animal waiting, silent, watchful, and motionless until the threat turned and moved away.

He gave her something very different. She had never realized before how used to loneliness she had become; it was the price she had willingly agreed to pay to satisfy the deeper, more fundamental life hunger for her work. What amazed her was the discovery that she could have both her creative work and a companion in creativeness; someone who was with her all day, who was there too in the darkness at night. Even when he was rapt and silent in some private thought of his own, his concern for her was always ready—like a dagger that lay loosened for instant use on her behalf. At night it was he who blew out the candle next to the bed. In the morning, it was he who rose and opened the window on the Rue Champollion, the narrow charming little street that ran from the Place de la Sorbonne down to the Rue des Ecoles.

All the things she used to do by herself—reading, preparing for a lecture, correcting papers, contemplating her current laboratory problem—she now did with him. Their lives had the same inner rhythm. Their two-room flat was crowded with books, his and hers, some in the bookcases, some on the floor. One particular pile of treatises—the individual books in the pile were continually changing—was always in the process of being moved from the dining table to make room for them to eat, then back again from the chair or window sill where it had been placed, so that they could return to their work. They were even fussy in similar ways. He was convinced that he understood wicks better than she and so the lamp in the center of the table could be trimmed only by him. The stove became Julie's province by her demand. She insisted that the laying of a fire was a purely American talent. Whenever she came in to the flat she went first to the stove, lifted the lid for an expert glance at the glow within, poked it deftly for its own good, and then—satisfied that everything was as it should be—she was ready to say "good evening," take off her coat and hat, and stretch out on the secondhand divan to rest a while. She was always on her feet all day in the laboratory.

She enjoyed his presence—even his silent presence as he read and she read. He could sit at the table with a book propped before him; Nernst's *Treatise on Physical Chemistry* for example, had been sent to him for review, and while he read it, his hands beyond it were deftly paring an apple to make one long continuous curl of red rind. The way he could read and peel fruit at the same time fascinated her. She caught the apple-eating habit from him, but ate them American style. They argued once for hours—his proofs unread before him and her students' papers unmarked—because she insisted that an apple tasted insipid without its rind. His passionate denial astounded her until she realized that he was defending not peeled apples, but French civilization itself.

Mostly he paid no attention to what he ate. She made a New England boiled beef; he thought it was *pot-au-feu*.

It was a relief to both of them not to have to break off their working lives to go home to bedmates who were shut off from what was innermost in their hearts. Their talk at supper, when they both didn't have to read for the next day's lecture, was about the experiment. But he could break off suddenly from the most concrete discussion of experimental detail to make abstract speculations on the largest scale on matters far removed from their own work.

She listened, fascinated and impressed whenever she allowed herself to follow his train of thinking across the enormous horizons in science. He brought the same large point of view to music, history, and art. She had no simple name for her feeling for him; it had too many facets. She was awed by his mind, chastened by his goodness, warmed by his protection and infinitely puzzled by the fact that he could have a passionate intensity without having passion itself. It was as if —unlike the planets—he had a core cooler than his surface, which meant she would never have to simulate an awakening desire. It was a relief, but also, no matter how she insisted on denying it, it was heartbreaking for he was fully content and fulfilled with her as she was, and she was not with him.

24

AT WORK, THE SITUATION WAS REVERSED. THERE HE fulfilled her completely. Everything he did in the laboratory made her aware of his superiority. It was actually pleasurable to watch and follow him and lose all awareness of herself; even time itself lost its meaning. The day could end at ten o'clock at night as often as at six in the evening, depending on when the last measurement, the last weighing, or the last filtration, was finished.

Actually, marriage took them into the laboratory even more than they had been before. They would usually go home twice a day to eat dinner and supper. After supper, if there weren't some reading or lecture preparation, they might easily walk down the four flights of stairs again and walk the few streets to the laboratory for another hour or so of work. Around eleven o'clock they'd stop off at a café on the way home to talk a little more, or simply to sit in the warm night by gaslight and feel Montparnasse pulse by them.

The increased attention to work began to produce a stream of results. Research papers with their names on it appeared in the journals. "Displacement of Particles in Disperse Systems"; "Some Physical Properties of Colloid Solutions"; "The Electrical Double Layer and the Isoelectric Point."

More than anything, Georges shared with Julie his fascination for the electrical means by which the particles maintained themselves in suspension.

The winter was spent in perfecting their techniques. Georges continually improved the micro-observation chamber which he had made from a thistle tube. Eleven variations were put aside before a twelfth suited him.

During that time, the journalist whose description of their laboratory was quoted everywhere six years later, hunted them down for an interview. He had been completely misled about what they were doing. Someone with a *fin de siècle* taste for diabolism and a hodgepodge familiarity with the lore of witchcraft and alchemy had told him that the gold colloid they were using was actually the same thing as the medieval medical nostrum: the mysterious *aurum potabile*— and he and his editor thought that there was an ironical story in the fact that the most advanced Parisian science was only realizing the fantasies of the alchemists. A few years earlier the Curies had discovered radioactive elements and could finally effect the age-old dream of transmutation. Here now was another young couple of researchers working on what was supposed anciently to be the fabulous elixir of youth. He wrote in the *Echo de Paris*:

"One soft spring day, I found myself on a twisting narrow Parisian street of broken-down houses and exhausted trees in Montparnasse. I wandered for some time through watery sunshine looking for a trace of the two modern alchemists of whom I had heard such provocative hints, and finally, a student who looked at me curiously directed me to the basement of a small gray institutional building down through the same sooty door through which coal passed.

"It was deathly dark and quiet down there in the cellar when the door closed behind me. Then I made out some slivers of light through a wall of boards in front of me that had been carelessly put together. When my eyes became accustomed to the gloom, I saw what I had been looking at: a bin opposite the coal bin, but larger. The bin of coal was dark and silent; the bin of light contained human beings: I could hear their murmurs and a steady prolonged hiss. Would I open the door and find my magicians murmuring incantations among the salamanders? I entered and found that I had surprised two young tired people at work with modern test tubes and a microscope even beyond anything in Jules Verne. They looked almost like brother and sister except that the man was at least twelve years older than the woman. She was in her early twenties. Then I saw that their tiredness was not in the way they moved, spoke, or thought—in that there was true fire. Exhaustion was in their eyes and around their mouths. They lacked only sleep, not dedication to their work which fascinated them. This was the young research pair—Professor and Mme. Claudet—they have been married for only seven months.

"I asked what progress they were making with their elixir of youth, and how their formula differed from those of Rhazes and Paracelsus and whether or not it would have fitted the requirements of that fantastic Emperor Rudolph of Germany who devoted his fortune to the quest of the *aurum potabile, potable gold*, the philosopher's stone for transmutation of metals, and the elixir of life. I marked that in his great gloomy palace in sixteenth-century Prague they might have met the charlatans John Dee, Michael Sendivigus and 'Count' Marco Bragadino as well as such great savants as Tycho Brahe and Kepler who had also played with alchemy."

Georges's politeness turned glacial the moment the man had stated his business, but Julie sympathized with the journalist's plight and agreed to talk to him. Even then, he took what she said and transformed it into the near-magical.

"Mme. Claudet informed me that the modern *aurum potabile* is no longer considered to be an elixir of eternal youth.

On the other hand a single drop of it may be considered all Nature in miniature: the gold particles in it belong to that newly-discovered twilight world of size which is neither molecular nor large enough to be seen. It is now known that this is the exquisitely fine state of subdivision in which matter exists in living blood, in each of the seven seas, in the elements of the sacrament; in wine and in the very dough of the wafer, even in mother's milk. To know the secrets of the colloid state is to move one step closer to the secret of life itself. One of the secrets which the young Claudets have so far ferreted out is that in this state one must forget our usual world of three dimensions. Imagine, if you will, a simple piece of matter the shape and size of a dice cube. When subdivided into smaller cubes with each edge a hundredth as large, there will be a million cubic particles having a total surface a hundred times larger than the surface of the parent cube. This means, Mme. Claudet explained to me, that the colloid world is really a two dimensional one because surface effects are of prime importance. Mme. Claudet, born in America, speaks French with a charming accent and discusses their project with a fervor that transforms her face even in the poor light in which they are obliged to work. At a moment when Professor Claudet, a taciturn man with sensitive features, was not busy with their remarkable microscope, she allowed me to glimpse through it at a world that is utterly startling—inanimate things move, dart, leap, jump together and fly apart with a vitality which she assures me can go on forever without any energy ever being added from the outside. I asked why I could not report then that they had found in the *aurum potabile* the secret of perpetual motion?"

That was too much for Georges who was so exasperated that he said, "Excuse me, monsieur," and left the basement altogether to pace up and down in the yard clasping and unclasping his hands. Julie, though, never lost her patience with the reporter and tried to explain the difference between the random movement of particles which he had been watching through the microscope and the production of useful work.

"In any event, M. and Mme. Claudet have so thoroughly explored the laws of their twilight universe in terms of the behavior of the subvisible particles of inorganic matter that now they are about to commence a series of experiments on molecules of organic matter.

"Their relentless search spirals in ever closer to the question of life itself. How strange, though, that the avant-garde of science should find its field of greatest interest in a drop of an elixir described almost two thousand years ago by Pliny the Elder!"

When the article appeared, a student who was pleased that his favorite professor was being given so much journalistic notice handed the article to Georges. He read it with increasing rage.

"That idiot!" he said to Julie, his voice silken with tautly suppressed fury as he strode up and down their tiny living room. "How ignorant can a man be! I ask you; *twilight universe! elixir of youth! elements of the sacrament! perpetual motion!* And *that* considers himself a cultivated man, a gentleman of letters! *He* is the one who actually belongs in the entourage of the mad Rudolph. Only two things he got right —the fact that we're dealing with the chemistry of surfaces, and the fact that we're about to begin to work with organic compounds." He ceased his springlike walk and stood squarely before her. "Julie, my dear, I beg you not to do it again. I'll speak to these people myself. If I don't feel like talking, then there is to be no story!"

"Very well, Georges," she said, very subdued.

"And we are *not* brother and sister!" he said. He was intensely quiet at what was to him a murderous insult.

Their friends were pleased that they had received some notice. That the piece was fatuous was only to be expected, they said. That was the price one had to pay for being a scientist in a world that had no true interest in science unless something sensational was happening.

"It's possible to blabber about art without knowing anything about it, or even about music or literature. But science —well, the day of the charlatan is over! Still, my dear Georges," he was told in the café one evening, "you must learn to suffer fools. Perhaps your rector will be so impressed by the newspapers that he'll give you two a proper laboratory!"

Few visitors came to the apartment on Rue Champollion during their first year of marriage. For one reason, they had so little furniture that five people could not sit down together. Then, too, Georges was not too good a host. He loved to talk, but every so often someone's chance remark would make him thoughtful and he'd want nothing but solitude to puzzle his way out. In a café, when he'd turn silent, he could pay his reckoning and walk thoughtfully away down the boulevard, leaving his companions to continue without him. At home, he couldn't get rid of others so easily. He'd begin to pace, or tap his foot until everyone had been made too nervous to stay.

But if he inadvertently discouraged visitors, he lost no friends. He and Julie were continually being invited to the quarters of other young scientists. He had that quality that made others want to reach out and take him in—but he in turn gave himself freely only to the group of friends he selected for himself. He rejected the young scientists who made careers out of knowing the right people. He had the same abrupt intolerance for those whom he considered to be the dutiful plodders without originality. What was remarkable was that a man so intolerant of anyone who fell even a hairsbreadth below his private standards should be so widely beloved. The invitations he accepted were very few. Those he gave were fewer still. Julie was content to live by his mood. She never for one moment doubted that he had entire worlds of knowledge and perceptions to teach her.

Early in the spring of their first year together, they began the new experiments which the newspaper article had mentioned.

Now when the star points danced, darted, and leaped in the field of the ultramicroscope, the electric charge of each one was protected by an invisible shield, a super-atmosphere. A massive organic molecule surrounded each electrified gold particle as an outer bastion.

Georges was drawing up a table of the comparative protecting powers of various starches, stearates, and albumins to see if he could get any insight into their structures. One day in May he remained at the laboratory while Julie went on ahead to prepare supper. Late that evening he walked into the little flat, still so involved with what he had been doing that he didn't notice Julie's strange silence as she moved back and forth from the table to the stove.

When he sat down though, he couldn't miss the envelope on his plate. He frowned and examined the postmark.

"It's from Marcel," he said.

She didn't reply.

"What does it say?" he asked.

"I didn't read it."

"Why not?" he asked quietly, turning to look at her. He still hadn't touched the letter.

"It was addressed to you."

"Any letter addressed to me is also for you. Especially from Marcel." He took out the letter. "It says he'll be back in Paris in August."

"We'll be in the country then, won't we?" she asked.

He could hear what was in her voice so there was no need to turn to her, and he sat looking down at his clasped hands. Then he said: "Yes, we'll be away if you like," and there was such kindness in his tone and so much sadness that she came to him on an impulse and kissed his cheek.

25

ON A STIFLING DAY IN THE FIRST WEEK OF SEPTEMBER, Paris shimmered in a bright gassy heat. Then an avalanche of thunderstorms rolled up from the south. Smoky clouds sped overhead, low and fast. Winds roared down the boulevards and through the parks, breaking heavily leaved branches from the trees. Flower gardens were blown flat, making a swirl of wreckage of blue-, yellow-, and purple-smeared petals; lightning forked and veined the sky. At first the bombardment seemed heaviest in the south of the city and the Parc Montsouris was struck several times. Twenty minutes later, a totally different crackle and roar came down on Montmartre and torrents of cloudburst poured down the Rue Lepic.

At the height of the storm, Georges and Julie arrived at the Gare St. Lazare. Rain was whipping the city as they came out of the station and sought a cab. Julie walked beside Georges, taut and wary, as if at any moment, from some unexpected hiding place, Marcel would step out and, with a demoniacal snap of his finger—like a jab of lightning—call up in her feelings that were better left dead.

She had been terrified for each of the ten days they had spent in Normandy. Georges was silent most of the time, but then he began to urge her to return to the laboratory.

"It's almost two years," he reminded her. "A few days

more or less can't make the difference now if the difference hasn't already been made."

The logic was unanswerable even if it never touched her secret dread, and so she gave in; but apprehension went on.

In the silent apartment, rain splashed and chattered on the windowpanes. She was alert for some sign—a note or a letter or any indication that Marcel had been there in their absence looking for them. There was nothing. Her surprise felt almost like disappointment.

When they finally did meet, there was no shock because she was already numb from anticipation. She had given up trying to imagine what it would be like to see his hands and feel nothing, to see his mouth and be able to glance away as if it had never touched her, to be in the same room with him and feel more allegiance to another man than to him. It was all incredible, and yet it was all going to have to happen unless the rest of her life was to be one long hell. When she went with Georges to Marcel's study to report on what they had been doing, and to hear his verdict of their performance, she felt as if she might very well be going to hear her own sentence of death.

He seemed unchanged, although she had forgotten how huge a man he was until he rose and dominated them with his outstretched arms. His embrace though was for Georges. For Julie, he had only one brief, piercing glance that was instantly veiled as he turned away.

"I hear you've found a laboratory," he said. "I went to pay a visit in your absence, but everything was locked. Your concierge is so devoted to both of you that the President of the Republic himself couldn't get in without you being present."

He seated himself in his tufted black leather armchair and waved to the blackboard. He hadn't one word for their lives, for their feelings. It was as if he had been away no more than a week or two and wanted only to be brought up to date.

For two hours, Georges spoke, outlining the train of thought that had led to the study of colloids, and what they had learned so far. Marcel listened without a word, but he was increasingly restless: shifting his position, tapping his foot, his finger, a pencil against his teeth. Julie became so nervous that she wanted to command him to be still.

At length with a deep sigh, he held up his hands as if he could bear no more.

"Stop!" he said. "Stop!" For a long moment, he said nothing. "You want me to be honest? Very well! I can't see why any of this could have seemed interesting to you. Perhaps I'm wrong. Perhaps I've been so immersed in my own work that I'm blind to what you see. I know it sounds brutal, but I think you've wasted valuable time on trivia. Leave me your notes," he said. "I'll look it all over again at my leisure, and then we'll talk once more."

Georges was so stunned that he didn't know where he was walking when they left. He would have been run down by a pair of trotting horses if Julie hadn't caught his arm. When he turned into the Rue St. Jacques, a huge van pulled by four percherons came along and again he would have been trampled. This time she held his arm firmly and led him up the hill. In the Luxembourg she walked with him through the nursemaids and children to a bench, but she still held his hand because his stricken eyes, his silence were breaking her heart. She hated Raubard. She had only one allegiance now: to Georges and to the work they had done together.

"You're the one who's right, Georges, not he," she said again and again.

He shook his head, still stunned, deaf to her assurance and support.

"He does *not* know everything," she insisted.

"No, Julie, no! You mustn't talk that way," Georges said at last, with sadness and affectionate amusement. "I'm not a child. If he's right, we'd better know it now."

"He's too self-centered to see anything but what's of immediate interest only to him," Julie went on. The flood of feeling that had made her decide to marry Georges in the first place had returned in one enormous surge. Thank God, it was all clear again! Thank God for the peace, even if everything else might be in shambles. "You're a better judge than he is!"

That night Georges hardly slept. He sat hunched by the window in the darkness, raw with disappointment and humiliation, looking down into the empty street, and Julie shivering in her wrapper could not get him to come back to bed. Something seemed to have been broken inside the man. He was in mute agony because he could neither submit to the pain nor could he bear it stoically. She kept repeating her conviction that in the end he would prove to be absolutely right, but that

the time had come to break with Raubard. Georges mustn't
think of working with a man who was so blind.

She laid a fire in the stove. It was three o'clock in the
morning, but she made the room bright. She cooked a huge
American breakfast and she induced him to eat it. Around
four-thirty, he began to concede that perhaps she was right;
he had better leave Raubard and turn to someone more sympathetic to the research, or even to go ahead alone, just the
two of them on their own conviction. The idea of breaking
with Raubard at last flooded her with intense relief.

At six-thirty, they were awakened by a pounding at the
door. Dizzy with exhaustion, they answered it together. There
stood Raubard fully dressed, smiling, brandishing their data
book.

"I must have been out of my mind to say what I did yesterday! How could I have been so wrong? I would have come
at one o'clock in the morning, when I finished, but I didn't
want to disturb you!" He looked at their numbed faces without the slightest idea of what was behind their stupefaction.
"Don't stand there like idiots! How much sleep do you want?
Get clothes on. Let's celebrate! Let's get to work!"

Georges's eyes filled with tears. He was too moved to
reply. Impulsively the two men clasped hands. Julie watched
them, as deeply moved as they were, but in the back of her
heart was the surging return of foreboding and fear: the door
to escape had been closed against her.

26

MARCEL TALKED WITH THEM FOR DAYS, SOMETIMES IN
his study, sometimes in their little laboratory, ceaselessly playing with new possibilities. It was intoxicating to work with him
on this level. Each day they expanded the program of research to be done. For the first time, Julie was seeing Marcel's size as a working scientist. He was a giant—a mover of
worlds and men.

"Something keeps eluding you about this ability of the organic molecules to 'protect' colloids from precipitation," Raubard insisted one day when he was visiting their little labora-

tory. "I don't know what it is. Intuition tells me that perhaps you have here the makings of an analytical tool."

"Or perhaps it's the other way around," Julie said. "We might also develop it into a test to identify substances whose precipitation properties we know in advance."

The two men turned to her in some surprise. The idea seemed to her to have come spontaneously on a throb of excitement deep in her body; and she knew it meant that she and Marcel were still tied in such a way that she would strike a spark every time Marcel pointed to flint. At that moment, both she and Marcel felt the pulse; their startled glance at each other asked with terror if it were really so.

"It's an idea worth examining," Raubard said slowly, his voice completely controlled. "Play with the possibilities a bit."

She instantly improvised for him a method that depended on the fact that a gold-colloid solution required a corresponding amount of sodium ion to precipitate it. Differing amounts of sodium ion would be required when some organic protecting substances were present.

"Ideally, the difference could identify the unknown 'protecting agent,' " she said.

"But that's of no real interest," Georges objected impatiently. "It tells nothing new about structure. Actually, it's a trivial application!"

"No, it's certainly not theoretical chemistry," Marcel agreed at once. "But then I wasn't thinking of the chemist."

"Of whom, then?"

"Of the diagnostician, the medical clinician. Specifically, I was thinking of blood."

"Blood?" Georges frowned his distaste. "But blood is a jungle to a chemist! A simple system like pure water is complicated enough."

"Blood," said Marcel again. "And jungles can be cleared. We could filter out the red and white cells. We could even remove the fibrinogen and the entire clotting complex."

"But what would be left?"

"Serum," Marcel said. "A water solution of salts and protein—including possibly the proteins of pathology. If the gold colloid could be used to identify just one of them, to medicine, at least, the contribution would be a real one. I must say—it's not a bad idea at all!"

Georges stood looking after him thoughtfully when he left.

His silence was a burden to Julie. Had he sensed what had flashed between her and Marcel for that one instant from their past lives? She dreaded what he would say.

"Well, of course, your idea is possible," he finally said. "Your method though has too many drawbacks. Here's a better procedure."

He outlined it for her. The maturity of his scientific understanding was so obvious that she was humbled by the realization of how far she still had to go to be really worthy of him —as a laboratory colleague, as well as a wife.

27

ON A GRAY WINDY DAY IN EARLY DECEMBER OF THAT year, a portly gentleman sat leaning on his cane in the crowded omnibus crossing the Pont Neuf toward the Latin Quarter. The wind slatting along the river rattled the glass windows. The man bundled his collar at the sound of what was waiting for him outside and he sighed.

"This weather will be the death of all of us." He spoke to the world at large. "Winters never used to be this cold," he sighed to the young woman sitting next to him with a paper package in her lap. "Ever since they discovered that disease came from germs, there has been more illness."

She was young, plainly dressed, and she had a serious but absent look, as if her mind was a million miles away. Still she nodded. "You can't be too careful, they say," he went on. "I wash my hands after I touch anything at all. I never breathe if I can help it." Again, she nodded. "Pasteur was a great man, they tell me, but the world was a better place before germs," he grumbled. He leaned against her hard as the omnibus started again up the hill. She clung tightly to her package, and he approved of her carefulness. "Hang on to whatever belongs to you, and there'll be no thievery. Nothing really well-guarded is ever stolen," he told her. "Except health. Germs get by anything."

He grumbled on, confiding to the young woman who nodded from time to time, and he decided that she was a pleasant little nobody, destined to live a colorless little life, engrossed in her little duties. She rose unsteadily as her stop approached.

"Ho-la!" he said aloud, because she stumbled. He supported her and the paper-wrapped box she clutched so desperately.

"*Merci, monsieur,*" she said and looked at him with gratitude. Automatically his hat came up in his hand, and mustache was stroked by the other because—he told this later with a rising inflection of wonder—when you *really* looked at her she was beautiful! But magnificent! Those eyes!

As fascinated as he had been by her eyes, he would have been even more interested in the contents of that plain little paper-wrapped box which he had handled so gallantly. It had contained nine cotton-stoppered test tubes: four of blood serum taken freshly from hospital patients suffering from meningitis, three from patients with lobar pneumonia, and two more from patients in advanced stages of leprosy. The identification experiment which Georges was always to call *Julie's test,* had begun.

Actually, Georges detested the experiment. The whole conception directly violated his idea of the kind of work a true chemist should be doing. His own taste ran to the more austere, more elegant, purer sort of scientific abstraction. Julie seemed to him to be rummaging around blindly in some dark damp attic full of the most senseless rubbish—a sort of blind man's buff. He couldn't understand how a man like Raubard might think it worth a scientist's time, until he reminded himself philosophically that since he himself had recesses to his soul that would always be completely unknown and incomprehensible to everyone else—then everyone else—even Raubard, must also be capable of the unpredictable. How Julie could play so calmly with the exudates of disease was beyond him. To a certain extent, it disgusted him. However she was his wife, and his desire for her happiness was far greater than his revulsion at the sight of the paper-wrapped package clutched under her arm as she came into the laboratory after making her periodic rounds of the hospitals.

"Look at you!" he said once with gentle wonder. "Do you know what you look like, arriving with your little test-tube batches of nightmare? In one month: 3 cc. of cancer, 2 cc. of pleurisy, 5 cc. of pneumonia, and 1 gram of powdered rhinitis! The next month's menu: syphilis, meningitis, epilepsy, sclerosis! Like a good little housewife bringing home the latest bargains! Then you go to work, concocting one loathsome stew after another, and always the same null result! Yet back you go to the Hôtel-Dieu, to Le Pitié to the Salpêtrière for still more, and still more beyond that! Why? Why?"

"I don't know why, Georges, but I wouldn't want to be doing anything else!"

He spread his hands in resignation. Then he proceeded to help her unpack her terrible test tubes and set up test schedules. He even continued to refine and improve the technique for her.

Julie's tenacity fascinated him. Her long apprenticeship under Salomon-Delachet had taught her that the recurring disappointment of a null result was very often the price one paid in advance for the moment of success and elation that could be still coming. She showed a toughness that impressed him. Only very slowly did he begin to sense the nature of the inner fire that had kept her going for an entire year.

"This whole thing is personal with you!" he said. "You should see your face when you're working. You're fighting a private vendetta!"

"Perhaps."

"As if you felt that death owed you something."

She flushed.

"Perhaps," she said again.

"As if there had been one death too many for you to bear remembering."

Her face hardened. "Each one was too many," she said quietly. "Georges, before I can go ahead with work in chemistry I must first do something with it that will at some time, in some way, spare someone."

He said nothing. She had appealed to him on the one level which he found unanswerable: she had made it a matter of family. In her house, he knew, his elderly parents would always be seated in the places of honor. In the same way, through marriage, he felt that he had assumed kinship to all her dead. His attitude toward the work changed. It never took on the high passion she had for it, but it became an honorable duty. He would have been ashamed to shirk or slight it even in the privacy of his heart.

Her first hint of success—like the cool swirl of air before a summer thunderstorm—came when she had been at work for fourteen months.

Before her on the workbench stood the test-tube rack hold-

ing a stoppered test tube with almost 5 cc. of amber liquid—
the serum of a woman with glioma of the brain. She dipped
the tip of the pipette beneath the surface of the clear straw-
tinted serum and, as if she were using it as an ice cream soda
straw of glass, she sucked up a fine column of serum to
within two inches of her lips. She had no time to think
whether or not it was dangerous. Actually, she didn't even
know—to her it was pure chemistry. Her finger replaced her
mouth and held the liquid column in tact while she reached
out to a florence flask into which she released it all for the
hundred-to-one dilution.

In another test-tube rack on the worktable stood five test
tubes with different concentrations of colloidal gold—each
one a tenth as strong as the preceding one. She dropped into
each test tube 1 cc. of the diluted serum which was to be the
"protecting agent" of the gold particles. She shook them all
vigorously, and then proceeded to pass down the line from
one to the other with the test amount of sodium ion.

In the first three test tubes, the glioma serum reacted to the
sodium ion exactly like serum from normal blood. She began
to sense something unusual only with the fourth concentration. To her surprise, there was no precipitation when she
added the sodium ion. She tapped the still clear test tube
lightly on the off-chance that supersaturation had taken place,
but still no precipitate as there would have been with normal
serum. Her heart began to pound. She added a little more sodium solution. Again no precipitate. She had difficulty
breathing. She added a third measure of sodium ion; then a
fourth. This time the fine yellow-white cloud of precipitate
formed a mist and slowly drifted down as sediment. She had
to go through the same thing with the fifth concentration. Exactly what Marcel had predicted! She had found a pathological protein of the blood that could be differentiated and perhaps identified by her method!

The beat of her heart had an intensity that actually pained
her, but she forced herself to repeat the entire process from
the start. She made up new colloid solutions, pipetted a new
measure of serum for dilution, and once again separated her
concentrations. Again, the fourth and fifth test tubes showed
no precipitation for the normal amount of sodium. Again,
they required three times as much as the others to form the
precipitate. She was almost limp with the excitement. This
finally was the excitement of discovery. She made the test a

third time. Her result still held. She put her hands to her cheeks: unless she was out of her mind, she had found a laboratory blood test that could show glioma. She had just enough serum left to make one more independent test, but she decided to hold it until Georges came down and witnessed the whole procedure. She was beside herself with impatience.

When Georges arrived, she tried to tell him calmly what she had seen, but she was almost incoherent. She repeated the experiment from the very beginning. Again, the wonder repeated itself: within thirty seconds, the first, second, and third tubes began to turn misty. The fourth and fifth remained absolutely transparent. At the end of ten minutes, they were still clear. With the twenty previous experiments there had been no such manifestation.

"You see?" she said quietly. "Exactly what I told you!"

"Get some more glioma serum," was his only reply. "Be very sure."

That night, she hardly slept. Next day she had her own classes. The day after she was back at the hospital laboratory to get another sample of the serum. The pathologist glared at her. Only Raubard's prestige protected her from his irritation.

"This is a hospital, mademoiselle. Not a bloodletter's stall. We don't bleed glioma patients the way you milk cows. What the devil are you up to?"

"It's too early to say," she had to reply. "But I need more serum."

"Come back tomorrow. It's highly unethical, but I'll try to get you some," he grumbled.

The second sample from the same patient repeated the performance of the first. She finally went to Raubard herself to report what had happened.

For the first time in the three years that had passed since he had gone to America, they were together without anyone else being present. Her life with Georges, her students, her work—a century stood between that time and now. Yet in another, more private life, no time at all had gone by; he had kissed her good-by and walked out through her door. Here, less than a moment later: the same man. She yearned to touch him, to have him rise and come to her. Yet all through this, she went on talking steadily in an even, dispassionate voice of what had been happening with the glioma serum.

She saw him watching her with an unguarded sadness of

his own. He too had a self behind the self with which he consciously faced her.

"Glioma!" he murmured. "What a piece of insane luck, if it's true!"

"You don't really believe it?" she asked.

"First, let's see it work on the sera of twenty-five different cases. I'll have to ask around among the hospitals for you. Glioma is not the most common disease in Paris."

She rose and left hurriedly without meeting his eyes. There were too many things to say and too many questions to ask that were better left stillborn in silence.

On the following Friday, by chance, two other samples of glioma serum became available at the same time. One had been prepared for her at the Necker, and the other from Salpêtrière. She made the rounds herself by omnibus. After hours of traveling around Paris, she carried her little package into the basement laboratory, nodding at the college concierge as she went past. Both women simultaneously exchanged their hurried little *"Bon jour, madame!"*

Her heart was pounding, whether with hope, fear, anxiety, or what, she didn't know, but her fingers felt numb and clumsy. She no longer had any illusion left about her scientific objectivity: here was a test she passionately wanted to come out. She went through the steps of preparation and knew that if there were any way to influence the result she would shamelessly have taken it. What stood in her way was the procedure itself: step by step, she and Georges had evolved a system that was itself the epitome of objectivity, and she had become only its attendant priestess, the performer of the ritual.

Georges came in just as she was pouring sodium ion into the five test tubes of increasing gold colloid concentration and serum. The crucial thirty seconds ticked by in silence. Then simultaneously in all five test tubes, the transparency began to dull and be replaced by turbidity. Exactly like normal blood. She could hardly believe the disappointment. Neither she nor Georges said a word. They didn't even look at each other. She set that sample of serum aside and tried the second one to check herself. Again, all five precipitates formed at once. There was no way to evade the obvious.

"Either what happened with the first glioma sample was a wild accident or else the two sera may have been prepared differently. They *did* come from different laboratories," he reminded her.

She went back to the hospitals to interview the pathologists. They were all busy, and they all resented being cross-examined by someone who had no business breaking in on hospital routine in the first place. The woman whose serum she had used for the first test was gone. No one knew her. Julie spent the next weeks and months checking and cross-checking procedures that took her deeper and deeper into questions that had nothing to do with the nature of the colloid world. Georges at last became openly rebellious at the drain on her time and talent. In the meantime he himself had embarked on two simultaneous studies of different aspects of colloid movement in electric fields. These were questions of real theoretical importance. He invented a name for what she was doing: "rag-picking."

Her "rag-picking" began to become obsessive. The same dream battened on her again and again. She came to know it as an old friend. She could almost predict the outcome, but the dream teased her with surprising turns. In it she was pouring sodium ion into a rack of five test tubes and getting an unequal reaction. Sometimes the first and fifth remained clear, sometimes the fourth only. The last time she dreamt it, it was disturbingly erotic in sensation. Halfway through the test, someone told her that this was her own blood. The reaction was markedly positive: the third test tube remained clear. Her father told her that the result meant that she had cellrobotulism and the disease had a hauntingly familiar sound, but when she awoke, she hadn't the slightest idea of what it was. She looked it up in La Forge's *La Pathologie*. No such disease was listed.

The strange accident with the glioma kept her at the serum experiment all through the late winter months, longer than she would normally have put into it. In April she had to surrender. She told Raubard of her conviction that the experiment had been a failure. He listened gravely, pulling at his beard. His lips had fallen into their habitual sardonic twist, but his eyes were apologetic.

"I'm afraid you're right," he said. "My intuition seems to have gone dead with advancing age. And I doubt if there's anything to be found in the sputum or urine that wouldn't also have shown in some way in the blood. However there is one body fluid I'd like you to try before you give up the experiment for good: the extract from the cerebro-spinal system. Certainly any protein associated with neurological diseases should be strongly concentrated in the spinal fluid. It's worth a look, at least." His tone was unusually considerate. He had done her a grave hurt in his own terms: robbing her of almost two years of precious creative time. Betraying her with a dozen mistresses wouldn't have been as serious in his eyes. He held her arm as he escorted her to the door of his study. At the last moment, his fingers tightened slightly as if to detain her for a question and her heart began to pound because she wanted to turn into his arms, but instead she forced herself deliberately to remove her arm from his grasp and to hurry down the dark steps toward the Rue des Ecoles entrance. She was breathless with the effort, with rage at her life. On the threshold that led to the street, dizziness made her lean against the massive door: Suddenly, like a gas bubble erupting up through a marsh, came understanding of the dream she'd had months before: the dream affliction that had been haunting her—*cellrobotulism*—was only a brutal childish pun, a play on Marcel's name: *'cel Raubardulism* . . . It was that foolish! She was stunned and humiliated. An elderly attendant asked her if she were ill, but she went past him and down the steps as if the place itself were a danger to her.

It was no longer a question of making her own life bearable: she would be willing to settle for any amount of deprivation if only she could be absolutely sure that nothing would happen to hurt Georges. But what could happen? Her own answer came from a clarity of vision that was almost surgically objective: the most potent threat to Georges was from herself, not really from Marcel nor anything Marcel might do. If only Marcel had brought his girl back to Paris with him, the danger to everyone would be less. For the first time, Julie prayed for that other girl's hold on Marcel to be overwhelming. At that moment, it seemed infinitely easier to go on without the man she really wanted than to have resentment deprive her of the respect and affection she felt for Georges. The very possibility was as terrifying as a glimpse of possible evil within herself. She did have a disease, but its victim could only be Georges.

28

IN THE DARKNESS OF THE LABORATORY, THE ULTRAMIcroscope's bar of golden light threw off enough glow to illuminate everything nearby on the worktable: the little glass-walled Daniell's electric cell, its pair of coiled wires like curling Victorian mustaches that led away to the stage of the ultramicroscope, the open ledger with Julie's finger pointing to the line she was checking. She herself as she peered down into the eyepiece was beyond the glow. Her hand closed the electric switch.

The Daniell's cell's electric tension surged immediately through the wires to the droplet on the slide and the darting colloid star points within Julie's field of vision began at once to stream sideways, as if some miniature dream sky of comets and meteors had suddenly begun to flow toward the black western horizon. Her fingers reversed the switch's polarity. The streaming motion of particles halted abruptly, and the stars moved back the way they had come.

That this simple and obvious a demonstration that the particles were electrically charged worked on the micro-scale with such deceptive ease was, Julie knew, a tribute to Georges's masterly technique—his very fingers seemed to have an ingenuity of their own as intuitive as a farmer's green thumb. He was one of the born experimental scientists and he had come to his *métier* with all the naturalness of a primitive, not by the groping way of angular intellectuality. She sat there working at his work, using what he had made, sensing Georges's far closer identity with the silent reaches of the cosmic universe and the cold fire of inanimate forces than to the immediate world of men. In this little laboratory, at work on these problems, using these ingeniously contrived devices, his blood really flowed at its warmest; not at home in their flat on the Rue Champollion. There he was the polite visitor, as kind as anyone could ask, but abstracted. He never touched her with any sense of his body's need. It was in this laboratory realm, here at work, that he needed her presence. This was the love they had in common. This was the life she had asked for without ever realizing she might need more. Then her line of thought stopped: Georges had come in and was standing at her elbow.

"Julie," he said quietly, and she raised her head at once. Not only was his tone shorter than usual, but he was interrupting her during an observation.

"Why did you tell me that you didn't want to do any further work on the medical experiment for Raubard?"

"I told him that I felt the serum experiments had gone as far as I could take them. It was pointless for me to go any further," she said.

"But he says that you agreed to try the procedure on the cerebro-spinal fluid."

"Yes," she said calmly. "We did discuss it, but I wanted time to think it over. Then I realized that I preferred to come back to what you were doing and to work with you."

Georges was silent for a moment, because she had touched a conviction of his that no one should be made to do work not of his own choosing. He was now uncertain. "But he has the impression that you really agreed. He went to the trouble of communicating with the neurosurgeons for you!"

She said nothing. She turned away and wrote down the observed velocities of migration in the ledger.

"My dear Julie," he insisted. "You can't lead a man like Marcel to think you are going to work on something and then tell him he was mistaken. Even if he misunderstood, you can't embarrass him by refusing."

Beneath her calm appearance of stubbornness, she hated herself for putting Georges in this false position—she was making him plead with her to do what in her heart she really wanted to do; but a man like Georges could never look ludicrous. Instead she knew that she was the one who was losing size by it.

"You're right," she said abruptly to put an end to it. "The truth is that I *do* want to go on with that work. I thought I didn't before, but now I do."

She held a conference with Raubard in the morning about the work on cerebro-spinal fluid. It was all business on both sides. She came away feeling that perhaps she had only been imagining undercurrents between them during the previous meetings. The second conference too held them both exclusively to the scientific problem. Only after she left him, Julie realized that the meeting had run straight through the time

he used to spend with her after a day in his laboratory before
he went home. The next meeting too again ran through the
same *heure verte*—that hour at dusk when the café lights
began to come on and little green glasses of absinthe glinted
on more than half the tables. For Marcel, that hour had always been precious. When he made still another appointment
at that time she couldn't stop herself from asking:

"Are you sure you can see me then?"

"And why not?"

"Your friend has no objection?"

"Which friend?"

"She didn't come back with you?"

"She? Back? What *are* you talking about?"

"Nothing. Very well, let's make it Tuesday afternoon, same
time."

"Just a minute." He blocked her departure. "You didn't
answer my question. Who is this *she?*"

Julie looked up at his hugeness; so familiar that she could
have closed her eyes and still seen him, so dear that she suddenly felt only pain to be in the same room with him.

She spoke with difficulty: "I'm talking about that girl you
took to America with you. There *was* a girl."

"There was no girl I took to America," he said, his face
dark with anger. "Nor is there any girl now—if that's what
you mean. Everything Emma told you was a lie. She invented
it all."

"You should have written. You should have told me so!"

His face turned darker and now he was stubborn. His
voice was low.

"Because it *was* true, in a way. I took no girl *onto* the ship.
I didn't live in New Haven with any woman. Someone else
did come along. But none of that had anything to do with my
feeling for you!"

"Oh my God!" she said in a suffocated voice. "Now we're
finally to hear about your feelings for me! After all that.
After all the times you told me how it disgusted you to use
the word *love?*"

"You're a bookkeeper!" he said angrily. "Words have to
add up for you like francs and centimes! You want so much
logic in life! What difference does it make what words I use?"

She closed her eyes tensely and gestured him to stop.

"I don't want to hear any more about your feelings! I don't

want to hear any more about your women! I'm sorry I started the conversation."

"And I'm still answering your question: I didn't write you any denials because I wasn't going to lie to you," he retorted. "That would have been too degrading!"

"And the truth wasn't?"

His face was strong with feeling. "The women I was with meant nothing. But *you*—you really gave yourself! *You* married. I couldn't marry—you or anyone else. But you always knew that no matter who I was with, I was yours—"

"How could I know that? You always said—"

"Don't keep telling me what I *said!*" he shouted. "You know there are things I *can't* say! You know *that* in your heart, and that's why it's a crucifixion every time you try to nail me to words! I don't know about words; I know only about feelings! Whatever other women there were, had nothing to do with what I felt for you. Nor did whatever I wrote or didn't write. Nothing ever changed that. Nothing ever will!"

"It makes no difference any more," she said struggling to free herself from the hold of his rushing voice. "I have another life now."

"Yes, the one you ran to the moment I left Paris. You were with him one month after I went away! I said you wouldn't stay faithful and you didn't!"

"That's a lie! Who told you that?" she demanded. "Was that also from your wife?"

He didn't answer, but she wouldn't release him. "I asked you: who told you that?" she said again. "What made you believe such an insane thing?"

"You *are* married to Georges, aren't you?" he asked softly. "That at least did turn out to be true, didn't it?"

"Two years later, yes. And if it did," she said pitilessly, "it was because she *made* it happen. You let her. Yes, you let her. In your heart, you must have really wanted it that way."

"I could have killed you for it!"

"And the fact that you have a wife and other women— none of that changes your right to feel that way?"

"No!" he replied strongly. "I get my right to feel that way from you. Directly from you! And you know exactly what I mean. That's why there really *was* no other girl! Why there *is* no other girl! Why there never will be!"

"Oh God!" she sighed, because he was right—in her heart,

she understood him. "How I wish there were! How monstrous to think it was all for nothing!"

He had the eyes of a crucified man. Then he shook his head with his bearlike stubbornness.

"Don't talk that way, Julie. I'm a long way from dying and so are you. We've got the rest of our lives to work and to live."

"To work," she said. "And that's all!"

"To live too. You'll see!"

"And Georges?"

Marcel didn't answer. He stubbornly refused to meet her gaze. He rose, opened the door to his study for her, and stood aside to let her pass. All the while, he was in cold command.

"Until the next time," he said curtly.

29

A FEW DOORS DOWN THE SLOPE FROM THE PLACE DE LA Sorbonne on the Rue Champollion was a little *crémerie* run by a widow, Madame Lorant, and her daughter. Behind the shop, where Julie bought her eggs, milk, butter, and cream, was another little room curtained off. It held four square tables, with a stove in the corner. The stove heated the little room and the huge pot that rested on it all day long—a pot of meat or mutton stew or *pot au feu*—Madame Lorant's *plat du jour*. The dessert was always one of her cheeses. Those who wanted wine got it from the coal dealer two doors down. Occasionally when Georges and Julie worked too late for Julie to have made any supper, they would stop in at Madame Lorant's *crémerie* where they were counted among the habitués —the regulars—along with a young mathematician from Montpellier who was living with a Rumanian girl studying medicine. There was also a tall bearded Danish physiologist who was a ferocious bachelor and bored everyone to death with his dissertations on why women like Julie and the Rumanian were the beginning of a barbarian horde invading and ruining science. Soon, however, he was taken in hand by a young Parisienne who worked all day as a dressmaker. The first few times he began his tirade in her presence she said amiably, "Oh, shut up!" and winked at the two girls. After that, he was quiet. Another regular was an engraver, and still another was a shoe-store clerk who worked on the Boulevard St. Michel and once had had ambitions to be a painter. A girl he met had so much more talent than he that he put away his brushes and easel, married her, and settled down to support her so that she would be free to develop her ability. The shoe clerk and his painter-wife were a gay and devoted couple. She kept staring at Julie whenever they were there at the same time. Once she turned her chair around, and said impulsively, "There's something in your face I don't get—I won't get it until I paint it."

Julie shook her head.

"A portrait!" Georges said. "What a good idea!"

"Maybe you won't like it," said the painter laughingly.

But Julie shook her head again. She was alarmed by the painter's awareness of something undisclosed.

"In the first place, I don't have the time," Julie said. "I'm too busy in the laboratory at the moment." She softened her refusal. "I'm just getting a new experiment under way. Perhaps later on."

"But there's no need to wait," said the painter. "It's in the laboratory that I want to paint you."

"Oh my God!" cried the Dane who had stopped eating when the conversation began. He had followed it with his blue eyes twinkling with malice. "See what I told you? It's the damned women working together again!"

"Oh, be quiet!" sighed his blond seamstress. She looked at Julie too. "Listen, I have just the dress you should wear for the portrait."

"I don't want any dress except the one she has on right now," said the painter. "Just as she is: and with just that expression."

"I don't have any expression," said Julie, trapped by all these well-intentioned people. "The light in the lab is poor. Besides what I'm working on at the moment may be dangerous to you."

The painter's husband came alert at once; his fork paused halfway to his lips. "What is it?" he asked.

"Meningitis," she said. "I have some extract from the spinal cord of a patient in the Hôtel Dieu."

"No picture," said the shoe salesman, and resumed eating.

Then he looked askance at Julie. "Do you carry that stuff around with you? Are you contagious or something?"

"Of course not!" Julie replied. It was a reflection on her technique. "I'm as careful as anyone could be."

The painter was insistent, though. "Can you catch meningitis simply by *looking* at a test tube full of it?" she asked. "Don't I have to get closer to it than that?"

Julie was caught. As a last resort she tried: "But your husband said he wasn't happy about you being exposed that way."

"That's right," said the salesman.

"If it were only a matter of looking," she said to him. "Some of *your* old friends had worse things than meningitis. If I could sit and look at them, I can sit and look at her!"

The artist came every day and installed herself in a little corner of the laboratory. She was out of the way. At first she did only charcoal sketches, one study after another. She was as silent and intent on her work as Julie was. She never asked any questions about what was going on, and once when Julie tried to explain that the cerebro-spinal fluid bathed the central nervous system in a circulatory system all its own, or that her present method of testing with a scale of ten concentrations was far more searching than the one she had used on blood serum, the other young woman simply shook her head. "You're wasting your time. I don't even *want* to understand!"

Julie became so used to her that she took her for granted. So did Georges and so did Marcel.

After a few weeks, when they were all together again in Madame Lorant's *crémerie*, the Dane asked if the portrait had ever been painted.

"Ask her," said Julie. "I haven't seen any of it."

"It's coming along."

"And that 'elusive something'—did you ever get the secret of that?"

Julie's heart started to pound, but she kept her face expressionless. The artist glanced at Julie and then down at her wine. She drank and answered very gently. "No, I found no secret."

The completed painting shows a woman—Julie—by the plain hanging light with one of the ten test tubes in her hand. It has a baleful red-gold glow. The rest of the picture is dark with the woman's loneliness—unusual in a post-impressionist work. The intense concentration in her face is compelling in its monasticism. Behind Julie there is a man in a black hat who waits by the door and watches her with a disturbing indolence and assurance. It's in the tilt of his head, the way his hand is thrust into his trouser pocket.

The artist, of course, was Amélie Cailleoux, and the painting is the one that hangs in the National Gallery. Cailleoux was asked why the man in the background was not Georges Claudet. She said: "I don't know. When I began the figure, it was just a man. Something in my hand, I suppose, decided who it had to be. Perhaps because he was dark, he made a better contrast for her than Claudet who had the same coloring. Or maybe something in the air down there made the decision. Maybe he willed himself into the picture. Maybe she pulled him in. Whatever it was, that's the way it came out, and there he stands: waiting."

30

HER NERVES WERE TAUT WITH STRAIN. ONE HOT, CLOSE night, when the Dane's mistress wasn't with him in the *crémerie* to restrain him, he went into his usual tirade again. Ordinarily Julie would have laughed at him, but now so much effort was required to keep her mind on the work that she had no reserves of strength or patience. For the first time she lashed back.

"Don't ever talk that way again when I'm present!" Her voice was so full of compressed feeling that everyone became still. Forks halted halfway to open mouths; pieces of bread dipped in gravy remained in mid-sweep. Only the candle flames continued to flicker in the hot night. "I work too hard to have to listen to your damned mindless ranting at the end of the day!"

The Dane had finished more than half his bottle of wine. He had no sense of her seriousness.

"What I said goes for you too," he retorted cheerfully. "I don't—"

Whatever he had been about to say became a gasped squawk. Georges's hands were on his throat, his eyes glinting with murder. He bent over the sprawled man who clutched frantically at the choking hands and gasped for air.

"Apologize to my wife!" Georges's voice was so low that hardly anyone heard him. The *patronne* and her daughter mopped the sweat from their faces and necks as they watched. Now they began to scream. A moment passed before Georges dazedly realized what he was doing. He released the dumbfounded man, and stepped back, horrified himself.

Madame la patronne's screaming voice found words: "Shame on you! *Apaches!* You're cultivated men! My poor shop!"

The Dane immediately tried to console her and awkwardly apologized across her to Georges, to Julie, to everyone; but Georges turned away with a sick face and went out into the street. Julie followed him. She found him walking swiftly with his hands to his mouth. He was in a dazed flight from himself. He crossed one street after another without looking to see where he was going.

"Did you see how horrible it was? I might have killed him! How ghastly to look down and see his face in my hands! Ghastly! And the joy I felt while doing it was even more ghastly!"

Julie could hardly keep up with him in the hot night. "It was my fault. He was only a little drunk—not drunk enough for me to have been so angry."

"No!" Georges insisted. "He was revolting! But in the end I was worse than he was!"

Julie was startled by a revelation of violence in him, but she was even more surprised to see him so violently heartsick over it. As a girl on the Vineyard, she had grown up used to seeing men fight, always averting her head from the thudding fists, the curses, grunts, and blood, and so she was resigned to the existence of violence and brutality of some sort in every man. They existed in Georges, but they sickened him. He walked like a heartbroken man.

He didn't once turn to see if she were keeping up with him, but she hurried along. She took his arm.

"Georges—I tell you again: it was my fault. These last few weeks I've been too short-tempered—"

He shook her off without a break in his tormented stride.

Eventually though she led him home through the empty streets. He was crushed and docile. All the next day and the day after, his silent self-condemnation was as violent in its own way as his original outburst against the Dane. She kept thinking back to the man who had first awed her at Cambridge—the vibrant ethereal shimmer of his personality must have come from just this suppressed intensity. On the third day, the Dane came to their flat. He stood awkwardly in the candlelit doorway, towering over Georges.

"I must tell you how very sorry I am," he said. "I'm never really serious when I speak that way. Certainly I never thought you were serious, madame. I apologize, and I ask for your friendship again. I don't know what got into me! There's something in the air these days!"

Julie watched the two men shake hands, and she turned away. The Dane was right: anger *was* in the air; frustration *was* in the air; so was silent rage at life; and all of it, Julie knew with infinite regret, was emanating from her. There was a poison torment within her that was proliferating beyond the point where it could be contained. Invisibly and impalpably, it was beginning to infect everyone around her.

She was in panic. It had to stop. One afternoon when she knew Raubard would be away from his study, she put on her hat and coat, hurried to his office, and slipped a note under his door: "Cannot meet you Thursday as scheduled. Here are the results of the last four runs—each one inconclusive."

She was ready to use all her will to refrain from seeing him again, but Georges the next day himself insisted that she make a second appointment. She knew she couldn't cancel the meeting, but she could postpone it. She told Georges that they both needed a few days of change—complete change.

"Let's go to Switzerland!" she pleaded. "I've never been to the mountains. Let's find a little village where we can go and walk. I want to stand in sunlight and breathe cold, clean air!"

He was puzzled, but without arguing or questions, he arranged the entire thing. Late Thursday morning they took the Simplon express and by early evening they were thousands of feet high in cold, thin air walking along the curving lane that served as the main street of the village of Zermatt. Above them—still higher in the hard blue dusk was the pale, starlit, glacial hulk of the Winterfall.

Georges was the one who most appreciated the change. He stood with his bare head raised to the sky the following morning and breathed deeply.

"How glad I am you made us come!" he said. "The air, the

sky, the snow, every blade of grass—everything is pure, everything is clean!"

He led her up the mountain and they rested below the snow line. He was far more lighthearted than he had ever been on their previous trips to Brittany.

"This is where we must come back again and again!" he said. "Here finally is the place that was meant for me!"

Julie's smile was wan. For her, the weekend had been no escape. She was imprisoned for the rest of her life within a cramped state of being where there would never be enough air for her to breathe, enough space for her to stand fully upright, enough time for her ever to be free of this tortured sense of waiting. She hated what had happened to her.

When she finally appeared in Marcel's study, pale, with averted face, almost rudely abrupt—he said nothing about her absence. He too looked strained and exhausted as he took her notes and glanced through them.

Standing behind him she watched him as he read, looking at the hands that were holding her papers, at the strong neck and the heavy line of those shoulders, at his hair, at the beard —how familiar! how familiar! how dear! Then she wrenched herself from desire and turned to watch the rain fall past the window and form rivulets on the pane.

She turned at the sound of his voice. He was looking at her with the torment of a physician who shares a pain he is powerless to alleviate. She had never seen his eyes so deep with suffering.

"What did you say?" she asked.

He made no answer and turned away back to his reading. His hugeness remained averted as if to spare her. Then slowly, he put down her papers and raised his head to stare straight ahead—anywhere but at her. After a moment, he closed his eyes out of weariness.

"Julie," he said in a low voice. "Get out of here at once and never come back! Or else stay and *really* be with me! I won't go on like this any longer. It's for saints, not for human beings!"

Her lips parted helplessly. A warm flow of readiness for him paralyzed her entire body, and she couldn't move. Then, with her ultimate strength, she turned and ran from the room and down the stairs.

"Julie!"

She stopped. He had come out of his study and stood at

the head of the landing above her, his presence demanding her return. She could go no farther.

"Julie!" he said again, more softly, and she was helpless. He stood up there until she walked by him with her head lowered and preceded him to his study. Then before he even touched her, she went to him as he stood with the door closed at his back. She clung to him, weeping shakily out of shattered nerves and relief that the war of feelings was over and she had lost it. As they kissed, she knew that one entire mountain range in her life was avalanching into tragedy; yet she was suffused with the singing sunlight of relief. Impaled to the exploding moment, each drugged the other to the world outside the room. The study door was unlocked; the window blinds facing the street were undrawn; at any instant someone could come upon them. Diamond points of reason within their minds still knew it, but the jeopardy was less than the sweetness. They suffered the terrible risk helplessly until a growing loveliness in the veins exploded into an aeration of the soul. Then they were at peace—stunned, panting, awed—neither one yet daring to turn and see what the earthquake had done to the landscape of their lives.

She watched him as he bent over to kiss the palms of her hands which still carried the scent of laboratory reagents, she knew, but he was kissing her in them, even after he had had all of her. She felt the softness of his beard; and her love for him was as dark as his hair.

At any moment, though, the precarious happiness could plummet. She was tied irrevocably into the lives of two men —both of them of enormous stature in her eyes. Georges was still the man with whom she shared her life of work; her life in time and place, but if he were to know what Marcel was to her now, he would die of it. She knew she was holding Georges's naked beating heart in her two hands.

Marcel asked her: "Could we live together now? That's what I really want—a life together."

For a moment she was too shocked—too moved—to reply —and even then she could barely be heard: "You should have offered me that before you went to America—"

"I wanted to, but I couldn't make myself do it then," he replied. "I wasn't that man."

"And I'm no longer that woman. Everybody changes."

"But do you really still think you can go on being the same to Georges, feel the same for him, appear the same to him?"

Chill made her shudder. "What do you think will happen?"

"Some part of him is sure to know," Marcel replied. "He'll see that you're happy," he said quietly. "No one knows how to hide that for any length of time."

31

SHE WALKED BACK TO THE LABORATORY, LITHE AND joyous. She hardly recognized herself: in her blood, in her heart, in her step, there was buoyancy and release from a life that until now had been too dry, too unfulfilled to contemplate without a shudder. To look back now was like looking back to a time of sickness.

At the entrance to the college, she hesitated for one more moment of sunlight. She dreaded Georges's first glance at her.

She crossed the basement darkness and paused at the closed laboratory door. Georges was at work within. He would see everything in her face the moment she entered; and now she was sorry she had refused Marcel's offer to make a clean break. There was no dignity in what she was doing. She would look as if she were hiding the truth out of fear when her only motivation was kindness. She steeled herself and opened the door. Georges didn't turn from the workbench: he was in the midst of preparing a formaldehyde solution. The light was on the far side of him, and he was in silhouette: a man in darkness with an outline of golden glow. She waited a moment, then realized that her waiting there was a demand that he turn to see what was wrong. She came in then, taking off her hat and coat, watching him all the time, but still he didn't turn from the beakers and boiling flasks. Suddenly she realized that she felt no guilt, only a strident joy because what she had done had come from a need as profound as the need to breathe.

"How did it go?" he finally asked over his shoulder.

"Very well."

"You sound happy about it," he observed as he poured.

"I am," she said simply, and at last it occurred to her that there never would be any guilt for her—her happiness was going to go on and on! She was amazed: it was like a nightmare in reverse, but just as in a nightmare, there was nothing she could do about it. What frightened her was that there was nothing she wanted to do about it. She wanted only to go on just as she was, terrifying risk and all.

32

EACH DAY AND EACH NIGHT FOUND HER WORKING AND living alongside a man from whom she kept the most important secret of his life. She never lost the sense she had of holding his life in her palms. Should she press a featherweight too hard, even inadvertently or carelessly, he would die of the agony. What was frightening was that she so quickly got used to it. In the laboratory, during the working day, from the moment he came in to the moment he left, she was aware she was telling him a lie about herself. Whether they discussed colloidal behavior, or molecular boiling points, or the number of the page in the data book where a certain experiment had been recorded, it was all a screen for her lie. She told the same lie at home in the apartment when she asked him if he wanted more cheese, of if he wanted to go to bed, or to go on reading. She told the lie in the street, in the tram, and on the train. The lie became part of her being, as inextricable as her memory of her mother. It made her feel apart from life. Other people still walked straight lines through time, she now had to dart in and out of the days and hours; slipping behind the hands of the clock to steal from the ticking gears and wheels a few hours with Marcel in order to complete her life.

Yet she was happy. She was lying to Georges with silence, but she felt kinder to him, less critical of his lack of physical passion, more tolerant of his distance from the world. She loved him because the unused emotions he had never felt any need for were now absorbed by Marcel. All of her at last was being used and needed. Finally she was completely happy.

Georges marked the change in her with relief, at first.

"You're easier to be with," he said. "Where it comes from, I don't know. It's as if overnight you came to terms with life. Do you feel it in yourself?"

"Yes," she replied, continuing with her work. "I *am* more at ease with myself." She didn't want to say any more. "I didn't know that I'd been difficult."

"You were dissatisfied, I think," he replied with prompt frankness.

"And you never told me this until now?" she asked. "Why? Because you wanted to spare me?"

"Not to spare you," he said mildly. "But because there wasn't anything you could have done about it. Either it was something that would go away by itself, or else I'd have learned to live with it."

"The truth is then that all along you were dissatisfied with me?"

"More to the point, I was aware of a difference between us."

"Which you were perfectly willing to live with?"

He looked at her with surprise at her persistence over the point.

"It's the least we owe each other, isn't it?" he asked simply.

Her life now stalked across the landscape of time with the looping rhythm of a telegraph wire—swinging in high, taut arcs from Wednesday to Wednesday, diving down the loop after every meeting with Marcel only to soar upward again as the next Wednesday approached. Each Wednesday morning, she was tight with dread that something would happen, but once Georges left the lab to go upstairs for his four hours of classes—one to five—that fear was gone and she had only another half-hour to wait to put on her hat and coat, her hands trembling, and go to the Rue Cujas from where it was merely a walk—studiedly held to a decorous pace—down the cobbled hill of the Rue St. Jacques. Then—safely out of everyone's sight—she could hurry up the steps of the Collège de France, make the rustling half-turn on Marcel's landing, and take the dozen heart-pounding paces along the dark corridor to knock on his oaken door, always remembering the cold surprise, on her first visit, of his wife's presence, and steeling herself against a repetition of the rebuff.

But each Wednesday, he was waiting, as anxious for her as she was for him. His strain was in his face as he opened the door. She returned his for-appearances'-sake nod, stepped decorously inside, heard the door close behind her, turned, and, intoxicated with relief, clung to him as he to her, their eyes closed with the sweetness—aware, both of them, that this was the purest happiness either would ever possibly experience for the rest of their entire lives.

"Sometimes I think that if Georges knew how things were perhaps he'd understand. Perhaps he already does know," she said.

"He doesn't know," Marcel replied slowly. He was looking down at her with grave pity. "Nor would he understand. Is that what you find unbearable?"

"No," she said. "And that's what haunts me." She turned to him with a plea. "I love him now in a way I never did before; yet why don't I feel remorse? What's wrong? Am I different from other people? Am I cruel?" She sighed and walked to the window. "Sometimes I have a sense that I'm not living in my own time. I get this sudden stab of terror that I shouldn't be wearing these clothes, seeing these sights out there, even speaking this tongue: that I *am* something—or that I *know* something—from thousands of years away. I can be sitting with Georges in a little café with Paris walking by and—like a spell of dizziness—I close my eyes and feel myself in a landscape I can't remember seeing before yet which I know very well; and all around me there are sounds I can't quite hear but which something in me recognizes—something that's wild, free, and can be—I'm afraid—utterly without pity!"

"You are different," he said. "Whatever it is, be glad of it!"

"No. I'm terrified. I'm terrified that I can deceive Georges. How can he *not* know? He always has such an insight into me. Could it be he doesn't want to know?"

Again Marcel shook his head. "Georges isn't that kind of man. What he knows, he takes action on. What he doesn't know, no part of him can know."

"And he couldn't bear it if he did," she said with resignation.

"He couldn't bear it if he did," Marcel repeated after her quietly. "And you're as aware of that as I am."

"I am," she confessed.

If what she shared with Georges was work, with Marcel she was sharing inspiration. He shaped her mind, so that it began to grow as dexterous as her fingers and to move as deftly among hypotheses as her hand could move past a reagent shelf and select the one bottle that she needed. Ideas became simple. She learned to solve problems by starting at either end or from both ends at once—fitting answers, intuitively arrived at, to circumstances, or the other way around.

Georges was instantly aware of her progress. Once his own electrolytic work was caught in an impasse, and he was confused by contradictory evidence, while she, coming fresh to the problem, was able to examine his data and sort out the relevant from the irrelevant with no idea of the mastery she was demonstrating. She found him looking at her with a shining gaze.

"My God!" was all he said in gratitude for the inexplicable way she had flowered. Then he leaned over and kissed her forehead. "You delight me!" he said simply.

She turned away.

33

THE HEAVINESS OF HER PREGNANCY MADE HER TIRE easily. Whenever possible when she was alone, she hoisted herself slowly on to the work stool for a few minutes' rest. She was always afraid she was going to fall and that the nightmare fluids with which she was working would splatter out of smashed test tubes. She didn't know how infectious syphilitic serum really was, but the idea horrified her. When she had started to work with syphilis, she had hoped that the experiment would be one she could get through quickly with a clean and decisive null result. Instead, like the glioma, the very first test had given her one of those heart-stopping responses, implying that perhaps here too was a possibility; but she had learned how to be callous to hope. There had already been a number of will-of-the-wisps among the spinal-fluid tests. By now, Julie could look at a rack of unequal precipitations with the same irritable skepticism with which a veteran gold miner hefted a lump of ore that he could swear was going to be pyrite—fool's gold—the trap for amateurs, not for those who were experienced in disappointment. And each time, sure enough, after sufficient repetition, she had always been able to prove out the null result. Syphilis though was turning out to be stubborn in its appearance of responsivity. The second test had also been responsive, although not exactly duplicating the first.

A clear-cut *yes,* or an irrefutable *no* was all she wanted now; but no *yes* could be accepted until it had withstood a hundred attempts to tear it down. So far, only syphilis serum's *yes* had been this tenacious. She was too steeled against hope to believe that this *yes* could be taken seriously; she felt only the irritation of someone who has been put upon one time too many.

Georges came into the lab before she heard him enter the basement, and he caught her still sitting on the stool. He glanced at her shrewdly and went past her to the worktable. A test-tube rack stood there with its implied promise of selective precipitation: the concentrations in the sixth and seventh test tubes were both almost clear where all the others were turbid. If the test tubes could be believed, the result meant that an isoelectric point was to be found somewhere between the two concentrations, and a diagnostic test was really possible, but Georges was as skeptical as Julie by now.

"I don't like it at all," he said turning to her abruptly. "And I'd rather postpone the rest of the tests until after we have our child. It's wrong to be working on a dangerous serum like syphilis at a time like this."

Until after we have our child. The words touched a dozen different awarenesses in her—and then she slowly lowered herself off the stool. He watched her with concern, but also with anger for not taking enough care of herself.

"You're tired!" he said accusingly.

"Not at all!"

"Look at the way you move! You shouldn't even be here!"

It was Wednesday. Georges's wish to send her home alarmed her, even though for the past month she and Marcel had spent their stolen time only in talk and work and gentleness. Habit was now too ingrained for her to want to give that up too. She had no intention of allowing Georges to coddle her too much.

"There isn't a reason in the world why I can't work right up to the last moment," she said. She had to straighten her skirts; they continually pulled up now over her protruding belly.

"Ordinarily I'd agree," he said. "But you're too unsure. Look, you can't move without holding on! If we were working with anything else besides syphilis, I might say all right. But this is too dangerous!"

His concern was warming, but it was going to irritate her if it went on much longer, she knew. A massive flood of withheld anger was waiting somewhere within her, and she didn't want to know too much about it or its cause.

"There's no danger," she insisted. She was secretly frightened, but she wanted to spare him anxiety because he had said *our child*. Along with all the contradictory things it had evoked in her it had also touched her with irritated tenderness. "Either with this next run, or the one after, we'll track down this discrepancy and the series will be ended. It can't go on this way much longer."

"You could have followed the glioma forever," he reminded her.

"It's not the same thing. There we got a positive response from only one patient. The moment she disappeared, it was all finished. Here, we keep getting some kind of selective precipitation from almost every syphilitic sample we've tried. I must say," she added in a different tone, "if we had got this kind of result back there last year with the glioma, we would have been positive that we really had something."

"But you don't give up anything," he protested. "You insist on making the rounds of the hospitals. You insist on going to see Raubard every week—listen!" He turned to her with a sharply changed manner. "Did you hear what you just said? You said: *We keep getting some kind of positive result from almost every sample we've tried!* The fact is that this *is* the first time we get roughly consistent results from so many different donors!"

"So far," she added.

"Almost ten," he pointed out. "With other false alarms, it never turned out to be consistent in more than two or perhaps three out of ten different sources of fluid. But with syphilis, it's been eight out of ten."

"It has been positive eight out of ten," she conceded slowly. "But not all of the eight cases reacted identically."

"I don't care!" He was getting excited now that he was allowing hope to rise. "I'm even more cautious about these things than you are, but we may have a right to begin to take this thing seriously! Show all the figures and graphs to Raubard this afternoon. Even he'll begin to think it's more than a succession of accidents!"

He took out the data book and excitedly began to organize the presentation. She watched him with tenderness for his transparency. He had said *after we have our child* as if the pain, anxiety, pleasure, the wonderful secret sense of containing within herself the child's entire being was something to be shared. But it wasn't *our child* at all. It was *my* child, she thought. Georges was a kind man, but what she felt and would feel would always be too intensely private. Still, the fact of his expectation was a gift emanating from the blood of his heart. God alone knew how much she owed him, but she did want every happiness for him. If, indeed, his enthusiasm was justified, and they really had discovered an analytical test she mentally made over to him the glory and wonder of it. Let him have it all—but the child was *her* child, and her time with Marcel was *her* life, belonging to her by a right that could never be recognized nor even defended, but which existed just the same.

These days Marcel waited for her with his door open so that when she began her laborious climb up to his study, he would be able to hear. By the time she was a quarter of the way up, he had come down the staircase to help her.

"I can do it myself," she said, but she leaned heavily on his arm.

"That idiot you've taken on for your confinement ought to be shot," he muttered. "Why he ever let you get so big so soon, I'll never know."

"He says it's a good sign."

"Then let him carry you up the stairs himself a few times!"

She laughed, but she had to pause on the steps because she was panting from the exertion.

"If I'm so much trouble, perhaps I shouldn't come until after the child is born."

"Who knows if I'll ever see you after your baby comes," he rumbled. "You may turn out to be one of those fatuous mothers who'd let civilization crumble rather than be diverted from your child."

He had a special way of saying *"your* baby," *"your* child" that was part of the unspoken question that was always in his eyes nowadays when he watched her speak and move. He was obviously yearning for her to tell him something. He already had three children. Did he really want a fourth that badly? Or was it simply that he wanted a child with her? She toiled up the dark stairs beside him, resting her full weight on his arm without the slightest hesitancy because she was used to his physical strength, to her own closeness to him. Still, she couldn't bring herself to talk to him about what he wanted. It was *her* child, *her* baby, she thought stubbornly. That was one point that would never be negotiable.

In his study, he didn't release her arm until he had led her to the hard straight chair which she preferred now. He lowered her into it, watching her sharply all the time. Then he went back and closed the door. He stood there, frowning down at her, legs spread, his hands on his hips: the very picture, she thought, of a man determined to impose his will.

"All right, now, let's talk straight," he said.

"Georges thinks we ought to begin to take the syphilis reaction seriously," she replied. "I've brought all the data."

"That's not what I want to talk about."

"Still, it's what you *will* talk about!"

He stretched one of his arms toward her, and the commanding finger began to unfold into its full authority, but she was unmoved. She rested her hands on her belly as if to draw calm strength from it.

"Don't do that," she said quietly. "Don't lay down the law to me. There is no law any more. Not from you. Not from anyone. The baby is mine. All mine."

Slowly, his arm fell back to his side, and the glint of anger in his eyes softened to hurt. For the moment, he looked like a boy wearing a black beard touched with gray.

"I only wanted to tell you to take better care of yourself," he said.

"I take very good care of myself," she retorted. She threw back her head and laughed. She loved the ease she felt now that she possessed in herself this totally unexpected completion. She impulsively held out a hand to him to make up for her impertinence. He took the hand and smiled wryly.

"You're the lady in charge of the world these days, aren't you?" he asked. "You're not frightened?"

"I'm terrified!" she admitted. "I wake up at night, convinced I'm going to die! I wake up and suddenly feel that the baby will die or be killed to punish me. I cry because it's so sad. But then in the morning, I'm like this. No tears, no sadness. All day, for that matter. I came to talk about the work. Here's the data."

He didn't take it, but continued to look down at her. Behind his eyes was that sad questioning concern which never went away any more.

"All right, about the work: do you still get positive reactions with every syphilitic sample?"

"Eight out of ten so far."

"No matter which patient is the source? No matter which hospital prepares the fluid?"

"Eight out of ten. All eight are positive one way or another. The ways differ from one to the other, though."

He shrugged. "You'll iron that out after a while," he said calmly. "I agree with Georges: you may really have something."

She said nothing for almost a minute, feeling more than she could put into words.

"My God!" she said finally, and it was almost a murmur. "At last! How wonderful if it turns out!"

"Yes, how wonderful!" he said, echoing her, without removing his gaze from her. "And what happens if your child's hair turns out not to be blond like yours or Georges's?"

She flushed but didn't look away. "Blond or dark—it'll make no difference," she replied quietly. "It's still my child!"

34

WHITE STERILE BRILLIANCE REFLECTED FROM THE TILED walls and floors of the hospital laboratory, and the reek of carbolic acid disinfectant made the air glitter with points of light and scent. The only sound in the crowded room was the hushed breathing of the white-coated laboratory analysts who had stopped work to watch the demonstration. Occasionally there was the *ting* of glass touching glass and the gurgle of cautiously poured liquids from the two men at work in the center of the group—the chief of the hospital service, Du Croy, and the tall, carelessly elegant non-medical visitor who was demonstrating the new technique to him.

The third man there in the center, the legendary Marcel Raubard, stood watching on the opposite side of the worktable. He was the one who had arranged for the demonstration of the Claudet syphilis test which had been in process of refinement for almost two years now. Raubard always acted as sort of liaison between the medical world and the world of pure science. Now he had to be mediator in another sense as well. Du Croy was a violent anti-Dreyfusard, an extreme rightist. His eyes were forever glinting nervously with suspicion and malice on guard against his being stealthily surrounded by Jews. At this very moment, he was convinced that Georges was a Jew. He also believed that Raubard was at least half a Jew—Du Croy had an elaborate scale for measuring such fractions. And if Georges Claudet was a Jew, he reasoned as he watched the preparation for the demonstration, then certainly that white-coated little wife of his working alongside him was a Jew too—a foreign Jew, perhaps, but then everyone knew that all Americans were Jews.

That Du Croy was more than half mad himself hadn't stopped him from becoming chief of the pathological service of the Hospital for the Insane.

"I refuse even to talk to such a man," Georges told Marcel. Georges had grown a beard in the year and a half that had passed since the baby was born. He claimed with a laugh that every little girl deserved to have a bearded father, but the beard was so much darker than his fair hair that his anger made him look almost white when the suggestion to meet Du Croy had been put to him. "The man's very soul is filthy!"

Raubard shrugged off Georges's description. "But as a chemist, Du Croy's no fool. I studied medicine with him and I know. The fact is that you did not perfect a test *only* for use by physicians of the left, for left-wing syphilitics. The Hospital for the Insane has by far the largest number of paretics in Paris. Its new laboratories in six months can give you more corroboration than any other hospital could give you in five years! Besides it's now time you two moved on to something else in chemistry. Let the technicians take it over from now on."

"But I don't care about having the method put to work so widely on so large a scale," Georges said, still angry.

"Perhaps not, but the paretics do," Marcel retorted quietly. "You forget that the purpose of the test is not to prove a chemical theory. If it's at all possible to make a faster, surer diagnosis than ever before, so that treatment can start even one day earlier, it would be cruelty to deprive anyone of that means of diagnosis."

Georges sighed. "Very well. Arrange the test then."

"What time would be best?"

Georges turned to his wife. Julie said, "The afternoon is

best. I'll have nursed the baby and she'll be taking her nap. Make it two o'clock." She told Raubard, "But warn Du Croy. He's going to have to be on his best behavior. If he as much as looks cross-eyed at Georges, out we walk!"

Du Croy needed no urging. It was obvious that if the test was all that Raubard claimed, then everybody connected with it was going to be famous. He was notorious for his boast that one fine day he was going to catch a couple of smart Jews of his own, harness them and ride them all the way to glory. Of course, if the test was a failure, he could have the pleasure of exposing the Jew fraud: the pleasure *and* the glory. He couldn't lose, either way.

"Bring your colleagues by all means, Raubard," he said cordially. "Should we invite the press too?"

Raubard put his arm gently around Du Croy's elegant shoulders. "My friend," he said. "You'll be famous soon enough I promise you that. But don't frighten off the Claudets. The press is not their style."

Du Croy nodded and said nothing. When the day came, he had everything prepared for the Claudets to make their demonstration. He had five samples of cerebro-spinal fluid ready for them to work on. Numbers one, two, and three were recorded as syphilitic; numbers four and five were recorded as non-pathological. He was the only one who knew that the sample number five was really meningitis. He could not resist this little extra trap to catch the Jews. Could their test really distinguish between syphilis and meningitis?

Raubard came to the lab on the appointed day five minutes earlier than the Claudets who arrived punctiliously on schedule. Du Croy made a number of attempts at ingratiation, but Georges was unbending. Julie was no warmer. They ignored him altogether as they selected from the glass stock the apparatus they'd need, and then proceeded to add insult to injury by rewashing each flask, beaker, and test tube with acetone, nitric acid, and double-distilled water as if they trusted no one else's technique. Some of the hospital staff appeared outraged, others were intimidated. The two Claudets were too busy to notice anyone's attitude to them. The two of them might have been working in their own laboratory, as aware and as sure of each other as a pair of experienced trapeze artists spinning in mid-air.

On the soapstone table opposite them, Du Croy stood with an identical array of glassware in front of him to duplicate the

Claudets' procedure step by step. But he ostentatiously folded his arms. He had no intention of cleaning glassware that had been already prepared for him by his staff. For the rest of his life, no one would ever be able to convince him that Georges and Julie were acting purely out of habit and that he was not the recipient of deliberate insult. They ran a poverty-stricken laboratory with their own hands. They no more knew how to do with the services of laboratory assistants than an ordinary man who all his adult life had dressed himself every morning and undressed himself every night would know what to do if suddenly presented with a valet.

The colloidal gold-test solution could certainly have been prepared for them in advance to their specifications, but it never occurred to them to ask anyone to help them. As they saw it, they themselves were perfectly capable of setting up distilled water to boil. In the same way, they had prepared the 1 per cent gold chloride solution so many times that when Georges went through the meticulous step-by-step procedure of adding 5 cc. of it to 5 cc. of a 2 per cent potassium carbonate solution, it was almost mechanical. At the same time, Julie was preparing the 1 per cent solution of formaldehyde, and she had it ready the precise moment that Georges's mixture came to the boil. Du Croy had not thought to supply himself with an assistant and he had to work with all his skill to keep up with both of them working together, particularly since they were doing what they had done at least a thousand times before.

Taking each of the fluid samples in turn, they made their sets of eight dilutions, and again he imitated their operations, but he was going so fast that he didn't have time to calculate the concentrations at each step. Yet he couldn't stop to protest. Fear got into him that his sweaty fingers were going to let one of the test tubes slip through and break. But before he had a chance really to realize what he was doing, there was a burst of applause from his staff. The precipitation pattern of his first sample was exactly the same as the Claudets: the first four test tubes had turned turbid with precipitate while the remaining four were still clear. Du Croy expanded with gratification at the appreciation of his technical staff. Claudet was saying, "Unknown Number One is syphilitic." Raubard, the referee for the demonstration, consulted the list before him on which Du Croy had identified the unknowns. The applause was not for himself, Du Croy realized, but for the Claudets who had not only made a remarkable identification, but had designed a test so simple that any novice could make it work.

Almost immediately they swept him into the procedure on the second unknown. Again he had the grotesque feeling that each of them had taken him by an arm and were forcing him to run faster than he knew how so that he was being dragged along with his legs flying, slipping, tripping—the tails of his frock coat waving fatuously—then again there was the miracle before him: the same pattern as with the first sample, and again Claudet was saying:

"Unknown Number Two is syphilitic also."

Once more Raubard nodded his corroboration and added, speaking to the staff in general: "And may I point out gentlemen, that once again Dr. Du Croy's precipitation pattern completely duplicates that of the Claudets."

The third time, the strain on Du Croy was not so bad. He was able to discern the pattern of successive dilutions which he was carrying out. He could even—in those areas of his mind which were not poisoned by hatred—appreciate the simplicity and delicacy of what he was doing. But just as he was permitting himself generously to feel admiration, the third test came to completion with the same precise verdict:

"Unknown Number Three is also syphilitic," Claudet said quietly. "Madame Claudet will work on Unknown Number Four and I'll do Number Five at the same time. I think by this time, the steps are sufficiently clear. Dr. Du Croy, you can follow whichever one of us you choose."

"I'll do Number Four with Madame," he said with a gallant little bow, and followed Julie.

"Unknown Number Four shows no syphilis," she reported to Raubard, who nodded his corroboration for the fourth time. Again there was applause. All this while, though, Du Croy's attention had been straining for Claudet's verdict. He now turned and looked at the rack of test tubes in front of the man. By now, everyone could recognize the pattern on the syphilis precipitation and sure enough the meningial fluid had given Claudet a reaction that was neither clear nor syphilitic. In the very high dilutions, there was a definite ghostliness in the test tubes. Claudet was looking down at them thoughtfully and saying nothing. Du Croy lowered his glance to hide his exultation and impatience. It was like waiting for the roulette ball to come to the end of its spin. He had a superstition that if one turned one's eyes away at the last moment, the ball would fall into the right hole; but he couldn't help noticing and delighting in Claudet's long hesitation and the way he turned to hold a whispered consultation with his wife. Du Croy kept his face grave and then with bland eyes looked frankly across the table at the Claudets. Madame Claudet seemed to be asking her husband a decisive question, and he was nodding in reply. Then Claudet turned to the waiting group.

"We report that Unknown Number Five shows definite pathology—" he began, but Raubard, frowning, interrupted him.

"But Number Five is not syphilitic, at least according to this group."

"Not syphilitic," agreed Claudet. "I hadn't quite finished what I was about to say. Perhaps it's premature to be too definite, but on the basis of other work we are doing, it's possible to guess at the presence of something else—"

"Come now," said Du Croy soothingly, anxious now to forestall anything more. "Four out of five isn't bad at all for a beginning. All the test needs is the kind of detailed work and polish that we here are fully equipped to do—"

"Not syphilis," Claudet continued implacably, "but meningitis."

Raubard shook his head again as he looked down at his list. "I see nothing here except that it is from Patient 200–546— non-syphilitic."

"Did you say Patient 546?" Du Croy's face went hard with vexation as he heard his assistant, Gallard, speak up—that idiot was always breaking his neck to please! Right now he had the pale, righteous look of a man reporting his own father to the police for having stolen bread to feed the children. "As I recall, Patient 546 from the 200 group *was* meningial. If the Claudet test can also detect it as distinct from cerebral syphilis, it is all the more remarkable!"

This time the applause from the staff was greater than at any time before. Du Croy could only smile and join in; but he could have been crying to himself, I'll go along with you and get what I can out of it, but I'll make you pay for it! I'll make you pay!

Without interrupting his smile, he shook hands with Raubard.

"A fantastic success! I'm delighted that you brought them to me."

And to the Claudets, he said, as they stood side by side, as alike in their reserve and their cool poise as brother and sister.

"I would be honored to be associated with you both," he said quietly. "I hope only that you agree with me that we go on with the work without any publicity at all. I assume you hate it as much as I do."

For the first time, the Claudets' expression lightened a bit. They glanced at each other and then at him again, and he could see that he had finally said one thing of which they approved. What ninnies they must be! They themselves didn't even know yet how big a thing they had accomplished.

Julie left the laboratory with Georges and Marcel. The May air was soft and fresh after the laboratory stench of disinfectant. Full white clouds floated over Paris, casting islands of shadow between bursts of sunshine. The ceaseless change gave the city a pulsing excitability—like the delicate throb of risk that ran through every day for Julie now, so that her vigilance never fully relaxed, no matter how hard she worked, no matter how she smiled, talked, studied, or lectured. She was closer to Georges in many ways than she had ever dreamed possible with any human being, but the watchfulness hidden in her never abated—and she felt it would go on this way for her every minute of every day, every day of every week, for all the years of her life ahead. It was the price she had silently agreed to pay, and so she lived with it.

Of the three, as they left the laboratory, Marcel was the most cheerful. He was delighted with the way the demonstration had gone; he was delighted that the colloid test was to be given at last its real trial of being used day after day by chemists of widely different skills. His approach to medical research was very different from his attitudes in pure chemistry. His years in medicine had made him unendingly aware of the patient: medicine was an applied science, and its only application was the ease of human suffering. In theoretical chemistry on the other hand, he couldn't have cared less if his ideas had a fruitful application or not.

Julie was as used by now to Marcel's contradictions as she was to Georges's remarkable self-consistency. Two more different men never existed. Marcel had such contempt for Du Croy that he had no qualms at all about using him to achieve the desired end of having the colloid test adopted by the hospital laboratory. Georges, on the other hand, was acutely unhappy. He had compromised himself in his own eyes to please his best friend; and he suffered within himself because of it. She took his arm and squeezed it reassuringly. His face brightened a bit in gratitude for her understanding.

"Let's celebrate!" Marcel exploded at last. "One drink together, at least! And Georges, that long face! Enough! You haven't sold your soul to the devil! You honor anti-Dreyfusards by the depth of your concern. To hell with them! To me they're simply idiots, cretins!"

Georges shook his head.

"We feel differently," he said.

"But as far as the test itself is concerned, you must admit that the best thing in the world has happened."

"I already agreed to let Du Croy take it over," Georges said quietly. "There's no point in discussing it again. What's done is done."

Marcel was suddenly quiet. Georges's remark had touched in him the same inner watchfulness that was in Julie. The huge man looked momentarily open with regret and tender with pity.

Georges misunderstood their silence. He lightened his face.

"Look, I don't want to be the skeleton at the feast," he said with artificial cheerfulness. "Of course, let's celebrate. With more than a drink, and with more than a bottle! Come home with us and have dinner."

"At last!" Marcel said in relief. "That's more like it! But why not a restaurant!"

"No." Georges had gone as far as he could. Beyond that he was stubborn. "It's better at home!"

The reason for his insistence was clear the moment they opened the door to their flat—the upper half of a little villa on the Rue Gazan. His face lit up at once as he took off his hat and called out loud: *"Suzy?"*

A child shrieked happily in the rear of the flat, and a moment later, she came crowing and crawling into the room. Her eyes were bright with love and delight as she made straight for him. He swooped her up, radiant with happiness. He kissed her neck, her little arms, and it was always at this moment when Julie was most watchful, when her heart stood still with pity, tenderness, terror, and helpless defiance. Marcel too watched him in silence, but Georges's eyes were closed as he pressed his face against the baby's jet black ringlets—hair that had never been seen either in his family or in Julie's.

35

Two afternoons each week—every saturday and
Sunday—Julie took the time from work and study to go
across the street into the park with Suzy. To a child, Parc de
Montsouris was filled with wonders. It had a real mountain
with mysterious twisting paths, through woods and glades; it
had huge trees hundreds of years old—older than fairy tales.
There was a waterfall, a pond with swans, swings, a café that
sold ice cream and sweet drinks, a puppet guignol that played
every week just for children, and even a train that ran along
a concrete chasm straight through its center.

That train was the reason Julie and Georges had moved to
the Rue Gazan along the park's eastern face. Two years after
she received her license, Julie found a good post teaching
general science in a girls' school in Sceaux. Three mornings a
week she took the twenty-minute train ride out there away
from Paris. On the opposite platform on those mornings
Georges stood waiting for his train to take him into Montparnasse. Each afternoon she rode back to Paris to join him in
the lab. The modest neighborhood suited them both. It was
inexpensive and quiet. A baker's widow—Annette—who
lived behind them on the Rue de l'Amiral Mouchez—an old
gray street below the hill in back of the house, waddled in
every morning to make their breakfast and to take care of
Suzy.

For a long time, Suzy thought the Parc Montsouris belonged to Monsieur Roche, who limped with a big-bellied
possessiveness along the park paths in the semi-military uniform of park warden. He still had the gruff voice of a non-
commissioned officer and a strict air, but he saw to it that no
one fell off the swings in the playground while he was
around, and when he saw a child sliding too fast down the
chute, he always managed to hobble over in time to keep her
from banging her white-frilled bottom on the ground. Children could fight and scream all they wanted; M. Roche never
bothered to notice; but any child who managed to get lost
found itself firmly led back to its nurse or mother, being

scolded all the way in that terrifying deep voice. Actually he had no other voice—not even for compliments. Once when he barked at Julie: "Your newspaper photograph last week was very poor, madame. No one thinks it was as good as the one in *Echo de Paris* in the winter," Suzy was embarrassed: obviously her mother had been naughty and careless about having her picture taken. She looked up in astonishment for her mother was laughing and saying: "Thank you, but it's not important." It came to Suzy as a shock that the ferocious M. Roche was actually being deferential!

The publicity which the work was beginning to attract left Julie unmoved. It had less to do with the scientific advance than with the sensational nature of the disease itself, and the easy melodramatic contrast journalists love to make:

BEAUTIFUL GIRL-SAVANT DEFEATS SCOURGE OF LOVE.
"A latter-day Jeanne d'Arc, Julie Claudet, a beautiful young *licenciée* in science of the Sorbonne and her husband of the staff of the Collège des Sciences, after a long period of dedicated research, have finally succeeded in attacking mankind's foulest affliction: syphilis. Two years of application in the Paris Hospital for the Insane, enables Dr. Du Croy, head of the service of Pathology, to announce that the Claudet test was almost infallible in its early detection of paresis, and that research work was already going ahead on a still broader attack."

She and Georges had become used to interviews, even from the foreign press. The test had been adopted in Vienna's Krankhaus, in Edinburgh's St. Andrew's Hospital, and in Stockholm's Royal Municipal Hospital. No publicity had yet been released on the meningitis test, but it was already clear that meningitis too was detectable by the gold colloid.

For the first time she felt an inner peace that she was in some way vindicating the drive that had originally taken her into the research. She was infinitely sorry though that Georges would never share her satisfaction. To him, it was all still a second-rate venture, merely an application of a much larger principle, a piece of work he had given time to only because of his devotion to her. For his part, the first pleasurable recognition had come with an invitation from Prague's Charles University, asking him to give a series of five lectures on the electrical properties of colloids from the theoretical point of view. The prospectus made only an incidental reference to the gold test, referring to it as further experimental evidence of the existence of the isoelectric point; but his satisfaction came to an abrupt end when the expense money was sent: there was train fare only for one. "I just won't go," he said. "I'm embarrassed to ask them to send me more money, and I won't appear there alone as if the work were all mine."

"Georges, what difference does it make?" Julie said. "Only one of us can talk at one time. Besides, if I were to go, it would mean both of us spending an entire weekend away from Suzy, and she sees little enough of me as it is. You must go. You must have the recognition."

They still lacked an adequate laboratory. Du Croy was only too willing to offer them space in the hospital, but it would have to mean subordinating themselves to him.

"You can't please the Claudets," Du Croy said, whenever the question came up of helping them. "God knows how many times I've offered them a completely equipped laboratory along with a staff of assistants, but they always refuse me. They prefer their little basement cubbyhole. It's a waste of time to talk of moving them!"

After Georges's lectures in Prague, he was invited to Berlin, to Oslo, to Amsterdam, and to Milan. He asked for a laboratory again, and this time the rector replied: "My dear Claudet, you know how proud we are of you. Each time you go abroad, you add international fame to our college, and we're deeply grateful. Unfortunately we still have neither the space nor the funds to grant your request. We can move the coal bin once again so you can add another eight feet to the space you already have. This doesn't match Du Croy's princely offer, but it's the best we can do."

However, funds and space were offered within ten days when Georges showed the rector a letter he had received from Brussels, offering professorships to himself and to Julie —the first time a woman would have been so honored in Belgium. It sounded highly tempting: the two good salaries would have ensured the best care and a pleasant home for Suzy as well as adequate lab space for them both. Julie didn't press either way.

"What happens if you go to Brussels?" Marcel asked her.

"We part," she said simply.

"But I need you."

She shook her head. "No. We'll find a way to survive. Our lives will change a little. They changed when you went to America."

"Ah, are we back to that?"

"I forgive you for going. I don't forgive you for what you allowed to happen while you were away. I should never have married Georges."

He was silent for a moment. "I don't understand what you wanted. We couldn't have married."

"We would have lived together," she said shortly. "You would have left her and come to me. You would have had to. We mean that much to each other."

"Still, you're willing to let Georges accept the Brussels offer if he wants it."

"I wouldn't raise a finger to stop him. I owe him happiness in his work even though each week we take it away from him all over again in every other way."

"Would it be a relief to go to Brussels and break off with me?" He asked it without any accusation. If there was any expression in his voice at all, it was resignation.

"In one way, yes. In another way I would die, I think. What I don't know is whether I would come to love Georges more, or whether I would come to hate him. If I thought I'd love him more, I'd urge him to accept."

"And be rid of me?"

"And be gloriously rid of complication and the risk to Georges's feelings."

"You said something before," he turned to her directly. "If I left my family, right now, would you leave Georges? We'd live together the way we should have years ago."

"It's too late," she said quietly, without an instant's hesitation. "I love Suzy too much to leave her to Georges. Georges loves her too much for me to take her away from him."

"But she's *my* child!"

"You don't *know* that," Julie retorted. "What *I* know is that she's mine. I won't give her up. I won't ask Georges to."

"You've never forgiven me," he said slowly. "I don't think you ever will. Perhaps it really would be better if you did go."

"Would *you* prefer that?" she asked in the same tone he had used to her.

"No," he said with prompt honesty. "If I can have you only one afternoon a week, I'll settle for that. If I have to have you with half your heart angry with me, all right, I'll settle for that too. Apart from my work, now, I live from one Wednesday to the next. That's all I have."

She put her arm through his like an old old friend, and leaned her head against his shoulder. "And I too," she sighed. "I too!"

Georges decided to stay in Paris.

"I'm too French," he said. "It's no more complicated than that. If there's to be any credit to the work we've done, I'd like France to have it. I owe it to France, not to the highest bidder. We stay."

One spring morning in the year when Suzy was four, a pale blue telegram arrived while they were at breakfast. They came fairly frequently now, invitations to lecture or to attend conferences. Julie was in a hurry and handed it unread to Georges. His silence made her glance at him. The pale blue telegram lay on the kitchen table where it had fallen from Georges's nerveless hands, and the morning sun fell strongly on it. She read it herself: they were to be awarded the Nobel Prize in chemistry. Julie's tears of excitement streamed down her face, and she too couldn't talk. What moved her so was the wonderful tact of the wording of the award: *for the development of a theory of colloid behavior and its fruitful application.* It meant that her gold colloid test for syphilis and meningitis had not been enough, but neither had Georges's theory of colloid electricity. The two complemented each other perfectly. On impulse, she leaned down and kissed him.

"For letting me be your partner," she said, and he stroked her hair without saying anything.

The rector of the college came down to their laboratory for perhaps the second time in the years they had been working there and stood beaming at them with his hands clasped on his rounded belly.

"What a victory! What a glorious victory! And I enjoy it, even though it means that I'm soon going to lose you."

"Does it?" Georges asked.

"My dear boy, it's intolerable that a man like you should be kept on here. A professorship must be found for you at the Sorbonne. It's a scandal that one hasn't been arranged already. We here are only a small new college, but you've made us famous all over the world. The least we can do in return is help you get where your talents entitle you to be even if it means our loss. You must also present yourself for membership in the Academy."

Georges looked at Julie helplessly, appalled at the prospect of calling on several dozen strangers who knew nothing about him and detailing to each one a list of his virtues and accomplishments as if he were a door-to-door vendor of toilet articles.

"But Georges can't ask for things," Julie explained. "It would be too humiliating to be refused. I'd ask for him, if I could: I don't have his pride—"

"It's not pride," said Georges faintly. "Julie, you have to let me explain myself. Certainly I'd like a professorship at the Sorbonne, and certainly I know I'm qualified for such a post. I'm not ashamed to ask for it or even to be refused because of another man who has superior qualifications. I would be embarrassed to ask and then lose out to a man with superior connections."

"That would certainly be degrading," agreed the rector with a smile. "But, my dear Georges, at this moment you have the most powerful friends in the world of science—the Nobel Committee. Any important professorship that comes open at the moment—either at the Sorbonne or at the Collège de France—has to go to you. Let Raubard continue to be your intellectual mentor—I take on myself the role of being your adviser and guide in more mundane things. Have I your permission to act on your behalf? Yes? Then the first step in the campaign will be a formal reception for you both. I personally guarantee to have an official from the Ministry if not the Minister himself on the receiving end with us."

"Raubard too," Georges reminded him. "He belongs with us wherever we go."

The reception took place a week before they left for Stockholm. Julie bought a new dress for the occasion, one that she could also wear for the official presentation by the king. The black silk and wool dress looked very grand at home when she tried it on for Suzy's round-eyed approval, but it became insignificant when compared to the elaborate gowns, feathers and jewels of the throng which crowded into the rector's reception to meet the celebrated and mysterious young couple. Georges wore the same suit of tails, worn and shiny, which was his daily uniform when he lectured, but he wore it with elegance. He was giving his attention to his surroundings only out of kindness. Julie knew that he was really thinking of the experiment he had worked on that afternoon; it had gone badly and he would not allow himself any rest until he had found the flaw.

Raubard, who was usually the difficult one on such occasions, was surprisingly a model of charm and graciousness. Homage to himself would have irritated him and made him uncomfortable, but recognition for his protégés gave him intense pleasure. Each couple that came along the receiving line—past the rector and his wife, past the Deputy Minister and Madame Lagrange, past the Claudets, found Raubard waiting at the end of the line with a warm clasp and a hearty smile, really grateful that they had come. Madame Raubard had excused herself, murmuring an excuse that no one quite heard. She neither stood on the receiving line, nor passed along it to pay her respects.

"Why should I?" she asked her husband when he at last left the receiving line. Her voice was low but hard as tempered steel. He was completely taken aback by her vehemence. "You can make a fool of yourself all you please, but not with me standing by your side!"

He was so astonished by her attack that he said: "What are you talking about?"

"But perhaps you have no pride?" she went on. "Your own students receive the recognition before you do! Why doesn't the Deputy Minister attend a reception for *you?* Why isn't the Nobel Prize being awarded to *you?* Doesn't your family need one hundred and fifty thousand francs as much as they do? Or shall I tell you why?"

"Don't bother," he said in a low voice. His face was dark, and he turned to leave, but she caught his arm and held him.

"I'll tell you anyhow. You've debased your entire career to help glorify your mistress and to pay off the cuckold. It's that simple! I've waited too many years for you to make up to me for what you once did! Your family deserves the money and the prestige that's going to others. Well, it's too much this time! I'll make a scandal that'll turn Paris upside down!"

"You won't open your mouth!" he said so quietly that she scarcely heard him; but there was no mistaking the murder in his eyes. She was past caring, though.

"Threaten all you want!" she retorted. "You can't stop me!"

She whirled around. People had been turning to look at her, but she ignored them all for Julie, who had by chance

been standing behind her, paper-white, aghast, and sickened,
too paralyzed to move away. Madame Raubard raked her
with her hatred, and nothing had to be said.

36

AS THE TRAIN NEARED STOCKHOLM, GEORGES AND JULIE
were limp with exhaustion even though their compartment
was the most elegantly comfortable one in the entire Wagon-
Lit. The service they were given was as swift and deferential
as royalty received. They had both worked so hard for so
long without any real rest that a day and a half of idleness
and true comfort had begun to untie the million little knots
of tension which held back their true exhaustion. Then too,
the hypnotic click of speeding steel had vibrated them into
lassitude.

"Or perhaps it's the sky and the light," thought Julie, letting herself sway against the headrest and cushions behind
her. They were passing through birch woods; the delicate
white tree trunks had the fragility of deer poised at the alert.
Above the woods, through the branches, the sky had a pale,
obliquely lit lemon-light. It was eleven o'clock in the morning, but it looked already as if the day were dying. To have
the moment of early dusk go on for hours and hours was
heartbreaking to southern eyes—like a long mourning, a grief
that held the promise of endlessness. Julie lay there, her eyes
half-closed, without resistance to the train's motion. At that
moment, they were the most celebrated couple in Europe according to the newspapers in the Gare du Nord: their names
had been given greater prominence than the Kaiser, who had
made a speech, or the retreat in the Balkan War. "M. and
Mme. Claudet—" ran the detailed account: were leaving
Paris—were to be received in Berlin after accepting the Nobel awards—were to be greeted at the Palais de l'Elysée. An
order from the Austrian Emperor had reached Paris too late
to be bestowed on them and was also—like the President of
the Republic—waiting for them to return.

"My God, if I had to live with this sky, I'd die!" Georges

sighed. He too was reclining on the opposite banquette. "How sad it is!"

"It's melancholy, all right," she agreed quietly. "At the moment, though, it suits me."

He continued to look out the window with his head propped on a pillow against the corridor wall. He was wearing a new pepper-and-salt English tweed belted traveling suit, which the rector had insisted that he buy, and dark brown shoes with light tan suede uppers and elegant glistening buttons.

"An entire wardrobe," said the rector stubbornly.

Georges had smiled. "Now, what difference could it make! Besides I have no money."

"Soon you will have a great deal of money. Both of you need to be dressed completely. Now! I will advance you what you need."

Georges began to relent a little. "For Julie, yes. But for me—"

"You don't understand," said the rector, interrupting. His hands fluttered. "It is not for you. It's for France. What will people think if you travel around looking like that?"

"What do you mean 'looking like that'?" Julie said indignantly. She straightened Georges's cravat a little. "Georges is one of the most elegant men in Paris. If his clothes aren't new it is precisely because of the way France treats him. Let the world know!"

The two men looked at each other silently and exchanged an understanding. Georges patted her hand affectionately, but said quietly: "I'll get the clothes."

The rector himself took Georges to the tailor; the rector's wife took Julie in hand. When they were finally outfitted in every detail, the day before the train left, they looked at each other in the privacy of their bedroom on the Rue Gazan.

"You look beautiful, like a society lady," he said regretfully. "Too beautiful for me, I don't know you."

"And I don't know you. Your hair is too short. Your beard and mustache are trimmed too neatly. They have made us bourgeois!" she sighed. "We look commonplace, expensive!"

He smiled a little. "Perhaps *I* do, but you're beautiful. Perhaps I've given you the wrong life. You're too tired!"

"Georges, the first time I ever saw you in Harvard more than ten years ago, there was a certain life I wanted. That's exactly the life you've given me. There was also a recognition

I was ambitious for you to have. You're getting it now. I'm happy for you, Georges. I couldn't think of anything more to ask."

"I could," he said.

"What is it?"

"That you be really happy. God, how I want that!" he said with a burst of passion.

"I just finished saying that I was."

"I know you did," he said quietly. "But I know what I see in your eyes. For years I've been seeing it. Come," he said, breaking in on himself because he didn't want to talk further about it. "We've got to hurry to get ready."

It was a mistake to let him break off like that, almost an admission, but she had been afraid to pursue it further.

For a day and a half, they rode side by side on the train, and neither one referred to his remark that hung in the air about them like the ghost of a child who had died long ago. From time to time Julie forgot that he ever said it. Then she would remember, and each time it hit her more forcibly. He lay there across the compartment from her, half a stranger in his new clothes, suddenly harder, older, cryptically wiser. It was far more than the new clothes—he had changed very deeply far within himself. How much did he know about her that she didn't even suspect? How much didn't he have to be told because he had already divined it? She wanted to put her hands in his—but to ask him for what? She didn't know.

The birch woods outside the train were giving way to villas and meadows, rich and darkly verdant in the lemon-colored light, then to city streets, lined with stone houses that had massively curved baroque façades, then into the coal-dust echoing gloom of a city railroad terminus. They rose in the train and stamped their feet a little and adjusted their clothes. Then he looked at her again with that sudden discernment that made her feel again that she was with a changed man— older, even more masculine than before.

"You seemed surprised the other day when I said that I had noticed you weren't happy," he remarked suddenly. "Why should you think I wouldn't notice?"

"Why do you start to talk this way when we're about to do something else?" she asked. "It's almost as if you want to be sure you're going to be interrupted. Do you or don't you want to talk about it? An official welcoming committee is going to burst in on us by the time you count five."

He laughed unhappily. "It's the other way around. I *don't* want to be interrupted. It just takes me so long to bring myself to say it."

"But why?" she pleaded. "Why? I don't say I'm divinely happy. A long time ago I learned that it's painful to live. I think it's supposed to be painful. There's never been a time in my life when there wasn't a hurt of some sort somewhere in me. We have a life together, we have work together, we have Suzy—" She couldn't finish the phrase, but said, "And now things will be easier. What more should I want?"

He threw a fur-collared coat over his arm—the coat of a completely different man. He looked down at it, thoughtful at the change that was being thrust on him.

"I think I would be satisfied if only you hadn't looked so surprised at my remark," he said slowly. Then he looked directly at her. "It was the surprise that came as a stab."

"But why?"

He was speechless at her lack of understanding. "Because it meant that some part of you had forgotten that I love you," he said. Before she could answer, there was a knock on the door: the reception committee had arrived in time to interrupt him. She smiled mechanically as the tall, pale, darkly dressed men came in and bowed from their heights, but in her heart the ache of regret was deepening into something else, something close to dread. Her partner and colleague with his too smartly clipped hair and beard, his expensive man-about-town clothes, his easy grace with strangers, looked himself like a stranger to her now, and the wounded man who only a moment ago had said with true pain: "You had forgotten that I love you" seemed to have disappeared forever. Who was she with?

They filed down out of the train and up into waiting black limousines, as high, square, and elegant as carriages. Georges sat back easily on the soft black leather that had the finish of watered silk. His natural grace made him seem at least as much the aristocrat as any of his titled escort, but his coolly gracious air was a danger signal to her: in self-defense he was making himself aloof from an outside world that might, at any moment, insult him. She knew him too well to miss the meaning of the change in him, and she longed to call him back, particularly at this moment which was the culmination of so much work and sacrifice.

All during that day in Stockholm, she waited for him to

give her just one glance of that wordless understanding and affection which until now had been so much a part of their lives. Only during the actual ceremony itself, the following morning when the citation was being read aloud in the presence of the king, did their hands surreptitiously touch, clasp, and press each other in a fleeting instant of silent comradeship. Then he had to disengage his fingers and take the notes for his formal acceptance from the inner pocket of his elegant new tailcoat. For the rest of their stay in Stockholm—the receptions, presentations, and the public lecture which was made by Georges on behalf of both of them—she waited for him to look at her and to touch her in that intimate way again. She herself could not take the initiative: it seemed to her too cheap a lie; too cheap to tell, too cheap to perpetrate on a man like Georges. If he could have made himself come to her as she yearned for him at that moment, she would have given him anything he could have asked, even to breaking with Marcel.

In Berlin, she continued to wait for him, crying in silent anguish: *Save us both,* as she stood by his side during scientific meetings and formal receptions at the Kaiser Wilhelm Institut, at the University, at the Opera, at the Imperial Palace. Everywhere crowds overwhelmed them. She received scrolls and awards from delegations of women students, from socialist women, from women for international peace, from a deputation from the German Theatre. Celebrity on a scale undreamed of in Paris shone on them at every stop they made on the way home. Gifts of all kinds were sent to their train as it stood in the successive stations. Georges became continually more aloof, more constrained. He was exhausted. She could feel it in him and urged him to rest; yet when he did, he lay with his eyes closed so that he couldn't see her.

Back in France, with the train speeding toward Paris, she could stand it no longer. They were going to be received by the President of the Republic; there were going to be more receptions, meetings and deputations; and these few hours they still had left was all the time there would be for themselves. If the moment had come to face the fact that Georges knew about her and Marcel, then let it be faced—now—once and for all. Let there, finally, be an end to this drag of regret.

Georges was reclining on the train banquette in his vest and shirtsleeves. His coat was hung away, but he hadn't removed his high starched white collar and brown knitted silk tie. His feet, in the suede-topped boots, were crossed.

She sat down on the banquette, touching him. He moved slightly away without opening his eyes.

"Georges," she said quietly. "Look at me."

His gaze was on her, calm, questioning but guarded.

"Now, tell me," she said, in the same tone she had used before. "What is it between us?"

"Why does it have to be put into words?"

"Because I find I can't live without understanding the man I live with. I have no clarity unless you give it to me about yourself."

He shrugged slightly. "There was a time when that clarity didn't have to be asked for. It was there—without words."

"All right," she said, still calmly. "Then let's face the fact that the time has come when I need the words to tell me what you think and what you feel."

"I think we're in a worse case than that," he replied. "What happens when you *do* know?"

"Whatever I can do to make you happy."

He smiled slightly and looked away.

"It's all too cerebral," he said. "Too mechanistic. But you see, I know I have no right to complain," he added, putting his hand on hers. He turned back to face her, and now for the first time his eyes were full of feeling. "I'm simply paying the price for what I extracted from you, and the terrible lesson is very clear to me now. I had no right to come into your life."

"Why do you say that?"

"Because it's true. I made the mistake of settling for less than I really demanded of life. This is always the fatal error. If you need clean air to breathe, fight for air that's clean. To settle for less means that in the end you suffocate, so you settle to no avail. I needed a woman who loved me the way I loved her, and you couldn't love me that way. I half-knew you couldn't from the very beginning, yet I settled and now that is what I have to pay for."

She said nothing, and his hand on hers moved with gentle intimacy.

"I knew you loved Marcel and that you would never really love anyone else. You had to give him up for me, because by the time he came back, we were married. All these years you have done without him because of me, and I have to pay for that. I don't ask if you continued to love him. I don't even want to hear you say either yes or no. It's beside the point. Something else happened between us. In the lab, we're close; in work; in the teaching; with Suzy whom we both adore, we're absolutely one. Yet between us as man and woman, even whatever little we had together in the beginning is gone. I told you then that I wanted you as more than a colleague. That's still true, Julie. I still love you the same way, and I haven't made you happy. It came finally clear to me when we were given the most tangible recognition the world could give of what we did together. If there's fame to be found in science, we've found it; if there's money to be won in science, we've won it; but if there's happiness to be gotten, you didn't get it. Your eyes are too heartbroken to fool me."

Again it was the moment to give him sworn assurance, but she was once more unable to make herself lie, and so she said nothing, too devastated by the mixture of truth and innocence in his insight. He overestimated her, she saw. Also he underestimated the way life could drive people with deadly relentlessness into streams where drowning was a certainty— even after he had just finished telling her how he himself had been impelled into a marriage that he knew from the beginning would be fatal to him.

"Sometimes I think Marcel is right," she said aloud. "How feeble a thing it is to *know!* How little you have of the thing you *know!* How distorted a vision *knowing* gives you!"

"Yet I *know* you."

"No, I don't think so," she said sadly. "Perhaps, in the end, all one really *knows* is how to torment oneself. Not how to live. The wisdom for living seems to come from some other impulsion—deeper than the 'knowing' mind—from a necessity within the cell plasm itself."

His smile was small and tired.

"And if you're one of the people who don't have it?" he asked.

"Then God help you," she replied. "Because no one else can and nothing else will!"

She rose from the banquette, and, with a sigh, he followed her.

37

A LONG LINE OF GLEAMING CARRIAGES, BERLINS, broughams, motorcars, and electrics moved slowly along the Rue du Faubourg St. Honoré, and halted every few minutes as guests alighted for the presidential palace within the gates. The line curved around and back to the Champs Elysées, where it turned again around the corner. Two thousand guests had been invited to the President's reception for the Claudets. They in turn were watched by ten thousand Parisians on the street, and the parade of carriages was flanked by two files of Guards in full dress—plumes, gaiters, swords, bayonets bright in the sunshine. The wait in the full sight of the sidewalk crowds, and the opportunity to complain about it later to each other and to those who had not been invited was as satisfying as actual presence within the Palace.

On the line after the President and his wife stood the two people everyone had come to see—the Claudets—a still-young couple, pale, tense, and obedient to their social duty, but painfully out of place. Also on the line, to everyone's surprise, was Dr. Du Croy, beaming his pleasure and standing somehow so that his decoration—equal to that of the Claudets—could not be missed. There had been an enormous outcry from the right that he had been maneuvered out of his share of the Nobel Prize by the Claudets, and that actually he deserved it even more than they did. One could not control the actions of foreigners—said their editorials—but France could not afford to show itself ungrateful. There were threats to boycott the reception unless Du Croy was included.

"This is what was going on here in Paris while you were away," the rector explained as he had ridden with them earlier that morning from the train to the reception. Georges turned away in disgust.

"I don't care if they decorate him with a forest of palms," Georges said. "I just don't want to stand with him. Didn't you get a chance to say anything?" he asked angrily.

"I did." The rector was calm. "And when I finished it was clear that they thought I had been making a demand. In turn they made a counter-proposition: in exchange for his decoration today you are to be accepted into the Academy and given a chair at the Sorbonne!"

"My God! And Julie?"

The rector's smile was ironic. "In the Academy? If even Marie Curie is unacceptable, then what chance does Julie stand? At the Sorbonne, though, she would be appointed Chief of Laboratory under you. Unfortunately there is still no laboratory arranged for. I hope to arrange that with the President himself later this afternoon." He spread his hands. "Georges, you know how it is! It's a disgusting business to have to do for oneself; but not for one's friends. The truth is I enjoy negotiating on your behalf. Leave it to me, and I'll arrange it all. In a few weeks it will be all over, and then you can settle down to enjoy the life of one of France's recognized scientists."

They arrived finally, and Georges was relieved to find Raubard already there to support them with his huge commanding presence.

"Make just the one more compromise," the rector advised. "And stand on the receiving line with Du Croy at the reception. After all, you've stood in the laboratory often enough with him."

Georges gave that silent sigh that kept Julie from looking at him.

"I can make any compromise now," Georges said, "I've lost my anger."

He and the rector walked away, leaving Marcel and Julie alone. Marcel watched him go and then looked questioningly at Julie, his eyes instantly alert with darkness.

"I don't know," said Julie. "I can't reach him any more."

After the formalities, she lost Georges in the throng. She was continually being stopped and congratulated by elegantly dressed strangers who claimed to have met her years earlier through her cousin Prissy. She always nodded and smiled, but she was distractedly searching for Georges. She caught a glimpse of him for only a moment, and to her surprise he was talking to Madame Raubard. She was stopped by her cousin Prissy's old friends, Lyman Mead and his sister. Lyman had the same monocle, the same glance, only his graying hair was cut differently. They asked permission to give an *evening* for her. Again she saw Georges through the moving crowd, still with Madame Raubard. Julie began to have a foreboding.

When the day was over, he came for her to take her to the limousine which had been put at their disposal. It was to take them back to the Rue Gazan; the little flat was still the focus of their lives.

"I was looking for you everywhere," she said.

"I was with Madame Raubard," he said. "Do you know, I had never really spoken to her before? She can be charming. And kind!" he added with a distant surprise. "How kind she was!"

"Madame Raubard can never be kind," she said quietly. "You know that better than anyone."

"To you, she never was," he agreed. "To me, though, she is. Perhaps she's softening, now that she feels she has won."

Julie closed her eyes and breathed very softly. Her foreboding tightened to terror.

The full reality of her celebrity dawned on her two weeks later as she walked past the salutes of the two United States Marines standing guard beneath the United States seal over the embassy entrance. The two boys were so unmistakably American that she momentarily forgot the lines of carriages and automobiles up and down the avenue filled with guests for the American ambassador's reception; but nothing prepared her for the nostalgia that drenched her when she heard the familiar language of the waiting crowd in the embassy salons: entwined in the American murmur she heard the voices of her father, her mother, Ronny, Joey, Amelia, Monty, Asher, Prissy. Tears blinded her, and she was voiceless. All around her were her own people who were gazing at her with awe and pride. She saw faces of American girls who looked exactly as she must have when she first arrived. They were staring at her nakedly, with gaping mouths and dazzled eyes, absorbed by the sight of the young woman of whom they had read so much. For the first time, it struck Julie that the newspapers at home had been full of her—the first American woman ever to win such renown. Until this moment, it had been a European adventure—with uniformed kings, emperors, and premiers. Its very grandeur had made it unreal. Now though it was clear that everyone on the Vineyard knew of her; at Rotch's store in West Tisbury, they had read about her in the Vineyard *Gazette;* her classmates and teachers at Radcliffe knew; it had been in all the Boston papers.

The guests came crowding around her now to grasp her hand, to tell her how pleased they were to see her, to tell her that they had daughters, cousins, sisters, aunts, friends, neighbors who had been with her at Radcliffe; to ask her help and advice for young girls who were just beginning careers in science, in the arts, in medicine, in politics, to return to the United States and lead the movement for women's suffrage. They submerged her with themselves; and even though she had been besieged so many times before, this was the first time it was in her own tongue, the first time it really touched her, even though they didn't really know what she had done, what it had cost her. They knew only that she was famous.

She looked around for Georges to share it with him—to feel his support, but he was no longer at her side. She caught a glimpse of him across the room—and a now familiar despair hit her—he was with Madame Raubard again who was speaking with intense animation.

These days Julie was mostly alone in the laboratory. For Georges, trapped in the negotiations for the post at the Sorbonne and the round of calls he was having to make on the Academicians to ask their support for his candidacy, all meaningful work had stopped. He knew that he was doing it all very badly. He was too reserved. The friends he had made in his lifetime had all come to him of their own accord: those whom he now had to seek out were being put off by his appearance of aloofness. He tried to arrange it so that he made his calls on men when they were sure to be out because then all he was required to do was to leave his calling card with one corner bent. Too often though he was surprised, and the man who was not supposed to be at home was there to receive him. Their entire life—their work—Julie thought, seemed permanently dislocated.

In June, at last there was the promise of some sort of resolution: Julie's old chief—Salomon-Delachet—finally retired and his chair at the Sorbonne became vacant—it went to Georges with a research stipend of twelve thousand francs and two workrooms for research in addition to his own study. Julie was officially appointed Chief Research Associate. Four days later, he was elected to the Academy, by the meager margin of two votes. The agony at last seemed to be over and all the prizes secured.

"Now let it be our turn to play host," Julie pleaded. "Remember the wonderful little ceremony your students gave us

when they first set up the laboratory in the basement? Let's
have another one for the new laboratory! We have some
money now. Let's invite all the people who have ever been
good to us—friends, colleagues, students—all the people who
aren't grand. Let's rent the wedding hall in the restaurant in
the park across the street. We'll have music! We'll start a new
time in our lives." She put her hands on his arms and shook
him with her intensity. "Ah, Georges, let's us take whatever it
is we have left and make it shine!"

He smiled a little with wistful eyes.

"Why not?" he said quietly. "We ought at least to try!"

38

ALL HER LIFE, JULIE FELT, SHE HAD FAR MORE LAUGH-
ter and gaiety locked up in her than had ever been tapped.
Each time she had ever reached out to grasp something that
delighted her, a shaft of tragic shadow had always fallen on it,
and her arms had had to fall emptily to her sides.

Now, in this brilliant green-leafed June, she knew that she
had come to an end of darkness; whatever it was going to
cost, she was turning her back forever on it. Everything she
had ever wanted was in one way or another being achieved.
In her heart there was no rancor that she would never be admitted to the Academy, or that there would only be second-
ary posts for her at the Sorbonne. It was enough for her that
Georges had the honors. What she herself had always wanted
was the way of life, and now she would have it in full measure. She prepared for the party with a heart so light that each
time she walked down the street from the house to the
brown-painted brick restaurant—the Pavillon du Parc—for
still another instruction for Vincent, the maître d'hôtel, about
the wine or the fish, she felt a new and irrepressible delight in
what could come—if only—*ah, if only!*—and she kept glancing longingly at Georges's thoughtful profile for some sign of
his willingness to share with her this yearning for a completely new tone in their lives.

"You see, this is really my first party," she said to everyone she invited, even to her own daughter. "I never in my whole life ever gave a party!"

"Not even when you were very little, *maman?*"

"Especially not when I was very little."

"Not even birthday parties like you give for me?"

"I give them for you because I know how it was *not* to have them, but finally, finally, finally, I'm going to give my own party! And after that Papa and I may give another one, and then still another! Perhaps one every month! Why not?"

"And will there be kings, and presidents, and generals?"

"Better than kings, presidents, and generals! There'll be friends, and *maman* is going to laugh and dance!"

"Dance? Do *you* know how to dance?"

Julie laughed. "I'll show you! We'll dance together!" Around and around and around they waltzed wildly together until the sofa got in the way, and they tumbled into the pale green cushions, both of them breathless with laughter.

She danced that way at the party itself. The Sunday afternoon was blue and green; flies buzzed softly in and out of the window; outside the park waterfall poured and splashed behind the music from the stamping orchestra of fiddle, accordion, and piano that jangled out the tunes from dance halls and cabarets. The more decorous guests—professors, teachers, and scientists' wives—were a little shocked at first to have come all this way down to the southernmost tip of Paris at the invitation of such an illustrious couple, only to find so much unscholarly gaiety, but the spirit was too infectious. Julie danced with everyone; Georges didn't dance at all. He had never learned. Not even the village dances into which they fell after a while, clasping hands to form squares, rings and intertwining serpentines. Even Marcel danced: red-faced and perspiring, but laughing at last because he too had been touched to an instinctive joyousness that had been almost completely suffocated over the years. Madame Raubard was not dancing either, and asked quietly in the middle of the afternoon to be excused. She hurried out alone with inexplicable speed and took a waiting carriage home; but everyone was having too good a time to pay much attention. The dancing went on, the laughter grew louder.

It was the rector's wife who whispered to Julie that Georges looked ill. Julie didn't hear her at first. She was drenched in perspiration, and fanned herself wildly while laughing at the clumsy cancan of one of Georges's old pupils.

"Georges is on the porch by himself," the woman said again. "He is absolutely white. He doesn't talk! Go to him at once!"

Julie hurried out with the woman right behind her. Georges was leaning against a pillar, as if rigid with pain.

"It's nothing!" he whispered. He didn't turn his head to look at her. She touched him but he pulled his arm away from her as taut and hard as if he had been made of steel.

"Don't touch me!" he said again in the same voiceless whisper.

"Does it hurt so?"

He closed his eyes to spare himself an answer, but the gesture itself was an answer.

"Go back to your guests," he whispered. "This will pass!"

"Come sit down. Lean on me."

"Go away!" he said again, swallowing convulsively. "Just go away!"

"I can't leave you like this."

He didn't answer, he merely shook his head.

"No," she insisted. "Georges, I beg you. Come to one of the carriages. We'll call a doctor."

"I don't want a doctor!" he said between his teeth. She could scarcely hear him. "I want to be left alone!"

She put her arm about his waist to support him, but his eyes closed even more tightly at her touch. The other guests came pouring onto the porch, staring. At the sounds behind him, Georges wet his lips; sweat poured down his white face, but he couldn't turn to face them.

"I'll be all right," he said over his shoulder. His voice suddenly was normal. "It's just the heat. In a minute or two, I'll be all right."

They paused uncertainly, but Julie said: "Help me to get him home. He's in agony. I don't know what it is."

"It's nothing," he said calmly. He walked by himself, stiffly and with a slightly dazed gait. He walked down the street to the house. At the door, he paused to rest; he was out of breath from the massive effort of keeping himself under control. "I don't want Suzy to see me," he said in a very low voice. "Keep her away from me until I get into the room. Then stay with her."

"I want to be with you! At least until the doctor comes."

His desperate glare had the intensity of hatred when he finally looked at her directly.

"Oh my God!" he murmured, and stared up at the sky. "Oh my God, my God! Go to Suzy, please!" he said to her. "I plead with you!"

"Who do you want with you?"

"No one." His teeth were clenched and rigid. "No one at all."

Then he closed his eyes again, either out of weariness or to shut himself away from the world.

Suzy was being entertained by others, and Julie didn't go in to her; her concern would have been too instantly visible. She sent for the physician and when he came she showed him into the room with Georges and closed the door. Julie went with everyone else into the little drawing room. It was almost an hour before the physician reappeared.

"I've given Professor Claudet a strong sedative, and he should be asleep quite soon. He's had some kind of shock. I can't be sure yet, but there appears to be nothing physically the matter. Do you know of anything that has happened to him that might account for his state of acute anxiety? No serious reverses of any kind? No death of someone very close?"

She shook her head slowly, but her soul was sick with dread: *Has it finally come?* she wondered. Is this the way it was going to happen?

"There doesn't have to be an overt cause, of course," he said. "The shock can be an interior one, brought on by any number of things."

"But he *is* in a state of shock, doctor?"

The man's expression was very grave. "A most severe state of shock, madame. He will sleep for at least six or seven hours with the dosage I've given him. And perhaps by that time, you may have discovered what brought this on—that is, if there *is* anything tangible." He looked at her sharply again. "You're positive that no change of any sort has taken place today?" he asked insistently. "It may seem very minor to you, yet he can have exaggerated it out of all proportion."

She made herself look him directly in the eye.

"No," she said quietly. "Nothing."

When the physician left, she went into the bedroom and stood looking down at Georges as he slept. The strain and anguish that had tormented his face was mostly gone. The lines that were there though hadn't been there ten years earlier at Harvard. The strands of gray in his beard touched her deeply, and she longed to have loved him the way he would have wished her to. He deserved gentleness, courtesy, and gratitude, yet he needed far more than that from her. What was in her, she wondered, that never let her break with Marcel on Georges's behalf? Was it strength or weakness? Did she have iron threads of ruthlessness that made her demand from life everything she hungered for? What really would it have meant, she asked herself, to have given up Marcel? She would have starved her own body and soul—but to what end? There was no new answer waiting for her. What she withdrew from Marcel she could never have given to Georges, who hadn't even wanted it. His appetites had always moved in far slower, more elusive, rhythms than hers. She looked down at the sleeping man without pity either for herself or for him and realized that there must have been times when she disgusted him; nights when he had known that she was wanting him and he had drawn away from her within himself and turned over and gone to sleep while she had lain there awake, tormented, unassuaged.

With an ache in her heart for him, she guessed that Marcel's wife had finally told him about them. Poor, dear man! She could feel only endless pity for his suffering. He should never have married her. She had been at fault when she had insisted on it because he himself had wanted to break away from her. She wondered what there was in him that was so fragile? She had had a far tighter tie to Marcel when he first left her to go to America, yet she had managed to survive the idea that he had taken another girl. Still, if it was this unbearable to Georges, she would have to break with Marcel for him, and she prayed silently that she could at last pay the price all by herself.

She fell asleep sitting by the bed and never heard him rise, dress, and leave. She never knew for sure what thoughts he had had in his turn as he must have stood and looked down at the sleeping wife and comrade who had betrayed him with his teacher, his closest friend, and only other comrade, the one man to whom he owed his entire science. Had he wanted to touch her, to awaken her for one last word to try to make her understand the utter loneliness and revulsion that he felt on discovering that the place in life he had taken for granted as his own had turned out not to be his after all? How it felt to find that it had all been a mirage—wife, child—neither of them his; and no place to go in life for anything worth having—no friend to be trusted any more, no career worth working for any longer; no truth to be believed in, no love worth feeling, certainly not any kiss or another's honor; not even a scent, a touch, a word—nothing—!

All she could be sure of was that he had gone past her finally, bent on escaping from the dark little house, and the darker, shabbier pretense to some high, clear place where the only sound was the clean wind, where the only light was from sun and stars, where only endless cold could remove the contamination of hot, dirty passions he would never either understand or feel. There had to be, somewhere, a cleanliness as clean as his own soul; and all the cold passion there was in the man must have focused itself into one overpowering drive of will and muscle—to find the one door he could thrust open into that cleanness and walk through it erect and with dignity. Once he had told her that as far back as he could remember, he had had the premonition in the depths of his heart that sooner or later he was destined to burst out of his life, impelled by disgust, and race to an icy height all by himself in order to breathe one clean breath—even if it had to be his last.

39

LATER, THERE WERE PEOPLE WHO REMEMBERED SEEING him go. His face was well-known, but even if they didn't associate it with the name when they saw him rushing to the station, or sitting hour after hour stiff and pale in the swaying railway carriage like a man in too much pain to trust himself to lean back against the cushion, they knew at least that there went someone famous—and several days later when the newspapers carried the story, they knew who it had been. In Zermatt they knew who he was even without the newspaper publicity because from the beginning they had identified him as the "quiet Frenchman who looked as if he were married to his little sister."

When he arrived at the village, no one knew that he hadn't bothered to register at either of the two inns—he went as if magnetized straight from the station to the path outside of town that led up the mountain. People who saw him thought

it a little unusual that he had come for the first time alone, a
little odd that he should start out all by himself at such an
hour, but neither unusual enough or odd enough to disturb
anyone. Husbands had come without wives before; men had
set out for late afternoon strolls. He seemed very sure about
everything he said or did although, they remembered later, he
spoke in such a low voice that several times he had to be
asked to repeat himself.

Death, though, added a darkness to every one of the reports; heightening them and distorting them to make insignificant things look significant, and certainly multiplied the
number of people who had either seen him or thought they
had seen him. One man descending the mountain, an Italian
engineer on vacation, had passed him on the way up and said
that it was inconceivable that he could have been out for anything more than a stroll: nothing he wore or carried indicated
that he was on his way up to the glacier—he looked simply
like a city man—a Parisian—dressed for a warm June day. He
was climbing when they passed each other, it's true, and he
didn't even glance at the Italian, but it was only natural that a
famous scientist should be absorbed in a problem.

"I turned and watched him for some time," the engineer
said. "I had read everything about his career and admired
him intensely. I had never been so close to so celebrated a figure
—and all alone too. It was something I would be able to tell
about later—even if he hadn't said a word to me. I turned
away at last when he became too small to see; but even then
he was still far from the snow line. It was getting on to dusk
in the valley below me. Sunlight was still strong on the peak,
though. It looked beautifully white, clean, and unearthly up
there; and there was even a sort of sadness in turning away
from it to the growing dusk in the valley but I wanted to get
down before dark came. So I stopped watching him and went
on my way to my inn."

Julie sat for the day and a half of waiting in silence, looking down at the heavily leafed summer park across the street.
The trees made a soughing sound everywhere in the air, and
playing children called and laughed far away. When the telegram came from Switzerland, though, she broke down and
wept with her face in her hands for her brother—her dearest
brother. It was impossible to believe that he wasn't going to
walk in the door as he had in the past; that he wasn't waiting
for her right this moment—breathing, frowning, thinking—in

the laboratory to check over her work with her and call her attention to some error or slip with that affectionate but slightly impatient, "Now, Julie—!"

She wept and Marcel sat near her. He remained after the others went away. He no longer had a home to go where for the sake of duty and appearance he had to show himself. The evening before he had come in late and bent down to excuse himself in an undertone because others too were present waiting with her for some word.

"I had to drop my bags. I've taken a room at the Hôtel de Brésil on the Rue St. Jacques . . ."

"My God!" she said quietly.

"Yes, she boasted of what she had done and said it was her duty: she said she admired him far too much to see him being treated that way!"

Now that it was all over and they were alone together, he put his hand on hers and left it there for a while.

"Let's talk to each other," he said gently. "Let me tell you how I feel. As if my brother had died—partly through my carelessness, partly through his, but I'm not sorry I loved you, or, for that matter, about anything we've done. I'm sorry that our being together hurt other people, but you and I were meant to be together the way I was born *meant* to breathe. You were *meant* to be my woman: and other women in my life were possible only until I met you. Nothing has changed that."

"No, nothing changes that," she agreed in a low voice. "The only thing is that the world in which you and I had to be together was a world in which he couldn't breathe. No, Marcel, nothing has changed between you and me, but everything has changed for me alone. I think I've lost half my life."

Yet her life had to go on, and once again friends had to intervene and arrange matters for her. Georges's old friend and support, the rector of the Collège des Sciences, came every day for at least an hour of condolence with Julie, and at last talked seriously to her.

"I take it, my dear, that you still have no plans for your future," he said tentatively. "Very well, then, let me offer you one possibility. It occurred to me that your research appointment at the Sorbonne had meaning only as long as you were going to be with Georges. Without Georges as your co-worker, it would be simply an embarrassment to you; so I took the liberty of asking my friends at the Sorbonne if they planned to ask you to fill Georges's professorship yourself there the same way they asked Marie Curie six years ago under very different circumstances to follow her husband. The reply, I'm sorry to say, is they do not have such plans. They feel that one woman professor in the sciences is about as much as Paris can take at the moment. I feel differently. I have still not filled the post which Georges resigned, and since I think it a disgrace that you have anything less than a professorship of your own, I and my colleagues very humbly offer that chair to you. It may not be the Sorbonne; it may not be the Collège de France; but it *is* a professorship and it *does* go along with your old laboratory so you can continue your research."

Her first surge of gratitude became a hunted look, and he perceived it at once.

"It was also anticipated that the basement laboratory would have certain associations for you," he went on. "And so we plan to ask for a special appropriation to finish off our top floor. I am sure we will get it; and we will then move the entire laboratory up there for you. We have always been very proud to have Georges with us, and we were always aware of you downstairs even though you were not officially a member of our family." He put his hand affectionately on hers. "We beg you accept our offer, Julie."

Tears stung her eyes.

"What a good kind friend you are!" she said softly. "May I think it over?"

"Of course, my dear."

"Do I accept?" she asked Marcel. He spent every evening with her now. He was bewildered by the change in his life. He ached for his children, but they were so hurt in their turn by his inexplicable desertion of them that every meeting with them was a torment to them all. He didn't speak of it to Julie, but she could tell that the brute suffering in his eyes was due to more than Georges's death. Yet she was too pressed by her own needs to be able to help him. "Do I hand in my resignation to the Sorbonne and go to the Collège des Sciences?"

"What else is there?" he asked. "Tell me what you'd like as an alternative, and I'll see if it could be made possible."

"There's only one other alternative I'd care for." She stopped. It was painful to realize that he still didn't know what she was talking about. Then she saw she'd have to put it bluntly. "Can't I work with you?"

He was too astonished to speak for a moment.

"But that's what I've been working toward all along," she went on. "And you always said I wasn't quite ready. That's how I got started working with Georges in the first place. Certainly I must be ready by now, Marcel!"

"Julie!" he said as if she needed to be awakened from a dream. "I have no position to offer anyone except as a laboratory assistant. *You* are the Nobel Laureate, not I."

"But I don't care about things like that," she said. "If I got a prize, it was because I performed a piece of research originally conceived by you, and carried out with your advice. I don't care what the Swedish Academy of Science thinks, I know who's the senior scientist."

"No longer, Julie," he said. "It was almost ten years ago that I said you weren't ready. We can do work together sometimes, if you wish; but not as senior and assistant. You can never again accept a post of preparator. You *must* take a professorship if only for the salary to support your daughter, and for the independence of your work."

"But I was never independent really. There was always Georges."

"Julie," he said almost sharply. "What sort of picture of yourself are you building up in your mind? You were not really Georges's assistant. You had long ago become an independent scientist. You didn't win a Nobel Prize by proximity or by marriage. You earned it by yourself—with your own work. You may have conferred with me, but you didn't need me."

"The idea of being alone terrifies me," she said in a low voice. "I'm used to being taken care of."

"I'll take care of you."

She shook her head. "No," she said thoughtfully. "Our lives have gone beyond that point, I see; just as they've gone beyond the point where I could be your research assistant. Time is so terrible; so insidious, so ruthless, so ironical, so stealthy. If I had met Georges and really known him before I met you, I would have found him entirely what I wanted. I would have been completely contented with him and he would be alive today with the true greatness of his career still ahead of him. If, on the other hand, there had been no Georges at all, and eight or nine years ago you would have come to me saying that you'd take care of me, I would have been deliriously happy. I would have made you happy too, I think. Two utterly marvelous different lives could have been mine; and instead of having either, time gave me both and, in the end, neither. Georges is dead and you and I are both suffering the agonies of amputated lives."

"You don't know what time will bring, Julie," he said in his growling voice. She had made him acutely uncomfortable. "Let's just get by this; let a little more time pass; let people forget a little, and then we'll see."

"I see it very clearly right now," she said with resigned calm. "How sad it is, how cruel, that it will have to happen!"

"What *are* you talking about Julie?" he said faintly.

"What you already feel in your bones, even though you hate to admit it. If I feel it, then surely you must too!"

40

WITHIN THE NEXT TWO WEEKS SHE ACCEPTED THE REC-tor's offer of Georges's chair. She set to work at once on the task of studying his lecture notes so that she could give his courses when the new school year started in September. The familiarity of his handwriting held him close to her. She could even hear his voice in the sentences before her. Many times she came across points which she would have developed differently, but on each occasion she subordinated her judgment to his. She worked in his study in the college, all his things about her intact. The new laboratory was being built for her on the top floor and at least twice a day she went up to watch the workmen to be sure that there was no departure from the plans.

Marcel was at loose ends. In previous summers, he had always taken his family to the seaside for a month of penitence and conventional fatherhood. However painful certain aspects of it had been, at least it gave a semblance of order in his life. Now he had nothing to substitute for it. He was unsettled in his evenings at Julie's: he was always the visitor, the caller, who would leave within a few hours.

"Why can't we go away together some place?" he said.

"Paris is an oven. Suzy needs the country air. You need a change. You're getting to be a spinster," he added pointedly.

"And how are we to go?"

"As M. and Mme. Dupont with Suzy Dupont. There are a thousand villages where we can lose ourselves."

"That's impossible!"

"All right, then you go as Madame Claudet and I'll trail along as M. Raubard in the *pension* next door. You find yourself a Villa Flora some place, and I'll go to the Villa Maris that's bound to be there too."

"Maybe next year we can do something—not this one."

"It had better be this year," he insisted sharply. "Otherwise it'll be too late. Do you realize that you're beginning to make yourself over into Georges? You've taken his study, his notes, his courses. Sometimes I even hear his inflections in your voice. I can understand and respect lack of physical desire under certain circumstances, but let it for God's sake be the abstinence of real grief and not an unthinking imitation of a man whose one tragic flaw was that he was born with every passion but sexuality."

"Don't talk of Georges that way!"

"I must," he replied, "because my life with you is at stake. It's that simple!"

"Wait a bit longer," she pleaded.

"No!"

"I beg you!"

"No!"

"I'll do as you say if you insist because I love you. But if you *do* insist," she warned him quietly, "it will be absolute disaster. There's something I have to live through inside myself first. For once, let time work *with* us."

Again he shook his head. "Life isn't something you let happen. You impose yourself on it. You force it."

"Don't force it, Marcel."

"I always have," he said. "Certainly in my work I have. What I got, I was determined to get. I was determined to have you. Now I see you starting down some side road that'll lead you away from me forever. That road has to be wiped out."

"For the last time, Marcel, I beg you to believe that this particular road is the only one that could eventually lead me back to you. Only be patient!"

His answer was to get up and go into the dark hall to see if

Suzy's door was closed. Then he stood there, silently ordering Julie to pass and precede him into her bedroom.

For the first time in all the years she had had love with Marcel, she felt nothing but his physical burden; for the first time, she heard the hot rhythm of his breath without an answering breathlessness of her own. There was something pathetic, hopeless, and impotent in this fruitless thrusting of his presence into this bed which she had shared with Georges for so many years, into this darkness where she had lain awake yearning for him for so many more nights than he could ever believe. As his tempo increased, she was finally seized with panic and dread that he would withdraw from her before she felt even the slightest wrench of pleasure to pull her back to him again against the rage and anger that was seething within her for his violation of her inwardly ordained period of mourning. She had been right and he had been wrong: he had pushed her still further away from him.

"But why?" he stormed at her later. "Why? You and I are alive. We didn't abdicate life. It's still ours!"

"Because Georges was far too big. If he had been less, we might have wept a while and then re-formed our lives over and around where he had been and there would have been no mark left. But where Georges was, what he did, what he stood for, can't be covered over with a simple bouquet of flowers and one crushed handkerchief damp with tears. If it looked as if I were, perhaps temporarily, stepping into his place, it was because only another whole life—mine—was required to fill the place where his life had been. I owed him that."

"I don't understand you," Marcel said. He was quiet: ashamed, embarrassed, and deeply angry. "Perhaps I'd better go away by myself for a few weeks. We'll talk when I get back."

By September, when he returned, she was busy with the beginning of classes, with the opening of the new laboratory on the top floor, a bright sunny room, with twice as much floor space as they had had in the basement. Gleaming new equipment was arriving every day, and she had three student assistants to help her unpack. The boys, all students in their final years, were bursting with pride to be able to serve her. They would have worked around the clock, but she made it clear that the condition on which they could apprentice themselves was that they must stand highest in their class work.

She went to see Marcel in his study, just as she always had, on the usual Wednesday afternoon, as if nothing had changed. They were no further apart than they had been, but no closer; and now both of them knew that they never would be in spite of Georges's death, in spite of Marcel's break with his family. There was heartache in that knowledge—unbounded sadness, a wrenching grief that had its roots in the very soul—and they shared it with such poignant intimacy that love almost started again.

For the two years that remained before the war began, they were intimate friends, sometimes colleagues, and once in a rare while, ghostly lovers revisiting with cool hand-in-hand affection a grave in which there had been a secret shrine until lightning had smashed it to dust.

With the war, Marcel went immediately into uniform as a major in the Signal Corps and set up a laboratory to perfect chemical detectors of wireless waves. The first paralytic stroke caught him seven months later in March. Because of army technicalities his wife was informed of his condition and called to take over his care five days before Julie even heard of what had happened.

When Julie tried to visit him, his son, a young private on leave because of a wounded leg, limped painfully out of the hospital room to tell her that his father was seeing no one. He stood there, very still on his canes, and waited coldly without a word more until she—with her own sense of dignity—turned and went away. She then sent a message to him through a friend, but the word that came back was total resignation: "Leave things as they are for a while. It makes no difference now."

It was a year before she saw him being led along by his wife: a man totally gray, eyes paralyzed and unblinking, jaw slack with blasted muscle. Julie hid her face in her hands with her agony for him, but she had a sense that this was not the first time she had seen him this way. Fifteen years rolled away and she was a girl who had only recently arrived in Paris, a Sorbonne student in love with the greatest man she had ever met and seeing him as one of the giants of the world until one hot Sunday morning she glimpsed him entering the railroad station trailing his family—wife, small son, smaller daughters—so laden with picnic hampers for all of them that he had staggered along with bent knees, his neck twisted in strain within the sweat-catching handkerchief he had shoved into his collar. The sight then had broken her heart for him—so plain and bedeviled by domesticity—but that fleeting moment turned out to have been the story of his life; for big as he was, in the end life had proven more of a burden than he could bear and here he was now, frozen into the agonized stance of a man under far too much strain.

Again she wrote, asking if she could come to see him, and again it was his son who replied with a brief note that his father was doing very well, but physicians had recommended absolute quiet with no contact except within the immediate family. At the moment she was swamped with work: her laboratory had grown until it occupied the entire floor and she had turned it into a special training course in chemical analysis for military sanitation for army medical officers. The trenches had become pestholes, more deadly themselves than enemy artillery fire, and she was spending eighteen hours a day in the rearguard action against bacterial infection. Yet with so much death around her Marcel's life was still her prime concern. She appealed to her eldest and now dearest friend: the rector—to help her to see him, but he shook his head: "Even I can't get to see him," he said sadly. "Madame Raubard has recovered full possession and he is put on display only for generals, members of the cabinet, and foreign ambassadors with decorations to bestow."

On a gray afternoon in the following February—the third winter of the war—Julie's uniformed assistant—the army had given her a full staff—came into her crowded little office, saluted and announced: "M. Raubard."

A wave of faintness made her dizzy as she stared stupidly up at the young sergeant. Above her, the student medical officers were still carrying on their argument.

"Raubard?" she asked at last, to be very sure of the name.

"Yes, madame."

"Who—who is with him?"

"He is alone, madame."

She nodded slowly, then raised her hand to silence the men around her.

"I have a caller. I want to be alone with him," she said, and they withdrew. She spent an agonizing moment trying to catch her breath. Then the door opened, and in limped the young man whose face was so like his father's in every respect but one—there wasn't a shred of affection for her in it. Even his stance told her he was still her enemy.

She sighed. "I had hoped it was your father."

His eyes suddenly glittered with tears, but nothing in him softened.

"My father died this morning," he said stolidly. "He died in his sleep."

Her sigh was a wordless sound wrenched out of her by life itself—a gasp of anguish, not only at Marcel's death, but at the way of his dying and at all that had died between them.

"Well, at least thank you for coming in person to tell me," she said in a low, dry voice. "It's better to hear it—even from you—than to have read it in a newspaper."

"That wasn't the reason I came," he said looking at a point just over her head. "I came to ask you please not to attend the funeral. This request is from my entire family."

She echoed the last words ironically, then shook her head.

"How much happiness did you and your entire family ever give your father?" she asked.

"He was my father," Jean Raubard replied tonelessly. The tears in his aloof eyes swelled still more.

"And you loved him?"

"I loved him."

"How much happiness did that love give him?" she asked again.

"He loved me," was the harsh reply. Then the young man's tears ran down his face, and his expression crumpled. "He *did* love me," he said in a choked voice. "He *did!* Always!" He stood still stiffly with his gaze on the ceiling above him in an attempt to regain his control. The tears coursed down his cheeks, and on to his uniform tunic. "Even when he left home, he loved me. He never stopped. And when he came back—" He lost his voice, and gasped for a few moments. "And when he came back at last, an old man, he took my hand and told me with his eyes that he was glad to be back with me. May I please go, madame?"

"Why did you feel it necessary to come and hurt me?" she asked quietly. "You know that your father and I loved each other very much."

"Yes? And how much happiness did *your* love give him?" he retorted.

Julie walked to the window. Soldiers were standing guard down in the doorway because of her. She thought *I am a military establishment*. But there had always been a far bigger war, one she had been in all her life. The war which man was always doomed to lose even though he began fighting it the moment he was born.

"I gave your father as much happiness as he was capable of taking," she replied. "I could have given him more, but he was always at odds with himself—he had so much that he was careless with treasures. You know, he had great insights —more than he was famous for—but those that didn't interest him, he threw away. It was the same with the way he loved. He had more than he needed, more than he could use. Yes, I know that he suffered in the years he was away from you because he loved you. And your sisters. I know that. I hope only that the day will come when you'll be able to say that about me."

Young Raubard still stared at the point above Julie's head. His throat worked convulsively, and several times he wet his lips, but he said nothing. Then he limped toward her swiftly, took her hand, bent, kissed it, turned, and walked as smartly toward the door as he had come in, his cane booming into the floor with every step he took. At the entrance he paused, "He loved you, all right," he said softly. "There was never any question about that!"

Julie waited several minutes alone to collect herself, then she rang for the sergeant. She told him to call in the student officers again: she was back in the war—in all the wars that made the fabric of her life, as long as she lived.

PART SEVEN—
HAL PRESCOTT: IV

1

I CONTINUALLY HAD TO REMIND MYSELF THAT THIS woman talking so objectively and with such compassion about her mother—this once-upon-a-time little Suzy—was older than Julie had been when I had first met her. The broomstick-thin little girl with haunted eyes had become a heavyset woman with straight hair of iron gray, cut short, a woman with an effortless smartness. She was Suzanne Claudet, director of the Institut Claudet, her mother's successor, and at fifty, she had long ago established her own reputation in science. What she had told me about Julie was a combination of what she knew, what she had been told, and what she guessed. I saw her several times while I was in Paris.

Whom she resembled most closely was fairly obvious. Her own feelings about it had been fixed as far back as she could remember, and were implicit in what she told me about that last night when Georges Claudet had fled from the flat on the Rue Gazan:

"Before he left the house, he must have stopped to take one final look into the other bedroom—the small one just before the stairs—because I swear I have a last memory of him in the early morning darkness looking down at me with love and sadness. I would have reached up to him for my usual hug except that I was too sleepy and warm to move. On the other hand, it's possible that I'm remembering any one of the hundreds of other times when he came and leaned over my bed that way. To an adoring little girl, he had a special warm smell that was a mélange of all the things he was, of all the things he used, in his everyday life: a black bitter ink he got on his fingers, the white lecture chalk dust that had got into the very fiber of his clothes, the chemicals of the laboratory, the soaps and the carbolic acid disinfectants with which he washed his hands—each one alone as faint as if borne on a zephyr, but all of them together mixed up with the stronger scent that was his very own. It suggested extreme delicacy and airiness and came from his light hair, his fair mustache, and that soft, darker beard that I loved so to feel against my cheek.

"I adored him. That day, when my mother, sick and dazed, told me that he was never coming home again, I refused to believe her. He *had* to come home. He knew how much I loved him. How could he know that and not come back to me? Even when I was told years and years later the way things really were, I accepted it with only the front of my mind. In my heart I still adored him. He was—and will always be—my father. Marcel has another place in my life, even though to this day I still don't know what it is. I was raised to call him Marcel—a genial giant, a rumbling dark man with dark gray hair—someone who was always kind, who always looked at me as if searching for something behind my eyes. I could ask him for anything in the world. I could even command him to be quiet, to stop speaking to my mother, to stand up, to sit, and for minutes at a time, he would go through the silent pantomime of absolute obedience and then say: 'All right, enough!' and the game was over. But if I wanted something that could be bought, I had it the next day; yet I never felt for him the same love. He was Marcel, not *Papa!*

"I didn't know who and what he was in my life until I was almost a grown woman—twenty-one and already working here between studies as my mother's first assistant. I was told by that same person who all her life had been telling others what would hurt them most: although she did it with such an air that for the moment, I was really fooled into believing that she had affection for me. She was in her late seventies by then, very small and pulled together, white-haired, and still smart with the chic of the era when Marcel had left her a widow. All her life she spoke her native English with that unquenchable southern accent—with all its warmth, honey-sweetness and slow croon of affection.

" 'My poor child!' she exclaimed fondly and stopped. She shook her head again, sighed, then said in a burst of confidence, 'I want you to know that your name is in my will, child, and I'm just going to have to tell you why.' No one looked further from dying at the moment. Her bright eyes were full of vivacity and pleasure. I had never liked her, nor did I then like the idea of being remembered in any will of hers. Still, I was human enough to want to hear what it was going to be and why.

" 'You mustn't think of us as strangers,' she went on, putting her hand on mine. 'We're related in a way—not through blood directly—you and I—but you are to my children. Unless, of course, your mother has already told you?'

" 'I don't know what you're talking about, Madame Raubard,' I said. I was sorry I had stayed to listen. We were at the tennis club, and my friend had already drifted away to the courts. I rose, swinging my racket. I didn't want to be related to her or to anyone in her family. Her daughters, older than I, I disliked. Her son, a good enough astrophysicist but an overgrown mother's boy I didn't like either.

" 'Your mother hasn't told you about any relationship?' she insisted.

"I shook my head.

" 'Oh dear!' she said. 'Perhaps I'd better wait to tell you another time, because I'm sure this would all come better from her.' Suddenly I felt she was obscene and frightening, playing this cat-and-mouse game with such obviousness. I moved back to leave her; but she put her hand on my wrist and drew me down in the canvas chair beside her and told me about my mother's life, just as she must have told my father on the porch of the Pavillon du Parc on that June day when I was a little girl.

" 'I don't believe you!' I said, and got up angrily. Within her elegance, she was dirty.

" 'That's what poor Georges said exactly,' she replied wearily. 'But he didn't say it twice. He knew at once what you looked like and what Marcel looked like. I don't doubt that he had known it all in his heart for a long time by then, but he hadn't the courage to face it until I helped him to. Look in the mirror again, child, and don't fear the truth. My daughters may look like me, but my son is his father's image. So are you!'

"I left the club at once and drove dazedly all the way to Paris in my tennis clothes and walked directly into my mother's laboratory. She had taken to working those afternoons to fill loneliness.

"I closed the door behind me and blurted out: 'Madame Raubard just told me the most horrible story about you!' I was crying, and I didn't know why. I suppose it was with rage. My mother had an open fountain pen in one hand and a slide rule in the other. She put the two things down on the white stone table top very carefully, then rubbed her hands against her lab coat.

" 'You'd better tell me what she said,' she told me quietly; and when I had finished, she said in the same tone: 'It's true, Suzy. I'm afraid that it's all true. I'm sorry only that it killed my dearest friend, the most precious man I ever knew.' She turned my face up to hers. I knew every fleck of color in those gray eyes, every hair in her dark lashes and heavy eyebrows. I knew the play of that face in weariness, impatience, laughter, or hurt. Even though she had an entire life that was not the life I had grown up believing it was, she was still the one human being I admired and loved more than any other. I had fought with her, I had nagged her, I had felt put upon, I had learned from her. I had followed her into the laboratory the way other girls follow their mothers into the kitchen: I learned to love to do what I saw her love to do. I knew all her faults. But no matter how we argued, whether over what I wore, thought, or wanted to do within the work, I knew every moment of every day that I was her entire army in life and she was mine.

" 'If I haven't told you up to now, it wasn't because I was ashamed,' she said. 'It was because I had shut it away—it hurt too much!'

"If it hurt her, it was because she had refused to give herself any absolution over the years: she had a line of steel in her soul that could make her—when she decided—ruthless and harsh with herself and everyone around her, but I was always softer with her than she was. She could be brutal to herself but I would rather have died than hurt her.

" 'I don't have to know, *maman*. Don't tell me,' I said. I was sobbing.

" 'No, you don't have to know,' she agreed slowly, smoothing the hair back from my face the way she did even when I was very little. 'But *I* have to tell you. Georges is gone. Marcel is gone. You're all I have. If I didn't tell you finally, I'd die of loneliness inside myself.'

" 'But don't tell me if it hurts! *Maman*, I love you so!' I couldn't stop my tears. She wiped them away with her finger-tips very gently, but I didn't know why I was crying.

" 'And I love you too, my child! It does hurt, still. It's never stopped. I don't think it ever will! But I don't look at it any more; I just live around it and keep on going without looking back. And you must learn to do the same.' "

2

SUZANNE CLAUDET WAS KIND TO ME. SHE EVEN OFFERED to go out to Orly with me when the time came for me to leave; but I was not ready to go and I postponed my flight. I had come to Paris to discover something about myself, and I could not bear to leave without the clarity for which I had come. I had come to Paris to discover once and for all why I had never lived up to the potential I had shown during the time I'd been with Julie. I had to understand what went wrong, but I knew I wasn't going to understand myself until I understood Julie. Did I know her now that I had most of the pieces of her life put together? Not really. I was haunted by what so many people had quoted of Marcel Raubard's conclusion—that in nature, man will always manage to ferret out the answer to every question he can think of asking, but there will always be an infinite number of questions that still evade his asking. For that reason, there must always be mystery. The same was true, I now felt, about human beings. All one's questions about any individual could be answered and yet there would always remain a certain elusiveness.

Julie seemed absolutely clear to me, but at the same time she was floating undefinedly half an inch above the ground. What was it in her? Was it that "line of steel" as Suzy had called it; or the "vein of iron" which Monty Crocker had referred to? Everyone else who knew her had felt something like that—some indestructible, unreachable source of inner strength that had always enabled her to elude predictability.

Whatever it was, it had made her survive; it had made her great.

I finally went out to the Rue Gazan myself at the south end of Paris. It's a quiet parkside street unknown to cab drivers or anyone else who has never actually been there. I went there by bus, not by cab, in order to feel it through the people who reside there now. There is a stop at the beginning of the street

—Parc Montsouris—and I got down there. Some of the old villas still stood facing the park from behind faded brick walls, but between them now are long blocks of modern flats with concrete terraces shaded by the huge trees across the street—trees fifty years taller, thicker, and more full of leaf than when Julie had first lived there. Even the restaurant was still there, and the faded and weathered lettering—PAVILLON DU PARC—had the old-fashioned thickness, the curlicue edge that belongs with horse trams, buttoned shoes, and parasoled ladies. I sat out on the terrace in the sun and I saw the same waterfall that had gone splashing into the same pool as on the day fifty years earlier when Julie and Georges had tried so disastrously to celebrate their new lives. I could see the swans, too, on the elegant artificially rustic pond nearby. Children played around me, and their mothers ate ice cream at little iron tables.

Like Julie, all the old wounds in my life were still in me, and like her, too, I was living around them. She said she didn't look back. I unfortunately had to—and I was looking back at her.

I had walked up to her that first time in London when she was already famous: when she had already survived the scars of a dozen bereavements and had paid every price in tragedy that life could demand. Yet she had merely smiled when I had challenged her right to criticize an obvious mistake of mine. When I pressed to come to see her at her Institute in Paris to force the argument, she had had the grace to lay her hand gently on my wrist to slow me down. She had simply said: "All right, Dr. Prescott, but come at eleven, not ten!"

What was it really that she had? Courage? Or a willingness to go on letting life happen to her and to live it as long as she remained true to who she was? Or a sense that tragedy—from birth to death—was the true wave-beat of life?

I saw her again in her lab coat the way she had looked that first day I came to her Institute—a youngish woman in her middle forties, beautiful, absorbed, with something about her which I sensed even then was unquenchable, untamed—

The word *untamed* broke the elegiac mood and started the explosion in my mind: the beginning of the answer I had sought so long! Why, Julie had been no intellectual with occasional adventures in passion! As long as I had tried to see her in those terms, she was elusive, even trivial. She was the reverse—I saw—excited by my own discovery—she was a primitive; a brilliant, gifted primitive—who still retained the atavistic drive of the hunter! That's what had taken her into science in the first place: into the only remaining wilderness where pursuit is eternal. Which was why Raubard's belief in the endlessness of mystery had never dismayed her. Why hadn't I seen it earlier? She, like him, had no real passion for abstract absolutes—those were simply the illusions nervously required by intellectuals—what she and Raubard both cared for was the quest itself. If the quarry renewed itself every day in still more complex guises—as the questions arising out of yesterday's discoveries—then so much the better!

She had to be the huntress, a Diana, a priestess of the chase for the greatest game in the universe: the universe itself! And because all her life in moments of crisis, she had intuitively treated herself as a primitive, she had always been able to tap that enormous primordial strength within herself. No wonder no one had ever caught her! No wonder no one had been able to deflect her from her path! And that was probably why she had been a mortal danger to every man who treated her as if she were less than she really was. Even if she had loved him, she had been compelled to remove him from her life.

It all seemed so clear; for here, if anything, was the reason for her strength—and the reason for my defeat. I had temporized with my time and with the values of my time—not like Julie. I had mistakenly tried to domesticate myself as a man and whatever it was in me that had taken me into science. Once long ago I had been strong enough to break with my father, but that one single break had been only the end of my own revolution, where it should have gone on every day of my life. Only with Julie had I kept up my momentum, but that had been merely contagion.

Julie and everyone like her, I saw, is born wild and timeless: more attuned to the sub-audible murmurs of the cosmos than to the reasonable gossiping voices of men; with more affinity to the wind, to the breaking of seas, to the ooze and drift of mountains than to the call of friends. They hear and commune with the spirits of trees and rocks, with atoms and stars. They are the strangers in whatever time they live.

This was Julie—as close as I would ever come to understanding her, and finally I knew it.

I took a cab back from the park to my hotel and telephoned Pan American to reserve my seat for the flight home on the following morning. I had nothing to keep me in Paris.

There was nothing and no one in my room but me. I called Suzanne Claudet to thank her once again, and to tell her there was no need for her to come out to Orly with me. To my surprise she insisted, and I was warmed by it.

We really had very little to say. We stood on the concourse as flight time approached and watched people hurrying past. The woman announcer's voice—dehumanized by the amplifier—droned out numbers and named the cities of the world. All around us, people were hurrying to their private futures, rushing—half of them—to the places where they were going to die. Beside me, the stocky, gray-haired woman who had been once a dark-eyed little girl asked out of politeness of the white-haired man who had once broken in on her and her mother: "And so you finally got all you came to Paris for?"

I had never told her precisely why I had come to Paris, but I simply nodded.

"I got as much as I could," I said. "I have to be satisfied with it."

From the loudspeakers throughout the airport, the mechanical woman called my number, my flight, my city, my destiny. It was my time, and I got up a little stiffly. Gray-haired Suzy stood up too. Once, forty years earlier, she could hardly bring herself to give me her hand to shake, but now after a moment of wistful uncertainty she held up her face. We were each of us the last the other had of Julie, and neither of us could bear to let her go. I was feeling exactly what I could see in her dark, haunted eyes; so I bent and kissed her. Then I turned and walked away to where it was my time to go.

FAWCETT CREST BOOKS
On Top With The Big Bestsellers

THE CHOSEN Chaim Potok	M1146	95¢
YOU'RE MY HERO, CHARLIE BROWN		
Charles M. Schulz	D1147	50¢
THE GIFT SHOP Charlotte Armstrong	R1137	60¢
SILVERHILL Phyllis A. Whitney	T1135	75¢
A MOST PRIVATE INTRIGUE		
Leo Rosten	T1116	75¢
OTHER PEOPLE'S MONEY		
Jerome Weidman	M1117	95¢
FATHERS Herbert Gold	T1107	75¢
WINTERWOOD Dorothy Eden	T1104	75¢
WHO DO YOU THINK YOU ARE, CHARLIE BROWN? Charles M. Schulz	D1089	50¢
THAT QUAIL, ROBERT		
Margaret A. Stanger	R1090	60¢
PHYLLIS DILLER'S HOUSEKEEPING HINTS Phyllis Diller	R1082	60¢
THE COUNTRY TEAM Robin Moore	M1069	95¢
APPENDIX TO THE I HATE TO COOK BOOK Peg Bracken	D1063	50¢
GILES GOAT-BOY John Barth	P1052	$1.25
SATURDAY THE RABBI WENT HUNGRY		
Harry Kemelman	R1036	60¢
COLUMBELLA Phyllis A. Whitney	T1037	75¢
ECSTASY AND ME Hedy Lamarr	T1035	75¢
THE DOUBLE IMAGE Helen MacInnes	T1013	75¢
THE SOURCE James A. Michener	C1122	$1.95
THE RABBI Noah Gordon	M954	95¢
THE I HATE TO HOUSEKEEP BOOK		
Peg Bracken	D830	50¢
THE I HATE TO COOK BOOK		
Peg Bracken	D777	50¢

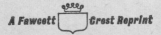

A Fawcett Crest Reprint

Wherever Paperbacks Are Sold